DEXTER

J. Peter MacAllister

DEXTER

New York   Ottawa   Toronto

National Library of Canada Cataloguing in Publication

MacAllister, J. Peter
     Dexter / J. Peter MacAllister.

ISBN 1-894508-38-6

     I. Title.

PS8575.A433D49 2002   C813'.6   C2002-902894-9

PR9199.4.M24D49 2002

For further information and for orders:

LEGAS
P. O. Box 040328   3 Wood Aster Bay   2908 Dufferin Street
Brooklyn, New York   Ottawa, Ontario   Toronto, Ontario
USA 11204   K2R 1B3   M6B 3S8

http://www.legaspublishing.com

Printed and bound in Canada

DEDICATION

Wesley, Tina, Carol,

And

Paul Williams, an extraordinary criminologist who through his
devoted service over the last 40 years has changed the direction
of the lives of many inmates and criminals in Canada
and the United States.

His trustworthiness and realistic approach to criminality has
enabled him to guide many back into the world of legitimacy and
out of the pain and despair that suffocates them in our gulags.

Thank you Paul for the many, many hours of consultation,
encouragement, and interest in this project.

The fat man is still around but his anxiety attacks have become
more subdued and no longer overwhelm him when
he sees his fridge is empty.

TABLE OF CONTENTS

INTRODUCTION

Much is written and portrayed on television about crime and delinquency. The general public is informed through the jaundiced eye of a sensationalized news media, usually after a spectacular event. Practitioners occasionally describe research based on data gleaned from incarcerated offenders. Within correctional institutions, studies have been conducted and evaluative tools have been developed.

Apart from the theoretical meanderings of certain armchair social scientists, most of the information brought forth comes after the fact. The crime has been committed, the offender arrested and the courts have rendered their sentence. Those interested in helping the prison inmate reintegrate into society hold out hope for motivation to change, on the part of the individual offender.

Change from what? Return to what? What is known generally comes from those who have failed miserably, the recidivists. What about the winners… those who have succeeded? Their monetary gain is unquestionable; what about the rest? What about the allurements and pitfalls of the lifestyle unceremoniously referred to as "the underworld?"

MacAllister takes us to a new and interesting level. Drug trafficking is the most lucrative of crimes today; also, the most complex. Could it succeed without the complicity, tacit or otherwise, of legitimate people? What combination of sound judgement and paranoid thinking is required to survive in this lifestyle, mired in deceit and violence?

Having practiced as a psychologist in the correctional field over the past four decades, I appreciate the need to explore the realities of these nether regions.

A must-read for concerned students and practitioners in the field!

Paul J. Williams
Executive Director,
John Howard Society, John Howard House Inc.
Montreal, Quebec CANADA

FOREWORD

Hi, my name is the Shadow. I'm a broke-down old bank robber who has spent more than half my natural life in a prison or penitentiary. I have done time in Atlanta, Georgia; Lewisburg, Pennsylvania; St-Vincent-de-Paul, Québec; Milhaven, Ontario and many other jerkwater jails in the United States and Canada. I'm an example of a life wasted in the world of crime; I'm a loser!

This story isn't about me or my life. It's about a young Turk I met many, many years ago, when Montreal was the Bank Robbers' Capital of the World. In the sixties and early seventies, banks went down like sale signs after Christmas. It wasn't unusual for two or three banks to be robbed in a day. On some days, as many as five or six jugs went down before noontime. It was the in game at the time, and I was considered an old campaigner, and I had the battle scars to prove it.

I hadn't been out of jail very long, so I was bunking up with a guy named Jake the Snake. He, too, was an accomplished bandit. We were both snooping around trying to find a score. The phone rang, it was the Old Owl on the line. He wanted Jake and me to meet with him that morning in a coffee shop on the north side of town. The Owl was a respected bandit who had the brains and the connections to put together some of the best heists the city has ever seen. Some of the biggest money I'd ever made was with him, so when he called, Jake and I were half way out the door before the dial tone went dead.

Jake and I strolled into the coffee shop and saw the Owl sitting at an end table with another young guy at his side. This was his friend Dexter. He introduced us. He was an average-looking teenager with a firm handshake and a pleasant smile. Dexter didn't dress flashy or carry himself in a demeanor that would attract attention. It was all in keeping with what I learned to be his calculated way of facing the world. He wasn't interested in the glory; his primary objective was to make money and enjoy the good life by mingling unnoticed with the crowd. He was not a boisterous person, and there really wasn't anything particularly outstanding about his personality or his looks. The Owl didn't waste any time in asking Jake and me if we wanted to go on a score with them. The take was to be between three and four hundred thousand dollars. That was very big money in those days. The Owl had the bank accountant in his pocket. The accountant was giving him the inside office on the score. On the surface it seemed like a walk in the park.

The Brinks Armored Car Company made a payroll drop at this particular bank every second Thursday. They would arrive at the bank, take the money into the bank and place it on the bank counter. The accountant would sign for it and then the Brinks guards would take the bags of money to the counting room, which was at the back of the bank. The bags of money would be deposited on the table in the counting room, then the Brinks guards would leave. Within seconds they would be back in their truck and on their way to do their other deliveries and pick-ups.

The game plan was simple. We would wait for the money van to drive off and then we were to go charging into the bank, hop the counter, and head straight for the counting room. We were going to scoop the money into a suitcase. The new kid, Dexter, would stand on top of the bank counter, playing centerfield, keeping control of the bank employees and the customers. The Owl would be outside in the getaway car, ready to deal with any unforeseen problem that may arise. The whole operation wasn't going to take us any more than ninety seconds, in and out!

Jake and I said we wanted in. We all shook hands on it and then we left the coffee shop to look over the bank and the getaway route. The bank was located on the corner of a busy boulevard. There was no parking on the boulevard. A one-way street ran down one side of the bank. Behind the bank was a large school and playground, which filled up the block behind the bank. At the end of the street there was another one-way street that ran along the base of the schoolyard, then another one-way street that ran up the other side of the schoolyard back out to the boulevard. In other words, the only possible getaway was to make a square around the bank. There were two major expressways within a quarter of a mile of the bank, one going east and west, the other going north and south. We drove around the bank and the school several times and all was quiet. It was now approximately 11:15 a.m. We waited to see the Brinks truck make its drop and check the timing. The armored truck always arrived between 11:30 a.m. and 11:45 a.m. We waited patiently for the dry run to play. The Owl had done his homework on the score. There was one regular police patrol between 10:15 a.m. and 11:00 a.m. and one in the afternoon between 2:15 p.m. and 3:00 p.m.

We were parked on the side street when we saw the Brinks truck pull up behind us at 11:30 a.m. Three guards got out and proceeded to deliver the money to the bank. The Brinks guards were in and out and on their way in a couple of minutes. We gave the Brinks truck two minutes to go down the one-way streets and leave the area. We backed our car up to the side of the bank and punched our stopwatches. Thirty seconds later, the Owl pulled away from the bank and headed down the one-way street beside the schoolyard. Kids were pouring out onto the street from every which way; it was their lunchtime. We had heard the school bell ring at eleven-thirty, but none of us paid any attention to the school or the street in front of us. We were all too busy looking in the side-view mirrors and the rear-view mirror, observing the action of the Brinks guards, to pay any attention to what was unfolding in front of us.

When the Owl moved the car out, he was immediately forced to tap the brakes in order to avoid hitting the kids who were scampering back and forth on the street. At fifteen miles an hour he was forced to come to a complete stop several times on his way around the schoolyard. When we got back to the top of the boulevard, we checked our stopwatches. Four and a half minutes had elapsed. That was too long a time to get a thousand yards or so from the bank, and we all knew it. The rule of thumb was to have changed cars and be at least two miles from the bank in that amount of time. We drove back to the coffee shop to get our cars.

A heavy silence blanketed the car as it pulled up. Finally the Owl stopped the car, looked around at each of us, and said, "Well let's hear it." Dexter spoke right up. "It's a beautiful score that can't be done. There is only one possible getaway, and that route means you're gonna have to run over a kid making it out. One kid if you're lucky. No, it can't be done. I don't want any part of killing or crippling some kid. I like money but that's a no-no!"

Jake piped in, "Screw that, if we hit a kid it's not our fault." I sat there silently. I knew Dexter was right. Dexter waited for the Owl to give his assessment of the situation. Jake looked at the Owl, trying to goad him into doing the score. The Owl just leaned his head forward on the steering wheel of the car. His body language said it all. The score wouldn't go down. With that, Dexter opened the door on his side and stepped out. Jake was still trying to convince the Owl to go through with the heist.

Dexter leaned his head back into the car and said, "If you guys go through with that score, you're gonna kill a kid. If you do, don't worry about the cops getting ya, because I'll be coming. It's bullshit and we all know it." With that, he slammed the car door and walked off.

Jake turned and looked at the Owl and said, "Who does that punk think he is?" The Owl responded, "He's young and a little fast with the lip, but he can hold up his end. Take it to the bank, he means what he says!"

The score never went down, and that was the last Jake and I saw of Dexter for many years. The reason for that was because Jake and I got slammed on another bank score some three weeks later. We did laundry and made license plates for the next five years. We were, you could say, in the government employ — not exactly civil servants — but on the government payroll for a buck a day, with room and board and a photo thrown in for the family album.

Upon our release, Jake and I started hanging out at a well known watering-hole in the west end of town. We were once again looking for work. A big Brinks score had gone down that day. There had been a shoot-out, and some of the Brinks guards had been wounded as well as some of the bandits. The TV announcers babbled away about the robbery; it was on everyone's lips at the club that night.

No one seemed to have a clue as to who the crew was and if they did, nobody was talking. Jake and I were standing at the bar, when we noticed the Owl's girlfriend walk in and give a quick glance around the place. The moment she saw us, she casually walked over to us and ordered a soft drink. I looked at Jake, and we both instantly knew who one of the players in the Brinks heist was. She greeted us, sat down at the bar beside us and casually sipped on her soft drink. When no one was within listening range, she leaned in close to us and said. "The Owl is hurt and he needs your help."

Neither Jake or I said a word; we just nodded our heads and looked up at the TV over the bar. She finished her soft drink and slowly walked out of the bar. Jake and I looked around to see if anyone had paid her any particular attention. Seeing that all was kosher, we followed her out to the parking lot. She told us to be careful, gave us the address where the Owl and Dexter were holed up and left.

The Owl had been shot twice and Dexter three times. They still had managed to grab the money and make it out. They were seriously wounded, but the Brinks guards — even though their injuries were minor in comparison — had surrendered the loot and had decided co-operation was the order of the day.

We got a doctor and with the help of some other bandits, we nursed Dexter and the Owl back to health. They paid us well, which was greatly appreciated, because we were broke. Now that Jake and I had a bankroll we could bide our time and take it easy while on parole. The Owl took a sabbatical and Dexter started his little computer service company. From that time on, Dexter, Jake and I were close friends.

Whether you be a Punter or a Player, Dexter's life experiences may help you decide, if a life of crime is really the journey you want to live. Today, the name of the game is drugs. Dexter developed his rules for survival in the Drug Game. He developed them over years of experience in playing the game. Decide for yourself if you think it might be all fun and games, or if you think it's worth it. After all, you shouldn't play the game unless you know the rules!

Many square johns are getting involved in the underworld without having the faintest idea as to what kind of life they are embarking upon. Millions of lives are being thrown onto the trash heap because of drugs and our blindness to the reality of its destructiveness, or because of that youthful mantra, "it can't happen to me!"

Today, drugs are commonplace. There is practically no one who doesn't have a family member involved in drugs. Never before in the history of humanity has a criminal activity permeated society to such a degree as the drug trade has. Many hard working, otherwise honest, law-abiding citizens (normally referred to by criminals as square johns) are getting involved in the drug trade. This way, the average joe participates in the Drug Game by laundering drug money, stashing drugs for a brief period of time or in many other seemingly inconsequential ways. Most would not consider themselves participants in the criminal world. But they are — whether they like it or not! As the old adage goes, "You can't be a little bit pregnant!" If you listen to your teenage children, your friends, your neighbours, the talk around the water cooler at work, you will hear how normally law-abiding citizens are participating in the drug game, albeit superficially or casually. They have no idea of the danger that lurks within the drug trade. When confronted, most would say that they were not deeply enough involved with drugs to be party to the death and misery of the trade.

Whether you are an experienced con, a housewife, a novice drug user, a small part-time dealer, or simply a part of the gullible public, if your greed for easy money sucks you into the web of lies and deceit that are the hallmark of the Drug Game, then this book is for you.

I found out too late in life that staying out of jail required a lot of work, and not just luck. I wish somebody would've told me that before having done twenty years. In the beginning, I thought it was all fun and games. In the end, all my Mother's tears couldn't wash away the pain of my wasted life.

Be you a Punter or a Player, a kingpin or a casual user, remember what recovering drug addicts always say, "In the Drug Game, there are no Victims, only Volunteers!"

The Shadow

CHAPTER ONE
INTRODUCTION TO THE RULES

The six o'clock train rolled up to the Dorval train station. The passengers began to disembark like ants out of an ants nests, scurrying left and right. Fred, a young college student, stepped onto the train platform. He was carrying a large suitcase in each hand. He was clean shaven, had medium length blonde hair and wore a freshly-pressed red plaid shirt, clean blue jeans and cowboy boots.

He walked about twenty feet in the direction of the train parking lot. He stopped, put the two suitcases down on either side of him, pulled out his pack of cigarettes and lit one up. After a few puffs, he reached down, gripped the handles of each suitcase and continued walking toward the parking lot.

Billy, a young man, dressed in blue jeans, a gray pullover sweatshirt, with the name of McGill University imprinted in bold lettering across the front, stood on the train platform, scrutinizing Fred's every move. Billy's shoulder-length brown hair, clean attire, and unobtrusive demeanor allowed him to blend in with people milling about the train station. Billy looked younger than his twenty-two years of age because of his small five-foot-six frame and his baby-face complexion. The innocent looking young man kept his eyes fixed on Fred as he made his way toward the big white Pontiac Bonneville sitting in the parking lot. Fred was almost at the white Pontiac when he stopped, put the suitcases down, reached into his front jean pocket and pulled out some keys. He then slipped a key into the trunk lock of a blue Ford Escort and popped the trunk open. Without hesitation, he reached down and grabbed the two cumbersome suitcases and threw them into the trunk of the car. Closing the trunk lid tight, he pulled the key out of the lock, slipped it back into his pocket and casually walked back to the train station platform. The train was just starting to roll out of the station. Freddie jumped back on board the moving train in one quick stride as it left the station.

Billy stood on the train platform with a puzzled look on his face. He then joined the remaining column of people making their way toward the parking lot. He got into his little red pick-up truck and headed straight for Dexter's house.

Dexter was a drug distributor and importer. The fifty kilos of hashish that Freddie had been delivering were for Dexter. Billy raced to tell Dexter about the screw-up. He rang Dexter's doorbell. The moment Dexter opened the door, Billy pushed himself inside and blurted out to Dexter in a panting voice, "Dexter, that runner you hired is a real fuck-up. He put the hash in the wrong car! Then he jumped back on the train. What an asshole."

Dexter's face clouded over. A shock of electricity went through his body and mind as he tried to envision what had gone wrong. He told Billy to go over to Hank's house and tell him to meet at the Bug. Hank was Dexter's partner in crime. Billy wanted to know what was going on, but Dexter just waved him off. As Billy stepped through the door, he could hear Dexter open the closet and grab his jacket — the hangers clashed and tingled together — because of Dexter's abrupt treatment of them. Driving away from Dexter's house Billy looked into the rear-view mirror to see Dexter pulling out of his driveway in his big Lincoln Continental, heading in the opposite direction.

No one knew who Dexter's runner was. Billy only had a description of him. He didn't know his name, where he came from, or even how Dexter had come to know him. That was between Dexter and Freddie. Dexter and Fred had a simple back-up plan. If Freddie saw something he didn't like, or if he thought he was being followed, he was to put the suitcases in the blue Ford Escort and get back on the train, ending his journey at Central Station, where he was to wait for Dexter to contact him.

Dexter had known Freddie from the hippie days. He was quiet, didn't deal drugs and had no criminal record. In fact Fred was attending college working toward a degree in accounting. He liked to toke a joint now and then, but he never messed around with hard drugs or known druggies. He had worked as a runner for Dexter for years. He was always punctual, followed the game plan to the letter and was very observant. The added income helped pay his tuition; he also never lacked personal smoke. During his many years as Dexter's runner, he had never lost a gram of hash.

Dexter's mind raced faster than the pistons pushing the big Continental down the expressway. He arrived at Central Station and went inside. When Fred saw him, he moved slowly in his direction. Dexter, catching sight of him, continued walking. Freddie planted his butt on a bench and watched Dexter walk toward the men's washroom. Fred scanned the station, checking the people to see whether anyone was following Dexter or if anyone had paid him any particular attention. Satisfied that Dexter wasn't being followed, he got up and walked briskly to the men's washroom.

Dex was waiting for Freddie as he entered the washroom. Dexter had checked the johns. All was clear, they were alone. Dexter didn't say a word; he just looked at his runner, waiting for an explanation. Freddie got right to the point.

"Man the cops were all over the Dorval station. What in the hell is going on?"

Dexter looked directly into his eyes, trying to determine if maybe his runner had lost his nerve, had a panic attack, or had really seen what he said he had seen. Had all the years of being a runner finally caught up to Freddie, or was he still the bright, observant, calm worker he had always been? The answer came flashing back from Fred's eyes and manner. He was the same collected and observant Fred he had always been. He had followed out the game plan with the stealth of a cobra.

Dexter asked, "How many did you see, and where were they?"

"One inside the station looking out the window, two on the platform, one at each corner of the station building, and one in the parking lot — he had the hood of his car up, toying with the engine, looking around. That's what I saw. There could be more. Do you think it's for us, or did we walk into somebody else's steam?"

"I don't know," replied Dexter. We'll try and play it out and see what we can do, if anything!"

"Shit" said Freddie, "If the hash gets busted in my car, I'm screwed."

"No, you're not. You catch the next train back to Ottawa. If it goes down in your car, I'll call you. If I call you, you immediately report your car stolen.

The cops might not believe you and you may be in for a rough time, but remember, just stick to your story and keep your mouth shut about everything else, you'll be home free. Remember, no matter what the Man says, all you know is that your car was stolen. If they ask you what time, tell them you don't know. When you got home from class you hit the books and you didn't notice the car was gone until, whenever. Got it? Now wait for my call; don't report the car stolen unless and until you hear from me. If it all works out I'll have someone drive the car back to Ottawa late tonight. We'll leave it on the street in front of your house. If there's any screw-up, call my office first thing in the morning. If your car's not in front of your apartment by nine o'clock tomorrow morning and I'm not at the office, report it stolen. OK?"

Fred nodded his head; it was going to be a long agonizing night for Fred and a stressful one for Dexter. Dexter turned, walked back out into the station and headed for the parking lot. Dexter's mind was spinning like a secretary's hands flipping through a Rolodex file, trying to come up with the right number to placate a tyrannical boss. In Dexter's case, he was reviewing the rules of the game, asking himself, what went wrong or who went wrong. He navigated the big Lincoln down the expressway to the Lachine Hotel. Dexter knew there had to be an answer to the problem — there always is — but first you have to figure out how the problem came about in the first place, and at this point Dexter was stymied. In order to continue playing out the hand, he had to get some answers. Dexter had learned long ago that whenever you have a problem in the Drug Game, you have to put the brakes on quickly, figure out exactly where the problem is, and make a decision based on facts, not on a wing and a prayer. If he didn't or couldn't figure out what was going on, he'd be like a rat in a maze, running around, being watched, and going nowhere but to jail.

He reflected on all the details of the deal. Starting at the beginning, he thought of Ace. Ace was an old hippie who had never left the flower fields. He liked to toke and rap with his friends. He didn't have a mean bone in his body. When the rest of his friends grew up and moved on from the hippie world into legit society, Ace continued doing what he loved best — smuggle hashish, toke up, make love and have as little responsibility as possible. The game had gotten a lot more serious since the hippie days. Today, people were ripping one another off, beating those hippie fools up and in some cases, even killing them. Ace hadn't made the transition from peace and love to big business, but reality was beginning to set in. It was all business nowadays, serious business, and hippies like Ace were getting rolled over because they couldn't or wouldn't deal with the violence that was now part and parcel of the game. Dealers had ripped him off for half of the last deal he had brought in and for part of the one before that. That was why he had contacted Dexter.

Dexter was from the old hold-up school. He had been taught the ways of the street by bandits who worked banks and Brink's trucks. Another hippie, his partner Hank, had introduced him to the hash game. He and Hank were now importers and distributors of hashish and grass, nothing else. They had a good reputation as distributors and smugglers. They brought in top quality hash; and as distributors, if they took your grass or hash, you always got paid. No song and dance, no head games, no short-changing your end. If you gave them a product that was unacceptable to them (quality was always the issue) they would return it to you without a word. If you bought their product and you didn't like the quality, all you had to do was bring it back and they would give you back your money. By running their business in a straightforward manner they had built up a solid reputation. That way, they avoided the headaches that some of the more dishonest players had.

The drawback with Dexter was you had to sell him the merchandise a thousand a kilo cheaper than you could get if you went directly to a dealer. That was why Ace had tried to move his last two deals himself. Selling directly to drug dealers and not going through a distributor like Dexter or Hank, meant more money for Ace. However, after his second experience, he realized it was better to take less from Hank and Dexter and get paid, than to opt for more money from a guy with a bullshit line, fancy footwork, and an NSF check. Take it to the Bank of England and get paid, or take it somewhere else and get shafted. Ace knew that the drug dealers were aware that he was not a violent person and so they could rip him off at will — and they did.

This time was different. Ace was now relaxing with his girlfriend, having a fine meal, drinking some vintage wine, and waiting for Dexter's runner to bring him the money that he expected in a couple of days. It didn't add up that Ace would burn his own deal. Besides, he still had another fifty kilos to move. If the Man were on to Ace, they would have busted the whole hundred keys. This wasn't what the cops called a "controlled delivery" where they have a stool pigeon or an undercover cop make the delivery. If Freddie had rolled over and been with the Man, he wouldn't have played it the way he did. He just would have dropped the shit off and let Dexter and his people go down with the hash. If the runner had somehow gotten heat and had been followed, they would have been waiting for him at Central Station, because that was the destination on his ticket. No, they were set up and waiting at Dorval. The way it added up, Dexter could eliminate Ace and Freddie as part of the problem. That meant trouble lay ahead.

Arriving at the Lachine Hotel, Dexter wasted no time in walking up to a six-foot-two, two-hundred-and-twenty-pound guy standing at the bar, drink in hand, bumping his gums. He was known as the Mouse. He was a car salesman and a small-time dealer. He had a reputation of being slippery with other people's money; but when he was kept in check on that account, he could move a fair amount of hash. This was the first time Dexter had worked with him. Dex had been observing him and had decided to cultivate him as a dealer. A good distributor needs many contacts who can move the hash or grass fast. The faster you move it, the faster you get paid. And the faster you're off the track, the harder it is for the Man to nail you! The Mouse had arranged for a square john friend of his to park his car at Dorval station for the drop. The square john had no criminal record and wasn't supposed to know anything other than that his car would be used for a couple of hours, and he would be paid three hundred dollars. If any problems developed, he would be contacted and told to report his car stolen. If by chance his car were stopped and the hash discovered in it, he wouldn't have a serious problem, because before the cops could get to his house, he would be on the phone reporting it stolen. Dexter and Hank always tried to provide an out for anyone they worked with. A little forethought could prevent a lot of trouble.

When the Mouse saw Dexter walk in, he turned to the barman to order another drink. Dexter grabbed him by the arm and said. "Let's go. We have to talk."

From the look on Dexter's face, the Mouse knew this was no time to come out with one-liners. He left the bar on Dexter's heels. Outside, Dexter told the Mouse he would meet him at the Bug.

The Mouse pulled up at the Bug right behind Dexter. As soon as they were out of their cars, Dexter asked the Mouse if he had told the guy he borrowed the white Pontiac from, anything other than what he was supposed to know. The Mouse shook his head. Did the guy have a problem with the police that the Mouse hadn't told Dexter about? Again, his answer was no. Dexter spelled out the problem of the Man sitting in wait at the Dorval train station. Dexter stopped talking and looked at the Mouse. The Mouse was a big mouth, a real talker (what car salesman isn't?). If he were lying, there would be no point in listening to him; he could shovel it out faster than a bull could make it. If he was holding out, Dexter hoped to pick up on it in his body language. Dexter wasn't sure. The Mouse was dancing a little bit, but it could be that he realized that Dexter was looking at him suspiciously. Then again, maybe he was holding out! Dexter asked the Mouse to call the guy and find out if he had a problem and at what time he had parked the car at the train station.

Inside the Bug, the Mouse went to the pay phone and called his friend. Dexter stood right next to him with his ear to the phone; he too wanted to hear the guy's response. The square john was so anxious to make the three hundred dollars, he had parked his car at the train station the day before. Hearing the answer, Dexter moved away from the phone, the Mouse finished off the conversation with his friend. Turning to Dexter he said, "That jerk parked the car there yesterday. No wonder the Man's watching it. They probably figure it's a switch car for a hold-up or something like that!"

Dexter didn't say a word; he just motioned for the Mouse to join Hank and Billy who were sitting at a table waiting for Dex. The reason Dexter held the meeting at the Bug (its real name was the Green Hornet Tavern) was that Jean — the owner and only waiter — knew everybody who walked into the place. It was a small beer joint that was about the size of a cabin. Thirty-five feet long by twenty-five feet wide. It had a seating capacity of forty people at most. The little one-storey building sat on a small plot of waterfront land on Lakeshore Boulevard, a winding road that ran along the shore of Lake St. Louis. It passed through several west end communities, uniting them as it had done for over a hundred years. Most of the traffic took the expressways that connected the West Island communities with downtown Montreal. The Bug was a kind of throwback in time to a less hectic pace of life. Inside, the stucco walls were a pale shade of green, twenty-five years later the walls cried out for a new coat of paint, but nobody noticed or cared. The worn, dark brown wooden floor, contrasted the mousy colored walls in art deco style. The chairs were the typical dark brown, round, wooden ones with the bent rattan arms that good beer drinkers associate with comfort. There was a mix of round and square tables with laminated tops of the same art deco green that graced the walls. Faded and scratched, the tables were mute testimony to many a scholarly discussion about how to solve the world's problems, who would win the Stanley Cup, and, undoubtedly, the age-old mystery of how to understand women.

The smell of beer and smoke wafted in the air. Two TVs were hung from the ceiling, one for the patrons at the front of the little tavern and one at the back. The main attraction for most of the patrons was the cheap beer and — probably just as important — women weren't allowed in the place! I guess some of the guys liked to drink their beer undisturbed. Jean only sold beer — draft or bottled — and if you were hungry, you could buy chips or a bag of peanuts. On a good day, Jean might have a ham and cheese sandwich he could pop into the microwave.

Jean knew his customers so well that, after you'd been there a few times, he knew what beer you drank, how many you ordered at a time, and had a general sense of who you were. There was a potpourri of clientele: the usual losers or drunks, the guys who worked with their hands, the executives and the wheeler-dealers. Jean was not a nosy guy. He was just on top of his game, which was serving all of his customers with equal respect and dexterity.

Two more dealers walked into the Bug and sat down at Hank and Dexter's table. Initially they just made small talk; the main thing on their minds was hash. Because of the problem Dexter and Hank were faced with, they wanted to move the hash expeditiously, meaning cash on the spot. When importers and dealers know one another, the hash or grass is usually given out on the front end for a day or two. This avoids having money and drugs in the same place at the same time. The hash or grass is given up first so that if there's a problem with quality, the merchandise is returned and that's the end of it. There's no point in risking moving the money and the drugs at the same time. This, of course, is only when you have honourable dealers who are not hold-out or rip-off artists and who have the financial backing to pay for the merchandise, even if they lose it. Once a dealer takes delivery of the drugs from the importer or wholesaler, they're either paid for or returned.

In hard drugs like cocaine, heroin, or crack, the game is different: no cash no candy. That's because the people in that part of the game tend to be unreliable. They are often users of the product themselves, so you can't trust them or their noses. Even in the hash and grass game, you have to know the people you're dealing with, and they have to know that you're not someone to mess around with.

In this case, if Dexter could get his hands on the hash, he wanted to turn it into cash right away. By splitting it up into smaller amounts, he could accomplish this within a couple of hours instead of a day. Dexter noticed that the Bug was unusually busy that night. Nobody was playing pool on the one pool table that was stuck off in the corner at the back near the washroom, nor was anyone banging on the pinball machine that sat blinking away in the other corner.

Hank and Billy sat across from Dexter, not saying a word, just waiting for some indication from him as to what the next move was going to be. They mumbled small talk about sports, politics, and broads for about forty minutes. The Mouse was blowing most of the wind. Then Dexter waved at Jean to bring the table another round. He reached into his pocket and pulled out some money to pay for it. He kept his hand low to the table so that Jean had to lean forward in order to tell Dexter how much was owed. Jean leaned close to Dex and in a quiet voice mentioned the amount in Dexter's ear.

Staring down at his hand with the money, Dexter whispered to Jean, "Are there any new customers here tonight?"

Jean responded quietly, "Yes, the four guys at the table, right behind you."

"You've never seen them in here before?"

Jean replied in a curt muted voice, "Never."

Dex paid Jean with an extra special tip and joined in the small talk drifting around the table.

Then a few minutes passed, Dexter's eyes met Hank's. A movement of Dexter's eyes told Hank it was time to go to the washroom. Dexter pushed his chair back, got up and went to the bathroom. Moments later Hank joined him.

"Did Billy tell you what happened?"

"Yeah," said Hank. "Now fill me in on the details."

Dexter immediately reviewed all that had past, including the Mouse's call to the guy with the drop car.

Then Hank said, "That Mouse makes my skin crawl; what do you think?"

"I dunno, it could be a legit screw-up, or somebody has fingered us. In either event they don't know that the shit's in the Ford Escort. They've gotta be looking at that big white-ass Pontiac. Only you, Billy, Freddie and I know about the Ford."

Hank and Dexter did some emergency brainstorming while standing at the urinals, holding onto the family jewels. They added up what they had and the game plan was born. They knew that the four guys sitting at the table right behind them were undercover cops. Hank had noticed how little they talked, as if they didn't want to pollute the atmosphere with more noise that would interfere with their listening mode.

Dexter left the washroom and returned to the table. Hank came out and went over to the pinball game. He dropped a coin in and began banging away at the machine. Billy looked at Dexter; he caught the motion of Dexter's eyes directing him to the far corner, where the pinball player was enthusiastically engrossed in his game. Billy casually got up and joined Hank at a game of pinball.

About twenty minutes later, the pinball addicts returned to the table just in time to be greeted by a new round of beer. Well into their third or fourth pint, Dexter said in a voice loud enough that the boys at the table just behind him could overhear. "Hey partner, we gotta get that white-ass Pontiac out of there."

"Jesus," said Hank, "Keep it down! I think you've had enough beer. Keep it down man, keep it down!"

"Ah," Dexter responded, "Don't be so paranoid. If you don't want to get the car, I'll get it myself."

"OK, I'll do it, just keep your voice down. We don't have to tell the whole world what we're doing, do we? You've had enough to drink, let's go!"

Dexter pushed back his chair, stood up, and advised the Mouse and company to wait for him there. He'd be back shortly with the goodies. Hank shook his head disapprovingly as he made his way to the door with Dexter. They both noticed how remarkably quiet the four guys at the table behind them had become. Hank jumped into the passenger side of Dexter's big silver Lincoln Continental with the matching gray Gucci interior. He turned on the radio to hear Elton John's version of "Johnny Be Good" come thumping out of the big speakers that vibrated the passengers in the car. The loud rock 'n' roll music gave a kick-start to the adrenaline rush that was soon to surge through their bodies as they played tag with the cops. They drove to Dorval station in a very leisurely manner, staying on Lakeshore Boulevard following its meandering path around the lake into Dorval.

When they arrived at the station, Dexter pulled his car right up beside the Pontiac that sat in the parking lot like an old broad on a bar stool hoping to get picked up on a Saturday night. Hank got out, walked over to the car and opened the door. The Pontiac growled as Hank started it up. Just as Dexter was backing out, preparing to leave, Hank sprang out of the Pontiac and went over to the driver's side of the Continental. Dexter zoomed the electric window down and asked Hank if there was a problem.

"No problem," said Hank. "Just get out and give me a big hug and a hand-shake. You know we gotta make this look good, like this could be the end."

Dexter smiled, shook his head, got out of his car and gave his partner a big bear hug and the handshake and palm shake they always did when greeting their special friends.

He said to Hank, "You're an actor, you know that. You're loving this shit. If this works and the Man finds out about it, we'd both better leave town. They're gonna want a kick our asses so hard our eyeballs will register tilt. Let's not piss'em off too much."

Hank just chuckled as he got back into the Pontiac, put the car in reverse, backed out of the parking slot and headed for the exit. Dexter was practically on his bumper as the two cars made their way to Dorval Circle, which would take them to the expressway.

They hadn't travelled five hundred yards on the Dorval Circle when Hank stopped his car in the middle of the road. Dexter didn't know whether Hank was acting dumb or whether he was just overacting, but in either case he didn't think it was funny. Dexter braked his car and jumped out as Hank walked toward him. Before Dexter could say a word, Hank blurted out, "The bloody car just went dead on me."

They put their emergency flashers on and then they pushed the big Pontiac off to the curbside. They checked under the hood to see if they could figure out the problem. Neither of them knew a muffler from a carburetor, but it's a guy thing, even if you don't know anything about mechanics you always look under the hood. Hank jumped in with Dexter and they drove to the nearest service station. The attendant informed them that he could tow the car in, but there was no mechanic on duty to service the car, so they would have to leave it until the following morning. The two actors took the news in a somber manner, left the keys with the attendant and headed back to the Bug. The Mouse and the other dealers were sitting at the table waiting for news as to what, if anything, was going to happen that night.

The gang of four who had been sitting at the table next to them had left. The Mouse told Hank that Billy had a date with his girlfriend so he had checked out. Dexter sat down at the table and ordered a beer for himself and Hank. His throat was parched and he knew Hank's was too. Hank went to the pay phone and made a quick call to Billy's Mom. "Yes," she said, "Billy called a few moments ago. He said he would be home in twenty minutes."

Hank thanked her. Returning to the table with the boys he sat across from Dexter. He flashed him a wink, and a sly grin crept into the corner of his mouth. From this Dexter knew that Billy had picked up the Ford Escort, brought the hash to the stash, and was awaiting delivery instructions.

They had saved the game, but now they knew they had to move the hash fast. One by one the dealers went into the bathroom with either Dexter or Hank. They paid for their orders right on the spot and gave the drop off address for the hashish. The Mouse was kept in the dark. He had no idea what was transpiring. After the dealers had left, they told him he would be receiving his package the following afternoon. Dexter drove Hank home and returned to his. The cops were all over Dexter and Hank, but now it was too late. Sitting on Hank or Dexter at this stage of the game was a waste of time — like waiting for the last dance when the band has gone home.

Billy's girlfriend stopped by Hank's house and picked up the delivery instructions for Billy. The little scheme Hank and Dexter had devised was simple enough. They knew that the four guys at the table behind them were cops. They also believed that the cops didn't know that the hash was in the blue Ford Escort. They felt that if they went into acting mode and talked loud enough for the cops to hear their conversation, all eyes would be on them and the big white Pontiac sitting in the parking lot — even without Hank's little impromptu act. By focussing attention on themselves and then taking the attention with them when they left the train station, they felt that Billy would have a window of opportunity to get the Ford Escort the hell out of there. Billy snuck up to the station and observed the action. If he felt he could make his move, he would; if not, he was told to pass. Needless to say it was bonus time for Billy.

The Pontiac had died on the road because the cops had drained the gas tank. There was enough gas in the fuel line for the car to make it out of the parking lot and a little ways down the road; far enough for the attention to shift away from the station and give Billy his shot at the roses. The car had been left with a full tank of gas. Even the Mouse wasn't so stupid as to screw up like that. Had the police not drained the gas tank, they would have gone for a long two-hour joyride. As it was, the next day Dexter and Hank went to the service station to pick up the Pontiac and the cops were still sitting on it. It wasn't the most brilliant plan you'll ever hear, but it worked and that's what counts. As the RCMP always say, "Close only counts in horseshoes."

RULE NUMBER TWO
KEEP THE CIRCLE TIGHT
KEEP EVERYTHING ON A NEED-TO-KNOW BASIS

I've decided to start with Rule Number Two and save what Dexter calls Rule Number One, for the end. If you can't get a handle on the next nine rules, there's no point in worrying about the first rule, so we'll save it for the end.

Rule Number Two is a rule that many guys never seem to learn, even after going to the can several times. Dexter had this rule drilled into his head by the old bandits he worked with way back when. He was told then that if he didn't learn this rule, you will either go to jail, get killed by the cops or your own associates. And if you're in the Drug Game, you can add getting ripped off for your drugs, your money or both.

There are no exceptions. Players either learn it and live by it, or die by it. Either slowly in prison or quickly with a bullet in the pumpkin. Dexter and Hank never told anyone anything more than they needed to know. In the war story you just read, you can see how vitally important that was to their success and survival.

Greed is what motivates our society, both legitimate and criminal. Greed unchecked is like a whore with birth control pills. The experience can only end in abuse and exhaustion. Dex and Hank had kept their circle tight by doing business only with people they knew. The exception was the Mouse. They had watched him, but they had never done business with him before. They decided to try him out because they wanted to expand their market. They knew his credit and word were no good, but they were confident they could keep him in check. They wouldn't give him any credit, he was cash only. Nothing bad ever seemed to happen to the people he did business with. Well, maybe some of them had been shortchanged, but at least no one around him went to the can. The Mouse's market would have broadened Hank and Dexter's capacity to move merchandise. Once the Mouse realized they weren't going to be played, he would concentrate on the business of selling hash. He could move at least fifty kilos a week. Hank and Dexter had been rolling along without incident, but greed motivated them to gain new contacts.

Ace was good for two trips a year. Add that to their own smuggling operation and it was clear that they had to expand if they were going to accommodate the increased volume passing through their hands. They could always have said no to Ace or smuggled less themselves, but greed, wonderful greed, propelled them forward.

Reviewing this war story, Dexter explained that by following Rule Number Two, he was able to isolate the problem. Ace was already in their circle — they had known him for years, as a hippie, as a player and a friend. Billy and Freddie were also in their camp. They were tried and proven runners. The two other drug dealers who showed up at the Bug that night were long-standing customers of Hank and Dexter. They had never had any problems with either of them in the past. The only new ingredients were the Mouse and the guy he got the car from. The guy who rented his car knew nothing, or at least he wasn't supposed to know anything. Only the Mouse knew that his car would be used for a drop. He didn't know by whom, how or exactly when. The obvious thing that jumped up into Dexter and Hank's face was that the problem, whatever it was and however it started, commenced at the point of the white Pontiac. Bells went off, but you can't accuse anyone of anything unless you're sure. In this case, the Mouse barely got a passing grade. Pinpointing your problem is a big help, even if you're not perfectly sure about its source. That's where the second part of Rule Number Two came into play.

Everything must be on a need-to-know basis. Dexter and Hank were partners so each knew the entire game plan, but they were the only ones who did. Everyone else only knew their particular role in the scheme, and that's all they had to know.

For instance, Ace knew where to make the drop to Freddie, but he didn't know Freddie or what Freddie was going to do with the hash once he got it. All Ace had to know was where the drop was to be made, at what time and how long his car would be gone for. Ace left the keys to his car underneath the front seat. Freddie drove Ace's car over to another shopping center and put the shit in his car. He then returned Ace's car to where he had picked it up, and left.

Hank and Dexter had driven up to Ottawa, picked up Fred's car and parked it at the train station. That night Freddie hopped on the train to Montreal with the two suitcases of hash. He knew what to do and he also knew the back-up plan. If everything went well he was to drop the two suitcases in the trunk of the white Pontiac. If he had a problem he was to do as he did.

He had no idea Billy was going to be at the station watching him, and Billy had no idea who the runner was or where he was coming from. He just had to make sure a guy with two suitcases made it to the white car, at which point he was to let the guy leave and then drive the Pontiac away. Billy was told that if anything different went down he was to leave the Pontiac where it was and to see Dex immediately.

Because each person was told only what he had to know, it was easier to track where a screw-up might have occurred. Everyone understood and everyone kept their mouths shut, because to do otherwise would have meant putting their own lives in jeopardy. Street sense at it simplest and best.

By operating in this manner Hank and Dexter made it very difficult for the cops to infiltrate them. As for stool pigeons or double agents, it made ferreting them out a lot easier. Stool pigeons are careful not to sell out the same crew twice, unless the crew is composed of morons — and that happens too. Usually they'll take a shot at informing on someone or some crew just once, and if it doesn't work, they'll back off. When stool pigeons are too persistent, they end up on the watch list. It's not a long nor a patient list. The Mouse was now on the watch list.

Hank and Dexter had had many a stool pigeon take a run at them over the years. Sometimes stool pigeons get cocky; they get to thinking they are ultra-intelligent, and that's when they get bold and brazen. It is usually at that point that they get their wings clipped. However, stool pigeons can do a lot of damage before their luck runs out. One of the best insurance policies Hank and Dexter had against becoming a victim of a rat was by adhering to Rule Number Two.

CHAPTER TWO
THE DEAL

Hank and Dexter had lost their connection in India. Through the grapevine they had been introduced to a new connection in Pakistan. Preliminary introductions had been made, and a deal was struck for five hundred kilos of hash.

Hank, Dexter and a guy named Checkers flew over to Karachi to put the deal together. They departed on different dates via different routings and met up at a small hotel near the airport. From there Dexter and Hank registered separately at the Intercontinental Hotel in downtown Karachi.

Checkers was brought along for two reasons. First, he was the best hash expert that either Hank or Dexter had ever met; and second, because this was their first deal with the Paki, no money would be turned over until the container was packed and ready to be loaded at the port. This meant that someone had to be sitting on the cash at all times.

Pakistanis have to be the slipperiest bastards in the world to do business with. No honour, no integrity, no nothing. You have to watch them every step of the way. Dexter swears he has never met a greedier race of people in all his life. The boys had their misgivings about dealing with Pakistanis, but on the other hand, the Pakistanis do have hashish processing down to a fine art. You can get the quality you want, packaged the way you want it, and the "out" is always guaranteed. In Pakistan, unlike India, Morocco, or other countries, everybody is corrupt. At least that's how Dexter saw it.

In many other countries that make and sell hashish, it is still processed the same way it has been done for thousands of years, using rocks for scales, wooden presses for molds. Often it's simply molded by hand into balls or spaghetti-like strands, sometimes called rope hash. The Pakis have imported modern industrial equipment to process it, weigh it, and package it. The hash is tagged, bagged, and made ready for export in one systematic production process.

Most people believe that if hashish is wrapped in red cellophane it is of high quality. This is a myth, a marketing ploy the Pakis have instituted worldwide. You can choose any colour of cellophane wrapping paper — red, green, or gold, whatever. It makes no difference to the quality.

The people who cut and re-press hashish in Europe and in Canada know this, which is why they, too, use red cellophane to wrap their hash mix. Some of these hash mixes are absolute garbage. Because of rising costs and the difficulty of smuggling hashish into Europe, Canada and the United States, people called mixers cut the real hashish when it arrives and re-sell it as the natural product. It is common practice with all drugs - heroin, cocaine, even grass. It's called stepping on the product. The amount of times a product is stepped on depends on the original quality of the product. It is only when a very big deal is smuggled in that the real product, the uncut version, hits the streets. Most of the time people are smoking the mixed or cut hash. There are many different ways to step on hashish. Two of the most common are by mixing dates with the hashish or by mixing hemp powder with it. Hemp powder is dried marijuana leaf passed through a food processor. It is then died black or dark brown with black or brown hemp hair-colouring. Black or brown hair dye can be purchased in any drug store; it is commonly used by women to colour their hair. The hair colouring takes the green colour out of the hemp powder and makes the hash black or dark brown in colour, thereby imitating the natural colour of top quality hashish.

The point of all of this is simply to demonstrate that when one smuggles in quality hashish, you don't have any problems selling it. Either the mixers gobble it up or the street buys it like cotton candy at a fair. Many old hippies — who are now doctors, lawyers, or captains of industry — buy a kilo at a time when the real shit hits town. Hash connoisseurs savor and cherish real hashish for their own personal smoke. It is not uncommon to hear dealers talk about their special clientele, people who will fly a thousand miles just to buy a kilo of the real stuff when it's available. They are always willing to pay top dollar for it, too. To have a cube of real hashish at a party is a status symbol. A great way to reminisce about old times is to have some quality smoke, Bob Dylan playing in the background and some old friends to smile away the hours with.

The police have never answered a call for domestic violence when people were toking on some quality hash or pot. Cannabis is not a violence-inducing drug like alcohol, cocaine or crack cocaine. Although the bureaucrats and politicians would have you believe otherwise, it's just not so!

Salim, the Pakistani hashish exporter, called Hank in his room from the hotel lobby. While he was riding the elevator up to the fourth floor, Hank walked down the hallway and rapped on Dexter's door, advising him of the Cricket's arrival. Checkers stayed in Dexter's room guarding the money. Hank and Dexter greeted the Cricket in Hank's room. The first thing out of the Cricket's mouth was that he wanted to see the money. The answer was a resounding "No!" In this game, cash can cost you your life. You don't flash it or let the other side know where it is until the appropriate time.

They called him Jimmy the Cricket because he reminded them of Walt Disney's cartoon character, Jimminy Cricket. He was about two apples high and had a mouth full of teeth enough for two people. He had large black bulging eyes and a handshake like a wet fish. His black greasy hair was slicked back and parted in the middle. Salim was a sleazy looking little guy, if you ever saw one.

Dexter poured three large double scotches. Then they sat around the small circular table, which was pushed up against the sliding glass door that led to a balcony that overlooked the front driveway entrance to the hotel.

The Cricket was a talker. It made him uncomfortable that Hank and Dexter just sat across from him not saying a word, not even responding to his questions or small talk. In short order, the Cricket got the message: "Let's get down to business." He reached into his pocket, pulled out three small sugar cube-sized pieces of hash and said, "Which quality do you want, Sir?"

Dexter didn't respond in words, he just scooped up the three samples in his hand and left. He knocked on the door to his room. Checkers opened it with a drink in his hand.

"Shit," said Dexter, "How in the hell are you going to tell us which sample is the best, if you're half smashed on booze?"

"Don't sweat it," replied Checkers in his gruffly voice. "I know what you're looking for."

Dexter returned to Hank's room, leaving Checkers to his own devices. They made small talk with the Cricket, giving Checkers time to sample the hash. About twenty minutes later, the phone rang. It was Checkers. Hank nodded to his partner, who got up and left the room to hear what Checkers' verdict was. Entering the room, Dexter observed that his tester was as stoned as a rock star at a music festival. A good sign, Dexter thought to himself.

"Well, which one is it?"

"None of them," replied Checkers.

Dexter didn't ask for any explanations, he turned on his heels and headed right back down the hallway to Salim and his partner. Hank and the Paki looked up expectantly. The looks turned dour when Dex informed them that the quality of the samples was unacceptable. The Cricket started to protest, but Hank cut him short.

"We didn't fly five thousand miles to buy crap. If that's the best you can do, get lost. We have other contacts!"

Now the Cricket saw all that money floating away. He quickly changed his tune from confrontational to accommodating. He reached into his pocket and produced a fourth sample. It was the size of an aspirin. Dexter looked at it, then at the Cricket and exclaimed, "You've gotta be fucking kidding! You expect us to put up three hundred thousand dollars on this? How would you like to go downstairs by the balcony route?"

The Cricket put his hands up in a subservient manner. "Please Sir, these are initial samples only. Once you have approved of the sample you want Sir, I will bring you a whole kilo sample. Upon your approval Sir, you will be taken to the godown to examine and select the entire shipment. Please Sir, I am an honorable man. I am your humble servant Sir."

Hank and Dexter glanced at one another; words were not necessary. They knew that Jimmy the Cricket was a sleaze. Dexter took the aspirin-sized sample back to Checkers, who was gleefully pouring himself another drink. Dex didn't say anything; he just looked at him and let out a sigh. He extended his hand with the little brown sample sitting in his palm. Checkers had to take three stabs at it before he was able to pick it out of

Dexter's hand. This time Dexter stayed with Checkers while he rolled himself a joint made from the little aspirin-sized sample. Checkers sat in a sofa chair that was off to the corner of the room up against the sliding glass doors and lit up the joint. He took two good tokes, put his head back, looked up at the ceiling and smiled, "Yeah, that's the shit."

Dexter bounded to his feet from his sitting position on the corner of the bed. His hands placed firmly on his hips, he growled at Checkers. "How the fuck would you know? You've been sitting here drinking all day. You take two tokes and say, yeah, that's the shit. Come on Checkers, get serious. We've got a lot of money on the line here. We approve this shit and we're stuck with it."

Checkers responded, "You'll never get stuck with this shit. Take a toke yourself."

"I'm just a casual smoker, you know that. Why in the hell do you think we brought you here in the first place?"

Checkers sat up and pushed the joint toward Dexter, "Take a toke."

Dexter sat on the corner of the bed, took the joint from Checkers and dragged on it. Then he passed it back, "I don't see anything special with this shit."

Checkers barked, in his deep gravelly voice, "Take another toke!"

Dexter wanted to prove a point to Checkers. He was screwing up big time because he was boozing too much. Dexter reached over and grabbed the joint out of Checkers' fingers, then he took a big drag, filling his lungs up with the almond-tasting smoke. As he exhaled the smoke from his lungs, he passed the joint back to Checkers. Dexter looked at his friend with an expression on his face that said, are you satisfied now? He was about to get up and return to Hank and the Cricket when all of a sudden he felt an electric tingling sensation starting at the base of his spine, rushing all the way up to the base of his skull. Dexter was stoned! So stoned that he had to lie down on the bed. He could hardly talk; he managed to mumble to his friend to call Hank. The last thing Dexter remembered hearing was Checkers' raspy laughter before he drifted off to sleep.

While Dexter lay comatose on the bed, Checkers got up from his chair, drink and joint in hand, and sauntered down the hallway to Hank's room. After hearing the condition his partner was in, Hank adjourned the meeting with Jimmy the Cricket. The Cricket advised Hank he would return to the hotel that evening with a kilo brick of the hashish they had approved. Several hours later they woke Dexter up and razzed him about teaching Checkers a lesson.

Spirits were high among the foreigners as they awaited the return of Jimmy the Cricket and his kilo of hash. Checkers said it was the best hash he had ever smoked — this coming from a guy who had backpacked his way around India, Nepal and Afghanistan. The three were unanimous, however, that the Cricket was a sleaze bag who had to be watched closely.

The phone jangled and Hank grabbed it; the Cricket was on his way up. The hashish was called Mazar. It was a dark brown, Swiss-chocolate colour. It was so fresh and pliable you could easily bend the whole kilo into a U shape without its breaking apart. The smell was heavenly, an aroma so poignant that you could taste it.

The boys were ready to go on to the next step in the game. They needed to confirm the preferred means of transport. The hash would have to be concealed in a shipment of some legitimate merchandise. They informed the Cricket that their choice of export product was cotton bales. In preliminary discussions, Salim had suggested several different product options, one of which was cotton bales. Dexter and Hank had developed a contact with a textile manufacturer who imported large bales of cotton for his factory. Their proposition was that the manufacturer got to keep the bales of cotton plus a fifty thousand-dollar bonus in return for the use of his company. When the shipment arrived, it would be cleared at customs. Once cleared, the container would be diverted to another warehouse, not that of the manufacturer. If anything went wrong, the manufacturer was in the clear — he simply had to keep his mouth shut and deny all knowledge of the shipment. If everything went according to Hoyle, he got the fifty thousand and the cotton bales.

The next morning, the Cricket's chauffeur picked up Hank and Dexter. He drove them to the godown, where Salim was awaiting them. They walked into the warehouse office, through a door that led to the warehouse area. The hashish was stacked floor to ceiling. The boys wasted no time in getting to work. They immediately walked over to the pile of hashish and began the selection process, pulling out one kilo brick at a time. By selecting the kilo slabs of hash at random, they were trying to ensure that no games were being played on them. It was all Mazar and what a beautiful sight it was! To a hash man it would be tantamount to an archaeologist discovering an untouched pharaoh's tomb or a treasure hunter finding the lost gold of Cortez. What a magnificent sight!

Once they had finished the selection process, the Cricket offered them a cup of tea. They now had to await the delivery of the bales of cotton. A half-hour later they heard a truck blaring its horn at the warehouse door. When the huge metal door was raised, an army of workers scrambled onto the back of the awaiting truck, and fired the large bales of cotton onto the warehouse floor. Once the truck was emptied, it left immediately.

The creaking metal door was drawn down. The workers swarmed over the bales of cotton like bees over a honeycomb. They opened each bale, placed ten kilos in the center, then bundled it up as it was before. When they finished, you couldn't tell the difference from before and after. The boys were satisfied that their goods had been properly packed.

Shortly thereafter another truck pulled up to the warehouse. Its diesel engine could be heard idling away, waiting impatiently for the rusted steel door to rise. The clanging, creaking door slowly raveled its way skyward, revealing the big truck with the sea container on its back, ready to be loaded. The driver of the container truck jumped out of the cab and quickly moved around to the back to open the doors of the container. The bales of cotton were deposited in the container by the same crew who had stuffed them with the hashish. When the container was fully loaded, its doors were closed and a customs seal was secured on the door handles. The driver then handed Salim the shipping papers, duly stamped and inspected by the Pakistani customs. The container truck departed for the port of Karachi to dispatch its precious cargo for Canada.

The smugglers were impressed. Perhaps they had unfairly judged the Cricket. Things were really cooking; the Cricket produced the shipping papers and the export documents. After handing the smugglers all the necessary paperwork, he paused and flashed his big toothy grin, "Now, if you please Sir, the money."

Hank and Dex smiled at one another. Hank advised Salim that his money was waiting for him at the hotel. The drive back to the hotel from the industrial park took them along an open sewer that served the City of Karachi; however, not even the acrid urine and feces smell bothered the two foreigners who were high on the adrenaline rush that was surging through their bodies. The deal had been set in motion. A wrong move from here on out meant ten years' imprisonment for each of the smugglers. The rewards were great, but so were the risks.

The chauffeur drove the car up the circular drive that graced the hotel entrance. When the car stopped at the front steps, the doormen quickly surrounded the car. They opened the front passenger door as well as the rear doors almost simultaneously. They stepped back and saluted the disembarking guests. The Cricket moved smartly out of the front seat of the car and headed straight into the hotel lobby, continuing through to the elevator banks. He had to wait momentarily for Dexter and Hank to catch up to him.

Hank said, "I didn't think that little midget could walk so fast."

Dexter chuckled, "He's either got sex or money on his mind. His wife has definitely got to be a two-bagger."

"I don't know Dex, maybe she's a beauty. Maybe she puts a bag over his head and counts his money."

Checkers was waiting in the room when the entourage arrived. They offered the Cricket a drink. He waved his hand, saying, "No thank you please, I am a Muslim. Drinking is not good for me."

Dex couldn't resist smiling. He asked, "What was that you were doing last night?"

It was obvious the Cricket didn't want to drink or socialize. He wanted to get his grubby little hands on the money. Dex had no problem with that; he just didn't like the Cricket's hypocrisy.

Hank nodded to Checkers, who reached behind the chair in the corner of the room and pulled out the briefcase with the money. Putting it on the bed, he popped it open for Salim's examination. The Cricket's lower jaw dropped when he saw the tightly jammed contents of the briefcase awaiting his embrace.

Dexter looked at Checkers and said, "Must be the heavy teeth." Hank looked over scornfully at Dexter, as if to say, "Cut it out!" Dex just smiled, and made his way over to the dresser, where Checkers was busily pouring himself a tall scotch. The Cricket was about to count the money; he stopped, looked over at Hank and said, "Please Sir, the total amount present is three hundred thousand dollars?"

Hank nodded his head and the Cricket closed the briefcase.

"If you please Sir, may I obtain the use of your executive case? I shall return it promptly to you this evening."

Hank nodded his head again and, with that, little Jimmy the Cricket bolted for the door, excusing himself on the way out for not being more hospitable; however, he "Had to pay the workers, you know." The boys lifted their glasses in the air toward the Cricket, he bowed his head, and in the next instant, he was gone.

That evening he returned with the briefcase. They went over their agreement again. It was simple enough — he would receive another two hundred thousand dollars when the shipment was cleared in Montreal. Included in the price were the shipping costs as was the cost of the bales of cotton. The Cricket began whining about the cost of the bales of cotton. The partners agreed, they would pay him an extra ten thousand for the cotton bales, when the shipment arrived safely. With that out of the way, the Cricket abandoned his Muslim beliefs and joined the boys in a couple of drinks.

Dexter, Hank, and Checkers were leaving at various times that evening and early next morning. Nobody hangs around Karachi any longer than they have to, not even the Pakis.

Dexter and Hank were going to meet up in Rome, do a little shopping and sightseeing for a couple of days, and return home. It would be three weeks before the shipment would reach Montreal. Checkers was stopping by London to do a little "bird chasing." He would be homeward bound in a week or so, depending on the birds. He was called Checkers because he was always ready to jump on something. The time, place or even looks of the bird didn't concern him. He would jump on anything in a skirt!

When Dexter met up with Hank at the Cavalieri Hilton, perched on one of the seven hills that overlooks the City of Rome, he discovered that his buddy was sick with the Pakistani version of Montezuma's Revenge. Hank who had never been to Rome before, was looking forward to seeing the sights, and Dexter had some of his favorite spots all lined up for him to see. Italy — the land of great food, Chianti Classico wine, quality shopping and fascinating historical sights to captivate the desire of its tourists — awaited them. The Italian climate had saluted the smugglers with bright, cool, autumn weather. It couldn't have been a more perfect time to visit the Fontana di Trevi or the Vatican, enjoy the excellent cuisine at Piccolo Mondo's, and maybe even catch a little Italian sparrow just to add to the ambiance of it all. Time to blow off a little steam and prepare for the pressure cooker that was going to engross their lives in a couple of weeks. Unfortunately, all Hank wanted was a toilet bowl — not very cultural but paramount in his life at that moment.

The difference between Pakistani Montezuma's Revenge and all others is that with the Paki version, you can shit through the eye of a needle at fifty paces! Man, that's power! Pepto Bismal? Tums? A joke! The only thing that ever worked for Dexter were the pills he had purchased in Pakistan. They know what they're dealing with over there — forget the pink stuff! Dexter pulled out his emergency kit and handed Hank a pill. Hank popped it down with a sip of scotch and dove between the sheets. Dex went to Piccolo Mondo's by himself and ate and drank for two people. Dex never ordered dessert when in Italy; if he had space left after his meal, he would order an extra side dish of pasta, quenching his thirst with a bottle or two of Chianti Classico.

The boys returned home and awaited the arrival of the deal. The closer it came to the arrival date of the shipment, the higher their stress level. One mistake — just one mistake — and it was all over but the crying. Three weeks to the day the shipment arrived, and the deal went down like an old whore's panties on a Saturday night. No problem.

The distribution of the hash went quicker than they had anticipated. Once the dealers realized the quality of the smoke, they came running back to Hank and Dexter with bags full of money. They wanted more, more and more. There wasn't enough to last a week. The hashish was out, the money was in and now they awaited the arrival of the Cricket.

In between the deals and the hustle, Dexter relaxed and enjoyed his success with his family. The most important thing in Dexter's life was his wife and children. While still in his teens, he fell in love with a gal who was mature and shared the same goals he had. Even at that young age, Dexter realized that one of his shortcomings was his immaturity. He was the third of a family of five children. He had two older brothers and two younger sisters. His older brothers left home as soon as they could, and they stayed away like an asthmatic from smoke.

Dexter's father was an alcoholic. His binge drinking forays brought instability and insecurity to the family. When his father was sober, he was a real gentleman; when he was drunk, he was all mouth. His mother and father were constantly involved in verbal battles. When his father was sober, everyone walked around on eggshells, not wanting to do anything that might trip Dad off on another drinking binge. They also had to be careful of what they said around Mom, not wishing to send her off on some tirade about the injustices of the world or marriage, or whatever. The family environment was one of denial and low self-esteem. Dexter never brought his friends home because he was never sure when his father would come home drunk and create a scene. Even when his Father was OK, there was a chance his Mom wasn't. Sometimes she was a very warm and affectionate person, but other times she could be off in la la land and say something stupid or embarrassing.

His Mom was a very attractive, hard working, law abiding person. Her inferiority complex led to wild-eyed episodes of loss of touch with reality. In short, she lived in a world of denial, playing a martyr's role that grew with each passing day. She would often be heard to say, "If I had a husband like so-and-so's, I'd divorce him in a minute." Yet she never realized the catastrophic effect her drunkard husband had on his family. The family atmosphere was generally chaotic, interspersed with moments of peace. Each period of tranquility brought hope that maybe things would finally settle down. They never did, and the family crisis became the norm. One by one the children left home as soon as they could.

Even though Dexter was part of this confused milieu, somehow he was able to see the insanity of it. He knew it wasn't normal, but then again, he didn't really know what normal was. The confusion of his family made Dexter more distant from them. While they continued in their world of denial, Dexter searched for a way out of the fog.

Dexter fell in love with his wife and the maturity of her ways. She, with this man who could make money like a baker bakes bread. It wasn't that she was a gold digger, because at the time of their meeting and subsequent marriage, Dexter wasn't anywhere near wealthy. Her attraction or fascination was more with the differences in their backgrounds. She, from a hard working, law abiding, middle class family; he, from a wild 'n crazy family that worked hard, played hard and didn't seem to give a damn about the rules of society. It was the age-old fatal attraction that women succumb to — the chance to change a man.

They began to raise their family with the hopes and dreams that all parents have. Dexter grew up believing that money was the way to happiness. The more he had, the happier he'd be, and the happier his family would be. As Dexter would put it, "Money, money, money, the royal road to happiness." He was convinced that if only his parents had had lots of money, then things would have been different. He would have had a happy childhood instead of the raucous, tumultuous and embarrassing ordeal that it was. Others have had it a lot worse — at least there was no physical abuse — but the verbal and mental abuse wasn't exactly a walk in the park.

With the money rolling in, Dexter bought a house. His wife hired an interior decorator and furnished it to the hilt. Hell, Dexter didn't know an interior decorator from a milkman and now he was having this pansy come into his home and talk about beige walls and milky ceilings. Dex just smiled and left it all to his wife who seemed to enjoy every minute of it. Dexter was called in for the big decisions such as fuchsia wall coverings, pastel pink lampshades or a coffee and porridge fabric for the living room sofa. His wife worried about the cost of things, while Dexter answered every query with his patent answer, "If you like it, get it." He wanted so much for his wife to be happy. He wanted a very different family environment than the one he had come from. He had money, so everyone should be happy.

Dexter lavished his attention and his money on his wife and his children. The only competing issue with Dexter's devotion to his family was his booze and his crony friends, for whom he'd walk through fire. Dexter was a binge drinker like his old man, except that Dexter had better control than his father and also a better personality when drunk. In fact, Dexter was a gregarious drunk. He liked to dance and sing and have a good time. His major problem was that one drink was too much and a hundred was not enough.

He never missed a hockey game, a baseball game, a ballet class, a school performance or a family function. Dexter spent most of his free time with his wife and his children, he grew up with them. He provided them with stability and good self-esteem. He emphasized education, love, family values and trust in each other. On Hallowe'en, Dexter would walk the streets with his children, watching them have fun. Sometimes he'd really get into the act and dress up in his Pakistani or Indian clothes.

Christmastime was a wondrous event for the family. Dexter always started his Christmas shopping early. He wanted his kids to have all the "in" things of the day, so he'd get a head start the moment the first Christmas decoration hit the malls. For his wife, he'd search the boutiques and shops all over town buying those special gifts not easily found. He loved to surprise her with gifts she'd not imagine he'd think of getting her. Dexter got off on the Santa Claus role. A very special day was when the family would have breakfast with Santa Claus at one of the downtown department stores. After breakfast, the kids would sit on Santa's knee and have their photos taken. Dexter loved watching the expression on the faces of the children as they spoke to Santa. The family would all join in the selection of the Christmas tree and then decorate it. Dexter and the kids would decorate the tree and Mom would do some baking. Mother would always do the final inspection of the tree and make whatever little touch-ups she deemed necessary. Christmas Eve, the kids would be tucked in bed and Dexter and his wife would pack the presents under the tree. In the morning, the screams of excitement coming from the children would get Dexter and his wife up to inspect all that Santa had brought. In the beginning, his wife was distressed at Dexter's extravagance. Sometimes she'd take some of the gifts back because she found them too expensive. Over time, many of the boutiques and store employees came to know Dexter and his wife by name. If Dexter wasn't shopping on his own, he was shopping with his wife. His wife was the one who was more concerned and careful about the family finances, but in time she, too, became accustomed to the higher lifestyle. In one aspect they epitomized the burgeoning yuppie culture.

His family was number one; booze and his buddies ran a close second. Dexter's wife recognized the blind trust and loyalty he placed in his friendships. She realized that he didn't see through their games of deceit and that they didn't share Dexter's value of friendship. In that sense, Dexter was very naive, and this caused many a heated discussion between him and his wife. Dexter matured and began to see that many of his friends weren't sincere, nor did they appreciate his devout, almost fanatical loyalty to friendship. Dexter regarded loyal friendship above money and personal safety. Many times he risked his life to assist friends; and in some cases, people who weren't even close associates to him. Once, he drove a bank robber, who had been wounded in a shootout with police, to a doctor he knew. The doctor treated the man and Dexter drove him back to his friends. Dexter never saw the guy again. Had he been arrested with the wounded bandit, he would have been charged and sent to prison. That is if the guy would have surrendered without a fight. A friend had reached out, and Dexter was there. He did it out of loyalty to a friend — no money, no ego trip — just friendship. Dexter's wife was relieved when he teamed up with Hank. She felt Hank was sincere and that his goals and character complemented Dexter.

Loyalty was a priority to Dexter, and betrayal was the lowest level one could sink to. Betrayal of friendship was as bad as betrayal of family. If anything could spark the electric flame of anger in him, betrayal was the catalyst that could make him explode. From being a mild, easygoing, polite person — to the heights of hell's fury — Dexter would be consumed with anger at the thought of betrayal. Betrayal took many forms, and sometimes people didn't understand that aspect of Dex nature. If you cheated him or stole from him, it was the same as stealing food from the mouth of his family, and at the same time you were betraying his trust. For the most part, his easygoing, almost docile manner was perceived as a weakness; but those who knew him, knew what lay behind the mask.

Dexter wanted his family to experience the opposite of what he'd experienced. His father was cold and aloof — Dexter was warm and affectionate. In his childhood, laughter was always at risk of disapproval, because no one knew what mood mother or father would be in. In Dexter's home, laughter abounded with practical jokes and plenty of hugs. Dexter could just as easily laugh at himself as others, and often he was the object of the jokes. In part, it was a childlike quality that was due to his immaturity and his belief that it was better to wear a smile than a frown. In time, Dexter matured thanks to his wife's prodding and life's experiences. After many disappointments with people, he learned to be guarded with his friendship and his commitments to people. In other words, he learned to say no.

Vacation time meant exploring the world, sharing and enjoying new experiences with his family. They spent many a vacation in the sun, bouncing in the waves, body surfing, splashing in the pool, exploring interesting places and dining in fine restaurants. His wife was his best friend and his children were his idols.

When Dexter made his first million, he wanted to take the family out to celebrate. The option of where to eat was put to the children. The parents named many of the finest restaurants in town that the children were familiar with. In the end the children decided on McDonald's. Dexter took his camera to mark the occasion and, to this day, his favourite photo is that of his wife, his children and himself, eating hamburgers at McDonald's.

During this period of great joy in his life, Dexter started seeing a psychiatrist. With everything going right for him, there seemed to be a stone in his stomach, something telling him that things weren't kosher. He thought that money would solve all his problems, and to some degree it had. But there was still a hollow emptiness inside that cried out to be smothered by booze. He wanted to be normal and for his children to have a happy, normal life. He knew he was somewhere off in centre field, but not knowing where centre field was, he searched for guidance. He suspected he was an alcoholic but he never admitted it to himself or anyone else. Besides, he thought that it was normal to get drunk every now and again. He just didn't admit that his every now and again was a lot more frequent than the norm. He continued on with his work, his wheeling and dealing, and his shrink. Slowly, he made progress on all fronts except the booze.

The Cricket arrived about two weeks after the shipment had cleared. He met with the boys, received his balance of payment and the program for the next deal was set in motion. Salim wanted to up the ante to a thousand keys. Naturally that would have required a larger deposit. Hank was all for it, but Dexter was not. Dexter reminded his partner of their first impressions of Salim, and he was still not convinced that the Cricket was a straight shooter. In the end, Dexter prevailed. They were just getting acquainted with the Paki, and Dex didn't want to make a possible honest man a thief.

The Cricket tried to sweeten the deal by dropping his price if the boys put up a bigger deposit. When they didn't jump on that proposition, he offered to send more at the lower rate, if they would put more cash in his hands. It all sounded a little too good to be true. Hank was chomping at the bit, but Dexter remained resolute. They'd stick with the original game plan — three hundred thousand down with the balance of two hundred thousand to be paid only after the deal arrived safely. They decided to give two hundred thousand of the three hundred thousand deposit while he was in Canada. It freed them of the hassle of bringing all that money over to Pakistan. The one-hundred-thousand-dollar balance would be brought over by Checkers in three weeks. This would give the Cricket ample time to have the next shipment all ready to rock 'n' roll for Checkers' inspection. This would mean less time for Checkers to spend in Pakistan. They wanted Checkers in and out of Karachi faster than a Paki taking a shower.

Three weeks later Checkers was on a plane heading to Karachi with the one-hundred-thousand-dollar balance of deposit. He was instructed by Dexter not to give the money up until he had seen the hash packed and loaded on the container and the Cricket had given him all the necessary documents for customs clearance in Canada. Then, and only then, was he to turn over the one hundred thousand to Salim.

The Cricket started into sleaze mode the moment Checkers arrived. The Cricket advised him that because of security reasons, the hash hadn't made it down from the mountains. The delay would be temporary. In the meantime, the Cricket was the congenial host, supplying Checkers with broads, booze and personal smoke. Checkers settled into the party scene at his five-star hotel like a dame in a bubble bath. The Cricket must have thought that Checkers would get fed up after awhile. Maybe he hoped that Checkers would make a mistake — leave the money in the room and go for a walk, or ask Salim to hold it for him (especially with all the strange women coming and going from his room). Maybe he thought Checkers would just give up the money and leave. He didn't know Checkers! The man could go through broads, booze and smoke like a preacher through a Bible.

Three weeks had passed and not a word from Checkers. Dexter was getting concerned that something had gone wrong, but Hank assured him there was no cause for panic. He assumed that Checkers had stopped by London again — apparently the birds were enraptured by Checkers' suave air. His six-foot-two frame, topped by a thick black mane of hair, his black brush moustache and his gravel voice were just too much for most women to resist. He also boasted that he had a tongue that could charm a beaver to heights it never dared to fantasize about.

Dexter was preparing to buy a ticket for Pakistan when Hank received a call from Checkers. He had returned and would meet them the following afternoon at the place he called his office — the Sex Club on St-Catherine Street. He loved to watch the bare-ass broads with their boobs flopping all over the place, dancing on his table or pouring him a beer. The man had an insatiable appetite for women. Hank contacted Dexter and the next day they sat at a table, the music booming off the walls, the mirrored ball fixture revolving at the ceiling, casting lights and shadows around and around the room, the bare-assed babes flaunting and taunting all who would be tantalized into giving them a tip for a little feel of flesh. Checkers walked into the club and found the boys at their table. Even in the dimly lit atmosphere of the club, he looked tired and drawn from his journey. They decided to go downstairs to the coffee shop and talk there. Checkers informed them he had flown directly back from Karachi, changing planes in Amsterdam, then on to Montreal. The jet lag made him lethargic in his motions and his speech, but he knew that Hank and Dexter were anxious to be filled in. He explained the reasons the Cricket had given him for the delay. He told them how the Cricket had showed up at his hotel all excited — Checkers had to get out of town immediately. Apparently the police had grown suspicious of him, and he was about to be arrested. The Cricket, learning of this information through his valuable contacts, had made reservations for Checkers to fly out that night. He advised Checkers to pack his bags, check out of the hotel immediately and take a taxi to his office. He would stay there until it was time for him to go to the airport. Without hesitation, Checkers did as Salim had suggested. He spent the balance of that day hiding out in the Cricket's office.

Hearing this, Dexter rested his elbows on the table, cupped his head in his hands, and stared down at his cup of coffee. When he looked up he saw the answer he didn't want to see in his partner's face. They knew the little weasel was trying to beat them. Hank asked Checkers if he had seen the hash. Had he given the Cricket the balance of the money? Checkers hadn't seen the hash and yes, he had given him the one-hundred-thousand-dollar balance of deposit. Apparently the Cricket was worried that if Checkers was arrested at the airport with the money, he would be charged with drug smuggling or with being a black marketeer.

Dexter interjected, "Geez, that was thoughtful of the Cricket to be so concerned about your welfare. He even took the chance of holding the money."

No one commented on Dexter's outburst. It wasn't necessary, they all knew what little Jimmy the Cricket was up to. They excused Checkers so he could go home and get some rest from his jet lag. He had already told them all they needed to know. Then the partners began reviewing their options.

Option number one was that they could let the Cricket slide and do nothing. Option number two was to go over to Pakistan and whack the little weasel. Option number three was to write him a letter, making it perfectly clear that they knew what he was up to and that they weren't going to let him get away with his bullshit. Dexter opted for option number two and Hank preferred the third option as being the most intelligent way to proceed. Dexter disagreed. His concern was that playing with Salim was going to land them both in jail. Dexter felt they should cut their losses and move on. The partners continued to argue. It was not that Hank disagreed entirely with Dexter's choice, he simply felt that it was not their next option but their last one, if all else failed. They both knew that letting the little Paki slide was not a viable choice. If they let him get away with it, word would eventually filter out onto the street. They would be perceived as weak and that would in turn make them a target of every coconut coming out of the can. The hippie era stigmatized drug dealers and importers as pushovers. Convicts sitting in prisons were frothing at the mouth to get out and rob those fat weak drug dealers as a first step on their road to riches. Robbing a drug dealer was easier than robbing a bank, and you didn't have to worry about the cops. At least that was the thinking until most of the hippies left the scene. Option number one was a non-option. Hank persisted and Dexter acquiesced.

The correspondence game started between Hank and the Cricket. First Salim sent them a phony shipping invoice. When he was called on that, he came up with a story about the ship the container had been sent on returning to port because of mechanical problems. Hank and the Cricket played postman bullshit for several months. Eventually Hank's patience wore out. He gave the Cricket an ultimatum: you come to Canada or Canada is going to you. Dexter had his bags packed, eagerly awaiting a response or more British science. Either way, he felt the inevitable solution was to exercise option number two. Dexter wanted to be finished with the little creep; he wanted to turn the page and move on. Hank insisted that they give the Cricket a fair chance to respond.

Two weeks later they received the Cricket's reply. He would be departing for Canada within the week. He implored them to be patient, he wanted to straighten matters out. Hank slapped Dexter on the back after reading him the news he had received by courier. Dexter was not quite so exuberant; he wasn't buying it. He told his partner that the Cricket was a sleaze. If in fact he did come, he'd probably have the Man with him. He warned his partner the little scuzzball was dangerous; he would try and set them up, put them in the can, or waltz them around the park some more. Hank wasn't listening, he couldn't believe Salim would stoop so low. After all, hadn't he made serious money with them? They had been honourable, there had been no problems other than the problems the Cricket had created with his delays and bullshit. Business could only get better. Why would he want to screw them? He could make ten times more money with them by playing it straight. It didn't make sense that he would want to screw them around and blow off a good thing. The Cricket had the hash and the guaranteed out, and the boys had the cash and the way in. They were like a football and a foot, they need one another in order to play!

Ten days later Hank received a call from his sister. A Mr. Salim had called and left a message for Hank. He was in Montreal, he was staying at the Queen Elizabeth Hotel. He would stay there until he heard from Hank. Immediately Hank got hold of his partner. They raced down to the Queen Elizabeth Hotel. Hank was jubilant, he was singing and slapping his knees to the beat of the rock 'n roll music thumping out of the radio. Dexter was subdued; he kept checking his rearview mirror suspiciously for a tail. When they walked into the lobby of the grand old hotel with its marble floors and bustling activity, they discovered the Cricket in all his glory, sitting off in the corner, lost in a big, high-back sofa chair, his feet dangling in the air beneath the seat. He sat there, perched like some little emperor watching over his subjects. He had been patiently waiting for the two mooks to show up, and they did!

The Cricket wasted no time in telling the boys another tale of woe. Hank's jubilant mood turned sour. Dexter didn't speak, he just sat there boiling, listening to the Cricket's line of crap. It took everything he had not to explode, not to grab the Cricket by the throat and rip his head off his shoulders, right there in the hotel lobby. Salim began to sense the danger he was in, so he put a new spin on things. The little sleaze ball now started appealing to their greed. He had the temerity to ask the boys for another two hundred thousand. Naturally, it was to be in the boys' best interest, because with that added amount, he would ship two thousand kilos. It was all ready to go, he just needed a bigger deposit before shipping it. Dexter had allowed his partner to do all the talking up to this point. However, when Salim came out with that proposition, Dexter started to get up out of his chair, his fist clenched. He was about to unload on Jimmy the Cricket! Hank was angry, too, and he could see that Dexter was ready to go over the top. He didn't want his partner to lose it, because he felt that as long as the Cricket was here, there was a chance that they might be able salvage the deal. Before Dexter could react, Hank jumped to his feet and stepped between him and the still-seated Cricket and adjourned the meeting to the next day. Hank wanted Dexter to cool off.

"You get some rest now. Tomorrow we can discuss this further. We'll take you for a drive and you can see the sights."

The Cricket bowed his head in approval at Hank's suggestion. His bulging eyes, slyly glancing sideways at Dexter, sized him up. "Mr. Dexter Sir, will I have the pleasure of your company tomorrow also Sir?"

Dexter, fighting to control his anger, couldn't speak. He just nodded his head and feigned a weak smile. Once outside the hotel, the boys walked along Mansfield Street, in the shadow of the tall aluminum cross-shaped building known as Place Ville-Marie. Dexter, in a voice crackling with fury, spoke to his partner. "You don't believe that little shit for a minute, do you? There is only one thing to do with that little bastard. Tomorrow we pick him up, take him to my country place and read him the riot act! He either comes up with the money or he sends the hash. If not, we bury the little putz in the ground!"

"Dexter, Dexter, Dexter, calm down. You don't think the Cricket has the balls to come here and ask us for more money if his intention is to out and out beat us, do you?"

"Yes," replied Dexter, "the guy is no good, he's a sleaze, his payoff is to beat us for everything he can. It's not a question of balls, he's a sleaze!

They get off screwing people to their knees. I'm telling you, we take him up north. One of us sits on him at all times. We give him a week, two weeks, a month, I don't care, but at the end of the day, he either comes up with the cash or the hash, or it's his ass! Hank, we can't let him slide, and he's too dangerous to play with any more. He comes up right or we turn his lights out. There's no other way. Do you want every punk on the street, every coconut coming out of the joint, taking a run at us when they hear we got beat by a four-foot-five Paki? We have no choice, he does the right thing or else he's history!"

"Now Dexter, listen to me. I don't like violence or killing. You know if push comes to shove, I'm there one hundred per cent; but this is different. The guy is trying to do the right thing, and you want to lean on him. You can't seriously believe he's here to screw us! He is offering to send us two tons, man. It's a sweetheart deal and you want to shoot the duck that lays the golden eggs. Dexter, what's come over you?"

"First of all, that guy ain't no duck, goose or chicken. He's a sleazebag! He's burying you in bullshit. Secondly, I don't like violence or killing any more than you do. We have to protect ourselves from him and the street. You know the first rule of the street. Have you lost your nerve? If so, get out of the game. You can't rewrite the rules just because it's convenient to you. Forget the crap he's been spoon-feeding you. He's playing to your greed, he's dazzling you with his footwork and baffling you with his bullshit. This guy is dangerous, he's trouble, and before this is over he is gonna take a run at us. I'm not only talking about money, I mean our lives! Now I don't want to hear about one ton or two tons, let's get our money back and walk away from him."

Dex we've been partners for a long time. We've been through a lot together. Please listen to me. Be a little more patient, we'll get it resolved."

Dexter looked at his partner and he saw him walking away from the rules of the game. He knew that you either play by the rules of the game, get out of the game, go to the can or die. It wasn't a question of being a bad ass or a tough guy. That's the way it is in the criminal world.

Try and live it any other way, and you'll get creamed. A lot of people get dumped everyday in the world of crime because they don't play the game by the rules. Dexter and Hank finally agreed that there would be no more talk of more money or a bigger shipment. They would stick to the original game plan. If he didn't send the deal within a month, they'd both be on their way over to Pakistan to settle it once and for all — no more talking, no more delays. The Cricket was to be told point-blank. No song, no dance, no stories. The hash, the cash, or else.

The next day Jimmy the Cricket was standing on the sidewalk in front of the Queen Elizabeth Hotel as Dexter and Hank pulled up in Hank's big black Buick. The Cricket wasn't acting like a little emperor now. He looked more like a puppet dancing on a string of nerves, the big toothy grin snapping open and shut like the shutter on a high-speed camera lens. Dexter sat quietly in the back seat as Hank played tour guide, steering the limo and its guest onto the expressway and out into the countryside. Dexter was checking to see if they had a tail; he had also made arrangements with Freddie to shadow them. If Freddie saw that they had company he would pass them and flash his lights. For a couple of hundred, Freddie took the day off school to play scout. Dexter had a back-up plan that he hadn't discussed with his partner. If the Man was following them, he was going to send the Paki back to Karachi in a box.

There were no police with them that day, at least Freddie and Dexter didn't see any. The Buick stopped at a little country inn, and they had their talk with the Cricket. Actually Hank did all the talking, Dexter just listened. Salim was playing Hank like a violin, he also realized that Dexter was not into music appreciation. Dexter sensed the Cricket's uneasiness with him, and that suited him just fine. They dropped the Cricket off at his hotel. It was obvious that his slippery little mind was spinning a web of deceit, but for now he had decided to keep his thoughts to himself. He had been given a clear mandate, and there was no wiggle room.

When the Cricket returned to Pakistan, he sent another crapola story, just stroking for more time. The deal that was supposed to have happened six months ago was no closer to realization than day one. Dexter called his partner and set up a meeting. It was time for them to take a trip to Pakistan!

CHAPTER THREE
BACK UP YOUR ACTION

Dexter and Hank went for a drive in the country. People often make the mistake of thinking their home, office or car are safe places to discuss business. The police often tap telephones illegally. Having your phone tapped is like having a microphone in your home, office or car that's wired to the local gendarmerie. All they have to do is call your number, let the phone ring once, hang up, and your telephone becomes a listening device, picking up sounds and conversation within a twelve-foot radius of the phone. The Man can't use this information against you in court, but he sure as hell can nail your ass to the wall with it. Many wise guys think this is all James Bond stuff. They refuse to believe the sophistication of the electronic eavesdropping devices that the police have. This is not to overlook the standard bugs they place in your home and car, or the parabolic microphones that beam a signal to a window, picking up your conversations from the beams bouncing off the window of the room you're in. Fax machines and beepers are also cloned and thereby spied upon. Some guys now believe that communicating via the Internet is secure. It's not — they can monitor the Internet, too.

To be a winner in the underworld is to be aware of how times change. If you don't keep up, you become a dinosaur, like a fossil in prison, locked up while the world goes by. Some might have said of Hank and Dexter that they were paranoid, but the cops would tell you that they were tough to nail. Criminal life is a very stressful one, more so than what the average square john has to cope with. That is why almost all of them abuse alcohol, or drugs, or both. Dexter and Hank saw many a loser spend their lives in the revolving door of the penitentiary system. (I was a good example of that.) They call going to prison for short stints of time (anywhere from a year to five years) doing life on the installment plan. Unfortunately, about ninety-five per cent of criminals are losers. They never grow up, they never mature. They're still little boys playing "Cops and Robbers." Sometimes beginners in the underworld move up too fast. They get in over their heads. They never have the opportunity to become mature thinking adults. The first time they get caught, they get slammed hard.

Later on they may come to realize how foolish, reckless or downright stupid they were, but it's too late, they're already marked.

In their younger days, when they were coming up in the underworld, Dexter and Hank did many stupid and foolish things. Some say they were lucky, but they would tell you that they were blessed. One thing they did that helped them mature and stay out of trouble was to observe others. They learned from the mistakes of their friends and associates, they watched and listened to the old-timers. Even the losers have something to say. This insight helped them acquire the street smarts needed to survive. They both graduated with Ph.D.s from the street. It wasn't till later on in life that they earned formal educational degrees.

One of the best ways Hank and Dexter found to ensure a private conversation was to find a small restaurant or café off the beaten track, a place they very seldom frequented. The Man is intelligent but he's not Houdini — he can't wire every restaurant and café in the country.

After driving a little way out of the city, Hank and Dexter stopped in at a country café. The place was empty, so they sat in a booth at the back. They ordered coffee and lunch. The waitress brought them their order, and then she returned to the front. If the Man had been following them, he would have entered the restaurant by now. The only way the police could have gotten to the restaurant before them was if Hank or Dexter had told them. They didn't know where they were going, and even if they had they wouldn't have mentioned it on the phone. It was by taking precautions like this that the boys kept themselves out of trouble. Many a friend who was too lazy to make the effort wound up behind bars. Others were just too stupid to even bother to be careful.

Dexter reminded Hank of his commitment. They both knew the Cricket had no intention of sending the deal. If Mohammed wasn't going to go to the mountain, the mountain had to get up off its ass and go to Mohammed. Hank started squirming. He wanted to give the Cricket more time. He told Dexter that it was stupid of them to go over to Pakistan now. The Cricket would be waiting for them. They would probably wind up with knives in their backs or find a snake or a poisonous spider in their bed. Hank shook his head; he thought it was a suicide move.

Dexter saw that his partner had gotten soft with the money he had made. It wasn't a question of hiring someone to do the dirty work for them. They both knew that when you hire someone to do the tough jobs for you, you eventually end up working for them. Hiring someone to whack someone for you is like giving someone a stick to carry over your head. They had seen the results of that type of thinking come boomeranging back on those who took that route. They had been through many tough scrapes before, and they had always stood side-by-side. This time Hank knew it was going to go down to the wire, and he didn't have the stomach for it. He tried every excuse he could come up with to change Dexter's mind. It was no use. Dexter was going to Pakistan and, for the first time in their long close friendship, Hank was backing out of his sworn commitment. Dexter couldn't or wouldn't drop the ball. He knew there were too many repercussions for them if they did. He spoke calmly to his old confidant.

"Hank, I've gone along with you on this one all the way, but here's where the rubber meets the road. I'm going over there and one way or the other this problem is gonna come to an end. The Cricket sends the shit or I'm turning his lights out. If he sends, we split up our ends and our partnership will be over. You'll go your way and I'll go mine. If he doesn't, I'll do what I gotta do and we both share the loss. After this, it's all over between us."

Hank tried to skate around the problem once again. In the end he realized Dexter was right. He couldn't bring himself to live up to his commitment, and he couldn't proffer another alternative.

Two days later Dexter was on a plane for Pakistan. Airline security was tighter than a virgin in religion class. All Dexter could manage on this trip was a small six-shot thirty-two revolver. Good enough to get the job done but not a whole helluva lot of use in battle.

The plane tires screeched as it touched down at the Karachi Airport as if signalling to Dexter's hormones to start pumping the adrenaline. Dexter cleared customs with a calm exterior, but his heart pounded away inside like a pile driver sinking an iron beam into the ground. He followed a taxi driver, who had grabbed his luggage out of his hands the moment he stepped through the customs doors, to the taxi parking area. He instructed the taxi driver to take him to the small airport hotel he had stayed at before. He didn't want to register at either of the five-star hotels, in case Salim had people at the front desk on the lookout for him. After registering at the front desk he went straight to his room. There was security all over the hotel, soldiers in their drab khaki uniforms, with their well-worn dark blue berets pulled down around their ears and their WWI Lee Enfield rifles slung over their shoulders, inspecting people as they came and went. There were soldiers at the elevator banks, soldiers riding up and down in every elevator car, all day and all night long. When Dexter got off the elevator on the third floor, there were more soldiers standing in the corridors. Dex knew Salim had nothing to do with this, so he asked the bellhop who was struggling with his luggage why all the soldiers in the hotel?

"Oh, sorry Sir, we have convention of oil sheiks visiting Karachi. Security very important Sir. Karachi very safe now Sir!"

The musty smell of the dimly lit room rushed into Dexter's nostrils as he stepped in and looked around. The floor had a dusty, threadbare carpet, the two single beds were covered with well-worn faded but matching bedspreads. The room was small, not much bigger than a jail cell. Dexter pushed back the heavy dark blue drapes that covered the window. The view overlooked the rooftop and the service area of the hotel grounds. He closed the drapes and the dust shed off them and filtered into the air, causing Dexter to sneeze. He tipped the bellhop and when he'd left, he secured the chain lock on the door. It was now two-thirty in the morning; in a couple of hours it would be light. Dexter changed from his suit, shirt, and tie, into his jeans and long-sleeved sweatshirt. He checked the sheets on the bed for any creepy crawlies, not because he was worried about the Cricket striking so soon, but just as a conscious reaction to Hank's admonition. He slept on top of the sheets that night with his jeans, sweatshirt and cowboy boots on. He arranged for a wake-up call at seven that morning.

It seemed he had just closed his eyes when the phone rang. Pulling the receiver to his ear, he heard the operator say in her sweetest English voice, "Mr. Dexter Sir, good morning Sir, the time is now seven a.m. Is this call sufficient or shall I call you back Sir?"

Dexter acknowledged her call. One call was enough. Immediately the adrenaline in his blood started building. He thought about all the soldiers he was going to pass on his way out. He thought about the little sleaze bag who had forced him to call his hand. In an instant Dexter was wide awake. He turned the shower on and stepped back, watching the tea-colored water gush out of the showerhead. After a minute or two it turned whitish gray. "That's as good as it gets," he thought to himself. As the warm water splashed over his body, his mind raced with expectations about all that might go wrong in the hours to come. After he had showered, he reached into his clothes bag and pulled out his dark blue banker suit. The white shirt, tie, black socks, and polished black shoes dressed the smuggler in an air of importance. He carried his small black leather passport bag in his hand. He walked down the hallway to the elevator.

Normally Dexter was a friendly guy. He would greet everyone from the street sweeper to the hotel manager with equal respect and acknowledgement; however, this morning was different. He walked with an air of aloofness to discourage the soldiers from addressing him — or, better still, from searching him. Down the elevator, through the hotel lobby doors to the awaiting doorman, who blew his whistle for a taxi to come forth immediately. The adrenaline in his blood was revving up to a higher pitch now! His stomach muscles began to tighten, his throat tensed, as he gave the driver the address.

The taxi left him at Salim's office building at about eight-thirty. Dexter wanted time to check out the office complex. It was a six-storey, white-washed cement building. Walking through the arched entrance, Dexter found himself in an open courtyard. Off to his right was a man wearing traditional Pakistani clothing, a long-sleeved shirt that went down to his knees front and back, covering the matching cotton baggy pants, which were tapered at the ankles. He operated the one and only elevator servicing the complex. It was a large old rickety cargo elevator with a metal gate that he pushed back and forth to let passengers in and out.

The center of the building was an open square courtyard. Each floor had a railing that ran around the perimeter, giving the complex an open spacious feeling as the rising sun baked the stagnant, hot humid Karachi air in the courtyard. A wide cement staircase wound its way around the elevator shaft, giving one a choice of walking up to the next floor or taking your chances in the cargo elevator. Dexter walked over to the elevator, the operator stepped aside, and Dexter entered. He pushed the button for the sixth floor. The operator closed the metal gate, pushed down on the hand lever and the elevator slowly trudged upward. It seemed to take forever, but finally the elevator creaked to a halt at the sixth floor. Dexter stepped out, turned to his right and walked slowly around the sixth-floor level, looking down at the courtyard and the office floor levels below him. No one was hanging around the corridors; everything appeared to be normal. He made a complete tour of the sixth floor, ending back where he had started. The elevator operator had descended to the ground floor. Dexter took the staircase down to the fifth floor and repeated his walk-about. He examined Salim's office door. There was nothing out of the ordinary, no bodyguards standing in front of his door; nor were there any persons milling about the landing. Nothing was out of place. He checked his watch. It was shortly after nine. No sign of the Cricket. Dexter walked down the urine-smelling staircase to the fourth floor.

He approached the Cricket's outer office door. Hesitating, he listened at the door for any sounds of talking. All was quiet. Gently he opened the door, his eyes darting about as he stepped in and surveyed the office layout. The white tiled floor was stained and covered with sand and dust. There were two large oak desks, one to his right and one directly ahead of him. To the left were two high back wooden chairs with dark brown leather seats up against the wall. An old man had his head buried in the office ledgers to his right. A pretty Pakistani woman about eighteen or nineteen years of age stood up from behind her desk and smiled at Dexter. She had a warm friendly smile, beautiful white teeth, long brown hair, and a lovely olive complexion. She was the prettiest Pakistani woman Dexter had seen in all his travels over there. Dexter thought back to Hank's remark about the Cricket's wife. He thought to himself, maybe Hank was right — she puts a bag over his head.

Dexter asked for Salim. The girl advised him that her boss was expected shortly. Then she inquired as to who he was. The moment Dexter spoke his name, the atmosphere in the office changed. Dexter had learned long ago the importance of studying people's body language. Her body language told him there was a problem. Her smile became forced. Her open demeanor quickly regressed to a respectful but distant one. The old accountant's head bobbed up from his ledgers as he stared at Dexter. For a moment there was complete silence, then the receptionist introduced herself as Shama, Mr. Salim's secretary. She began to regroup her thoughts and quickly offered to escort Mr. Dexter into her boss's air-conditioned office. Dexter declined; he preferred to sit in the chair in the outer office and keep his eyes on the front door.

The old accountant offered to get Dexter a coke or a tea. Dexter thanked him, telling him that he had just had breakfast and didn't need anything. Actually, Dexter wanted to keep his hands free in case trouble blew in the front door. He glanced over at Shama and noticed that she was on the telephone, talking in a muted voice. Dex couldn't speak Urdu but he knew what that phone call was all about. Time stretched on slowly. He glanced at his watch. It was now 10 a.m. and still no sign of the Cricket. Dexter broke the office silence asking Shama when she expected Mr. Salim to arrive. Her stock answer was, "shortly." Twenty minutes passed, then Dexter heard footsteps advancing down the corridor toward the office.

The door opened and the Cricket entered. He flashed a phony, toothy smile. His eyes spirited around the room, checking his employees, trying to pick up a signal to know if there were any other guests with Mr. Dexter. Behind Salim stood a little man even smaller in stature than the Cricket. He wore a pale blue long-sleeved shirt, gray pants and plastic sandals.

The Cricket greeted Dexter with all the cordiality he could muster. Dexter kept his aloofness intact. The Cricket knew this wasn't a social call. He motioned for Dexter to follow him into his office. Shama leaped to the door and opened it wide. Salim brushed by her. Dexter stopped and looked into her face. She smiled and looked directly into his eyes. He could see in her eyes that she was troubled. He felt like telling her not to worry, but of course he said nothing and continued on into Mr. Salim's office.

If it hadn't been so serious it would have been funny, seeing the Cricket positioning himself behind his huge wooden desk. The thought crossed

Dexter's mind that the Cricket should have had a footstool to climb into his chair. He quickly threw his mind into gear to deal with what he had come to settle. For once the Cricket didn't talk, but waited for Dexter to open up the conversation. This Dexter did by going straight to the crux of the matter, namely the hash or the cash. The Cricket responded.

"Mr. Dexter Sir, I assure you that I have the most honourable of intentions of serving you, but what to do? There are no ships leaving for Canada this week. How can I accommodate you Sir?"

"First of all, I want to see the hash; then you are going to pack it in front of me and then you are gonna ship it out today."

"Sir, I have already made arrangements to take you to the godown and inspect the goods today. I cannot put the merchandise on a ship today because there are no ships leaving for Canada this week. None Sir. Please Sir, you must come to the godown and inspect the goods. We will discuss the program for shipment later. All will be done Sir, but now you must see for yourself that I am an honourable man Sir. I am your humble servant Sir."

Dexter came back loud and clear: "Salim, I'm not putting up with your bullshit anymore. You told us a while back that you could send by air. Well, we can also receive it by air. So get your act together, and if the shit ain't in the air today, you had better come up with the money. No more stalls. You do whatever you gotta do, and I'm gonna do what I've gotta do. Are we communicating Salim?"

"Oh yes, Mr. Dexter, perfectly Sir. Now please come Sir, you will see the merchandise, you will inspect the merchandise, and all will be taken care of. There will be no problems Sir. Ah, is Mr. Hank or Mr. Checkers with you Sir?"

"Salim, forget the small talk. Let's go!" Dexter knew that Salim was fishing when he asked about Hank and Checkers. He could almost hear the wheels turning in that little weasel's pumpkin. It was time to deal the cards, let the chips fall where they may.

The Cricket's chauffeur was jumping out of his skin. He was tripping over his sandals, stumbling with the car door handles, bobbling the car keys;

in short, he was an absolute mess. Shama and the old man hadn't even looked up at Dexter when he left. The chauffeur was driving so badly that the Cricket had to shout at him in Pakistani to get them where they were going in one piece. Dexter also noticed that the drive this time was nowhere near the open sewer they had smelled and seen the last time they went to the Cricket's godown. They seemed to be heading out of town. Dexter didn't know east from west, but he was aware that the buildings were getting scarcer and scarcer. The Cricket sat in the front seat not saying a word to Dexter. He was paying strict attention to his driver and the roadway. Dexter didn't mind the solitude. After a forty-minute drive, they pulled off the highway into a compound of three or four warehouses. They were situated about a half-mile from nowhere, rather bleak and abandoned looking. A nice quiet spot!

The car pulled up in front of one of the dusty old sun-bleached brown warehouses. Salim quickly disembarked and opened Dexter's door. Stepping out into the blaring sunlight, Dexter squinted his eyes and checked out the lay of the land. His stomach muscles were fully knotted into one big ball; his mouth was as dry as the dust blowing around the sun baked buildings. The adrenaline raced through his body like a Grand Prix race car heading for the checkered flag. Dexter knew this was it! Showtime, make-it-or-break-it time. All the experience of his old hold-up days came flashing into his mind. He knew the feeling of taking the bull by the horns; he knew how important it was to remain calm, to be aware of your surroundings. Panicking would only make matters worse, it would only add to the problems he had to face. The rules of the game tumbled through his mind like numbers in a bingo drum. He tried to bring it all back, all his life experience crammed into the next few moments — experience not related to smuggling per se but to surviving in the underworld, keeping your wits about you when something goes wrong on a score. So far so good, the Cricket didn't have the element of surprise, and as for the seclusion, that worked both ways. He had a little surprise for the Paki, who was strutting towards the warehouse like a fat little peacock general preparing to review his troops.

Dexter took off his suit jacket and placed it on the back seat of the car. Now it was evident to Salim that the foreigner wasn't carrying a gun, and the bright white shirt he was wearing just made him a better target. Dexter followed Salim and the chauffeur to the warehouse office door. Dexter thought about all the jealous punks who would grumble and complain about Dexter's wealth. How it pissed them off that he wouldn't loan money, and yet, here he was — alone. Dexter had approached a few so-called heavies or tough guys, but none wanted to come along on this journey. They liked the money but they didn't want any part of this action. Strange thoughts go through your mind when you are facing the moment of truth. Strange that he should think about those who would bump their gums and criticize him behind his back. Normally he wouldn't give a damn, but somehow they came to mind. Maybe it was just a way for him to psyche himself up for what lay beyond the door.

The little chauffeur was having all kinds of troubles with his sandals. It was obvious he didn't want to go into the godown. He stumbled ahead of Salim and his guest, grappling with the door handle, opening it wide for them to enter. Salim stood at the opened door and motioned for Dexter to enter first, but instead Dexter gave the Cricket a little shove, and in the Cricket went. Dexter stopped, looked at the driver, and with a stern expression on his face, he put his hand on the chauffeur's shoulder and pushed him through the warehouse door. Dexter stepped inside the godown and stayed at the entrance. The room was dimly lit by the natural sunlight that streaked through the dust-baked windows. He waited at the doorway as his eyesight slowly adjusted to the shadows in the room.

At first he couldn't see the other people in the warehouse office, but he could feel their presence. Gradually as his eyes adjusted to the amber light; he could make out five men standing off to his left, about ten feet away from him, their backs firmly planted against the wall, motionless, quietly waiting in the shadows. The Cricket had walked to the center of the room and he motioned for his guest to follow. Dexter didn't move. He continued to familiarize himself with his surroundings. To his right, four or five feet from him, was another man. As Dexter focused on him, he could clearly see that he was an older man with a white beard, broad shouldered and taller than all the others. He wore a rag around his head, not a turban, just a piece of dirty cloth, wrapped around his head with its tail trailing down the back of his neck.

Dexter had his hand inside his passport pouch. He was trying to figure out who the leader of the band was. His eyesight became sharper, having adjusted to the dim lighting in the office warehouse. His eyes scanned over to his left; the five seemed to be looking toward the older man for direction or some sort of signal. Dexter's focus returned to the white-bearded man, dressed in the traditional Pakistani attire, the long shirt down to the knees and the baggy pants, tapered at the ankles. He had a red cloth sash wrapped around his waist, much like a tuxedo cummerbund. His hand clenched the handle of a dagger that was tucked in his cloth belt. Dexter now knew who the leader of the band was. The Cricket stood impatiently in the middle of the room waiting for his guest to join him. The chauffeur stood off to Dexter's left, visibly shaking like a leaf; he was definitely not a threat.

Instead of walking to the center of the room to be with the Cricket, Dexter stepped to his right to stand toe to toe with the older sadage. He could see his eyes clearly now. Staring directly into them, Dexter cocked the hammer on his revolver.

The old killer had heard that sound before. His eyes widened so that the whites of his eyes made his pupils look like prunes in a bowl of milk. Dexter glared into his soul, through the old *sadaj's* eyes. The Cricket began abba-dabbing away in Pakistani. Dexter and the old killer stood eyeball to eyeball, neither moving an inch. Silence blanketed the place as the Cricket stopped talking. Then Dexter slowly stepped back from the rag-headed leader of the band and calmly walked over to Salim, his hand buried in his passport pouch, never taking his eyes off his main target. The Cricket didn't get it! Again he began abba-dabbing away in Pakistani, looking around the room, searching out his hired henchmen, ordering them into action. Not one of them moved. The Cricket was dumbfounded. He stopped talking and slowly looked around the room, trying to figure out what in the hell was going on. Still no one said anything and none of his hired thugs moved a muscle; they all just stood at their positions like silent, mummified sentinels.

Finally Dexter broke the heavy silence. "Salim, the shit had better be here and it better get packed now!"

With that the Cricket opened the door to the warehouse area. He turned on the lights and went in. Following right on his heels was Dexter. Before entering the warehouse area, Dexter glanced over at the old killer, who was still frozen up against the wall. Inside the warehouse Dexter examined the goods. All Mazar! He turned to the Cricket and said, "This shit ain't doing you or me any good sitting here, understood? Today, Salim — and I mean today — it had better be on a plane for Montreal!"

"Yes Sir, yes Sir, I assure you, it will be so Sir. No more delay Sir."

"OK, Salim, let's go back to your office. There's something I want to explain to you."

"You don't want to witness the packing Sir?"

"No, because if there is any more bullshit, you are going to regret it. And that I will explain to you at your office, so that you won't have any doubts as to what those regrets are all about. You haven't got time to waste, Salim. Get your boys into the packing, *jeldi*! Now let's return to your office and confirm the airline routing information."

Salim was still unaware that Dexter had a piece on him. He was still at a loss as to why his parking-lot hit men hadn't gone into action. When Dex and the Cricket walked back into the warehouse office, the players hadn't moved a stitch. Once again, Dexter stared into the old *sadaj's* eyes, then down at his hands. With that gesture the old thug released his grip on the handle of his dagger tucked into his sash belt and placed his hands by his sides. Dexter walked by him and stepped out into the bright sunlight. All the while, he had kept his hand buried deep in his passport pouch. The little chauffeur danced out of the warehouse. He sprang around the car, opening the doors for Dexter and his boss. He was smiling happily as he closed the doors after his passengers and jumped behind the wheel of the white Nissan. He had the car started and moving all in one motion. He wasted no time swinging the car around in a circle, heading it back out on to the main road to Karachi. Dexter could tell that he wasn't the only person happy to be leaving the desolate warehouse and its band of thugs.

The drive back was unusually quiet. The chauffeur had a smile on his face, as he guided the car in a velvety ride towards Karachi. The Cricket was lost in a world of his own thoughts. He had a puzzled look on his face and Dex could see that he was trying to figure it all out. The little chauffeur drove with exceptional dexterity, avoiding all the potholes, pedestrians, oncoming traffic and wayward animals that were a challenge to the right-of-way. The drive back seemed to take half the time it took to go. When they walked into Salim's office, the staff appeared surprised to see Mr. Dexter again. Dex figured that he wasn't the first foreign visitor to take the drive out into the country with the boss and never to be seen again. Shama opened the door to her boss's office. The Cricket brushed by her, oblivious to her presence. Dexter stopped and flashed her a big smile. As she looked at him, a genuine smile of relief graced her face. The Cricket had perched himself behind his old mahogany desk. He clasped his hands and rested them on the desktop. Dexter sat in the chair directly in front of him. Salim's face was expressionless as he awaited Dexter's explanation as to why the Cricket was going to do the right thing.

Dexter knew the little scuzzball was still trying to work out a way to weasel out of shipping the deal. The Cricket's posture seemed to be saying, "This had better be good."

Shama knocked on the office door. She wanted to know if anything was needed of her. Would we like her to get us a coke or a tea? The Cricket waved her out of the office; he made it clear he didn't want to be disturbed. Dexter slowly reached into his passport pouch and pulled out his shiny, nickel-plated, thirty-two snub nosed revolver. He didn't say a word, he just leaned forward on Salim's desk. Quietly he began to take the gun apart. First he flipped the cylinder open, ejecting the six bullets that were in the chamber. Then he removed the cylinder from the gun and gently placed the gun frame as well as the cylinder on the Cricket's desk. During this operation he glanced up at the Cricket. He had his undivided attention! He then took the bullets that he had ejected from the cylinder and stood them up on end in front of Salim's small grubby, hands, which glistened with sweat.

After Dexter had finished his little act with the gun, he calmly sat back in his chair, looked Salim directly in the face and said, "Salim, your little plan didn't work today because the old sadage knew I had a piece. He also knew that if the shit hit the fan, he was the first one who was going to buy it, and

I can also tell you that you were going to be the second. Now there are six bullets here. One of them was for you! The next time you see that old sadaj, you should kiss his ass. He saved your life and his today. I'm going to give you this gun as a present, because if you don't send that fucking shipment I'm coming back and I'll have a bigger one the next time! I don't want to have to shoot an unarmed man, so if you decide not to send the shipment or if you're gonna play anymore games, I'm gonna shoot you on sight. You have a choice: send the shipment today or carry this gun with you at all times. Remember, if you force me to come back, I'll bring a bigger gun and I'll put all six bullets in that sleazy pumpkin of yours! Are we communicating, Sir? No more stalls, delays or bullshit, Salim; that shipment had better be in the air by tonight and it had better arrive safely, not hot. If you tip it off we will know, and you know the end result of that game!"

Dexter relaxed in his chair, studying the Cricket's reaction. If you're wondering how Dexter smuggled the gun through customs and past various security checks, that remains his secret. Smugglers are like magicians, in that certain tricks they'll explain for all to see and certain tricks are for the initiated only. Salim saw the writing on the wall; he reached over to the other side of his desk and buzzed his secretary to come in. Shama immediately answered his call. Entering the room, she looked at Dexter, her boss and the strange objects on her boss's desk. Salim spoke to her in English. He told her to call Mr. So and so of the airlines. He wanted his airline contact to report to his office post haste. He ordered Shama to bring his guest and himself a coke. Dexter noticed Shama's eye's light up as she glanced over at her boss's desk and the chrome-plated, disassembled thirty-two, and the six bullets still standing perpendicular on the Cricket's desk. She closed the office door on her way out as she left to do her boss's bidding.

Salim looked at Dexter and, forcing a smile said, "Sir, Mr. Dexter please Sir, I am your humble servant Sir. I would do you no wrong Sir."

Dexter interrupted the Cricket, "Salim, I don't like you. I don't trust you and you can forget about the humble servant shit! You had just better do what you committed yourself to do. If you don't want to do business with us, that's OK by me. Just don't get cute and don't fuck around. After we receive the deal, you will be paid your balance of two hundred thousand dollars. Are we perfectly clear on this?"

"Yes Sir, yes Sir, I am simply upset that you think I am a cheater person, Sir."

"Salim, I know that you are a cheater person, just don't play that game with me. I won't let you get away with it! We are not friends and we are not going to be friends. Just do your job. If you don't want to do business with us in the future, that will be up to you, but make sure you fulfill this commitment. After this one, we can just walk away from one another. You go your way and do your thing, and we go ours and do our thing. It's that easy. Just do business honourably! I'm not just asking you, I'm telling you! Believe me, Cricket you play any more games, and I'm gonna enjoy shooting you! So forget the friend crap! Just do it!"

Shama entered with two cokes and two glasses filled with ice on a silver tray. She advised Salim that Mr. So-and-so was on his way over. She had sent the chauffeur to fetch him. Then she turned and left the room, closing the door behind her. Dexter took a small bottle of vodka out of his pocket, the one-and-a-half-ounce size you get on airplanes. He cracked the cap, poured the vodka into his glass and swished it around the glass and over the ice. He did this not so much because he needed a drink, but to kill the army of germs that were in the glass and the ice cubes. Then he filled his glass up with the coke and took a sip. The two men sat across from one another not saying a word, allowing the silence to settle down upon them. The Cricket was noticeably perspiring, even though the air conditioner in his office was blowing directly on his back. Dexter had the Cricket right where he wanted him. He had jammed him so that he had no wiggle room. With no time to develop another plan, and understanding clearly that the bottom line was ship today or else, he had no choice but to send the goods immediately. To be sure, the Cricket must have thought about tipping the deal off to the authorities, but Dexter had covered that base, too. The Cricket would have to wait for another day to be the sleazebag he was. The man sitting across from him was too real to be taken lightly. Dexter knew the Cricket was a treacherous son of a bitch, but he wasn't stupid. He would wait for a better opportunity to play his game of deceit.

When the airline guy arrived he was told the situation and what was expected of him. Dexter gave him the shipping instructions and the airline routings and schedules. He understood, and guaranteed Dexter that the shipment would leave that night as per instructions given. When he left Dexter stood up to leave also.

"I'm going back to my hotel now. There is nothing further for us to discuss. When the shipment arrives safely and is cleared, we'll contact you. We can bring the balance of money over here or you can come and get it, suit yourself. For now, I'll say goodbye. It's up to you whether the next time we meet will be pleasant."

Dexter turned and walked toward the door.

"Mr. Dexter Sir, my accountant will accompany you to your hotel Sir. He will fetch the chauffeur. Don't bother with a taxi Sir, you are our honoured guest."

Dexter knew what that was all about. The Cricket wanted to know where he was staying. Dex smiled. He knew Salim had blown his best shot at dumping him, but he was still hoping for Dexter to screw up and give him one more chance. If the Cricket could kill Dexter before he left Karachi, he wouldn't have to send the shipment. He would be home free. He didn't consider Hank much of a threat. The little weasel didn't give up easily! Dex knew he wasn't out of the woods until he strapped his ass on the plane heading down the runway. He decided to play it safe by giving the Cricket a little shuffle. The game was in motion, and there was no margin for error at this critical stage. Dex knew that the only way the Cricket could keep his cash and not send the deal was by nailing Dexter before midnight, when the cargo had to be at the airport. The aircraft departure was at 2 a.m. that morning. That left the Cricket with about ten hours to find Dexter and kill him.

Karachi is a big city with a population of about ten million. The odds on Salim being able to locate him and move on him were slim, unless Dexter slipped up. Dexter climbed into the back seat of the white Nissan as the accountant ran around to the passenger side and slid into the front seat with the little chauffeur. Looking back at his guest the accountant said, "Excuse me please Sir, which hotel are we going to Sir?"

"The Intercontinental," Dexter replied.

"That's a lovely hotel Sir."

"Yes it is. I only stay at the best."

The old man advised the driver where to go. Slowly they made their way through the congested, dusty, diesel-polluted streets of Karachi. Dexter sensed that the old accountant had something on his mind, but he was obviously nervous about whatever it was he wanted to say. Dexter began conversing with the old man, trying to put him at ease, making small talk and listening carefully to whatever the accountant said. Finally, when they arrived at the Intercontinental Hotel, the old man got out of the car with Dexter. He came up close to Dexter, obviously wanting desperately to say something, but he couldn't speak. His lips quivered but no sound came out.

Dexter smiled and covertly gave him his business card. He grasped at the card and buried it deep in the palm of his hand. The old man looked into Dexter's face, examining it to see if he could trust him or not. Dexter broke the impasse, "I'm looking to do business with an honourable Pakistani. If you come across one, drop me a line."

The old accountant smiled; he tucked the business card away in his wallet as though it were the autograph of some movie or sports star. Once again he tried to speak, but his lips just trembled. He was incapacitated by fear — fear of being branded a traitor for conversing with Dexter, fear of being accused of trying to develop his own contacts — fear that was based on the threat of death should Dexter or the chauffeur report to Mr. Salim. At this point, he simply put out his hand and grabbed hold of Dexter's. Looking around he said, "Be careful Mr. Dexter. *Inshallah*, we will meet again."

"You'll see me again, old man, you can take that to the bank."

Dexter walked into the lobby of the hotel. Inside he hesitated, looking back to see Salim's car leaving the hotel grounds. It merged with the traffic on the main road and was out of sight like a fart in a windstorm. Dexter went through the lobby to the bar on the ground floor. He turned around to see if he was being followed. The lobby was as quiet as an English pastor's wife. No one had come in after him; he knew he wasn't being followed. He turned abruptly and exited quickly by the side door of the hotel. He walked a couple of blocks down the street till he came to a taxi stand. He boarded a taxi and went to the airport. He got off at the airport, walked inside, and then walked out of the terminal and hailed another taxi, which took him back to the small airport hotel he had checked in at. Dexter knew the shuffle he had just thrown at the Cricket would keep him off balance and eliminate any last-minute heroics Salim might try to drum up. The Cricket wouldn't be able to track him down in the time he had left, and he would have no alternative but to send. He knew Dexter meant business, and Dexter had left him no wiggle room.

At a few minutes after two in the morning, the plane raced down the runway taking Dexter and his cargo on to Montreal. Changing planes in London, Dexter called Hank from Heathrow Airport. Nothing of any importance was said; no code was used. The phone call itself was enough to tell Hank to contact the airport crew at Mirabel. The airport ground crew knew the routing, the name of the company the cargo was destined to, and on what flight it should arrive. The cargo shipment would never make it to the cargo department or to customs clearance. When it landed in Montreal, the ramp crew would grab it right from the belly of the aircraft and boot it home.

Dexter arrived at Mirabel Airport exhausted. His wife was waiting for him as he exited the customs doors in the arrival terminal. Hank was waiting for him at his house; the moment Dexter arrived they went over everything. Hank would follow up on the finishing touches, taking care of delivery, distribution and the money. If Dexter were needed for anything, he'd be at work. That way, if the Man sat on Dexter because of his recent sojourn in Pakistan, it wouldn't interfere with what Hank had to do.

And the deal went down like an old whore's panties on a Saturday Night. No problems.

RULE NUMBER THREE
BACK UP YOUR ACTION

You've gotta back up your action; that's rule number three. When you're involved in anything criminal, you must always be prepared to back up that action with whatever other action is required. It doesn't necessarily mean that you have to carry or use a gun. It might simply mean being prepared to pick up the ball when someone else drops it.

For example, your runner is supposed to make a drop to one of your clients, but he has a car accident, and he can't make it. So you make the drop yourself and thereby do what has to be done.

Backing up your action may become an issue when someone has made a commitment to do something or buy something from you and fails to live up to the agreement. You have to confront that person and straighten the matter out. You cannot walk away, make excuses or simply ignore the fact that someone has not lived up to their end of the bargain. You must be able to stand up for yourself and not allow someone to blame you, lie about you or disrespect you. If someone is badmouthing you, no matter how big they are, no matter how tough they are, you have to confront them.

Failure to back up your action will only bring you grief. The sleazebags and the sharks are out there. They will eat you up if they realize you are unwilling or unable to back up your action. Sometimes backing up your action means carrying a gun and being ready, willing and able to use it. You can be the most honourable, the nicest, the most decent person in the world, but get involved in the Drug Game and all of that and fifty cents will buy you a cup of coffee and probably a bullet in the head. It happens every day! Square johns step over to the other side of the fence thinking that if they are honest and do business honourably they won't have any problems. Not so — take it to the bank!

If you can't back up your action — whatever that means you have to do — then don't play the game. Eventually someone is going to take a run at you, either for your money, your drugs, your life or all three. The only way you can diminish the chances of that happening is by letting everyone know from day one that you won't take shit from anybody! It doesn't mean being unreasonable or inflexible. You can compromise without letting people roll over you. In some instances you can walk away from a given situation because it is just not worth the risk or aggravation to pursue the matter further. You always have to weigh up the risks versus the rewards, and consider the circumstances you presently find yourself in. Sometimes timing is everything. Never let your ego rule your reasoning powers. It is always a judgement call and that's the way Dexter played it.

Dexter knew that people on the street don't and won't respect someone who can't back up their action. It is a rule he lived by and, like all the other rules of the game he lived by, he knew there were no exceptions. Like the people on the street say, "If you can't pay the band, get off the dance floor; if you can't do the time, don't do the crime; and if you can't back up your action, don't get involved in the Drug Game!"

Had the old sadage thought Dexter was just some punk with a gun, he would have made his play. Often punks play with guns, threaten people with guns, and even shoot their guns in the air to impress people. However, when it comes to crunch time, the one person you don't want to be bullshitting is yourself!

The old sadage knew Dexter wasn't bluffing because Dexter knew he wasn't bluffing. Reality has a way of coming through. One has to be honest with oneself, "To thine own self be true." You have to know your limitations. Dexter knew his, but Hank had begun to con himself.

You can bullshit in the square john world, and if you get caught at it you might lose your job or get tangled up in litigation. In the world of drugs and crime though, it'll cost you everything. Dexter and Hank had talked about this many a time; but where Dexter adhered to the rules of the game, Hank had begun to rewrite them. Later on you will see the results.

CHAPTER FOUR
RATIONALIZE

Hank and Dexter drove the two hundred kilometers from Montreal to Ottawa to meet Salim. They walked into the Château Laurier Hotel carrying a large black sports bag that was bursting at the seams with money. The Cricket sat in an oversized leather sofa in the lobby of the grand old hotel. He appeared all the more diminutive against the backdrop of the spacious foyer, with its high vaulted ceilings, marble columns and antique furnishings. The Cricket squirmed off the sofa to greet the two smugglers carrying the booty. He reached out to shake Dexter's hand. A phony, toothy smile was plastered on his face. Dexter couldn't dismiss that uneasy feeling he had whenever he shook hands with the limp-wrist Salim. Hank put the sports bag on the floor and exchanged greetings with the Pakistani smuggler.

The first words out of the Cricket's mouth were addressed to Dexter, "Please Sir, Mr. Dexter Sir, don't hurt me Sir!"

The two Canadians exchanged glances with one another. Befuddled by the Cricket's outburst, they assured him that they had no desire to harm him. In fact, they only wanted to pay him his money, which was in the bag. The Cricket seemed surprised that they had brought the money with them. Hank reminded him that it had always been their intention to do business honourably. In spite of all their difficulties, things had worked out well. The Cricket looked down at the big black sports bag, then back to the smugglers who were standing there waiting for him to make the next suggestion.

"Sir, I must leave immediately with this money. The banks will be closing in several hours. It may take some time for them to make the appropriate arrangements to transfer the funds to Pakistan. If you would be so kind as to meet me back here in several hours, we can discuss future program. If you please Sir."

Hank looked at Dexter, who gave a nonchalant shrug of his shoulders. It was obvious to the Cricket that Dexter wasn't all that enthused with his company. Hank conveyed to Salim that they would have supper together that evening. The Cricket stepped forward, reached down and grasped the handles of the sports bag. He stumbled around, unable to lift the bag up off the floor. He looked at Dexter, who began to turn away and walk toward the bar, just off the lobby.

"May I have your assistance Sir? If you would be so kind as to assist me by carrying this bag out to the front door, where I will hire a taxi. I shall return with the utmost of expediency Sir."

Dexter just stood there grinning. It was obvious he wasn't going to lift a finger to help the Cricket with his bag. Hank reached down, took the handles of the bag out of Salim's hand, and headed for the hotel entrance. Looking back at Dexter, Hank said, "See you in the bar — I'm buying. I think this guy is a big tipper."

The Cricket turned and bowed towards Dexter, then he scooted to catch up to Hank, who was making his way through the lobby to the doorman. He escorted the Cricket outside to a waiting taxi and deposited Salim and the big black sports bag into the back seat of the cab.

The bar at the Château Laurier Hotel had an air of opulent elegance and prestige. The smugglers felt comfortable talking in low voices; here it was considered etiquette, not deception. Ever since the deal had come in, Hank had been trying to change Dexter's mind about splitting up their partnership. Dexter listened as his partner talked about doing another deal with the Cricket. He pointed out to Dexter that if it weren't for him the Cricket might never have shipped. Hank was going to do another deal with Salim, with or without Dexter. He felt it only fair Dexter should be a part of it. He was adamant that Salim had learned his lesson. He was positive that there would be no problems this time. They agreed to do another five hundred kilos, this time they would put up two hundred thousand instead of three, and the Cricket would collect the balance when the deal arrived safely. If the Cricket agreed to the new terms, they would throw the dice again.

Dexter reminded his partner of the Cricket's treachery. He underlined the Cricket's opening statement about not getting hurt. This attitude re-enforced Dexter's belief that the next time would be the last time, because the Cricket was a sleaze and he would try to burn them or to send the deal in hotter than an old maid at a male strip joint. However, in the end Dexter allowed his greed to overpower his better judgement. He accepted his partner's rationale. He deserved to be in on the deal, especially in light of all that had come to pass. He made it clear to Hank that if the Cricket started dancing around and playing games, he was just going to write it off and walk away. He wasn't going to go back to Pakistan. If Hank wanted to go he could, but Dexter knew from past performance he wouldn't. Ultimately, Dexter went against his feelings, against what he knew he should do. If it worked, great. If not, they would all go their separate ways.

On this point, Dexter was bullshitting himself; we will see the results of that later. Jimmy the Cricket joined them for supper that evening. He was in a jovial mood. The Cricket agreed to a two-hundred-thousand-dollar deposit for the next deal. He agreed to the new terms without a fuss. This only made Dexter more leery. The deal would come by boat; apparently Salim was having difficulty with the airline people at his end. Dexter thought to himself, he probably didn't pay them. The deal was to be completed in six weeks' time maximum. The Cricket assured the two mooks that this would be so.

A month later Hank received a call from Pakistan. Their humble servant was on the other end. He wanted to speak to Dexter. Hank advised him that his partner was golfing in North Carolina. The Cricket said it was imperative that he speak with Dexter. Hank gave Salim the phone number and the room number of the resort where his partner was vacationing.

At about two-thirty in the morning, the ringing of the telephone awakened Dexter. Answering it, he heard the familiar whistles and crackles of a long-distance call from a third world country. Half asleep, he questioned himself as to who would be calling him. The Cricket's voice broke through the cobwebs in his mind.

"Hello Sir, hello Sir, it is me, Salim. Please Sir, you must take pen and paper and write this down. Very important Sir."

Dexter's mind, still in a fog, asked Salim to hold on for a moment. He reached into the drawer of the night table and retrieved a pen and a piece of paper.

"OK Salim, what is it?"

"AQ double zero 7295 double three AQ. This is the bill of lading number for shipment. It is scheduled to arrive on the twenty-third of next week Sir. I wanted you to know I am an honourable gentleman Sir. Your goods have been expedited according to our agreement Sir."

Dexter jumped out of bed as though hit by a bolt of lightning; his mind fully awake now, he stuttered to respond. Momentary silence passed through the crackling telephone lines. Dexter finally gathered his presence of mind and said, "Good-bye," banging the receiver down in its cradle. His wife awoke and asked him what the call was all about. He didn't respond; he couldn't get back to sleep. He paced the floor of his hotel room for several hours. He decided to wait until morning to call the airlines and book a flight back home immediately. He wanted to call Hank, but he knew there had already been too much talking on the telephone. He was unable to book an early flight back to Montreal, so he stayed with his original return flight that was for the following day. He knew he still had time to warn Hank and the manufacturer before the shipment landed on the docks.

Arriving in Montreal, he dropped his wife off at their home and went straight over to his partner's house. He told Hank everything that had happened; his partner, looking relaxed, responded calmly.

"He said he wanted to speak with you personally. He told me everything was a hundred per cent OK. He insisted on speaking with you. I gave him your number in North Carolina. Relax, everything is copacetic."

"Are you nuts?" boomed Dexter. "That son of a bitch is trying to set us up! The deal is wired! He's trying to put us down. I told you he'd try something like this."

"You're getting paranoid. He made a mistake. You're right, he shouldn't have given you the shipping invoice number over the telephone. I agree, but that doesn't make him a stool pigeon. The Man couldn't have tapped your phone in the States; they'd never get a warrant for it there. It's a Canadian deal, not an American deal. The Yankees don't give a shit about a hash deal in Canada. Relax, man, relax!"

"Now you listen to me, I'm not going to the can because you wanna be stupid! That little bastard isn't scared of you. It's me he wants to park in the joint. You're going to get hold of the manufacturer and tell him to refuse the shipment. You got that? When his broker calls him, he's to tell his broker he didn't order anything and he's not to accept it. Hank, I don't know what in the hell's with you. You used to be so sharp. Now you're walking around with your head up your ass. Listen to me; don't get cute and try and clear this deal on your own or behind my back. The deal is hot; it's got my name all over it. Don't play games, Hank, do as I say!"

Hank contacted the manufacturer immediately. The manufacturer knew he was in the clear if he didn't accept the shipment. Two days later, in the early hours of the morning, Dexter was awakened by the ringing telephone. Answering it, he heard the familiar squeaking, whistling sounds of a long-distance call from far away. His mind flashed to full consciousness; he knew who was calling and why he was calling.

"Hello Sir, hello Sir, it is your humble servant Salim calling Sir. I just wanted to give you…."

Dexter slammed the phone down, disconnecting the call. A moment later he picked up the telephone and laid it on the night table. There would be no more phone calls from the Cricket. The only sound he would hear would be a busy signal. He explained to his wife the problem he was having; he cautioned her not to take any messages for him, especially if they were long-distance calls or from someone called Salim.

Hank was jarred out of his sleep by the incessant ringing of the doorbell. Groggily he opened the front door to see Dexter, his face blackened with anger.

"Did you give that little bastard my home phone number?"

"Who, what are you talking about?"

"The Cricket called me at home last night!"

Stunned, Hank shook his head from side to side. He motioned for his friend to follow him into the kitchen. A strong black cup of coffee seemed to get the glaze out of Hank's eyes. Wrapped in his housecoat, he moved to the kitchen table and slumped over his cup of coffee. He mumbled something about the sleaziness of Jimmy the Cricket.

Finally looking up at his partner he said, "I never gave him your home phone number. I guess the Man did that. What I don't understand is why he would call you twice. He's making it obvious. Does he think we're that stupid? Oh, if I could only get my hands on that little midget, ooh, ooh ..."

Dexter interrupted his partner's oohing and ahing. "I've been thinking about why he called again. It goes back to what you said before. The Man may have recorded the conversation in the States, but I don't think they could use that against me here. I think that's why he called me at home last night. If I had bitten on that call, I'd be up shit creek without a paddle. Well, be careful, stay cool. I'll be in touch in a couple of weeks."

When the deal arrived, the manufacturer declined the shipment. The horsemen went barreling over to his office with a search warrant and an arrest warrant in hand. Needless to say it was a little bit embarrassing for the manufacturer. He spent two days in the can being grilled by the RCMP. They offered him the opportunity to call a lawyer but he refused. He was an innocent man, he hadn't done anything wrong and he wasn't going to waste his money on a lawyer. For a square john, he held up one hundred percent. In the end, the horsemen had to let him go.

They found nothing at his office; there was nothing to connect him to the deal and they had no legal means to even charge him. He was released with a stern warning: Big Brother is watching! (Those horsemen just can't take a joke.)

The boys had steam for a couple of weeks thereafter. The container sat in the customs yard for about two weeks under the watchful eye of the Feds. No one came to claim the container with the hash in it, so they eventually took it away. The Man got the hash, Salim got the cash, and the boys got away with their ass intact.

A month later Dexter tracked Hank down at one of the local watering holes. Hank was really blitzed. Dexter realized that now was not the time, or the place to talk. He also noticed a known coke dealer hanging around the bar with Hank when he first walked in. Dexter asked his partner what he was doing, hanging around with the Candy Man. A shit-faced grin was smeared over Hank's face. He put his arms around his partner's shoulder and told him to lighten up.

They sat down at a table off in a corner of the dimly lit bar. Dexter was a heavy drinker too, but seeing his partner all bent out of shape like he was made him suspicious as to what was going on inside his partner's head. A one-hundred-thousand-dollar loss was not the end of the world, so that couldn't be what was bothering Hank. He asked his friend point-blank what the problem was. Hank replied that he really didn't have any problems, pointing to the bar where two twenty-year-old floozies sat smiling and flashing their boobs at the boys. This was out of character for Hank. Oh, he'd grab a strange piece of ass now and again, but he wasn't no Romeo. Now he was acting like some wise guy who deserved the world's attention.

The Candy Man strolled over to the table and pulled up a chair. Dexter gave him a cold stare. Hank welcomed him like a long-lost dream. The Candy Man slid two ozies of coke over to Hank's hands, which were resting on the table. Hank palmed the coke and put it in his shirt pocket. The Candy Man looked around for the waiter. Dex leaned forward and told the Candy Man to leave, because he and his friend had something to discuss. At first the Candy Man gave Dexter a hard stare back; but when Dexter didn't blink, he got up and left their table without saying another word. Dexter looked at his partner of many years; he knew then that it was absolutely all over between them.

They had had a pact together; no coke, no pills, no hard drugs and no exceptions. They didn't buy, sell or invest in anything other than grass and hash. They had many opportunities to get involved in heroin, cocaine, designer drugs, you name it. They never did, they stuck to their game. That was their pact, and for all their years together their pact had served them well. They knew most of the major drug dealers in town. It was not hard for them to know who they were; they just never got involved, they never ventured out of their game. Undoubtedly the Man was convinced they were involved in it all, but they weren't. That was their saving grace, because when the heat came down on hard drugs, they were only given a cursory scan. They had known many a fine hash and grass smuggler who had stepped up to play the cocaine game. All of them, without exception, had gone down, been dumped or ruined in one way or another. Some had become addicts themselves, lost their pride and integrity and become liars, stool pigeons, or just unsavory individuals. Many of them had made big money for a year, two years, or even a little longer. All of them, without exception, if they hadn't gone down or been dumped, had been ruined in one way or another. Locked in a prison for the rest of their lives or dumped as human refuse in the waste heap of cocaine's broken dreams.

Cocaine has changed the underworld completely. It gives punks the courage of tigers. It gives them a belief in their ability to tell outrageous lies, never doubting their credibility with others. Eventually they become paranoid, greedy and egotistical beyond all reason. The cokers have made the already treacherous underworld even more treacherous. Convinced of the illusory powers that they take in with the powder they suck up their noses, they go on to oblivion. Inevitably the power they wield crashes down around them, and when their powder of courage runs out, or is unavailable, their cocaine paranoia turns them into withering schizophrenics. And the world of crack cocaine addicts is a whole other world, a world of sharks attacking sharks. They respect no boundaries and they allow no exceptions; it's death in a bag!

When Dexter saw his partner and close friend taking the stuff punks are made of, he knew it was time to part company completely. He knew Hank was on the road to hell with no brakes. It explained a lot of the changes Dexter had noticed in his old buddy. Saddened by what he saw, he stood up, put out his hand and said, "My friend, you and I have had a wonderful, interesting journey together, good times, bad times, and in between times; but this is where our journey ends. Do what you want with the Cricket. Remember this and remember it well, none of our contacts are to be used for that shit you have in your pocket. Hank, I love you like a brother, but don't ever have a wet dream about double-crossing me by using our contacts for coke. If you do and I find out, you're dead; is that clear?"

Dexter walked away from his old friend feeling depressed, angry, and sad — all the emotions one feels for a death in the family or the loss of a loved one. Cocaine has such finality about it. Rich or poor, black or white, big or small, they're all losers eventually.

RULE NUMBER FOUR
RATIONAL THINKING, NOT RATIONALIZATION

Don't rationalize a problem away just to make everything fall into place. This was a complex rule for Dexter and others, because oftentimes we use our reasoning to warn us of danger; and at times we rationalize and actually blind ourselves to the reality of a given situation. In our normal way of living, we survive by rational thinking. In the Drug Game or criminal world, rationalizing rather than rational thinking is sometimes employed and can cost you your life as you avoid the facts. You must be vigilant not to fall into the trap of rationalizing situations to suit your convenience.

Normally, we base our decisions on what we've experienced before. For example, you are driving down the highway well in excess of the speed limit. You see a police car parked on the shoulder of the road. You assume that he is there waiting to catch people who are speeding. You automatically reason that you have to slow down to the speed limit, or the police officer is going to pull you over and give you a ticket for speeding. That is an example of rational thinking.

Looking back you can see how Hank was rationalizing when trying to figure out the Cricket's actions. Why would he betray people who were honourable, trustworthy, and profitable; people with whom he could and would make an inordinate amount of money, as long as he did business with them in an equally honourable manner?

Dexter rationalized when he agreed to do another deal with the Cricket, motivated by greed and the belief that he deserved to be in on another deal. In the end, he rationalized away his better judgement. He ignored his instincts and experience which told him it was wrong — and almost ended up in the can. Many times people think they are being followed or watched, yet they still go through with the deal because they rationalize this feeling away and attribute it to paranoia. In some cases it is, but it is better to be a little bit paranoid than to rationalize your paranoia away and end up in the slammer.

Talk to anybody who goes to the can. If they are honest with you, they will tell you they saw something was wrong, they felt something was wrong, but they went through with the play anyway. Ninety-five percent of the criminals who go to the can will tell you it was bad luck, somebody else's fault or simply a fluke that they went down. They will always find someone else to blame. In the end, each of us is responsible for our own actions. If Dexter had gone down he could have blamed Hank, but in reality he would have been the signatory of his own sentence. Dexter learned early on in life that it was better for him to accept his own mistakes than to make excuses for them. There is no progress in an excuse. An excuse is an escape that will come back to haunt you! An excuse is a dead-end street.

Dexter learned the hard way that one and one makes two, it never makes two and a half or three. He realized that if he tried to rationalize that one and one should make two and a half or three, he probably could do it! The reality is that such thinking never works out; and in the end one and one always makes two. A big problem with the people he worked with in the Drug Game was that the more money involved, the more they rationalized problems away. Some guys would never think of walking into a set-up or dealing with a stool pigeon in order to sell a kilo of hash, but let that stool pigeon offer to buy twenty, thirty or a hundred kilos of hash and they'd do business with him. Why? Because they contrive a way to rationalize their thinking that makes doing business with a known informer OK. Instead of using reason and recognizing the fact that the person is an informer and not someone to do business with, they contort their thinking to believe that business can be done with an informer, just this one time, and they'll get away with it. In such instances the thinking is based solely on greed, other factors are rationalized away. Some streetwise people do it on the street every day, and they get tagged as a result.

Dexter has implanted the rules of the game in his mind; he tries never to rationalize the rules away. If he has known someone as a liar, a cheat or a rip-off artist, he won't do business with them, not for any amount of money. If he knows that someone has been unreliable in the past — a sleazeball, a bullshitter, a scammer or a rat — take it to the bank, they won't be doing business with Dexter. Dexter plays it straight, backs up his action, and keeps his circle tight.

CHAPTER FIVE
BE OBSERVANT AND PATIENT

Hank had his head in a bag of coke most all the time. He developed a new circle of friends, cokers and sleazebags. Up to their eyeballs in cocaine courage, they decided to roll over Dexter and use some of his contacts.

Dexter had cultivated an old man in a bonded warehouse. He had met this contact at the Bug one night, rather innocently. It was an exceptionally busy evening and Dexter sat quietly at a table in the corner, nursing a quart of beer. Jean brought an old man to his table and asked Dexter if it was all right for the gentleman to sit at his table, as there were no other chairs available. Dexter didn't mind, so the old guy sat down and ordered a pint for himself. They exchanged pleasantries and Dexter gave him the party line that he was in the computer business.

The old fellow told Dexter that he was a janitor in a bonded warehouse. Dexter's ears perked up when he heard where the old guy was employed. He knew how valuable a contact someone working in a bonded warehouse could be. It is tantamount to having a video camera watching your shipment. Dexter befriended the old guy, slowly developing a relationship with him. Jean filled Dexter in on the old guy's background. He had been a long-standing client, a quiet man who came in regularly for a pint or two. He was never rowdy or a problem, nor was he a drunk. He seemed a stable kind of person, married, two daughters in college, in the same house for twenty years.

Dexter checked him out further. His wife worked in a Zellers department store as a sales clerk and his daughters supplemented the family income with part-time jobs at McDonald's. Dexter made it a point to stop by and have a beer whenever the old man would be there. In no time at all they were good friends, to the point where Dexter propositioned him with a job. He would be on the lookout for Dexter's shipments when they came into his warehouse. Dexter and Hank referred to the old man as the Doc. He would poke around the warehouse to see if anything was out of the ordinary when a shipment came in. The Doc was sociable with everyone and no one suspected him or paid the old janitor much attention. When the custom officers took their coffee break, he would go in and clean up the cafeteria, eavesdropping on their conversations. He got five grand a deal, just for keeping his eyes and ears open. More than once the Doc had saved the day by tipping Dexter off to a hot deal that the cops were sitting on. The Doc became Dexter and Hank's ace. It was better to walk away from a hot deal than to go after something that was already lost and go down with it. Five grand was a lot cheaper than a lawyer!

The Doc had made it clear from the onset, hash and grass only, no hard drugs. The boys respected him for that, and he in turn respected them for not being involved in what he called "Satan's Revenge."

A few months after Dexter and Hank had parted company, Hank and his new acquaintances decided to ship some coke in from Colombia. The Doc was unaware of the split between the boys, and only when he saw the shipment did he realize that it was too small for grass or hash. The deal had arrived hot. It was all screwed up; the paperwork was wrong, the shipper didn't exist, and the company it was assigned to had declined the shipment. Doc advised Hank that the deal was hot! Hank's cokehead buddies decided to "put the arm" on the old janitor. They told the Doc he had to steal the package out of the warehouse. If he didn't, something was going to happen to his daughters. The Doc was traumatized by this new, heavy-handed action. He wondered why Dexter was acting this way. In the past, if the Doc said the deal was hot, Dexter took his word and let it slide. He decided to confront Dexter directly. He called Dexter and set up a meet at the Bug. When Dexter heard the story, he told the old man to go home and forget about the package and not to worry about his family. He also informed the Doc that he and Hank were no longer partners. The Doc told Dexter that he didn't want to have anything more to do with Hank or his friends. Dexter made it clear to the Doc that Hank and friends would never bother him or go near him again.

Dexter left the Bug and went home. He strapped on his piece and went to the bar that had now become Hank's court. When Hank saw Dexter entering the bar with that black look on his face, he froze. He sat quietly between his two wannabe tough guy friends, sheepishly looking up at his old comrade.

Dexter went around the table and stood behind one of the wannabes who sat in a chair with his back to the wall. Dexter told him to move. The guy looked up, and seeing the expression on Dexter's face, he gave up the chair without a comment. Dexter proceeded to read the riot act to the three amigos sitting around the table with him.

There were no ifs ands or buts. Dexter offered to hold court right then and there. Much the same as Dexter, Hank very rarely carried a gun, but his two partners had a reputation of being parking-lot hit men. Their reputation scared most people into submission; it only irritated the already irate Dexter. The meeting was brief and explicit. They were told the consequences of ever going within a country mile of the Doc or his family. Should they be so foolish as to challenge Dexter on this point, he told them he would kill them on sight! They knew he meant it. Bottom line, Dexter was a nice guy except when provoked, except when betrayed. When provoked he could be a complete and utter maniac; he'd go anywhere, anytime, and do whatever in the hell he thought had to be done.

As far as their deal was concerned, he told them they could go in and get it themselves. He advised them of the one problem they faced: the horsemen had set up a SWAT team inside the warehouse, which meant they'd probably be coming out on their backs! Their choice, he didn't give a shit, as long as they stayed away from the Doc.

He then turned to Hank and gave him three weeks to get out of town. If he were still around in three weeks, it would be showtime. He understood the essence of that. Hank and his stooges sat in their chairs with blank looks on their faces; there just wasn't enough cocaine courage among them to push Dexter's button. They could see it was blinking, armed and ready to explode!

Hank left town without saying good-bye to Dexter. His marriage was on the rocks, what with the broads, the booze, the cocaine and his nummer friends; his wife couldn't take it any more. She had begun divorce proceedings, packed up the kids and returned home to Calgary. The house had a sale contract pending on it, so there was nothing left to tie Hank down to Montreal.

He moved to Manila. He bought a beautiful home and moved into paradise, or so he thought. He became a vegetable. He stays in his house twenty-four hours a day, seven days a week, stoned out of his mind, vegetating away. He has a cook to prepare his meals for him, what little he eats; a maid to keep the house clean and serve him, even though he rarely leaves his bedroom; a chauffeur to drive his car, fetch his booze and buy his drugs. Women he can have at his beck and call for next to nothing, but he's lost interest in them. He has enough money to last him two lifetimes. Is he happy? Hell no, he's miserable. He's lost interest in life, in business, in sex, in everything except the junk he snorts, shoots or smokes. He's a junkie, wasting away the rest of his life. He may as well be in the can, at least he would have friends and the desire to survive. One day runs into the next for as long as his health holds out. His health? Well, most seventy-year-olds are in better physical and mental shape. His mind is constantly numbed in a drug-shrouded stupor. He's alive, medically speaking, if that's what you call living. Cocaine has taken another life and dumped it on the trash heap. Whose fault is it? Who can make sense of it? Only another dumb cokehead could give you the answer to that riddle.

Dexter received a letter from Salim's accountant. He advised Dexter that Salim had hired bodyguards. They were with him constantly. Everyone in his office was told of the problem their boss was expecting from Mr. Dexter. The front desk manager at the Intercontinental Hotel was on the lookout for Dexter; he was to inform the Cricket the minute Mr. Dexter requested a reservation or checked-in unannounced. The accountant stated that Salim was worried because his plan had backfired. Salim felt that Mr. Dexter would surely be coming to Karachi to avenge his treachery. Salim intended to resolve his dilemma by killing Mr. Dexter the instant he set foot in Pakistan. The Old Man also made it clear that his boss had no intention of paying the money or sending any hash. He closed the letter by offering his services to Dexter. He was confident he could do a better job than his boss and that he was a much more honourable person.

When Hank left town, the cops decided to concentrate on Dexter. Dexter put all his plans on hold and chilled out. He devoted his time to his small computer company. For one year, the Man sat on Dexter. They rented a house in his neighborhood that had a view of Dexter's. This allowed them twenty-four-hour surveillance on their pain-in-the-ass target, who was now a subdued company executive going about his business as any normal person would. It was apparent to Dexter that his name had been dropped in connection with the failed cocaine deal. Who dropped it and for what reason, he never found out for sure. But he guessed that it may well have been one of the two parking-lot hit men working with Hank.

There are many different roads revenge can take. It is very common in the world of drugs to have someone drop a dime on you out of revenge or jealousy. Someone has a hard-on for you, they're jealous, angry or just plain stool pigeons — they drop your name to the Man, anticipating that that will bring you down. Unfortunately, the cops rarely know or care whether the information is accurate or if it's simply a settling of accounts. From the cops perspective, even if the information isn't true, it helps them build a file or jacket on you. Later on, as that file gets thicker and thicker, the cops can justify spending overtime on surveillance, electronic eavesdropping and more manpower in trying to nail you. With a thick file, a punter can be made out to be a major player.

Police officers don't get promotions for putting punks in jail. They build their careers on busting so-called big time criminals. Half the stuff you read in the newspapers about criminals is nothing more than police propaganda. When a so-called big fish goes down, the public is happy, the lawyers' fees go up, and the cops get their promotions and accommodations with even bigger budgets. It's all part of the game, and Dexter was well aware of the consequences of notoriety.

In Dexter and Hank's case, the cops had created a beautiful bulging file. Do you ever wonder why so many ex-police officers become writers? It's because they get a lot of practice writing bullshit reports that aggrandize small to mid-size criminals into monster mob Dons, and the journalists and the public eat it up. The Drug Game has created bureaucracies within bureaucracies, ivory towers on top of ivory towers, all at the taxpayer's expense. And these bureaucracies must be fed criminals — criminals the public demands be locked up. Because he knew and respected the power of the various police agencies, Dexter was very averse to any kind of publicity if it could be avoided. A lot of guys think it's great to have their name in the papers, they get off on some kind of ego trip; if they only knew the price they would have to pay for every by line ever written about them. Dexter was never into empire building, for himself or anyone else.

The police create criminals on their computers who are larger than life. It is all part of the game. Small drug dealers often have the attitude that because they are small potatoes, they are not likely to become objects of a major investigation. It is this attitude that allows them to talk on telephones and do a host of other stupid things that offer them as fodder for the big government drug machine. If most small-time drug dealers or importers ever saw their police files, they'd freak out; they wouldn't recognize themselves. Dexter always assumed the worst. He never took it for granted that he was just a small-time player: he knew he had to be as careful as the big players. He didn't know what bullshit had been dropped in his jacket; all he knew that once it was there, it was there forever and a day. He knew that the Man would build you up to be some Capo in the Mafia or drug ringleader. If you're Italian they will invent a gang or title for you, such as the non-existent "West End Gang" of Montreal. The police will embellish the deeds of a small player to the point where he or she becomes a menace to society. They thereby ensure that their budgets and bureaucracies will grow in accordance with the "drug kingpins" they hunt down!

The amount of money spent on Dexter and Hank could never have been justified in terms of the small-time drug dealers and smugglers that they really were. However, their files obviously told another story, and when Dexter saw the steam coming down on him, he went into hibernation. He knew that there was no point in fighting the government, it wins every time.

A year passed, and the heat had gone on to easier pickings. Slowly Dexter started plotting some action. He wrote to the old accountant, whom he now referred to as Papa Gee. The response was positive. Papa Gee had made inquiries and established contacts; he could supply Dexter with top quality hashish, and the 'out' was guaranteed. The only fly in the ointment was Salim. He was becoming meaner by the day. He had reduced his entourage down to one bodyguard; however, Papa Gee cautioned Mr. Dexter to be prudent when coming to Pakistan.

Dexter booked a flight to Europe. He toured England, France and Italy. In Italy he purchased a ticket for Pakistan. On his flight over, he had kibitzed with a stewardess who was serving the passengers in the business class section. Her name was Sharoone Williker, she was cute, nice figure and she had a spunky type of character that gave her an air of mystery. There seemed to be a spark between them right from their first meeting, but she remained very professional throughout the flight. Dexter had given her the party line that he was involved in the computer business. That was his reason for going to Pakistan.

The plane landed in Karachi. The passengers cued up to disembark but as Dexter had no one waiting for him and no urgent need to rush to his hotel, he let the other passengers pass him by. At the exit door stood Sharoone. Smiling at Dexter, she grabbed him by the arm, leaned close to him, and whispered in his ear, "Mr. Computer man, can you give me a tip on the stock market?"

Dex smiled, and whispered the name of some technology stock in her ear. Again she leaned close to him, and with a mischievous sparkle in her eyes and a light chuckle in her voice, she said, "Yeah right. Mmm. If you were with me, I'd straighten you out in no time. A computer salesman in Pakistan - that's original."

Dexter laughed aloud. There was something about this gal that was special. He would have liked to invite her out for dinner and whatever, but he had to keep his mind on the game. He never mixed business with pleasure, especially with a woman like Sharoone. She was sharp, and like the old adage says, "When you have your head on the line, it's not wise to put your ass there too!"

"Well, maybe we will meet up sometime, stateside - New York, Washington, or Miami — we'll paint the town, and you can have a go at straightening me out!"

"I'd like that," she responded.

Dex said good-bye and left the aircraft. Even though he sensed the chemistry between them, he didn't ask for her phone number or her address in the States nor where she was staying in Karachi. He didn't want to weaken and invite her out for dinner while in Karachi. And when he returned home, he didn't want to start something he knew he couldn't finish. Once at home, his family took priority. For now he had to keep his eyes open and get on with his business.

He arrived at the small airport hotel at about three in the morning. He advised the front desk that he wanted a wake-up call at 8 a.m.. Once in his hotel room, he crashed into a deep sleep. He contacted Papa Gee the minute he awoke, advising him he had arrived and where he was staying. Papa Gee and his daughter Shama showed up at the hotel an hour later. Dexter went downstairs and invited them to join him for breakfast in the little coffee shop just off the hotel lobby.

Papa Gee wasted no time in advising Dexter about all the arrangements he had made concerning the two hundred kilos of hashish. The sample would be brought to his hotel in the afternoon. He would meet the airport man, who was responsible for placing the cargo on board the aircraft. They discussed the financial aspects of the deal, which Dexter had changed somewhat. He would only put up fifty thousand dollars to get the deal together and out. Preferably, the balance of payment would be made in Canada when the deal was cleared. However, if the old man didn't want payment in Canada, Dexter would have the balance of payment brought to Pakistan or any other country he wanted. This is where Shama came in. The old man wanted his daughter to go to Canada and live there permanently. That way, Dexter could pay her the money and she would do whatever was necessary to send it back to Pakistan.

"Mr. Dexter, can you help us with making the arrangements for the immigration papers for Shama to become a Canadian citizen?"

Dexter thought about it for a moment. He explained that he would need a little time to organize it. He would have to find a Canadian willing to marry Shama for a price. She would have to remain married, in name, to such a person for a period of three years. After that, she could divorce him and she'd be free to do as she pleased. Dexter didn't know how much it would cost, but he figured it might run to about five grand. If their business went well, he would cover the cost. He cautioned Shama and the old man that he was not a babysitter. Papa Gee extolled his daughter's virtues. She was intelligent, loyal and completely trustworthy. He was not concerned in the least about her giving Dexter or himself any problems. Dexter agreed to look into it. He promised Shama and her father that he would find someone and make the arrangements.

Shama, her face glowing with happiness, took Dexter's hands and thanked him profusely. She was so happy, she could hardly contain herself. She left with her father, arm in arm. Papa Gee reminded Dexter that he would return at two that afternoon, with the sample and the airport man.

Papa Gee was back as promised with the sample and the cargo man. Dexter had seen enough hashish to distinguish quality from garbage, especially when he saw a whole kilo at a time. He hadn't brought Checkers because he knew that even if he bought mediocre hash, he wouldn't get burnt. He didn't expect to get the super quality hashish he got from Mazar; however, he advised Papa Gee that that was the quality he expected. To Dexter, anything close would be more than adequate. The plans were made, the airline routings confirmed and everything was in place. The game would be in motion when Dexter returned with the fifty G's. Dexter didn't want to rush the deal. He advised the old man he'd be back in two or three months. He wanted to see if his trip had attracted any attention. Salim was another loose end he wanted to tidy up. As the two Pakistanis left, the old accountant invited him to his home for dinner that evening. He accepted the invitation. That evening, Dexter showed up with an unopened bottle of gin and some flowers for his wife.

Shama, her sister and her sister's young son greeted Dexter. Papa Gee arrived shortly after. He said he was late because he had been taking care of business. At the end of the meal Papa Gee and Shama escorted Dexter into the living room for some after-dinner drinks. The other daughter left with her son, while the servant attended to the dishes. Dexter asked to be briefed as to the goings-on of Salim. Papa Gee related how Salim had acted cocky and boastfully about the demise of the Canadians. (In Pakistani culture, it's all right to be an informant or stool pigeon.) When he was told that no arrests had been made, his mood changed dramatically. He immediately hired several bodyguards and a new chauffeur. He went about making preparations to deal with Dexter and his friends the moment they set foot in Pakistan. The more time passed without hearing from the Canadians, the more irritable he became. Last month, he dismissed Papa Gee and his daughter. No reason — he just threw them out onto the street. And there's no unemployment or social assistance in Pakistan. The old man with the thinning gray hair had been a loyal employee and servant to Salim some fifteen years. From one day to the next he was out on the street. Because of his lengthy service with the Cricket, he had learned the smuggler's game and had acquainted himself with all the contacts. The old man had been speaking to one of Salim's bodyguards who had also been fired. He told Papa Gee that Salim would be closing down his business shortly. What Salim's plans were, the bodyguard didn't know.

Dexter pressed Papa Gee for more information, anything, no matter how trivial it may be; he wanted to find out what he could about the Cricket's habits. What time did he arrive at his office, what time did he usually leave? Did he eat lunch in the office or did he have a special restaurant that he frequented? He grilled the old man about everything, to the point where Papa Gee suggested they talk about something else. Dexter persisted, so Papa Gee obliged him by saying whatever popped into his mind about his former employer.

At a given point he started to say, "Mr. Dexter, do you know a …"

Dexter interrupted him, "Papa Gee, Canada and the United States are such large countries, I'm sure I don't know the person you are going to ask me about." It always amazed Dexter, how people in Asia will say to a Canadian or an American, "I have a friend in Canada, or New York or whatever. Do you know him?" The old man had stopped talking. Dexter realized he had been abrupt in cutting him off mid-sentence.

"Papa Gee, I'm sorry for cutting you off. Please continue what you were saying. Maybe I do know the person you were about to mention."

"She is a very nice person Sir, a very pretty woman. Now Mr. Salim is going to put her in jail!"

"Put who in jail?"

"Her name is Sharoone Williker."

"Who?" Dexter blurted out!

"Her name is Miss Sharoone Williker. Do you know her Sir?"

"Yes, as a matter of fact I do. I just met her on my flight here. How is Salim going to put her in jail? Why is Salim going to put her in jail?"

"She is a smuggler person Sir!"

Dexter was floored. He knew there was something about that broad that made his adrenaline rush. Now he understood the look she gave him. She probably spotted Dexter coming a mile away. Dex leaned forward, listening intently to what the old man had to say in response to his question.

"She's a hash smuggler like me?"

"No Sir, she is heroin smuggler Sir. Mr. Salim is going to sell her to the DEA. They pay good money for such information. It is real tragedy. She is such a fine person Sir, very honourable person Sir. I wanted to tell her this myself, but if I do so, or write her a letter, and she would show this to Mr. Salim; my life would be in peril Sir. What to do Sir?"

Dexter asked the old man for her address. She would be leaving Karachi late that evening. Hopefully she wouldn't be carrying; maybe she was just setting up the next deal. All Dexter could do was write her a letter when he returned home. If her karma was right, she would get the letter in time and get out of the game. If not, her life would be flushed down the toilet! Doing fifteen or twenty years in some prison is not a walk in the park. Dexter thought to himself, what a waste.

Dexter was against heroin, cocaine and all the other chemical drugs. His principal reason was that he had children of his own. He didn't want to bring that kind of karma on his family. He also knew what he would do to any son of a bitch who offered that shit to his kids. Hash, or grass — hell he'd sit down and toke a joint with them. No worse than having a beer or a glass of wine with the kids; but that other crap was a ticket to hell, and Dexter had no sympathy for the merchants of misery. That was the moral reasoning behind his never getting involved in hard drugs or chemical drugs. Being a smuggler himself, he understood the smuggler's creed. Supply the market with what it wants and for whatever it'll pay. Smugglers don't create markets. They come in after the fact, after the market has been created. They are entrepreneurs, capitalists, the stuff the free enterprise market system is made of. In many countries around the world, smugglers are respected as persons of an honourable profession. It's the politicians, the bureaucrats and other self-serving groups that want their heads. In WWII, thousands of Jews were rescued from the holocaust by smugglers. When the Soviet Union's atheistic empire was at its apex, smugglers brought Bibles and news of the free world to the Soviet citizenry. In truth, smugglers are revolutionaries against the constraints of a bordered world. The world is their country and their commodity is their non-conformist spirit.

If Buffalo shit became the craze in the United States or Canada as lawn fertilizer and the governments banned its importation or taxed it excessively, guess what? Smugglers would smuggle in Buffalo shit!

Some smugglers subscribe to a high moral code, others never consider the consequences of their actions vis-à-vis the society in which they live. Some governments don't either. Which is worse: a smuggler of heroin and cocaine, or a government that supplies and smuggles guns and bombs into a foreign country, or tries to destabilize a regime, and starve a people into submission and allegiance simply because they don't accept their choice of government? The Contras in Nicaragua and the Cuban trade embargo are good examples, and I'm sure you can think of a few dozen of your own to add to the list. All of us must be responsible for our own actions. That applies to governments, to smugglers and to the drug addicts who blame the drugs, the smugglers and the governments for all their problems. You'll note that the smugglers are always in the middle. They don't create the governments, the drugs or the drug addicts. They are just entrepreneurs. We can only hope they will acquire the moral conscience not to value money so highly that they ignore the human misery they are participating in.

Was it her good looks, the chemistry he felt between them or just the little head ruling over the big head? Was tipping Sharoone off the right thing to do? Dexter rolled the debate around in his head for some time.

On the one hand, she was doing something Dexter was vehemently against; on the other... Papa Gee gave Dexter her address. He returned to his hotel that night, thinking about Sharoone wasting away in some prison for the better part of her life and that little sleazebag the Cricket laughing all the way to the DEA. His flight out was for the next evening. He had a day to waste in Karachi.

When he awoke the next morning, his mind was racing with thoughts of the Cricket. He began to review all the information the old man had told him the night before. After breakfast, he went up to his room and wrote down everything he had on Salim. He had discovered that sometimes this was the best way to find an answer to a problem. When he looked at what he had written down, the answer jumped off the page. Salim had one regular routine. At two o'clock every day, he sent his bodyguard out to fetch him a pot of tea. Previously it would have been Shama or Papa Gee leaving to get the boss his tea. He had no other office staff, and if Papa Gee had told the truth, the Cricket would be vulnerable for about five minutes. A window of opportunity, Dexter thought to himself! Dexter was not prepared to dump the little sleazebag. For one thing, he would have to take a taxi to his office and have him wait there. Foreigners stood out like pork chops in a synagogue, especially in that part of the city. He didn't have the proper artillery with him, either. In the event that a move on Salim went wrong, one could be facing some heavy action from his bodyguard. Clipping the Cricket would have to wait for a more carefully planned scenario. However, his inner compulsion and his anger compelled him to go over to Salim's office and check things out.

He took a taxi to the Intercontinental Hotel; from there, he took another taxi over to Salim's office, arriving around one-thirty. He walked up the six flights of stairs, trying to avoid contact with anyone and everyone. The taxi had been told to wait. He was walking around the sixth-floor corridor looking down at the floors below when a Pakistani gentleman approached him and asked him if he could be of service. Dex thanked the man and went on his way. This encounter confirmed his thinking — he couldn't whack the Cricket and make it out of Pakistan because he could be so easily identified. It would be insane to make a serious move on the Cricket without the slightest chance of getting away with it. He descended to the fifth floor and walked around the inner gallery, continuing to check out the lay of the land, always keeping an eye on Salim's office door.

Promptly at two o'clock, the office door opened. A big burly guy in baggy pants, sandals, and the traditional Pakistani shirt that went down to his knees, walked out of the Cricket's office. Dexter started down the decrepit cement staircase. He could hear the bodyguard's sandals smacking on the cement steps as he too took the staircase down to the ground floor. Dexter nimbly descended to the fourth floor as though his feet were wrapped in cotton balls. The adrenaline flooded his veins as he stepped on to the fourth-floor landing. He moved swiftly toward Salim's office door like an Indian Scout sneaking up on a wild pony. His stomach muscles knotted up like leather strands drying in the sun. He reached the outer door to his "humble servant's" quarters. Momentarily, he hesitated, putting his ear to the door. Not a sound came from within. He reached into his pocket and pulled out a little four-shot, twenty-two magnum derringer he had brought along in case of trouble. Not a great weapon, but better than standing there with your dick in your hand if the shit hit the fan.

He opened the outer office door quietly. His eyes scanned the reception area. The door to Salim's office was closed. The two large black desks were vacant. Dexter thought to himself, no one here but the Cricket and me — looking good! The anger was bursting from within, the adrenaline screaming through his body, his stomach muscles stretched taught like a guitar string, ready to snap. His mouth was as dry as a morning hangover, parched like a desert plain. Dexter tiptoed over to the Cricket's inner office door. His heart pounded away like a bass drummer in a marching band. He put his ear to the door, sucking in the all sounds coming from the Cricket's throne. He could hear Salim talking to someone. Dexter hesitated. Maybe it was a set-up, maybe he had other bodyguards with him, waiting for the trap to be sprung. His mind spun through the options he had at hand: back off and leave the Cricket for a better day, or make the move. The rage inside of Dexter spoke to him, 'Fuck it, that weasel has to get a taste!'

He turned the doorknob and threw the door wide open. In a laser-like flash his eyes panned the room, the little magnum cocked and ready to explode in the direction of the first tough guy that got in his way. There was no one in the room but Salim. The Cricket was at his desk in his high-back leather chair. His stubby little legs were crossed and propped up on the desktop. He held the large black telephone receiver to his left ear. He had been bumping his gums on the phone with someone when the tornado blew in. His eyes almost popped out of their sockets. The instant he saw Dexter, his feet went flying off the desk, the telephone receiver went in another direction, and the Cricket bounced around from behind the desk and scrambled towards Dexter with his hands raised up as if in prayer.

He was so scared that his lips and jaw were quivering, but not a sound was coming out of his mouth. Dexter transferred the derringer from his right hand to his left. Then he reached into his back pocket and pulled out a leather blackjack he had brought along just in case he had the opportunity to talk to the Cricket. As Jimmy the Cricket approached, Dexter raised the blackjack towards the ceiling; he brought it down and around as if he were trying to smash a grand slam home run ball out of the park. He caught the Cricket full force, smack on the face. Salim went reeling backwards, landing on his back on top of his desk. That one was just to get his attention. Dexter moved in for more. The rest was going to be payback time. Dexter's raging fury was at a full pitch as he brought the blackjack smashing down like a blacksmith's hammer on an anvil. The target was the Cricket's head. At the last instant the Cricket threw himself off the desk, landing on his hands and knees on the floor. Dexter had to follow through, and missed the little sleazebag's head completely. The blackjack smacked down on the desktop, creating a thunderous explosion that smashed the glass top that covered the desk. It shattered into a thousand pieces, particles of glass spraying about the office in every direction.

Dexter turned around to line up the Cricket once more. Salim was on his hands and knees scurrying toward the door. Dexter went after him. In his blind zest to get his hands on the Cricket, he tripped over one of the large chairs in front of the desk. Stumbling, his hands waving in the air like a high-wire tightrope walker, he managed to maintain his balance and prevent himself from falling on his face. He stopped. The Cricket, still on all fours, had reached the door. He stopped and looked back at Dexter.

He knew he couldn't make it! He turned around and crawled quickly back toward his unexpected guest like a fat little rat caught in a trap. Dex wound up again as the Cricket approached him on his hands and knees. He dusted him another shot off the top of his head, but it didn't phase him a bit. The Cricket kept on crawling toward Dexter like a yo-yo on a string. When he reached Dex, he threw his arms around his ankles. He began kissing Dexter's shoes, pleading for his life.

"Please, please, Mr. Dexter Sir. I am a married man, two wives, four children. Please, please Sir, I have made a terrible blunder. Please Sir, I am your humble servant!"

In between his pleading and sobbing, he kissed Dexter's shoes repeatedly. Dexter swung the blackjack at him again, but this time it only sucked wind. He couldn't get a good shot at the little weasel because he was fighting to maintain his balance while Salim had a grip on his ankles. Dexter managed to gain control of his blind fury, and he forced himself to come back to reality. He couldn't afford to start scrambling around on the floor with the Cricket and have his bodyguard walk in on them. He hadn't come to Pakistan to kill the Cricket, and this would do as an impromptu message for all Pakistani hoods: Dexter was not to be taken lightly. Dumping the Cricket would have to wait for a better, more organized opportunity. Gathering his senses, he bent his knees so that he was now crouching over the little weasel, who was still sobbing and pleading for his life. He dusted a half swing off the Cricket's ear. Salim was so enveloped in fear he felt no pain, he didn't budge or loosen his grip. He continued kissing Dexter's shoes and sobbing. Then Dexter spoke to him in a calm voice; at the same time, he stuck the barrel of the derringer on the bridge of the Cricket's nose.

"Let go of me you little bastard or else I'm going to turn your lights out!"

With that Salim relinquished his grip on Dexter's ankles. Dexter stepped back, reached down and gave him another swat with his blackjack. After that shot, he made his way to the inner office door; he turned around and looked back at Salim, who was still on his hands and knees sobbing. Dexter spoke, "I'll be back and you had better have my money for me!"

Dex knew the clock was ticking against him. He really didn't expect to collect any money from Salim. He just wanted the Cricket to sweat it out. The bodyguard would be returning at any moment. In the heat of anger it was hard to tell how much time had elapsed. He continued walking to the front door. Exiting the office, he went directly to the elevator.

He could hear the elevator slowly creaking its way up. He advanced to the staircase, hesitating, listening for the sound of footsteps in the stairwell. There was nothing. He stepped gingerly into the stairwell as he heard the elevator creak to a halt at the fourth-floor landing. The elevator gate clanged back as it was pushed aside, and he heard the familiar sounds of the bodyguard's sandals as he walked down the corridor to his boss's office.

Dexter descended the cement staircase like a nimble-footed mountain goat running down a mountain trail. Quickly, quietly, he raced down the four flights of stairs and walked out into the bright afternoon sunlight. He made his way across the crowded, bustling street to his waiting taxi. He jumped into the back seat and ordered the driver to take him back to the Intercontinental Hotel, *jeldi!* He made the same move at the Intercontinental Hotel as he had made before, walking in and out and down the street to hail another cab, which took him back to his hotel.

At midnight that evening, Dexter checked out and went directly to the airport, where he boarded his plane for Canada.

RULE NUMBER FIVE
BE OBSERVANT AND PATIENT

Dexter's rule number five is to be observant and patient. In the war story you just read, you saw how Dexter went into hibernation when he realized he had heavy heat. He could not see the police around him every day, because he was unaware that they had rented a house in his neighborhood as a surveillance point. However, he observed them around him often enough to know he had a lot of steam. Rather than guess when the steam would blow off, he simply backed off.

Dexter has noted that the problem with ninety percent of the criminals he ever associated with was that they had only one focus in life — crime. They had no diversions. By only focusing on criminal activities, they diminished their perspective of life and thereby their powers of observation. Time after time Dexter saw some rather intelligent and many not-so-intelligent criminals get their tickets punched because they had become complacent, perhaps even bored with their way of living. The minute one lets one's guard down in the Drug Game, the curtain falls, and it's drag time in some joint or another.

Dexter always had a job, either working for some company or other or for himself in his small, computer servicing business. One of his successful associates owned his own garage, another a bicycle shop and another a printing shop. Others who were successful had daytime jobs as car salesmen, parking-lot attendants, real estate agents, and so on. Those who hit the slammer early and repeatedly were those criminals who did nothing other than deal or smuggle drugs or rob banks. It was obvious to Dexter that having a legitimate job or career was important, because those criminals who had one developed a different mindset than those who didn't. The heat eventually comes down on every player in the game at one time or another. Having an alternative mindset can make the difference between putting your action on hold or sinking into the cesspool of the underworld. Of course, having a job, business or career other than crime won't help you if you're not keeping an eye on your environment, your other business and your associates. If you walk around with your head up your ass, take it to the bank, the Man will hammer you every time.

Dexter was observant when listening to the old man tell him all that he knew about the Cricket. He listened attentively, logging every detail in his head, and then he sat down in his hotel room and put the information to paper. In the Drug Game you have to be alert in order to be observant; if you're not observant you're history! This is where the stress comes into the game. You can't be wide awake one minute and walk around like a doofus the next. When you're in action, you'd better be on the ball. If the action is for a day, a week or a year, you have to be wired up and develop a keen sense of the reality of the game you play.

There are other observations Dexter made that will come into play later. It wasn't a matter of his being intelligent, it was a matter of survival. If you don't make the effort, then you're a piece of cake for the Man — it's as simple as that. Sometimes Dexter found himself in the middle of a scam that was going haywire; he couldn't back off because he had passed the point of no return. The game was on; he had to go through with the play — not nice, not fun. The only thing that saved his bacon, and sometimes the deal, was his ability to be observant. Sometimes when the heat comes down you can put the game on hold, because you have been observant; or you can back off completely. Better to pass on a deal that the Man has gloved, than to go to the can. Nobody ever made any serious money in the joint, except the bureaucrats who run the system.

The second part to Dexter's Rule Number Five is be patient. You don't have to be a rocket scientist to learn to be patient. It was because Dexter was patient that he was able to back off for a year. That was a perfect demonstration of how patience pays off. Eventually the heat passed and he slowly made his way back into the game. Dexter has learned that it doesn't pay to be in a rush; there will always be another deal. This seems to be a very difficult learning process, especially for those of the "me generation." We live in a time and a society that teaches us to expect instant gratification. If you want to survive in the Drug Game, you had better grow up and learn that all comes to the one who is patient. If you choose not to be patient, the Man will slap your ass in the can and you'll have no choice but to wait for the clock to tick away your time and the dates on the calendar to mark your score. Learn patience in the can or out of the can, the choice is yours. Again it's not a question of intelligence, it is just a matter of training and teaching yourself to be patient. Learning to delay your gratification in all that you do will reward you handsomely. In the Drug Game, patience can be almost as valuable as a gun.

Dexter demonstrated this up to a point, but then when he allowed his anger to overwhelm his intellect… He wanted the Cricket so bad he could taste him. He wanted instant gratification for the fury raging inside of him. Every time he thought of the Cricket, his blood boiled. He violated his very own rule, and it could easily have cost him his life or a life sentence in a

Pakistani gulag. He went to Pakistan on a fact-finding mission. He wanted to check the old man out. He didn't go there to clip Salim or even to beat him up. He knew that the best way to dump Salim was to find out all he could about him, learn his vulnerable spots, come back with a crew of two or three guys and whack him. No talking, no exposing oneself as a foreigner in a strange land. Just dump the little shit and walk away! It could all be over in a couple of seconds if done properly. If organized properly. Organization requires patience.

Doing what Dexter did was stupid. Allowing his emotions to rule his actions caused him to violate his Rule Number Five. You either play by the rules or you don't. If you don't play by the rules you're a moron. In this case Dexter acted like a moron.

Sitting on the plane on the way back to Montreal, he knew it, too. Even though it felt good, he knew that in future he would have to exert more self-control, or the next time he might not be so lucky. Violating a rule and getting away with it can lead to disaster because it sets you up for a worse fall later. Recognizing that you screwed up and being mindful not to do it again can correct your error. The important thing he had to accept was not to make excuses for screwing up, even if it did work out this time. If you learn to be patient, chances are you'll improve with age and experience. If you live long enough!

CHAPTER SIX
MOTHER

In a couple of days, Dexter had recovered from his jet lag. He went over to the Cavalier Motel on Upper Lachine Road. It was the hangout of his very good friend Duney. He was the biggest drug dealer in all of Canada. Dexter would stop by and have a couple of drinks with Duney every once in a while. The bar in the Cavalier Motel was known as the Zoo. Every type of criminal in the rogue's gallery could be found there socializing with one another. Drug dealers, drug importers, con men, B&E artists, boosters, petty thieves, prostitutes, safecrackers, hit men, psychopathic killers, bikers, bank robbers and, of course, Duney. The police had the Zoo under video camera surveillance twenty-four hours a day. The odd square john would frequent the place, but not many were welcomed.

Initially when Dexter would go to the Zoo, people would freeze up and give him a hard stare. He would usually be wearing his suit, shirt and tie, so they thought he was a cop. He didn't mix and mingle with the locals all that much; if Duney wasn't there, he'd leave. It was only after the locals saw him drinking and shooting the breeze with Duney several times that they realized he wasn't a cop. Dexter never explained anything to the locals nor did he try to impress them. He went there to see his friend Duney and that was all.

To most he was known as Duney, but to his inner circle of friends he was affectionately called Mother. He was called Mother because he looked out after a crew of people who would otherwise have been in jail or on welfare. Some of them were so stupid they needed a road map to get around a corner. Duney kept them busy doing little odds and ends for him. No matter how stupid they were, as long as they were solid, he found something for them to do. In that manner they earned a living and maintained their self-esteem.

Dexter and Duney were from the old hold-up school. They had successfully made the transition from the hold-up game to drugs. Duney was into everything from heroin to hot toasters — he was into anything he could make a buck at. To most legitimate citizens, he was a bad man, a criminal extraordinaire. To those of us who knew him, he was a kind-hearted man who helped more people than any bureaucratic rehabilitation program ever did.

Dexter walked into the Zoo looking for Mother. There he was, off to the corner of the bar, nursing a beer. The place was packed as usual. The bar stools were all taken, and the tables and booths up against the wall were jammed to the max. Some people just stood around with drinks in their hands because there was no place to sit. Mother sat alone at his table. Dex walked over and pulled out a chair. Duney acknowledged his friend's arrival, but not with the usual gusto. As soon as the waitress saw Dexter sit down, she came over with a beer for him. Not many people drank Black Label beer; however, Dex claimed it was the best beer on the market, so Duney had them stock it in the bar for his friend. It always gave Duney something to bitch about with Dexter. He would grumble how nobody else drank Black Label beer. He would admonish Dexter that if he were a considerate friend he would switch brands so that he wouldn't have to waste space in his beer cooler for a beer that didn't move. No matter how frequently he whined or cried and laid the guilt trip on Dexter, there was always a cold Black Label waiting for his friend.

Dexter noticed his friend's pensive mood. "What's up?" Dex inquired.

"Well, I suppose you've heard about the Mazar and now you're here to squawk in my ears too."

"No," replied Dexter, "I haven't heard a thing."

Mother let out a slight groan, as if preparing to inform his friend of some unpleasant news.

"The last time you brought in the Mazar, I bought it all up. I turned around and pressed it and sold it back with the Mazar label. It went so well I bought up a bus load of crappy Lebanese hash for six hundred a key, added a little hash oil, mixed it all together, put the Mazar stamp on it and bailed it out at three G's a key profit. Everybody loved the shit! There wasn't one complaint. They kept banging on the doors for more. The town has been dry for a couple of months now. There's just no hash around, garbage or otherwise. Anyway, one of the guys who did the mixing for me got drunk in a bar in the East End of town and bragged to everyone that I make the best press around! Now all these dealers come running back to me, asking me for their money back or at least a partial refund, because they paid top dollar for what they thought was Mazar, not a mix. I told those assholes that I never said it was Mazar. All I said was, I have some hash, here it is and this is the price. I'm surprised those assholes could read! I told them I'd be happy to give them a full refund if they would return the hash. They didn't have any left; sold it all, at a nice profit too. So I said 'You made money!' They said 'Yes, but.' I told them there were no buts. Some of them still have their noses out of joint. Now I suppose your beak is out of joint because I used the name Mazar!"

Dexter broke out in laughter. He yelled at the waitress to bring "Mr. Mix" a drink. Mother sat back in his chair with a big grin on his face. That was the kind of relationship they had with one another. Dexter never sold his hash directly to Duney, even though Duney would have paid top dollar for it. Dex's reasoning was that if Duney got control of the market he'd dictate the price the importers would get for their merchandise. It is almost impossible to corner the market in hashish or grass, but if anyone could have done it, Duney was the man. Dexter respected and admired his friend's shrewdness in business. By keeping some dealers independent from Mother, he kept the market open to all. It was a good-natured competition between them, not based on greed, jealousy or ego; just a little fun between friends. Duney was already a wealthy man, a multi-multi-millionaire; he was making money hand over fist. He wasn't selfish, egotistical or flashy, he was very down to earth. His motto was "Let everybody make a buck," and if you hung around Duney, you couldn't help but make a good buck.

Dexter enjoyed sharing war stories with Mother. He always had a new one. On one occasion when Dexter stopped by to see his friend, he was looking anxiously around the bar. Dex asked him about his obvious anxiety. Duney responded that he was waiting for his runner to return from a drop. The dealer had called and told Mother that he hadn't received his package. Mother thought, maybe his runner had been busted. Shortly thereafter the runner walked in. Duney waved him over to the table.

"Did everything go OK?"

"Yes," replied the runner, "I dropped it off a half hour ago!"

Duney was perplexed. All of a sudden the dealer who had been waiting for his package comes walking through the door. He goes directly over to Duney.

"What happened to your runner?"

"He's standing right beside you. He made the drop twenty minutes ago!"

"No way," the guy answered. "I never got no drop from him!"

Mother looked over at the runner, waiting for clarification. The runner said that he had rung the doorbell to 740 Elm Drive; a teenager, about seventeen or eighteen had answered the door. The runner handed him the package containing five keys of hash and left.

The dealer jumped in, declaring that he lived alone with his mother and there were no teenagers in his house. He asked the runner if he had gone to 740 Elm Drive or Elm Avenue. The runner just stood there with a dumb look on his face. Dexter looked over at Mother, whose face had started to become slightly flushed. Duney told the runner to go with the dealer and point out the house he had made the drop at.

"Don't do anything, just check it out and come back and see me. You hear?"

The runner left with the dealer. Forty minutes later they returned to the Zoo. The runner didn't speak. It was the dealer who broke the news to Mother.

"He left the shit at 704 Elm Avenue!"

The runner piped in, "Don't worry, Duney, I'll go back and get it."

At this point Dexter was trying his utmost to hold back his laughter. He held his hand over his mouth, glancing over at the dealer, the runner, and Mother, who was now beginning to heat up.

"Oh, you're going to go back and get it! What the hell do you think, we're delivering pizza here? If the kid opened the bag and called the cops, all we need is for you to go over there. Not only will I have lost the hash, I can add the cost of your lawyer's bill to my loss and make it a nice round number. No, you don't go back and ask for the package. It's lost. Forget about it!"

Dexter was doubled over. He was pretending to tie his shoelace. He didn't want to burst out laughing in front of the runner. It only would have humiliated him. The runner was a good man, but needless to say he wasn't a full hundred-watt bulb.

Some guys would have made the runner responsible for the mistake and forced him to pay for it. Others might have done that and given him a helluva beating as well, still others might have done even worse. Mother, squawking like an old crow over it's territory, ordered the runner to go to the stash and get another five keys and drop it off to the dealer.

Duney admonished him. "If you drop this package off to the wrong guy, just keep on going."

The runner left to get another five keys and make the drop. The dealer went home to wait for the delivery. Duney looked over at his friend, who was still doubled over, playing with his shoelaces.

"What's with you?" he asked.

Dexter straightened up, tears of laughter streaming down his face. A howling belly laugh roared from deep within Dexter. Mother started squawking all over again.

"You think it's funny. I blow thirty G's, and you think its funny!"

Dexter doubled over again. He couldn't talk. Mother rambled on. When Dexter finally managed to straighten up, he said, "Mother, you didn't blow no thirty grand. It's probably a mix that cost you twelve hundred or something."

A little smile broke out in the corners of Mother's mouth. It was all over just like that. Mother's bark was worse than his bite. Some might say he was a bad man. Those of us who knew him would say he was a man of compassion.

Dexter recalls another time he was sitting with Mother having a few drinks when two guys approached him. They wanted to talk with him urgently.

Duney got up and went to the back of the bar. After a brief conversation, he returned to the table leaving the two guys standing there. Moments later they came over to his table again. They wanted to talk some more. Duney told them it was OK to speak in front of his friend. They started haggling back and forth about toasters. Ten dollars, no, fifteen dollars, no ten dollars; finally the two guys agreed to ten dollars. Dexter didn't ask what the conversation was all about. Duney volunteered an explanation. Apparently the two guys had hijacked a truck loaded with GE Oven Toasters. They wanted fifteen dollars a piece. Duney had offered them ten, cash up, for the whole twelve hundred toasters. Once the price was finally agreed upon, they pulled their truck up to one of the motel units and off-loaded their cargo. Mother spent the rest of the evening hawking his toasters in the bar for fifteen bucks apiece.

When he had finished he returned to his friend, who had been sitting there in amazement. Here was a guy involved in cocaine deals for millions of dollars, hash deals, grass deals — you name it. Now he was selling hot toasters! He was the only criminal genius Dexter had ever met. He could appraise diamonds as well as any jeweller. He could tell you the quality of a mink coat on a woman's back and whether it was Black Diamond mink or dyed mink. When boosters brought him clothes, he knew if they were quality or if they were copies from Asia. Once some boosters brought in some swag that Dex thought looked like the real McCoy. The price tags were still on the garments; the labels were correct, everything looked legit. Mother began examining the merchandise right in the bar. After a while he looked up from the swag and said, "These are strikes from Asia. You guys printed up your own tags. Take a hike!"

The boosters protested their innocence. Mother just looked at them with a stern look. They made a hasty retreat, not saying another word. He kept track of all his wheeling and dealing in his head. Dexter never saw him write anything down. One guy would owe him for three keys of coke, another for seven keys of hash, another for fifteen pounds of weed, and on and on it went. If Duney had applied his intelligence to academics he would have earned a doctorate in something, maybe more than one. But he had no interest in anything legit. He was a complete, total, professional criminal. No one could shine his shoes!

With all the action he was in, he had to have muscle around him. He was a very powerful man who seldom exercised his power. He rarely carried a gun. He was not into threatening people, but he could back up his action and everybody knew it. To Dexter, Mother was a character with a heart of gold, not pretentious, not boisterous; just a regular guy who lived life on the edge, enjoying every minute of it. He used to crack up his friends by explaining to people who really didn't know his life that the reason he walked with a limp was because of the dangerous life he lived. The reason he walked with a limp was because some drunk driver hit him when he was walking across an intersection and almost killed him. Naturally, people who didn't know the real story assumed he had been shot in some bank robbery or something of that nature. Whenever the broads who drifted in and out of the Zoo would flirt with him he'd say, "Watch it girls, my body's a weapon."

One time about two weeks before Easter, Dexter stopped by to see his friend.

"Hey," said Duney, seeing his old friend come strolling into the bar "Do you want some chocolate bunnies?"

"Mother, what in the hell are you talking about? Black broads or hash?"

"No, chocolate bunnies. You know, those big three-feet-tall, solid chocolate bunnies. They sell in the store for a hundred and fifty a pop, plus tax. Do you want some for your kids?"

Dexter sat down at the table, a little confused. He knew Mother was into a lot of things, but chocolate bunnies? He looked at Duney, waiting for some clarification, not quite believing what he was hearing. He figured his friend was trying to play some sort of joke on him. But then Mother explained how some guys had hijacked a truck loaded with chocolate bunnies. He had bought the whole load and now he was selling them for fifty bucks each.

"Do you want some for your kids or not? They're going fast!"

Dexter was not quite sure if his friend was pulling his leg. Hesitantly he agreed to buy four. He handed Mother two hundred bucks and waited for the punch line. There was none. Mother was dead serious.

"Tomorrow at two-thirty in the afternoon be at the Lachine Hotel. I'll have your bunnies for you then."

They sat around shooting the breeze over a couple of drinks, then Dexter left. Arriving home, Dexter asked his wife if she had bought the kids their Easter eggs yet. She said she hadn't, so Dexter told her he would take care of it.

Normally, the Lachine Hotel was so empty at two-thirty in the afternoon during the week you could shoot moose in the place. Dexter arrived a little after two. The hotel was packed wall-to-wall. Men in business suits, laborers, rounders, people from all walks of life crammed into the main bar. At first Dexter thought there must be a union meeting or some kind of convention going on. Pushing his way in, he saw Duney sitting at a table in the centre of the bar, by himself, strumming his fingers on the tabletop. Dex walked over and joined his friend. Mother wasn't talking. He kept checking his watch, looking up at the clock that hung over the bar. The crowd was staring in his direction. Eventually, a tall skinny guy wormed his way to Duney through the throng of people. He didn't take a seat at the table, he bent down and whispered something into Mother's ear. Duney's face began to redden.

"Oh shit, you can't do that to me," Mother exclaimed, as the bashful looking man with his hands in his pockets, standing slightly bent over close to Duney's face, nodded his head.

The man said in a low voice, "I'm sorry." Then he straightened up, turned on his heels and disappeared into the crowd of people who were anxiously waiting for their Bunnies to come hopping through the door.

Mother looked over at Dexter. Dex had seen that look before. Mother was about to start squawking. Dexter sat back in his chair, awaiting Mother's next move. Mother just sat there for a moment, then he stood up and made an announcement.

"There's been a problem with the bunnies. I can't get them. If you'll come over here, I'll give you back your money."

The crowd moved quickly to Duney's table. It was truly amazing to watch. He knew how many bunnies each person had ordered. They'd come up and say two, or three, or whatever; he'd look at them, then peel off the money from the wad of cash he held in his hand. Dexter watched all of this with fascination. With all the many deals he had on his mind, it was amazing how he could remember details like that! When the last customer was paid off, he sat down and threw Dexter his two hundred dollars. Dexter leaned forward and said to his friend, "I want to hear this, and it had better be good. You just broke the hearts of a lot of little kids."

Mother answered, "Don't you have to go and play with your fuck'n computers or something?"

Dexter didn't budge from the table, he just sat there with a big smile on his face, waiting for Mother to explain. Normally he wouldn't be so nosy. He never asked Duney any questions. They shared with each other what they wanted to share. Dex knew this wasn't anything major and he knew it would be good, so he sat there staring at his friend, waiting for a response. Finally, Mother explained how one of the two hijackers had double-crossed the other. He stole the truck from his partner and parked it in a heated underground garage. After a week, the one partner caught up with the other and they settled their differences. When they went to get the truck, they discovered that the chocolate bunnies had all melted. Mother also explained that these two morons were supposed to have hijacked a truck loaded with cigarettes; instead they grabbed the bunnies. They went running to Duney to off-load their swag. Who else would pay, cash-up, for a truckload of chocolate bunnies? He had rescued them from disaster, and they had still managed to screw it up! Mother sat in his chair, percolating like a coffeepot left on high heat.

Dexter went to Hilton Head, South Carolina, to play golf for a week. While there he decided to drop Sharoone a line. He had wrestled the pros and cons around in his mind for quite some time. In the end, he decided that maybe if Sharoone got a break, she would quit the game and retire on her winnings. He had to be careful, because he didn't want to be associated in any way with a heroin smuggler. He went to Sears department store and typed out a short letter on one of their demonstrator typewriters.

Basically the letter read,

"Dear Sharoone,

You don't know me, I'm just one of the many thousands of passengers you have served on your flights. I'm writing to tell you that Salim is a double agent for the DEA and he's going to sell you out! You have made a lot of money in a dangerous game. Count your blessings. Be smart and pack it in girl!"

He made sure his fingerprints weren't on the letter or the envelope. He didn't put a return address on the envelope either. Once the letter was mailed, he threw away her address. He didn't want to get caught with a heroin smuggler's address in his possession. He never discussed it with anyone, not even his friend Duney.

One night after he had returned to Montreal, he stopped by the Zoo to see Mother. When he entered the bar, he noticed that the lights seemed dimmer than usual. He noticed four guys sitting around a table near the front door. Dexter walked by them, looked around and, not seeing anyone else, he went downstairs to the disco. The disco was closed. The hair stood up on the back of his neck. He knew something was wrong. He went back upstairs and was preparing to leave when he heard a familiar voice coming from the far end of the bar.

"Dex, come here."

The lights were so dim that Dexter couldn't make out the figure seated at the end of the bar, wearing a hat. Mother never wore a hat; however, Dexter recognized his voice.

"Mother, that you?"

"Yeah," he replied.

Dex walked over to the familiar voice, wondering what all the cloak and dagger was about. He knew something serious was going down; he could feel the tension in the air.

"Mother, what's up?"

"Come, sit down and have a beer. I'll tell ya."

Duney got up, went around behind the bar and pulled out a Black Label. He walked over to a table at the back of the desolate club. The four guys sitting at the table near the entrance door remained where they were. Mother began explaining.

Five guys had decided they were going to kidnap Mother's son and hold him for ransom. Their muscle was a hit man by the name of Donald Lavoie. He was a well known killer from the East End. Two of the remaining four punks were known to have done the odd parking lot hit. The other two were just asshole cokeheads, stepping way out of their league.

Mother had gotten wind of the plan; he moved like a tiger protecting her cubs. The first two to get dumped were the minor parking lot killers. Then he went after Lavoie, a little tin god who was about to get his mettle tested. Lavoie believed that his tough guy reputation would insulate him from Duney, especially if he stayed in his own end of town. Mother wasn't impressed, and the moment Lavoie heard that Duney was all over the East End looking for him the pins began to shake. The East End executioner ran to the first police station he could get to. He pleaded for police protection.

Protection they gave him. He rolled over on about forty murders, ones he had committed himself as contract hits for others and also murders he had committed with his friends and associates. He never forgot a name, a date, or a place. He was a hellavu witness. He put a bus load of people in the can for murder. He didn't forget anybody. There were a few who had been on hits with him who didn't go down, either he hadn't mentioned them or… well, you figure it out. Some of them are still walking around today… Hmm, I wonder how that works…?

The next two on Duney's list were the cokers with delusions of grandeur. When Duney mentioned that the Gearbox was one of the cokers he was looking for, Dexter volunteered that he knew him. Mother wasn't taking anything or anybody for granted. He was playing his cards close to the vest. He had to. For all he knew, others as yet unknown to him could be involved in the kidnapping plot. Unfortunately, he hadn't had the opportunity to talk to any of the principals known to be involved; so at this juncture even Dexter was under scrutiny.

Mother was having a problem in getting the Gearbox lined up. He was hiding at home. They could have gone in and nailed him, but Mother didn't want any part of that in front of his wife and kids. He also knew that accidents happen and maybe one of the kids or the Gearbox's wife might get hurt; therefore, he passed on the idea of going after the Gearbox when he was at home or with his wife and children. Mother had his morals, perhaps not as high as most; but still, what he had, he adhered to.

Duney knew that Dexter was not a gun for hire. You could put a million dollars on the table and he'd walk away from it. He was not for sale or hire; he was his own man, doing his own thing independently.

Dexter suggested that he might be able to set the Gearbox up.

"No," Mother said, "He's not leaving the house. He knows what's waiting for him when he does!"

Dex thought about it for a moment, then told his friend he'd give it a try.

"If you can get him to come out of his house, give me a call. We'll take care of it from there!"

Dex responded, "No, if I get him out of his house, I'll take care of it personally."

Mother advised his friend that he didn't have to do that. However, they both agreed that if the message wasn't made clear, every coconut, punk, and wise guy on the street or coming out of the can might decide that the best way to move up the food chain would be to jump into the kidnapping business. They knew that they couldn't allow that shit to start in Montreal, like it had in Europe. This was everybody's problem. Duney thanked his friend and asked to be kept posted. Dex just looked at him and said, "If there are any positive developments, you'll read about them in the newspaper."

As Dexter was about to leave, Mother made a strange request of his friend. He asked him if he could get him a snub-nosed thirty-eight. The one he was presently carrying was a long-barreled thirty-eight. He found it too cumbersome. At the time Dex didn't think the request strange. He advised Mother that he'd bring it to him the following night. Duney responded that in case he wasn't at the club he should leave it with the manager. The following night Dex stopped by the Zoo. Mother wasn't there, so he left the gun with the manager. It was only later that Dexter realized his friend had put him to a small test. Duney was checking to see if Dexter could be trusted, to see if he would come alone, or at all. Mother was just being careful, because in a war it's usually a trusted friend or a trusted associate that sets the other up for a hit. This all dawned on Dexter much later. In retrospect, he realized Duney could have gotten ten snub-nosed thirty-eights in an hour, along with as many machine guns and grenades as he wanted.

Dex had met the Gearbox over a hash deal a few years prior. He was a little guy who carried himself like some kind of bad-ass gangster. He was called the Gearbox because he was a little light in his slippers. The word was, he was AC/DC. Dexter wasn't impressed with his tough-guy antics, or his big mouth, and had refused to do business with him. That was about the extent of Dexter's contact with him. Duney had mentioned that he was a cokehead. Dexter called up the guy who had introduced him to the Gearbox. He told him he wanted to do business with his friend. The guy knew Dexter didn't like or trust the Gearbox. He was confused as to why Dexter wanted to do business with him now. To clarify matters, Dexter intimated that he had some coca cola for sale. The going price for coke at the time was around thirty five thousand dollars a kilo. Dex offered five keys on the front for twenty-two grand a seat. He figured he would flush the Gearbox out with his greed. One of the phones was hot and as a result, Dexter had "coke dealer" dropped in his file. (Even though he never bought, sold, borrowed or financed a gram of the shit in his life.) The middleman scrambled back and forth between Dexter and the Gearbox trying his utmost to put them together. If he was successful, he was going to make a substantial fee.

The middleman advised Dex that the Gearbox was very interested but for some reason, which the middleman didn't understand, the Gearbox was reluctant to leave his house. He offered to bring Dex to the Gearbox's house, but Dex refused for the same reasons as Mother. Instead, Dexter suggested that the Gearbox choose the time and place. The Gearbox hesitated, then picked a time and place to meet, but at the last minute he changed his mind. Dexter showed up at the designated spot, unaware that the Gearbox had backed out of the meet. Dex had a simple plan. No matter what restaurant, bar or shopping center the Gearbox selected, he was simply going to show up and shoot the little bastard on the spot! He'd take his chances with witnesses. The majority of people witnessing an underworld hit tend to mind their own business. That's the way it is in Montreal and most major metropolises around the world. Play hero, get involved, and your asking for a lot of anxiety and perhaps serious, if not fatal, problems. Most people tend to look the other way, and Dexter gambled that would be the case if he nailed the Gearbox in public. In those days they didn't have video cameras on every street corner, parking lot and shopping center, like they have today.

When the middleman finally caught up with Dexter to advise him of the change of plans, he asked him if he knew a guy by the name of Duney. Dexter said he didn't. Maybe Dexter made the deal too sweet, and that raised the Gearbox's suspicion, or maybe it just wasn't his time to die. In any event the Gearbox was so scared, he didn't leave his house for six months. Duney and company nailed the other cokehead and that seemed to put an end to the story. Mother felt at ease — four out of five wasn't bad. Besides, leaving one on the street to spread the gospel sounded like a good idea. The thought of kidnapping seemed to fade out of the criminal consciousness in Montreal, at least. The square john public never gave Duney a medal for putting the kibosh on kidnapping; the idea could have blossomed into a new crime wave that would have engulfed the public! Some would probably tell you that Mother was a bad man. Those of us who knew him, knew he was a good man in a bad game.

With all those things going on, Dexter had put his trip to Pakistan on hold. He had written the old man advising him of the delay. He reiterated his keen interest in doing a deal. He asked him to be patient. In the interim, he had received a letter from Salim. The Cricket wrote that Ajmal, a very important Pakistani, would be contacting him soon.

Ajmal called Dexter at his office.

"Hello Sir, hello Sir, I am Ajmal. I am here in New York City. I have met a very beautiful blonde woman last night. You must come down to New York and meet me Sir. Yes, no, thank you please Sir."

Dex held the receiver close to his ear. He thought to himself, if this guy is the general, I'd hate to deal with the troops in the trenches. Dexter had a policy of not doing any business in the United States, because he had had several bad experiences with Americans. He also felt that it was tough enough having the Canadian authorities on his case; he didn't want or need the Yankees on his ass, too. The U.S. was strictly vacation time, absolutely no business activities there.

In the era when Montreal was the Bank Robbers Capital of the World, an American crew had ventured to Montreal in search of a bandit with experience, a bandit who could handle a Brinks score, and one who had no criminal record. Dexter was tailor-made for the job.

Dex was offered in on the Brinks job they had lined up in New York City. He was willing to go, but he insisted on bringing one of his own crew along with him. This was going to be a multi-million-dollar score, and if everything went according to Hoyle, Dexter didn't want to get paid off with a bullet in the head. His second reason for wanting one of his own crew with him was that in the event things went bad, he knew from experience he could count on his own people going right to the wire with him. The Yankees talked a good game, but talk is cheap, and he wasn't going to gamble his life on talk. The Americans balked at the idea of bringing an extra guy along so Dexter passed on the score.

Eventually the Americans found another Canadian who fit the bill and he went down to New York. He replaced a Brinks truck driver who didn't show up for work and drove the armored truck around on its route. When the two Brinks guards got out of the truck to make their last pick-up of the day, the Canuck waited for them to enter the bank and then he started driving off with the armored truck loaded with cash. The guards, seeing their truck pulling away from the curb, immediately dashed out of the bank and began chasing the truck down the street, their guns blazing away at the bullet-proof vehicle. Half a block from the bank, the bandit in the car in front of the Brinks truck stopped at a red light. The Canuck could see the two guards in his rear-view mirror, charging closer and closer to the truck. Finally the light turned green. The bandit in the lead car is driving as if he's on a sightseeing tour. The Canuck pulls the Brinks truck past his numb-nut associate and heads for the designated switch spot. He can hear the police sirens wailing away, coming in his direction. He knows there is another bandit in a back-up car right behind him. He wheels the armored vehicle down a one-way street, going in the wrong direction. Pulling the truck up to the curb, he jumps out, runs around to the back door of the truck to open it wide and bail the bags of money into the back-up car. He looks around, and no getaway car. The criminal genius didn't want to go down a one-way street the wrong way! The Canuck is then forced to split on foot. He made it safely back to Canada. A year or so later, the Yankees go down for another armed robbery score somewhere in the States. One of them makes a deal with the DA, rolls over and stools on the Canadian. The driver of the ill-fated Brinks robbery is arrested in Canada, deported to the United States and gets fifteen years for his effort. Dexter counted his blessings!

On another occasion, Dexter was approached by a friend who had an American friend who had a contact for hashish in Europe. They needed an in. Dexter had contacts at the airport, so he agreed to clear the suitcases of hash for them. One day, Dexter picks up his newspaper and reads an article on the front page about a local hash man who had decided to move up to smuggling heroin. Arrests were imminent. Dexter thought to himself, what an asshole, he should have stuck to his own game. The next day his friend stops by to see him. His friend is coming apart at the seams. It seems that his American friend got busted in Europe with heroin. He figures the guy will roll over on him and he is about to get dropped in the toilet bowl. Dex didn't ask any questions — he knew who the asshole was!

However, it was a bad for a good, it smartened Dexter up. He would never again agree to clear something without opening it himself personally. Later on, he modified that principle even more: he would not allow anyone to piggyback something in on his shipments. From Dexter's experience, going down for something you're not involved in was not being nice, it was plain stupidity. Tell it to a judge, that you didn't know what you were smuggling, he won't buy it either!

Dexter was in the process of making his plans for his trip to Pakistan. An old bandit friend paid him a visit. He asked Dexter a favor for old-times' sake. The old bandit's pal had been released from prison and deported to

England. His friend had never taken out a Canadian citizenship, and because he was born in England the Canadian government shipped him back to the old country upon his release. He didn't know anyone, had no family or friends there, and was unable to hook up with any group of criminals he trusted. He was starving. The old bandit asked Dex if he could use him in his business, give the guy a job, a chance to make some money. In the old hold-up days in Montreal, the bandits stuck together. There was no bullshit French or English thing. When a guy got out of the can there was always a crew willing to invite him on a score, or to give him a score, or money to tide him over. There was camaraderie among the Montreal bandits, at least with the people Dexter knew. So he thought about the old bandit's request, even though he did not know his friend personally. Dexter made it very clear to the old bandit that the guy was never to use any of Dexter's contacts. The old bandit assured Dex that he wouldn't have a problem with his friend. His friend was solid, loyal and trustworthy. As for the old bandit himself, he was in the "candy game;" he had no interest in hashish. Dexter changed his routing to Pakistan; he stopped by London on his way over. He contacted the old bandit's friend whom he called the Putz.

The Putz showed up at Dexter's hotel five hours later. He apologized for being so late but he had had to walk half way across London because he didn't even have bus fare in his pockets. Dex went over the commitment he had made with the old bandit. The Putz wholeheartedly agreed. Dexter took him out for supper and gave him some pocket money and money for his plane ticket to Pakistan. He told the Putz to buy his ticket at an airline travel agency, not at the airport. The flight left the following day in the afternoon. The Putz had ample time to pack, get his ticket and meet up with Dex at the airport.

When Dexter arrived at the airport, he checked in and went straight to the departure gate. The Putz sat down beside him and they waited for the boarding call. Before they boarded the aircraft, the Airport Police approached the Putz. They checked his passport and his hand luggage, and they questioned him as to why he was going to Pakistan. The Putz answered that he was going to Pakistan to get married. (A real quick thinker, the Putz was!) The Airport Police then turned to Dexter and began questioning him.

They asked to see his passport, how much money did he have with him, did he know the Putz, and what was the reason for his trip to Pakistan? Dexter informed them that he was joining a trade commission in Pakistan, showed them his American Express checks, and also stated that he did not know the Putz. The Police took their notes and left.

Dex had told the Putz not to buy his ticket at the airport; he hadn't listened and had done exactly opposite to what Dexter had advised him to do. Buying an international ticket at any airport is like waving a red flag to the police, who are at every international airport. It is something the authorities watch out for, much like profiling prospective hijackers or smugglers. The Putz thought it was all a big yuk-yuk. Dexter knew he would have to have a talk with the boy later. Dex began to have strong feeling that trying to help the Putz out was a big mistake. Then he thought to himself, the guy hasn't been out of the can that long; he made a mistake, it would all work out once he settles down. The Putz was from the old hold-up school, so Dex reasoned that when he explained the Drug Game to him he'd catch on quickly.

CHAPTER SEVEN
RECOGNIZING THE ANGLES

Arriving in Karachi, Dexter had a good feeling. He now had two options, Ajmal and Papa Gee. When Ajmal had met with Dexter in Montreal, they had made a tentative agreement. Ajmal would send three hundred kilos of hash on the cuff. He wanted to demonstrate that he was a serious player. Dexter agreed to visit him in Lahore, go over the shipping details, and approve the quality of the hashish before it was sent. Dexter emphasized the importance of quality versus quantity. Dex knew the quality was there, it was a matter of convincing them that the best quality was in their interest as well as his. Quality was the glue that would hold their business relationship together.

He also informed Ajmal of his intention to work with another group of Pakistanis. His decision about which group to work with on a permanent basis would depend on results. He would assess each group's reliability in sending high quality hashish as per instructions. Dexter felt that a little competition would go a long way in resolving the game-playing that he had endured with the Cricket. He was terribly wrong; this turned out to be a major mistake.

Dexter was not aware of a Pakistanis need to "save face" at any cost. He goofed by not doing his homework on the cultural aspects of the people he was dealing with. He learned the painful lesson that you can't simply use the Western style of thinking to understand people of Arabic or other Eastern cultures. Dexter was often heard to say, "Don't expect them to think or act like you in business. If you do, you're in for a hell of a surprise!"

Ajmal told Dexter how he came to be introduced to him. The Cricket had been up to his old games, slipping, sleazing and sliding. He had sold a piece of land that he didn't own to a Pakistani army colonel. The colonel discovered the fraud and demanded his money back. The Cricket didn't give it up, so the colonel brought him before a military court, where he was found guilty and sentenced to prison. Ajmal came to the Cricket's rescue. The terms were simple: give up your hash contact in Canada and I'll take care of the colonel for you. Ajmal was considered a big *hodj* in Pakistan, and the Cricket knew he'd be able to pull the strings to get him out of prison; furthermore, the Cricket wouldn't have to make restitution for the money he had stolen from the colonel. It also meant that the Cricket could "save face" by not having to admit he had cheated the colonel. The trade was made, and Dexter was obliged to work with Ajmal.

Ajmal's father was the one who had established the smuggling business for his family. When he died, his son Ajmal inherited the family business. But as time went by Dexter became aware that Ajmal was not worthy of being a *hodj*, because he hadn't earned his stripes. Ajmal's biggest interest in life was getting laid, drinking and "saving face" at all costs. He had no concern for the people who worked for him or the woman and child who loved him. He was a spoiled mamma's boy. He always had an entourage of bodyguards and lackeys surrounding him. He was a very shallow person who wanted everybody to treat him as some kind of tin god.

For the first several days, the Putz and Dex stayed at the small airport hotel in Karachi. Papa Gee rented an apartment for the Putz and made arrangements for him to move in. The deal was set in motion; everything appeared to be progressing well. During the time the Putz and Dexter were awaiting Papa Gee's notice to move into the apartment, they discussed the Drug Game in detail. Dex went over the rules as he had learned them and tried to implant them in the Putz's mind. Dexter stressed how each aspect of the game functioned and how critical it was for him to observe all the rules.

Papa Gee informed Dex that Sharoone had returned to do another deal with the Cricket. One afternoon, the Cricket gave her four keys of smack. Sharoone told him she would pay him at her hotel the following night before leaving for the airport. He was to be at the hotel, in the lobby, a little before eleven o'clock. The bus for the airline crew left for the airport promptly at eleven. The Cricket fronted her the four kilos of heroin, certain that Sharoone would pay him as she had always done in the past. He figured he would get paid for the smack before she left and then tip the DEA off as to the identity of the heroin smuggler. In that manner he'd make it both ways: profit on the sale of the heroin and profit on the sale of information.

The Cricket showed up at the hotel at about ten-thirty. He sat patiently in the hotel lobby waiting for Sharoone. Fifteen minutes or so later, Sharoone stepped out of the elevator and walked toward him. She looked him straight in the eyes and kept on walking. The Cricket knew he was being stiffed. He went scrambling out of the hotel to his prearranged meeting with the DEA. He was going to make money one way or another. When Sharoone arrived stateside, the Customs Officers went through her luggage like a bear in a picnic basket. Nothing, nada, zilch! Instead of doing her usual suitcase and body trip, she had ditched the smack off to a runner who had left Pakistan the day before. By the time Sharoone arrived in the U.S., the heroin had been cleared and was probably already on the street. She had beaten the Cricket and the Man, one last time.

Dex had always felt that Sharoone was a woman of his own heart. He didn't like the thought of four keys of smack winding up on the streets. Actually it would have been more than four kilos, because heroin is cut many times before it is sold on the street. Still, Dexter couldn't get over the nerve of that broad; she was too much!

Did she go back into smuggling heroin after that? Did she develop another connection and get caught? Did she return to the States, only to be murdered by her friends who were now holding the heroin? Dexter never knew; he had done what he thought was the right thing to do. He never dreamed she would take a shot like that. "Crazy broad!"

The Putz moved into his new apartment in Karachi. He was more comfortable there than his one-room flat in London. Papa Gee was in constant contact with him; he ensured that all his needs or wants were addressed. The gray-haired old man had dyed his hair dark brown. He was constantly in the company of his daughter and they seemed very happy together; their lives were finally turning around and the future looked bright for them. Dexter was still trying to find some Canadian to marry Shama. He had a few leads but they were asking for ten grand, and Dexter felt that was much too much money for a piece of paper, with a wedding party thrown in. Dex figured five grand was plenty. He knew if he waited a little bit, one of the two guys he was talking to would bite.

Everything was a go in Karachi, so he left for Rawalpindi. Ajmal wanted to meet Dex there and drive to Lahore, rather than have Dexter fly into Lahore. He checked in at the Rawalpindi Hilton and waited for Ajmal to connect with him, which he did, two days later. From Rawalpindi they drove to Lahore, through the mountains of Pakistan. There is no amusement ride in the world as death-defying as the road through the mountains of Pakistan. The road is a two-lane highway, one in each direction. Everybody plays chicken passing oncoming traffic around curves bordered by three-hundred-foot falls off the precipice of the road. Dex thought, it must be a driver's training school course for them. The ones who survive get to go to New York City and become taxi drivers! Later on, Dex learned that Ajmal's chauffeur was constantly stoned on opium. Looking back, it explained a lot!

Ajmal didn't want Dexter staying at either of the two five-star hotels in Lahore. He had booked him into a small hotel, somewhere in hell's half acre. There he waited for Ajmal to get back to him with the samples of hashish Dexter was to approve before shipment. Ajmal made a major production out of bringing the samples of hash over to the hotel. It was obvious to Dex that the big *hodj* was scared shitless of handling the hash. Dexter had made it clear that he didn't want to meet any of Ajmal's workers or anyone else; Ajmal had to bring the samples himself. Ajmal kept making excuses and stalling. Finally, after two days, Dexter agreed to go with him to the godown to see the samples firsthand. In that manner Ajmal would never be in possession of the hashish at any time. Dex could see that Ajmal was a real coward. He was great at giving orders, but when it came down to his putting his own ass on the line, even in the slightest manner, the guy was yellow.

They drove outside of Lahore a little ways, stopping at a poor desolate no-name village where the hash warehouse was located. Most of the samples he was shown were either of poor quality or of just the standard commercial quality usually shipped abroad. Nothing wrong with the commercial quality, it was just that Dexter prided himself on superior quality hash. The cost differential for superior quality hash in comparison to commercial quality was negligible. The difference in moving it on the street in Canada was astronomical. Dexter tried to make Ajmal understand this, but Ajmal wouldn't or couldn't, or maybe he was such a sleazebag that he thought screwing around with the quality made him worthy of being a *hodj*. Dexter found it impossible to understand the Paki mentality. Throughout the day Dexter was presented with various types of hashish. He refused to accept anything they had showed him, even the commercial quality, which they assured Dex was shipped to his country all the time. Dex kept pushing for the good stuff, which he knew they had. Eventually they came up with a superior quality hash that Dex approved. The ball was now in Ajmal's court. He had to ship properly and promptly, according to instructions, along with the quality that Dex had approved. Dex had not put any money down with Ajmal; therefore, Ajmal knew that if he switched the quality of hash he risked not getting paid. Ajmal wanted to send a dummy shipment first, just to be sure the shipping instructions from Dexter were correctly followed. He wanted to be sure that there were no unforeseen problems. Dex reminded him that the other contact he had was also preparing to send a deal. The performance of either group would dictate which group Dex would work with. Nevertheless, he appreciated Ajmal's concern and thoroughness in wanting to do it right. Dex would therefore not consider timing as a factor, but rather the quality and the precision with which the shipment was dispatched.

Dexter returned home and waited for the play to happen. He got word from Ajmal that the dummy shipment had left Karachi. Two weeks later, and no papers for the shipment, no news, nothing. Two months passed and still no sign of the cargo or its papers. The old man too, was running into some unexpected obstacles. Dexter returned to Pakistan to see if he could get a handle on the situation.

He saw Ajmal first. He couldn't fathom the reason for the lengthy delay of the dummy shipment. He met with Ajmal and asked to see the shipping papers. Dex almost jumped out of his pants when he realized that the dummy shipment had been sent to Buffalo, New York!

"No wonder we can't find the shipment. You sent it to Buffalo, New York. How in the hell did you get Buffalo, New York, out of Montreal, Quebec, Canada?"

Ajmal looked over at Dexter with a deadpan face and said "Buffalo New York Sir."

"Yeah. How would you like it if I sent your money to New Delhi, India?"

"Buffalo New York Sir?"

Dexter glared at Ajmal. There was a momentary silence, as the two men stared at each other. Dexter broke the heavy atmosphere by asking Ajmal how such a blatant, glaring error could have been made without his noticing it?

Ajmal started shouting and barking orders to his workers in Pakistani. He calmed down after awhile, explaining to Dexter that he had to check something out; he excused himself and left the room with his associates. Dexter sat alone in his room thinking to himself that no matter what bullshit story Ajmal came up with there was no plausible excuse that could satisfy him for a goof like that. Especially in light of the fact that, as he had told Dexter, he had been educated in Europe. He could read and write English and had traveled to the United States and Canada. He had to know that there was a helluva difference between Buffalo, New York, U.S.A. and Montreal, Quebec, Canada. Dexter detected Ajmal's unfamiliarity with the shipping documents and reasoned that he had turned them over to a subordinate without doing any follow-up himself. Dexter asked himself if the guy was that lazy or just that stupid. In any event, Dexter intended to drive home the point that it was imperative that the paperwork be done as precisely as possible. There was no margin for error with the paperwork! Dexter and others had lost more deals than he cared to remember because someone screwed up the shipping documents, and the Man had picked up on it. That's one of the major tip-offs the customs people look for. Dexter thought that it should be simple enough to convey this principle to his Pakistani acquaintance. Dexter was now about to be introduced to what the Asians and Arabs call "saving face." Ajmal returned to Dexter's room, explaining that the shipping company in Canada had given his man the wrong directions. Dexter reminded Ajmal that it was he who had given him the shipping directions and that there was no way in hell he had ever mentioned Buffalo, New York!

Ajmal sat in his chair, his eyes rolling round in his head, contemplating a response that would counter Dexter's. The two men sat across from each other in silence. Ajmal didn't speak. He wouldn't admit he had made a mistake. As the silent moments passed between them, it was as though he hadn't heard Dexter at all. Dexter made his statement again, but Ajmal, having no answer other than to admit he was wrong, sat there, eyes rolling round in his head, ignoring Dexter completely. Dexter realized it was hopeless to try to confront Ajmal with his mistake, so he went back over the shipping instructions once again.

Because he didn't like loose ends lying around, Dex took the shipping documents for the dummy shipment in Buffalo and had the cargo shipped to Montreal and cleared. It was a wasteful expense, but on the other hand it would close the chapter on the shipment. In so doing, it would eliminate the possibility that either US Customs or Canadian Customs might make a notation in their computers about the shipping company or the receiving company having an outstanding shipment. Smugglers always try to avoid waving any flags that might attract unnecessary attention to their operations. He categorically spelled out to Ajmal that if the live shipment went anywhere near the United States, he wouldn't clear it and he wouldn't be responsible for the loss. He made sure Ajmal understood that the deal was not even to go via the United States, in transit! If a deal passes through American territory and is cleared in Canada, the American authorities can still press charges for smuggling goods through their country; it's like having a double whammy. If something should go wrong, one government on your case is usually more than enough for most people. The following day he hopped a plane from Lahore to Karachi.

In the old man's case, it was just a matter of start-up bugs that occur in any new enterprise. Dex informed Shama and Papa Gee that he had found someone to marry her. Once the deal was done, he would set up the arrangements for Shama to come to Canada and be married. She was exploding with joy. It made Dex feel good to see her so happy. Papa Gee was looking younger by the day. Dex asked Shama to bring her passport, her birth certificate and her identification card, as well as her medical card verifying her vaccinations, to the hotel the following day. She would need a chest X-ray also, but that she could bring Dexter anytime before he left. He had to take photocopies of all her documents and have a doctor in Canada check them out as well as her chest X-rays. There was no point in her arriving in Canada, only to be refused by Health and Immigration authorities because she didn't have proper documentation or had problems with her lungs. Dexter was just being methodical, making sure all was in order, avoiding any problems before they became an issue.

Shama visited Dexter at his hotel the next day, alone and on time. They had to leave the door to his room open, because in a Muslim country for a woman to be alone in a hotel room with a man who was not her husband was an offence punishable by death. Dexter had read in the Karachi newspaper about a seventeen-year-old girl and her eighteen-year-old boyfriend being caught in a compromising position — meaning that her bloomers were off and he had a hard-on that a cat couldn't scratch! They were both sentenced to death by public stoning. The public was invited to throw stones at the juvenile sinners. Knowing of this, Dexter thought that Shama was a gutsy gal for skirting the edge, so to speak. The door to the room remained wide open! Dex thought to himself, it's one thing to be the "stoner," but it wouldn't be a lot of fun being the "stonee."

Examining her passport and her papers, Dexter noticed that her family name wasn't the same as Papa Gee's. His name didn't appear on her birth certificate either. It really didn't matter what the story was; her passport and her papers were in order.

One question Dexter had buzzing around in his mind about bringing Shama to Canada was that if something went wrong, or if, for whatever reason, she were to be arrested by the police, would she stand up or could she stand up under pressure? Could she endure a police interrogation, or would she roll over and cop out on everyone, including Dexter? The question bothered Dexter ever since he had agreed to help Shama come to Canada. Was he exposing himself to a weak link? The old man had assured him that his daughter was solid, loyal and trustworthy, a story that Dexter had heard from a lot of so-called tough guys who eventually stooled on their Mother, priest and wife! Dexter had to be as sure as he could that he wasn't getting another snow job. A mistake of this nature would be disastrous. He knew that Papa Gee wasn't her father which was perhaps a minor detail, but he had to know if she was solid.

He confronted her with the obvious. "Shama, Papa Gee is not your father. I know that. Now I can't have you come to Montreal if you are going to lie to me. I want the truth, or else you can forget about coming to Canada!"

Shama's bright bubbly smile changed to a look of bleak despair. It was evident to Dexter that more than anything in the world Shama wanted to get out of Pakistan and live in Canada. She went from the height of happiness to the depth of despair in one short sentence. It was the truth or else!

She looked at Dexter; tears welled up in her large brown eyes, tightly clenching a silk scarf, she said in a soft, barely audible voice, "Papa Gee is my Father."

Dexter looked at her passport. Opening it up, he pointed to the name of another man as her father. The name wasn't even close to Papa Gee's. She stared down at her hands, twisting and turning the knotted silk scarf.

Dexter knew that what he was doing to Shama was very painful, even cruel; however, he had to know if she was solid. He knew that if something went wrong once she was in Canada, the police would threaten her with deportation if she didn't co-operate. Dexter didn't want to wind up doing ten or twelve years for importation and trafficking because some broad from Pakistan couldn't hold up her end. Dexter knew from Shama's reaction the first time immigration to Canada was brought up that the subject made her glisten with joy. He knew that taking that opportunity away from her was like threatening her with a death sentence.

Dexter didn't really care what the story was between her and Papa Gee. What he wanted to know was whether she would crack under pressure. Dexter leaned forward. His elbows resting on the arms of the chair, his hands clenched in fists, a stern, cold look on his face, he spoke to her in a harsh voice. "Shama, I know Papa Gee is not your father! Your passport tells me this, your birth certificate confirms it, and yes, even Papa Gee has told me all about you and him. Now, for the last time, tell me the truth! If you continue to lie to me, you can rot here in Pakistan!"

Dexter felt like a real shit for being such a bastard with her but he had to know if she was trustworthy. Was she solid? Dex was fishing a bit when he told her that even Papa Gee had revealed the truth about Shama not being his daughter. In truth, he had never discussed it with Papa Gee, and Papa Gee had never said any such thing. Dexter had guessed as to the true relationship between Papa Gee and Shama when he recalled the dinner he had been invited to at their home.

When he had first met Papa Gee, he had graying, thinning hair. He walked like an old man, slightly slouched over, with slow methodical footsteps. At the first meeting, they arrived as a father and daughter. They walked out of the meeting arm in arm, smiling at one another, more like boyfriend and girlfriend. The family supper he had been invited to was a set-up. It wasn't at the house address Papa Gee had given him as his home address, or the address he sent correspondence to. Papa Gee had arrived late, after everyone else. There was no need for him to have been so busy that he was late for dinner, especially in making arrangements for a deal that couldn't get under way for many months later. The other sister and the child had been props arranged to distract Dexter so that he wouldn't only be conversing with Papa Gee and Shama. The sister and child had left the house late that night. Why, if it was their house? Then there was the new Papa Gee, no longer slouched over, a little bit of spring to his step, and yes, the dyed brown hair! Dexter was fishing, but he wasn't exactly fishing blind. He didn't care who or how Papa Gee was getting laid. He was concerned that maybe Papa Gee's little head was controlling his big head, which could inadvertently lead to Dexter ending up in the can. In the Drug Game, you watch out for your own ass!

Shama sat in her chair facing Dexter, looking down at her hands, continuing to twist and wring the silk scarf.

"Shama, look at me! I want to hear the truth from you!"

Shama looked up at Dexter. Her eyes drowning in tears. She bit her lip, fighting back the tears. Not a tear spilled from those big brown eyes, which seemed even larger than before. Her heart must have been drowning in sorrow too, as she heard her dream crashing into despair. She swallowed hard and said, "Papa Gee is my father."

Dex chuckled to himself. He felt like getting up out of his chair, reaching over and giving her a big hug. She was a helluva lot more solid than ninety-nine percent of the guys he had ever met. She had passed the test with flying colours. She had put her future on the line, everything she had ever dreamed of; she had remained loyal to her friend, Papa Gee. He had told her to say she was his daughter, and come hell or high water she stuck to the party line! Dex now knew she was solid, and admired her strength and loyalty. Dexter was now confident that if anything ever went wrong, the cops wouldn't be able to break her. He smiled at her and said, "Shama, you will come to Canada. I only hope that I can always count on your loyalty as you have shown your loyalty to Papa Gee today. I really don't care about who your real Father is or what your relationship with Papa Gee is. Once the deal arrives safely in Canada, I will send for you. Everything is going to work out fine."

She looked up at Dexter, a bright smile graced her face once more, a smile that warmed Dexter's heart. She was glowing, beaming with happiness once again, and Dexter never broached the matter with her after that.

Papa Gee arrived with the Putz. They went over the game plan for the umpteenth time. After lunch, Shama and Papa Gee left, arm in arm. Shama was as happy as a bride-to-be with a diamond engagement ring. Papa Gee was as happy as a married man getting the signal from his wife — it was that once-in-a-blue-moon time.

Dex sat around with the Putz in his room, having a few drinks, shooting the breeze. Dex asked the Putz to give him the scoop on Shama. The Putz volunteered all he knew. She was apparently orphaned at the age of twelve. She had made her way on the streets of Karachi, working at what she could in order to survive; eventually she found employment as a servant in an office. She then taught herself to speak and read English, use a typewriter, and whatever else was necessary to become a secretary. Salim brought her into his office at the age of fourteen or fifteen and she had remained with him until he fired her and Papa Gee. Frequently, she would visit the Putz in his apartment, inquiring about books, mathematics, geography and Canada. She wanted to know all there was to know about Canada.

Papa Gee had gotten drunk with the Putz one night and had told him the whole sad story of Shama's life. Shortly after she had started to work for Salim, he began to abuse her and forced her to sleep with him whenever he wanted. In Pakistan, orphans don't get support or protection from the State. It's a game of survival. Shama was a survivor. The Cricket had kept her around not only because she was qualified and loyal but also because she was very pretty. He could have had a dozen orphans do his bidding and probably did. Shama became more attractive with each passing day; however, she was enslaved to Salim for as long as he wanted. The Cricket's wife had begun to turn up the heat with regard to his pretty little secretary. Perhaps he got tired of her, or maybe he just wanted to placate his wife; whatever, when he turfed the old man out, Shama got the boot too. Salim could have married Shama and that would have silenced the wife, but because she was an orphan, a used woman, she was valued less than a dog in Pakistan. It was OK to use her and abuse her, for she was not worthy of any higher social status than what she had already attained. Her prospects for getting married in Pakistan were none to less than zero. She was at the bottom of the social scale — no dowry, no parents, no family, no virginity. Her life in Pakistan was all laid out for her. Dex realized how much it must have meant for her to come to Canada. He admired her solidarity even more than before. As far as Dexter was concerned, Shama was a princess. Her marriage in Canada would be in name only. Whoever else she slept with would be of her own choosing. Dex felt she had paid her dues. That evening, he boarded a plane for Europe. He spent a couple of days shopping and returned to Canada.

Several weeks later, Dexter received a message from the Putz. The deal had left Pakistan, and he was going to Lahore for some R&R. He gave Dex the name of his hotel, just in case Dex should want to contact him. Two days later he received a message from Ajmal. He knew Dexter's man was in Lahore, and wanted permission to meet with him, to discuss a small problem he was having with his deal. Dex couldn't stop it, so he agreed to let Ajmal contact him. Dexter had told the Putz in no uncertain terms not to discuss Papa Gee's deal with anyone. He didn't know how it was that Ajmal knew who the Putz was or how he had come to know of his stay in

Lahore. He had a queasy feeling about it all; however, there was nothing he could do but hope that the Putz would keep his mouth shut concerning Papa Gee's deal.

The Putz met with Ajmal, got drunk, and told him about how the old man had shipped his deal out. He told Ajmal exactly how and when the deal had left. Ajmal is a *hodj* in Pakistan, which means he has money and power. In Pakistan, corruption is the name of the game, regardless of how pristine a front they have. The more money one has, the more power one has and the higher up the government ladder of corruption one climbs.

Ajmal had to "save face." Being the big *hodj* he said he was, he couldn't allow some peasants to usurp him by getting a shipment out when he couldn't. The reason Papa Gee and crew got their shipment out was that he was working with the little people at the airport. They had gone around all the bureaucrats, politicians and big *hodjs* in Pakistan. In short, they did it on their own! With the information the Putz gave Ajmal, he was able to have Papa Gee's deal brought back from half-way round the world. Had the Putz delayed telling Ajmal for another two days, the shipment would have been too far gone to bring back. It would have been in Dexter's territory. Unfortunately for Papa Gee, that was not the case, and the deal ended up back in Pakistan. Not knowing which crew had sent the shipment out, the authorities played it safe and fired a hundred and twenty people working in cargo and on the ramp at Karachi Airport. That's the way it works over there, the little people don't have the opportunity to get ahead. They pay them peanuts, but if they should dare go out on their own they crush them. Nice people! The *hodj* saved face, and a lot of little hard-working innocent people paid the price.

Ajmal was still unable to get his shipment out. He kept advising Dexter it was coming, it was coming, but nothing ever came. After several months of waiting, Dexter returned to Lahore. Ajmal claimed that the government had closed the door temporarily, for reasons of political relations with the U.S. Once they got some loan or grant, it would be business as usual. Ajmal was apparently first on the list to get a deal out. While speaking with Dexter, Ajmal made a slip of the tongue that made it clear that he knew Dexter had lost a shipment. Dex said nothing; he just made a mental note of it and moved the conversation on to their business. Dexter got hold of the Putz in private and confronted him with the problem of his big mouth. The Putz admitted he made a mistake, but Dex was not to worry — Ajmal was bigger and better than that broken down old man, so why sweat it! Dex looked at the Putz; here was a guy who wasn't much of a bandit in his day, and now he was telling Dexter how to smuggle. Dex left the Putz in Lahore and went to see the old man in Karachi. Papa Gee explained everything, to the point of telling Dexter what he already knew about the Putz and his big mouth and Ajmal's face-saving play. Dexter told the old man to cool his jets, and that as soon as the big *hodj* sent his deal Dex would take some profits from that and give him another shot at the roses.

Dexter returned to Canada and waited for Ajmal to do his thing. Eventually he did send the deal, but it came in all screwed up. It took a lot of finagling on the part of Dexter and company to rescue the deal from disaster. When they opened up the shipment, they discovered that Ajmal had sent two hundred kilos of standard commercial hash and one hundred kilos of dog shit. Dexter sold the deal and flew over to Pakistan like a tiger with a tin can tied to its tail.

Ajmal expected Dexter to greet him as some kind of big-shot hero. That was not quite the greeting he received from Dexter. When Dex laid into him, Ajmal puffed up his chest as if to say, "You can't talk to me that way." He looked over at his little bumboy, the Putz, who sat quietly on the sofa, not making a peep. Dex caught the look Ajmal gave the Putz, and at that moment he knew whose side the Putz was on. The Putz was now working for Ajmal, with his own agenda. Dex thought to himself, "That's gratitude for you." The Putz had obviously briefed Ajmal as to Dexter's background. He realized that Dexter wasn't buying the "face saving" bullshit, and he didn't care if the big *hodj* was insulted by his attitude. Ajmal ordered his men out of the room. The Putz remained seated on the sofa. Dexter looked over at the little drunk and told him to leave, too. Ajmal began to object, but the Putz wasn't about to press his luck, so he slunk out of the room like a little kid being ordered to bed. The atmosphere was very heavy. Steam was coming out of Dexter's ears as he stood face to face with Ajmal. The moment everyone had left the room, Ajmal turned into a marshmallow.

He explained to Dexter that he was mainly into smuggling gold and silver in and out of India — besides running heroin into France and guns into Kashmir, he had no real knowledge of the hashish game. He pleaded with Dexter to give him another chance. Next time Dexter would receive primo hash and the deal would be executed to perfection. Dex said he'd think about it. Then, before his men and the Putz came back into the room, Ajmal asked Dexter not to shout at him in front of his men. Dex looked at him, disgusted with the bullshit face-saving game they play over there; however, he realized that to humiliate Ajmal in front of his men would give him nothing. Besides, Ajmal had asked him nicely!

From Lahore, Dex flew to Karachi to meet with the old man. Papa Gee and Shama arrived at his hotel like two privates waiting to be court-martialled. Dex got right down to business: he was ready to shoot the puck with the old man once more. At this point, Papa Gee confessed that he was unable to send anything out. He needed more time to develop new airport contacts. He figured it might take him as much as a year to put together another crew. Dex advised him that when he was ready, he should contact him immediately. Dexter looked over at Shama. The sparkle had gone from her eyes and was replaced by a vacant, haunting gaze that seemed to have all its life sucked out. Dark circles beneath her eyes accentuated the expression of hopelessness on her pretty face. Dex noticed that Papa Gee was no longer treating Shama with the kind courtesy he once had. Dex gave Papa Gee some money to operate with, and then he turned to Shama. He told her that she would still make it to Canada. She managed a faint smile as she fought back tears. Dexter wasn't in a position to help her, or at least that's the excuse he used to convince himself that her future was out of his hands. He did his best to lift up her spirits by making light of how quickly a year passes. The reality was that for Shama, nearing her twentieth birthday, another year in Pakistan was an eternity. In retrospect, Dexter was like so many other people in this world — too self-absorbed to really consider taking time out to help another human being. He regrets not doing something for Shama. Regret sounds so compassionate; yet in the end, it's only a word.

Dexter returned to Lahore, where he met with Ajmal. He had no choice but to shoot the puck with him again. It was either that or sit around waiting for the old man to get his act together or go to Morocco or Egypt and work on connections he was developing there. He was fed up with the Pakistani bullshit, but he decided that after all the time, money and effort he had invested in Ajmal, he should give him one more try. He thought to himself, "Maybe things will improve."

The new deal was to be in a shipment of cashew nuts. They discussed the shipping arrangements and the problem of the quality of the hashish. Dexter was assured of top quality hash, not commercial and absolutely no more dog shit. Dexter approved a sample, and the Putz witnessed his selection. The Putz was running around Ajmal like a little suckhole trying to land a promotion. It was sickening to see a man from a first world country, kissing ass like some beggar in a bazaar. He was more like a trophy to Ajmal, having his little Irish bumboy blowing smoke up his ass all day long. Dexter didn't know the Putz's game plan, but he knew that whatever it was, it was contrary to Dexter's best interest.

Ajmal introduced Dexter to the other members of his clan. There was a fine young lad Dexter liked very much. He was intelligent and unspoiled by the art of face-saving at that point in his life. The lad's father was Ajmal's partner, a big fat guy who didn't speak any English but seemed genuine and sincere. His son would act as translator for Dex and his father. Dexter liked the fat guy and found out that he had earned his stripes in the smuggling game as one of Ajmal's father's loyal men. He had been wounded in shootouts with the border patrols in the old days; as a result, he had been elevated to partner status in the clan's hierarchy. Unfortunately, Dexter couldn't do business directly with him because of the language barrier. Dex had a feeling that things would have worked better if mamma's boy hadn't been in the way. Dex was compelled to do all business arrangements with Ajmal; sometimes life deals the cards all screwed-up, and you just have to play them as they are.

RULE NUMBER SIX

RECOGNIZE THE ANGLES

Another way of saying, recognize the angles is to say: learn street smarts or street sense. Street sense is simply the ability to recognize and adjust to the reality of life. It is the ability to see through the smoke-screen individuals use to cover their real purposes. Everybody has an angle and learning to accept this fact — and to decipher whether another person's best interest and yours are compatible — is what street sense is all about. Whether you're a Holy-Joe, a square john, a captain of industry, a housewife, a criminal or a player in the Drug Game, you have your own angle, and we all play our angles to suit our own best interest.

Here are some easy examples to explain what Dexter means.

A man sees an old lady struggling with a heavy shopping bag, waiting at a street corner for the light to change. He approaches her and offers to help her carry the heavy shopping bag across the street. He relieves her of the shopping bag, takes her by the arm and walks her across the street. What's his angle?

There are three possibilities. Maybe the old lady is his mother or his aunt, and he wants to stay in her good books so as not to get cut out of her will.

Or, he's a thief, and once he gets to the other side of the street he's gonna take off running with her bag!

The third reason could be that he's a nice man and by helping an old lady across the street, he is simply doing a good deed. In so doing, he feels good about himself and the society in which he lives.

In all three instances, the man had an angle. It was up to the old lady to figure out which angle he was playing.

We can think of a dozen other examples, of angles we see people playing at work, in their social life or in business activities. Angle-playing is often wonderful, if it is motivated by a person's desire to be constructive or compassionate. Sometimes it is self-centered and self-serving, without regard for the feelings or status of others. Sometimes it is vengeful, malicious and troubling. In the legit world, people who play the angles constantly for themselves are said to be "takers."

"Takers" are people who calculate everything they do for anyone in terms of real and tangible returns for themselves. "Takers" don't just do something for someone to be nice or compassionate. They do good deeds in expectation of a return for themselves. To a "taker," a good deed is an investment. Altruism isn't in their dictionary. If it is, they have it listed under the definition of "sucker." In our society, it is more common to be a "taker," because we live in a materialistic society that teaches us that winning is everything. How we win isn't important; it's winning that counts. If you doubt Dexter's observations, he would ask you to look no further than your political leaders. They say almost anything to win. True or not?

"Givers" are individuals who have managed to maintain a pleasure in giving. Not giving of themselves materialistically in expectation of receiving something in return but giving for the pure pleasure of making others happy. Often "givers" do not have a good sense of balance between giving and being used. Many times they wind up being used and not appreciated for their generosity or their compassion for others. They have altruistic ideals that most do not understand or accept. Unless they learn a balance in life, they become martyrs or fools — a polite way of saying loosers or suckers!

Still, all that aside, whether you be a "giver" or a "taker'" in the legit world, it is seldom going to cost you your life. In the Drug Game, it might. Many things that apply in the legit world are also equally applicable in the Drug World; it's the consequences that are manifestly and dramatically different.

People on the street develop an acute sense of the way others try to play the angles on them. They have to be on constant vigil. Dexter had trained himself to be a good listener, to observe every detail of other people's body language and to be highly attuned to every aspect of his environment. He knew himself, too, and above all he was alert to his own strengths and weaknesses. You don't have to be callous and totally self-centered in order to survive; but you'd better learn to recognize the sharks as they swim by you.

Dexter found that talking less and listening more carefully to what people had to say was the best way for him to stay on top of his game.

CHAPTER EIGHT
LIVING IN A CRISIS

An interesting observation Dexter brought to my attention was that almost all of the people involved in the drug world come from a background of crisis living, himself included. Psychologists call it a dysfunctional background. Dexter would tell you that not only did he come from a dysfunctional family, he came from a dysfunctional neighbourhood. And a dysfunctional family is always in a state of crisis.

Dysfunctionalism can be caused by any one of a number of things: alcohol, drugs, gambling or various kinds of abuse. Kids growing up in a home never knowing if one or both of the parents are going to be arrested, come home drunk and start a fight or flip out and beat them up. Or it may be the landlord knocking on the door for the rent, when the family hasn't the money for food or clothing, let alone shelter.

Doctors, lawyers, politicians, industrialists, entrepreneurs — people from all walks of life are subject to various types of crisis living. Living in a crisis knows no boundaries of race, colour, creed or religion. It is a common misconception that dysfunctional conditions are found only among the poor and the downtrodden. Not true, they are found in every stratum of our society. Perhaps the wealthy or affluent just cover up dysfunction better; or simply purge their confusion, hurt, anger and pain in more acceptable ways, such as bulimia, anorexia, overeating, introversion, hedonistic pursuits or simply detachment from the world.

Whatever its root source, it is the underlying reason people turn to drugs and or alcohol. If you know someone who abuses drugs or alcohol, check their background; it's there without fail. It is your environment and the degree to which you have to adapt merely to survive the growing years that determine your life's direction. If you don't recognize the effect that crisis living has on your life, you are doomed to live a life in constant turmoil and constant stress.

Yet, being raised in a crisis environment is not necessarily a recipe for failure. It does not have to be a disadvantage for someone to come from such a background. If it's recognized, it can set a person far above the rest in the workplace or in the world of crime.

Dexter's theory is simply this. Imagine an instrument that measures the level of stress in an individual's life, say on a scale of one to twelve. The average person lives in a stress range from three to six. People who come from stressful environments live in a stress range from five to seven. These are the norms for both types of people.

People who have been brought up and are accustomed to living their lives in the lower end of the stress scale, from three to six, can and do function well even when the stress factor in their lives goes up to a seven. It is difficult for them, it is uncomfortable for them; but they can and do function. If the stress factor climbs even more, they may be able to handle it for a very short period of time. However, if the stress factor stays at, say, an eight or a nine for any lengthy duration, they cave in. They cannot function at these stress levels for a sustained period of time. They quit their job or their marriage, bomb themselves out on drugs and alcohol or have a nervous breakdown.

The second group of people, those who come from stressful dysfunctional backgrounds, and are used to living in the stress range from five to seven, are completely comfortable when their stress level rises to nine. When it goes up to a ten, they are still able to perform their duties. They are able to function even when the stress scale goes higher for a short period of time. Any prolonged duration of a stress level, ten or higher, and they too turn to drugs or alcohol to assist them in coping with the stress.

It is therefore natural that people who had a stressful childhood tend to seek out jobs or professions that are stressful. If you were to take a person who has lived all his life in a large city and place him on a farm somewhere out in the boonies, he'd go nuts with the placid solitude and quietness. And the reverse is true, too. Police officers, firemen, airline personnel, actors, entertainers, stock and commodity brokers and risk-takers in the business world as well as the political realm are all attracted to these and other stressful vocations because of the stress factor. They actually thrive on a high-stress lifestyle. In the early stage of a criminal career, most criminals are drawn to the world of crime less because of money and need than because of the adrenaline rush that comes with living on the edge. Many criminals may think they started their career in crime for monetary gain, but if they take a reality check like Dexter did, they too will realize that the adrenaline rush was the real payoff. This is not to say that every single person who lives in the higher stress zone is from a dysfunctional background, but the overwhelming majority are!

Those who work in stressful professions but are not from stressful backgrounds never seem to excel or reach their potential as do those who were raised in stressful environments. Dexter has lived both kinds of life, and this observation has enabled him to pick out the winners and losers in both the legit world and the drug world. Those who can cope with stress are much more focussed and successful. Take a cop who can handle the stress when things aren't going his way and the pressure is bearing down on him. He'll stay focused and get results. Cops who blow their cool, use violence to get results or falsify evidence are those who can't cope. Whenever a cop slapped Dexter around, Dex knew he was dealing with a dummy and all he had to do was shut his mouth. When he met a cop who was polite, calm and courteous, it scared the crap out of him; he knew he was treading on thin ice. Dexter much preferred to have a blockhead working on his case than a brainy one.

In spite of this, Dexter would not suggest that anyone raise their child in an unduly stressful environment. He would however, point out to all those people who come from stressful backgrounds, whatever their social level, that their upbringing maybe a tremendous asset. In this very competitive society we live in, it can be an advantage and not necessarily a defect. Recognize it and run with it! Most of us don't. We sit around crying the blues, and "poor me," wasting a valuable asset that can't be bought in a store or gotten from a college education. It's a gift, if used properly. Imagine being able to function when the majority of people are caving in. But in order to use it advantageously, you have to know that you have it!

The downside to this gift of coping with stress is that if you let it guide your life totally, it will eventually crush you. It will constantly lead you to finding or creating stressful situations that could be avoided. In the shadowy world of drugs, it usually leads to either the revolving door of the penal system or death!

In the drug world, you won't have to look too hard if you're looking for a crisis.

For a long time, criminals who lived from one day to the next bewildered Dexter. He couldn't understand their dysfunctional approach to life, like if they had a couple of grand in their pockets, they would blow it all. They never seemed to give a thought about tomorrow or the day after, or have any real plans for their future. Dexter knew many who made big money, hundreds of thousands, even millions of dollars; yet they never put a penny aside for a rainy day. The vast majority never tried to establish any kind of legitimate income for their old age or the rainy days that inevitably follow the good ones. Dexter recognized that life goes in cycles; nothing remains the same forever. He found it difficult working with these one-day-at-a-time criminals. They never thought out their actions, and this often placed them and those who worked with them in dangerous situations — all of which could be avoided with a little forethought.

Sometimes in the Drug Game, you make money hand over fist for two or three years, sometimes more. You can be sure that as the night follows the sun, one day you'll wake up living in a toilet bowl. No matter what you do, everything turns to shit. This is also true in the legit world. But the difference in the Drug Game is that you or someone else is going to pull the chain, and you'll end up in the sewer. And usually the person pulling the chain is you. You guessed it: it's because you were looking for a crisis. You needed that kick — maybe not consciously, but subconsciously — that boost of adrenaline you get when you're in a crisis. A psychologist once commented to Dexter on this phenomenon of crisis living as being linked to hyperactivity. Whatever label you put on it, you have to be conscious of its devastating effects on your life and liberty.

Dexter had to go through a period of living from one crisis to the next, before he finally recognized what in the hell he was doing to himself. It's a tough habit to break; even tougher to harness. Dexter knew guys in the old hold-up days who would be out robbing banks before they'd even taken the time to put the money away from the job they'd done the week before. A drug dealer will often spend all his money on cars, drugs, booze and broads, and only then try to figure out how he's going to pay the people he owes. Most people in the drug world live one day to the next. In part, it's because they don't know how to manage money; but they also have no respect for it — they simply believe the good times are going to roll on forever. Dexter believes that behind it all is the "looking for a crisis" syndrome. It happens every time — when everything is going well, we do things that put us behind the eight ball. Our lives speak for us. To Dex, the common thread with all the people he has met in the underworld is that they were brought up in a crisis environment. When things were flying high, they looked for a crisis. They did stupid things like talk on telephones, get drunk and mouth off, attract attention by buying new cars, expensive clothes, jewelry that was out of place, or just flashing money around playing the big-shot. Eventually they got the attention they were looking for: either some shark took a run at them or the Man came down on them so hard their eyeballs registered tilt. Then they found themselves in a crisis.

Over the years Dexter was fortunate never to have had to pay the ultimate price for the stupidity of his crisis living. Not that he didn't pay for it in other ways; but he was fortunate enough to have had a good wife who had more sense than he did, banked his money and kept that crazy man's feet on the ground.

There's less stress, less excitement and not much in the way of adrenaline rushes if you manage to control the "crisis-living motor" that propels you down the highway toward self-destruction. Dexter learned that when you are in a bad part of the cycle, you have to cool it! You have to ride it out! That takes money. You have to put it aside for those rainy days. Push things when the cycle is going against you, and you'll get a crisis that will register twelve on the stress scale. Unfortunately for most players in the game, they team up with a spouse or a partner who is much the same as they are, and so there is no balance in their lives. Sometimes when they do have a good spouse, partner, lover, husband or wife, they get rid of them because they don't want to face the reality of dealing with life on an even keel.

Dexter hadn't seen his old buddy Duney for a while, so he stopped by the club to see him. A gradual but noticeable change had overcome Duney. It went back further than the kidnapping attempt on his son. It started about a year after a guy known as Jackie, or Jake the Snake, was released from prison on parole.

Duney had taken Jackie under his wing. Jake the Snake was a killer *par excellence*. Mother was an easygoing guy. Duney needed a visible stick to keep the sharks at bay. In the drug world, especially if you are of the stature of Duney, you need an enforcer on a day-to-day basis. Mother could always reach out and employ hired guns if the situation warranted it. You don't want to have an army of gunslingers hanging around all the time, but in Duney's case it was necessary to have a show of force. Having a high-profile button man readily available diminished the need to use him. That's the way it works!

If people in the drug world know you have the capability of having them dumped at the snap of a finger, chances are they'll mind their P's and Q's and do business straight up. Having a killer in your employ who everyone knows is a killer avoids the necessity of using extreme violence. It's kind of like putting the fear of God into people without having to make a big show of all that lightning and thunder. When you are lower down the scale in the drug world, people have to know with certainty that you're no pushover, or powder-puff. You won't have a hired gun walking around with you, because you want people in the Drug Game to know that you're your own gunman.

In our legal world there are different types of killers. There is the one who is charged with manslaughter, the one who kills for compassionate reasons, premeditated murder, and so on. The underworld is no different; we just have a different slant on what is right and what is wrong. There are many different types of killers. There are those who kill in self-defense only, the psychopathic killers, the serial killers and the professional hit men who usually act as enforcers for gangs or mobs or organizations.

There's a difference between someone in the legit world who kills in self-defense and someone who does so in the underworld.

Consider this situation. You are in your home asleep at night. You hear someone breaking into your house. You call 911, then you go to your closet and grab your shotgun. You turn on the light and shout down at the intruder, "Get out of my house!"

The intruder is a crack-head. He doesn't care. He shouts back up to you, "Throw me down your wallet or I'll go up there and kill you!"

You stand at the top of the stairs, hoping and praying the police are going to arrive quickly. They're at the doughnut shop having a jelly doughnut. The intruder starts to come up the stairs. You see he has a knife in his hand. He's about ten feet away from you. You point the shotgun in his direction. Boom! You blast him. You are a killer, but in the eyes of the law — and rightly so — you have killed in self-defense. Your life was in peril; you were forced to defend yourself. Society understands this and accepts your plea of self-defense. You are not punished. You do not go to jail. It is an acceptable killing in the eyes of the law and society. You have the right to defend yourself. On this, we all agree; nonetheless, you are still a killer.

In the underworld and the Drug Game, it works the same way; except that the law of the land and society don't see it that way.

Consider this situation. You are a drug dealer. You sell drugs to someone. There is no problem on either side. The buyer was happy with the quality of the drugs you sold him, or at least he accepted the quality of drugs you had for sale. He agreed on the price, so there was no conflict.

But let's suppose the buyer has different ideas. He knows you have more drugs and also more money. He decides to rip you off for your money and your drugs. By chance his scheme to rob and kill you comes to your attention. Perhaps he went around trying to hire some guys to help rip you off. Maybe he bought a gun and told the guy about his plans to eliminate you. In any event, you were tipped off. (Broads do this trip, too!) You can't call 911 and tell the police you're a drug dealer who is about to get ripped off and murdered. You're not going to confront the punk about his plans, because this would jeopardize the life of the person who tipped you off, in such a case he just might grab you right on the spot. You know of the punk's reputation as a parking-lot killer. You know he's been suspected of killing other drug dealers in the past. You just never thought he would turn on you! You have the option of either letting him kill you or going after the son of a bitch and whacking him before he pops you. If you are successful in defending yourself by killing the bastard, you are a murderer in the eyes of the law and society. You will be punished for defending yourself. If you get caught, you do not pass "Go," you go directly to jail. This is the gigantic mental step one has to make about a killing in the underworld, versus a killing in society. You have to be comfortable with this or you'll perish in the Drug Game. There is no second-guessing when it comes down to crunch time.

When you saw the intruder coming up the stairs with a knife in his hand, you thought about pulling the trigger before you pulled it. In the case of the drug dealer, he thought about his options before executing them. Both killings are premeditated.

A judge would argue that the drug dealer put himself in the position of having to kill by getting involved in drugs in the first place. Therefore, the dealer's actions are not self-defense. Dexter would tell you that he never met anyone who got involved in the drug business because he or she wanted to kill someone. People get entangled in the Drug Game to make money or buy drugs, pure and simple. It is a moot point to argue that the drug dealer brought it upon himself. It may be, but the overriding circumstances tell us something entirely different. The dealer had no choice but to defend himself. As for Dexter and company, they would say that neither person is a bad person, they were just doing what they had to do.

The other types of killers Dexter has met in the underworld are more clearly defined. You have the parking-lot hit man, usually a punk who thinks he has discovered water because he's able to take a human life for no rhyme or reason. At best, they are bolstering their low self-esteem by convincing themselves that their deadly actions make them revered as people of special importance. They are guns for hire, but only if the victim they are stalking is not likely to put up a fight or be in a position to defend himself. They usually kill their victims for a price, at night, in a parking lot or some secluded location. Lacking a whole lot of balls, they commit their murderous deeds whenever the victim will be unarmed, unsuspecting and vulnerable. They build their reputations on the trail of corpses they leave behind. They are usually paid according to their IQ which, as you can imagine, isn't that great.

Another type of killer we meet in the Drug Game is the serial killer. They lurk in the underworld seeking out a particular type of victim. Often they will be parking-lot killers as well. They kill to satisfy their morbid thirst for blood, all the while hiding their evil bent in the shadows of the criminal world. The underworld provides them with a vast quantity of victims who, they know, have no relatives or whose associates probably won't go to the police.

One such animal was released from prison after serving twelve years on a fifteen-year sentence. At one time he was a hold-up man. Upon his release, he wanted to get involved in the Drug Game. When he left prison, the boys inside gave him a few names and addresses of people he could hook up with on the outside. He contacted the people and began to make some money. His new friends introduced him to women as a natural part of befriending him. The strangest thing started occurring — every time he went out with a woman three or four times, she would disappear! When asked about it by his friends, he would play dumb. He would tell them that he had broken off with the woman or that things just hadn't worked out and that he didn't know where she was or what she was doing. He always seemed detached and uninterested. It all came to a head when a friend of Dexter's known as Patty introduced this serial killer to his girlfriend's best friend. Several dates later, the gal disappeared!

The punk's sick game came to light because Patty's girlfriend was very close to her friend. She knew that something was desperately wrong. She told Patty about her suspicions. Patty confronted the guy with an ultimatum, produce the girlfriend or else! The coconut maintained his innocence, denying all knowledge of what may have happened to the girl. He realized that Patty wasn't buying the party line, nor was he about to drop the issue. He decided to knock Patty and his girlfriend off, because they were the only two people who could expose him. Patty returned home with his girlfriend one night shortly after the confrontation. The killer lay in wait for them. He emptied his gun on them and fled, thinking he had killed them both. Patty's girlfriend was slightly wounded and Patty escaped unscathed. When their deaths weren't reported on the news or in the newspapers the following day, the killer knew he had to have a change of scenery quickly! Patty put the word out that the guy was no good; in fact, that he was a coconut who was better off dead. People were now keeping an eye out for the sicko punk.

Nobody goes to the Man — to do so would be tantamount to being a stool pigeon. The underworld is always better off doing its own housecleaning, at least that's the way the old-timers feel about it. Besides, what could the Man do? There was no proof; no bodies had or have ever been discovered, and Patty would never take the stand to identify the coconut as the shooter; he would be labeled a rat, and rightly so. The psycho punk was finished in the Drug Game, because he knew the word was out about him. He went back to his old game of bank robbery, but he got caught and was sent back to prison.

He gambled that the boys in prison didn't know about his sick game of killing women when he was on the outside. He didn't ask for protective custody. He went into the general population at Sainte-Anne-des-Plaines Penitentiary. Not long after, he was dumped by some cons in the joint. How many women did that sick killer murder in the nine or ten months he was on the street? No one knows. This is just one type of serial killer who lurks in the underworld. It is the best place for them to hide their thirst for blood. They are out there. You cannot recognize them by their looks, their manner of speech or their social mannerisms. If you associate with the underworld or play the Drug Game, you will rub shoulders with them whether you like it or not; just be sure you don't become a source of pleasure for them.

Another type of killer is the professional hit man. Hit men usually work for, and owe their loyalty to, a group, a mob family or an organization for which they act as policemen. Their moral code does not permit them to hire themselves out as professional killers. You may find this a misuse of the word "moral," but these men are not psychopaths who kill indiscriminately or for the thrill of the hit. They kill only as a matter of company business. Their murders are an expression of their commitment to their circle of associates. Psychologists or psychiatrists may put a different spin on it, but aside from their criminal activities, which may from time to time involve the taking of another human being's life, they are as normal as the people next door (at least on the surface). This does not justify, moralize, or defend them; that's just the way it is.

Freelance killers, guns for hire, are usually psychopath killers looking for an excuse to kill. They may be bombers, arsonists or gunmen; but they're all psychos who have made their perverse pleasure in murder reward them substantially by turning it into a career. Their principal criterion is money. If the price is right, they'll do it. They do not concern themselves with morals: they don't have any and they don't need any. They drift around the underworld cloaking their real passion for death by letting it be known that they are guns for hire. There are no "dial M for murder" clubs out there. These killers distinguish themselves by their ability to commit their acts of death without being caught. Usually, they kill with finesse tailored to order. They can make a killing look like a robbery gone bad, an accident, someone being in the wrong place at the wrong time, or just make the victim disappear.

The killer punks we read about in the newspapers are just that, punks who think that taking a human life makes them special, a cut above. Actually, they are just a bunch of assholes who are devoid of any feelings of compassion or decency. They don't necessarily kill for money; sometimes it's an ego trip, and sometimes it's petty larceny. No matter, they're a stupid lot who end up with short lifespans or long prison sentences before they reach the age of twenty-one. They are a part and parcel of a phenomenon of our times known as "wilding." More on that later.

The other type of killer is the psychopathic killer. They are the most deadly of all. They kill for the sheer pleasure of killing. They will do it for money: but money is not their only, or even a necessary, motivation. They murder for their deep-seated need to destroy. For them, the taking of a human life is the ultimate payoff, the ultimate expression of power! Their highest high, or thrill, comes with the taking of a human life. They crawl around the underworld because it is the best place for them to go undetected. The underworld is a breeding ground that gives them ample opportunities and excuses to ply their murderous skills while satisfying their blood lust. They may start out as a parking-lot hit man or as a killer punk, or even hide themselves in a gang or organization; however, once their desire to murder exceeds the demands of their position, they will seek out opportunities to be in on the next hit or kill. There is nothing normal about them. They are sick, deadly and dangerous. They are the most dangerous animal of all!

Jake the Snake was an old bandit who had been sent to prison for ten years on an extortion beef. Long before going to prison he had a reputation as a killer. All the killings he had performed up to that date seemed to have been justified, at least as far as the underworld was concerned. In other words, he had knocked off several stool pigeons or people assumed to have been stool pigeons. There have always been stool pigeons or rats in the community. The big difference between now and the old days is that back then there would be an annual housecleaning. The rats or stools had a much shorter lifespan then than they do today — another effect of the drug trade. Today, there are not only stool pigeons in the community, there are communities of stool pigeons.

Jackie was a quiet guy. When he smiled he had a boyish grin much like that of William Bonny, Billy the Kid. He was well liked by most people, because he was forever buying drinks for friends and acquaintances. If he had money in his pockets, he would spend every last dollar. When he was broke, he'd go out and rob a bank. He was known to be solid, and therefore he was highly trusted. Before going to prison, he had had a run in with a killer punk named McDonald.

McDonald was so stupid he wore sneakers because he didn't know how to get a shoeshine. He decided that the way to get into the major leagues was to become a killer. One night he was in a bar and stayed there till it closed. When he went to get his car, the parking lot was closed. There was a sign posted in big letters that said the parking lot closed at midnight. McDonald was obliged to walk several blocks to another parking lot, where his car keys had been left.

The next night he was back at the club, telling everyone he was going to dump the parking-lot attendant for being disrespectful to him. The parking-lot attendants shift had finished at midnight and so he did what the parking lot procedure demanded he do. He left the keys to any unclaimed cars at the central parking lot; it was open twenty-four hours a day. McDonald thought the attendant should have waited around till three in the morning for Mr. to show up. He bumped his gums all night long, telling everyone or anyone who would listen that he was going to kill the parking-lot attendant. No one took him seriously. Dexter's friends all thought he was just another punk mouthing off. McDonald left the nightclub around midnight, murdered the parking-lot attendant, and made off with a hundred and twenty-five dollars from the night's receipts. The next day the police went through the club asking questions. No one said anything. The police had no clues and no leads, so it went into the books as an unsolved murder. A week or two later, when McDonald surfaces on the night club scene, he imagines himself to be a real tough guy. He has proven to one and all that he's a killer! He lets it be known that he wants to make some real money, he wants to move up to the major leagues. He's ready for the big time.

Eric, an old bank and Brinks bandit was putting together a truck hijacking. He hired a driver to handle the big eighteen-wheeler. He offered McDonald the job of sitting on the driver for a half-hour after the truck was hijacked. With the driver incapacitated, they would wheel the truck into a warehouse many miles away from the scene of the hijacking and empty its contents. McDonald was paid ten grand to sit on the driver for forty minutes. The deal went down like a hot knife through butter, no problems. Eric sold the Michelin tires for eighty grand. He paid McDonald, the driver and his expenses for the warehouse. The balance of the money was his. At first McDonald was thrilled. He had never seen so much money at one time in his life. In no time at all, he had blown his wad. He found out how much money Eric had made on the sale of the tires and began to brood about it. He felt he deserved more. He decided to pay Eric a visit at his home. Eric welcomed him into his home, not knowing there was a problem between the two. They went downstairs to his basement bar and Eric began to pour him a drink. McDonald pulled out a piece and dumped him without ever saying a word as to why he was shooting him. When Eric's wife heard the popping sound of the gun going off she ran downstairs to see what the problem was. McDonald murdered her, too.

Now the punk had a real big head. He laid low for a week or two, then he surfaced. Some people had liked Eric, some were jealous of his success and others didn't like his boisterous ways. Eric was a crazy Irishman with a big heart and a big mouth, especially when he got into the booze — it was the reason he ticked some people off. But he did have some good friends who accepted him with all his defects of character. McDonald knew that some of Eric's friends would be looking to even the score, so he was very careful when he surfaced. Friends of Eric were looking for McDonald, but things became complicated when he started chumming around with Jake the Snake. That friendship bought him a pass for the time being. Because of his friendship with Jackie, people decided to sit back and wait to see if the friendship endured. No one wanted to mess with a popular and deadly guy like Jackie over a punk like McDonald.

Patience and time would provide a better opportunity to deal with the new psycho punk on the block. McDonald took Jake's friendship and the sullenness of Eric's friends as a sign of respect. Before his killing spree, he was nothing more than a punter doing small-time stuff; now he was a killer with a big ego. It was easy to label him a psychopath and most people did. He didn't have the smarts to make money on his own, so he went around the nightclubs borrowing money from people. A hundred bucks here, two hundred there, penny-ante stuff. He never had any intention of repaying the loans, nor did he ever pay back a dime. People didn't want to have a run-in with a psychopath for a couple of hundred dollars, so they'd avoid him and the places he frequented. In essence, the punk thought he could put everybody on the arm because he was such a bad ass. When the word got around about McDonald's new-found livelihood, he began to run out of people he could put the bite on for money. The only people left in the clubs he visited were heavies, people he couldn't mooch off of, people who wouldn't let him mooch off of them.

Dexter heard that Jake was in between scores and broke. Jackie had helped save Dexter's life once, and Dexter had never forgotten it. Dexter went down to the Dream Lounge Bar, a little joint on Mountain Street, to find his friend Jackie. He wanted to buy him a drink and give him some money to tide him over until his next score. He also intended to invite him to his home for a couple of weeks so Jackie could straighten himself out. Dex walked into the Lounge, and took a moment to allow his eyesight to adjust to the subdued glow of the golden lights that bathed the interior of the little drinking den. Jackie was sitting at the bar with another guy. He saw Dexter as he entered. Dexter walked over to a table at the rear of the club; Jackie left his companion at the bar and joined Dexter. They ordered drinks and made small talk. A short time later, the fellow at the bar came over to their table. Jackie introduced him to Dexter; McDonald pulled up a chair and sat down with them. Dexter wasn't a big fan of the night-club scene. For him it was a point of contact, and occasionally if the company warranted it, he would imbibe in drinks and stay longer. However, on this occasion he didn't like or want the company of McDonald. McDonald didn't know it, but Eric had been a friend of Dexter's. Jackie and Dexter finished their drinks (Dexter hadn't ordered a drink for McDonald) and pushed their chairs back from the table, Dexter prepared to depart. Jackie headed back to his seat at the bar. At this point, McDonald approached Dexter and asked to borrow a hundred dollars. Dexter told him he didn't loan money.

Dexter sensed McDonald was not happy about being snubbed. He gave Dexter a half-assed hard stare as he returned to his seat at the bar beside Jackie. Dexter paid the waitress for his drinks. On his way out he stopped at the bar and gave his friend Jackie a G-note. He also invited him to stay at his house for awhile. McDonald was staring straight ahead into the mirror behind the bar. He saw Dexter give Jackie the wad of hundred dollar bills. Jackie took the G-note and stuffed it into his shirt pocket. McDonald glared over at Dexter. His stare was met with an equally icy stare. No words were spoken between the two — no words were necessary! Dexter was letting the punk know in his own way that he had no respect for him. McDonald understood the message; he just couldn't figure out who the messenger was.

The following day Jackie showed up on Dexter's doorstep and stayed with him for two weeks. Dexter's wife's home cooking put some meat on his bones and brought some long overdue routine to his life. In a week or so, Jackie changed from a haggard-looking alcoholic to a healthy, robust man of forty. Near the end of his two-week stay, McDonald phoned Dexter's house wanting to speak to Jake. He was really pissed off. His father had died; no one had sent flowers or paid their respects. Jackie guessed there were no flowers at the funeral and McDonald couldn't afford to buy any. Jackie discussed McDonald's attitude with Dexter; it seemed to Dexter that Jake's friendship with McDonald had come to an end. The punk was getting uppity, and Jackie was starting to boil over at McDonald's disrespectful attitude toward him. Not satisfied with insulting Jake the Snake, he walked into the Bishop's club wearing black gloves and sunglasses and gave the Bishop and friends a hard-ass stare. The Bishop was a good man; he always minded his own business, did his own thing and didn't take shit from anybody.

McDonald either had a death wish or thought he could terrify everyone with his dastardly reputation. He was now walking around threatening everyone. It was only a matter of time before either he'd hurt someone, or someone would hurt him. One night he walked into the Cat's Den, another of the local haunts on Guy Street in downtown Montreal. The place was empty except for the barmaid and the bartender. McDonald sat down and ordered himself a drink, a drink he had no intention of paying for. Shortly thereafter two guys with hoods, brandishing M-1 Enforcers came charging through the door. McDonald was armed to the teeth and itching to kill someone. When he saw the two hooded gunmen, he knew it was Dad calling! He got his wish for death, and another psychopath picked up his shovel and reported to work.

The hit on McDonald was considered justifiable. Maybe not by society's standards; however, another psychopath punk killer was taken off the streets permanently, before he could kill anyone else. And that was all the justification needed for the street. Jake reaffirmed his status as a killer.

Jackie was involved in several other hits and, looking back, some were definitely questionable. At the time, nobody scrutinized Jake's hits either because no one wanted to see him as a psycho, or because ignorance is bliss. Eventually, he screwed up and went to the can on an extortion beef.

By the time Jake was released from prison, the hold-up game was (for all intents and purposes) passé. Dex stopped by the Zoo to greet his old friend Jackie. He slipped a couple of grand into his pocket as a home-coming gift. Jake joined Dexter and Mother in some small talk over drinks. They brought Jake up to speed as to how things had changed, who the players were and who the punters were. Some former players in the hold-up game were now nothing more than punters in the Drug Game. Some had tried to make the transition and couldn't; others, like Duney and Dexter, had. The two friends enlightened Jackie as much as one could expect on his first night out of the joint. They felt he would fit in, in time. They basically wanted him to understand that things were dramatically different in the Drug Game. If he wanted to survive, he would have to take his time and stick with known friends and associates. Unlike the hold-up game, the Drug Game is a bullshit head game, and the closer you get to the street the more bullshit you are going to have to deal with. They spent the evening knocking back a few drinks and reminiscing about old times.

Mother was getting bigger by the day in the drug business. He had reached the stature where he required a high profile back-up enforcer. Duney had begun by buying and selling small quantities of hash and grass, and then he ventured into cocaine, heroin and designer drugs. The deals got bigger and so did the amount of money involved in each transaction. Mother always had numerous transactions going on simultaneously. He gave Jake a room at the motel, carte blanche to order whatever food and drinks he wanted. Those were the perks that came along with a hefty salary of at least a hundred grand a year. Jackie didn't have to do a thing — just to have him around and have him known as Duney's enforcer made Mother's life easier. This way, Mother could prevent problems before they started. Just knowing Jake was on Mother's payroll made everybody ante up and pay their tab. For a year or so, the arrangement worked out perfectly for Duney and Jackie.

One afternoon, a big guy walks into the bar, sits down and orders a drink. Someone recognizes him as the guy who raped and murdered a little girl. He had been charged with the crime but he beat the charges on a technicality. Now this rape artist figures he's a tough guy. He's heard about the Zoo and wants to make some contacts; he wants to become a player in the Drug

Game. When Jake discovers who the guy is, he calls the creep over to his table and starts pouring drinks into him. Several hours later, Jake the Snake invites the rape artist back to his room for a little coke. Once they're in the room, Jackie pulls out a knife and stabs the guy to death. He puts the corpse in the bathtub and cuts it up into pieces. Then he puts the body parts in green garbage bags. He takes the guy out of the motel piece by piece with the plastic garbage bags slung over his shoulder. It takes him several trips on his motorcycle to get all the body parts out of the motel and to the graveyard.

The next day, the cops find the corpse. It had been reassembled in a sitting position and placed leaning up against a tombstone. The Man goes flying into the motel as soon as they discover the body. They want to know who saw the guy and who he left with. They have the rapist going into the Motel on videotape, but they don't have him leaving! The police search the Motel from top to bottom; they don't find any incriminating evidence. Strange as it may sound, no one in the Zoo ever recalled seeing the guy enter the place. Now some might say the hit was justified, but to Mother it indicated that Jake was acting weird. Not that Mother had any love for the rapist, or that he cared about the guy getting dumped. It was just that it wasn't Jackie's job to be an avenging angel and, in so doing, to bring down all kinds of heat on the Zoo. It was already under twenty-four-hour-a-day surveillance. How much steam do you need? It was at this point that Mother started thinking he might have a coconut on his hands.

Things got progressively worse. Jake made a few more hits that were questionable. Mother talked to Dexter about it; his concerns were mounting. He didn't want Jake coming around his house any more. It was a delicate situation that had to be handled deftly and subtly.

Jake starts hanging around with a guy called the Hulk. He was one of those guys who come out of prison looking like Arnold Schwarzenegger. No one was aware of it at the time, but Jackie was teaching this guy to be a killer like himself.

Late one night, Dexter pulls up to Nittolo's Restaurant Bar and Motel. As he's getting out of his car, Jake the Snake pulls up beside him in his car.

Jake rolls down his window and, in a friendly voice, yells at Dexter to get in. Dex tells him to come inside, he'll buy him a drink. Jake insists he wants to talk to Dexter privately. Dexter, thinking nothing of it, accommodates Jackie and gets into the front seat of his car. Jackie and Dexter had been friends from a way back when; there had never been a bad word between them, except for their initial meeting.

Dex noticed that Jackie was acting a little strange. He got into the front seat of the car. Turning sideways, he faced Jackie, resting his elbow on the dashboard of the car. Dex asked Jackie what it was that he wanted to talk to him about. Jake went off with a story about Dexter saying so-and-so was a rat. Dexter had never heard of the name mentioned by Jackie, and he didn't know anything about it. Dexter looks Jackie straight in the face, and senses something is amiss with Jackie's story, but he can't figure out what it is. Dexter starts to get bad vibes. The hair on the back of his neck starts rising, and he has that strange tingling feel in his neck and arms. Casually, Dexter reaches over and pulls on the door handle and starts to open the car door. At that point, the big guy known as the Hulk, pops up from the back seat of the car. Dex looks over at him, still trying to get a grip on what in the hell is going on. Jake asks the Hulk if Dexter is the one who has been bad-mouthing him. The Hulk looks at Dexter and shakes his head, no.

Dexter didn't understand what was going on; however; he knew that whatever it was, it was all bullshit. The bad vibes increased in intensity in the silence. Dexter pushed the car door wide open and stepped out. Jackie broke the dull silence by smiling at Dexter and telling him to save a place for them at the bar. When Dexter reached the bar door he looked back at Jake the Snake and the Hulk, who were now in deep conversation. Dexter goes into the bar and sits at a table, where he is later joined by Jackie and the Hulk. Neither of them mentions anything more to Dexter about who is calling the Hulk a rat. Dexter wrote their strange behavior off as being one of those things in life that has no real rhyme or reason. It was only later on, when Dexter discovered that Jackie was training the Hulk to be his protégé and that Jackie was a certified nut cake, he realized how close he had come to being one of Jake's statistics!

A week later, Dexter met Jackie in the Zoo. He asked him where the Hulk was. Jake the Snake points down to the floor. At first, Dex thought he meant the Hulk was downstairs in the Disco. Jake laughs, shakes his head, points to the floor again and stamps his foot down. Dex got the drift. Jake had murdered him!

Dexter was reminded of Jake's strange antics of the week before. It was at this point that he started to suspect that Jake the Snake was a psycho. Jackie left the Zoo, and Dexter joined Mother at his table for a drink. Mother wasn't happy. He confided in his friend that he was having second thoughts about Jackie. Jake had made several hits lately that were marginal at best. He was developing an aggressive attitude, even toward Mother. Mother ventured that maybe he was taking too much coke and booze. Jake wasn't his old self, and Mother wondered if it was something temporary or if Jackie was showing his real colours. Dex listened intently, but could not offer Mother any insight into the strange behavior of their mutual friend.

Several weeks later, Dexter stopped by the Zoo to see Duney. On his way in, he bumped into Jackie, who was walking out of the club. Jake takes Dexter by the arm and escorts him outside. Jackie seemed troubled. He wanted to confide in Dexter. Once outside in the parking lot, he began to ramble on about a hit he had done recently. Dexter would rather not know. He tries to convey this to Jake but Jackie insists that he must talk it over with a trusted friend. Dexter listens as Jackie recounts the gruesome tale.

A small-time drug dealer owed Mother fifteen hundred dollars. The punter was stroking Mother for payment. Jackie felt Mother was being too soft on the guy, so he decided on his own to pay the dealer a visit. He went to the punter's apartment and let himself in. Jake sat in the darkened living room waiting for the guy to come home. Some time after midnight, the dealer returned home. Jake said that he had tried to talk to the guy about the money he owed Mother, but that the guy got mouthy; so he whacked him. At this point Dex realized Jackie was trying to justify the hit. Dexter listened uneasily to the rest of the story. The dealer lived with his twelve-year-old daughter. She knew Jake well; he had been to their house many times. She always called him Uncle Jackie. The little girl was sleeping in the bedroom next to the living room. She heard the muffled sound of the gun going off. Jackie had a silencer on his gun, but silencers don't completely muffle the sound of a gun going off. She got out of bed and went into the living room to see what the noise was. Jake the Snake was calmly sitting in a living room chair across from the dead drug dealer, who was slouched over on the sofa. She asked Jackie what was wrong with her father. He told her he was sleeping. As she got closer to her father, she realized he was dead. She looked at Jake and screamed, "You've killed my father, you've killed my father."

Then she turned and ran toward the kitchen. She was trying to get out of the apartment by the back door. Jake chased after her, catching up with her just as she reached the kitchen door. She turned, looked up into his face and pleaded for her life.

"Uncle Jackie, Uncle Jackie, please don't hurt me!"

Jake looked into her face, raised his gun and murdered her at point-blank range.

After telling his story, he began demanding Dexter's indulgence. He had no choice, he said. He had to do it, otherwise the little girl would have told the cops on him. It was the punter's fault for not paying his tab with Mother. He was looking to Dexter for some kind of reassurance that he had done the right thing. Dex was speechless. Jake saw his reaction. He didn't like it. He started ranting and raving about how he had cleaned up the city of a lot of stool pigeons for guys like him and Duney. Dumbfounded, Dex just couldn't find any words to say. He was stunned to hear what he had heard. He now knew for sure that Jake the Snake was a sick-o. Dexter lost his zest for going into the club that night. Over and over the story rolled around in his mind. He never thought that someone he considered a friend would turn out to be such a sick son of a bitch!

Jake's story didn't add up. First of all, nobody would mouth off to a guy holding a piece with a silencer on it, especially a known enforcer like Jake. Add to that the fact that the guy is waiting for you, in your own home, with the lights off, just sitting there in the dark! Then there was the part about Jake sitting in the living room chair, calmly looking at the guy after he had murdered him. The correct part to the story was that Jake the Snake had murdered two people. The details didn't make any sense. His concocted story was about as coherent as he could make it. It was a poor cover-up attempt to mask his penchant for murder. From that day forward, Dexter never spoke another word to Jackie.

The following week, Dexter stopped by the Zoo to see Mother. Jackie was not around, and Duney sat alone at his table deep in thought. Dex joined his friend. The silence between them was heavy as each waited for the other to say something. The void between them was broken when Mother spoke up.

"You heard?"

"Yeah," Dex replied, "He's a sick puppy. What are you going to do? Whatever you do, be careful. You can't afford to make a slip with him!"

Mother nodded his head in agreement. He went on to say that recently Jake the Snake had become real nasty. He had indirectly threatened Duney when he visited him at his home. What pissed Mother off even more was that Jake had been carrying a piece on him at the time. It's an unwritten rule that you never enter a friend's house with a gun on you unless there is a very good reason, and your friend expects that you will be carrying a piece. To do so for no reason is an insult and an invitation for trouble. Dex knew where this was all leading, and so did Mother.

The issue was put on hold when Jake the Snake got himself into trouble with the law. He had to go on the lam for a while. Mother sent him down to New Brunswick to cool his heels. Duney had arranged for a fellow in New Brunswick to rent a farm so that Jake had a place to stay and lie low till the heat blew over. It also gave Duney time to prepare for the unpleasant task of doing what he had to do. Jake moved onto the farm with his girlfriend, his dog and the guy who rented the farm with his wife.

If you have a beloved pet dog and it goes mad, you put it out of its misery before it hurts anyone. In the underworld, when someone goes bad you put them out of their misery before they hurt you or someone else. A psycho is the most dangerous animal on this earth. Dark clouds of trouble follow them and anyone associated with them. Mother knew all of this, and he knew what he had to do. But he was a kind-hearted man, and this was an old and trusted friend. He just wanted a little time to figure out a way to deal with his problem, a little time to ease his conscience.

Jake could have stayed down on the farm quietly. Unfortunately, however, he decided to train the guy who was fronting for him to be his protégé. They went on a killing spree in New Brunswick. Killing, just for the sake of killing. Not criminal related homicides, just murder for the pure pleasure of murder. No one in Montreal was aware of Jake's activities in New Brunswick. Everyone thought he was sitting quietly down on the farm, watching the grass grow.

The news hit Montreal that Jackie was dead. His protégé turned on him one night. He killed Jake the Snake, his girlfriend and Jake's German shepherd guard dog. Then when the landlord stopped by with his son to collect the rent, the protégé flipped out, killed the landlord and wounded his son. The son made it out of the house and collapsed on the front lawn. A passer-by saw the action and called the police, who arrested the guy and his wife. The wife told the whole, horrid story about the killing games of her husband and Jake the Snake. When Jake's protégé was confronted, he confessed to it all. After questioning, he returned to his cell, where he hanged himself. When the police searched the farm, they dug up the hastily dug gravesites that marked the diabolical work of the two death merchants.

How many people did Jackie murder in his career? Nobody knows for sure, but conservative estimates put it at over fifty. None to soon, another psychopath picks up his shovel and reports to work.

Mother decided not to hire any more high-profile back-up muscle. He assumed people were well aware of his capabilities to defend himself and his business enterprise. He could reach out and hire guns if he needed them; he didn't feel the need to have a hired gun in his presence all the time. The stool pigeons took it as a sign of weakness on Duney's part and moved in on and around him. The vacuum created by Jackie's departure emboldened the informants and the shyster's to take a run at Mother.

RULE NUMBER SEVEN
LIVING IN A CRISIS

This rule, like all the other rules, was one that Dexter had to learn. From the foregoing, it is easy to see how Dexter and his friends involved in the Drug Game and the world of crime go from one crisis to the next. It is therefore imperative to know oneself. The adage, "To thine own self be true," was never more appropriate or necessary than for survival in the Drug Game. Everyone — from the punters (who consider themselves to be only marginally involved), to the drug dealers and upper echelon players — must learn to avoid the trap of living in a crisis. It means the difference between living, dying or spending the rest of your life in a prison.

In the Drug Game or the world of crime in general, you're always playing the percentages. The more you go to the well, the more apt you are to make a mistake. We all make mistakes. Crisis situations will invariably happen, but the odds of one walking away from them unscathed decrease with each incident. Dexter realized that he couldn't afford to be constantly adding to, or creating, crisis situations in his life. To survive successfully, he had to become aware of his penchant for creating problems when none existed. Very rarely do deals go down without a hitch. Sometimes they do; in many instances, everything goes a hundred per cent in your favour. It was on these occasions that Dexter learned to bank some money and time for those days when nothing went his way.

Dexter knew how things could be turned upside down in his life. As quick as a heart beat, you go from cloud nine to hell. A stool pigeon drops a dime in the phone on you. You are seen in the wrong place, at the wrong time, with the wrong person. Any number of things can set a crisis situation in motion. Therefore, when a problem does arise, one doesn't want to deal with two or three other crises at the same time. Nobody is that smart. People in the Drug Game try to do it all the time; but inevitably a situation arises that is so burdensome it crushes them. Living in a blind state of crisis is like dousing yourself with gasoline then playing with a blowtorch — you will get burned!

Dexter had to learn not to get involved in other people's crises. And that's not easy to do in the Drug Game. Most people who play the Drug Game are accidents looking for a place to happen. He learned that rushing in to rescue his friends from their crises only dragged him in; often he would end up bearing the brunt of the blame, because the other person's crisis wasn't resolved to their satisfaction. Someone once said to him, "Remember, your friends survived long before you came on the scene, and they will survive long after you're gone. Take care of your own troubles, and let others take care of theirs — unless it has something to do with you directly."

If you do not take the time to know yourself, to analyze yourself, you will go from one crisis to the next. Eventually, you will create a situation whereby death or prison will halt the cycle. If you think you're different or special, life will slap you upside the head and get your attention.

Throw your money up against the wall and when you need it, it won't be there. Don't expect your friends to loan you any money. Chances are they will be as broke as you. If they have any, why should they loan money they risked their lives to make to a guy who just pissed his away? If you're in the Drug Game for any other reason than to make money, you're an idiot! If you're an idiot, you probably don't have any friends anyway. Who wants an idiot for a friend?

Dexter recognized he was living his life from one crisis to the next. Sometimes it was excessive gambling, sometimes it was abusing alcohol or drugs and sometimes it was just stupid behaviour. It was a slow process, so slow that even today he has to be vigilant so as not fall back to his old ways. He learned not to look at others or blame others for his troubles. It wasn't his girlfriends' fault, his wife's fault or his friends' fault. Whatever happened, he took responsibility for his situation. Dexter swallowed his pride and went to see a shrink. The psychiatrist was able to put him on the long journey of self-discovery. Was the emotional pain worth it? A thousand times his answer is "yes!"

CHAPTER NINE
LISTEN TO YOUR VIBES

Time flew by for Dexter. Eight months had passed since he last talked to Ajmal. Finally, his man arrived from Pakistan with the papers for the shipment. It had left Karachi the previous week. When Dexter opened the papers in the presence of Ajmal's courier, his reaction was immediate and hostile. He exploded with a volley of curses when he saw that the shipment wasn't for cashew nuts. Ajmal had decided that the safest cover for the shipment was Mercedes-Benz parts rather than cashew nuts. Dexter had two problems with that. First of all, why would a company that imports cashew nuts be importing Mercedes-Benz parts, and why would anyone import Mercedes-Benz parts from Pakistan? Unbelievable, but true!

There was no way he could clear a shipment so blatantly wrong. He knew that customs would be all over the shipment like kids on a snowman. He sent Ajmal's courier back with a message. The message was in the form of a query. Did stupidity come natural to Pakistanis, or did they have to work at it. His message was punctuated with more curses!

Dexter started to recognize a pattern. The constant screw-ups by Ajmal, along with the poor quality of the merchandise, had to be intentional. He suspected that the Putz was purposely trying to sabotage his relationship with Ajmal. Dexter had a choice: walk away from the deal and give Ajmal the excuse he was looking for to do business with someone else; or try to salvage the deal. If he could salvage the shipment, he might be able to force the Putz's hand and get Ajmal back on track.

He went to see the Doc. The old janitor had been having a hard time of it of late. His wife was ill. She was forced to quit her job. His girls had been doing better in college since he was able to support them without their having to work and attend college at the same time. However, because of the lengthy delays, the Doc hadn't been making money other than his minimum wage job.

Dexter had changed their meeting place from the Bug to a little bar run by a gal named Sylvie. Sylvie had been introduced to Dexter by another woman known as Auntie. Auntie was an old friend from the hold-up years. She was one of the best wheel men in the city in her day. She was a heavy-set woman. She would wear shoulder pads, a baseball cap and sunglasses when driving a getaway car for the boys. She was solid and had as much balls as any bandit you could ever meet. One thing about Auntie, even if the Cavalry arrived while the boys were in the jug, she'd be waiting outside when they exited. She worked with several groups of hold-up people. The boys paid her less than they would have paid a guy — not fair or equal-opportunity employers those bandits — but that's the way it was. Besides, Auntie liked the action. She never let anyone down, and she was never pinched on or off a score. The cops suspected her; they had pulled her in many times. They threatened her with heavy jail time, losing custody of her children and whatever else they could think of. She never gave them the time of day. She was a solid, crazy old broad who lived life on the edge, travelled around the world; and when she was in her fifties she had a twenty-two year old boyfriend — a "boy toy."

She accepted the terms, because it was still more money than she would have made boosting. She had a checkered career in boosting. Auntie had met a guy who worked at a slaughterhouse and meat-packing plant. One day she was driving around with her partner in crime, a paraplegic named Cory. He drove a big Cadillac convertible that was fixed up with all the controls for the brakes and the gas peddle on the steering column. Their arrangement was that he drove Auntie around and she did the boosting. Things hadn't been going well for the dynamic duo. Between the two of them, they had twenty dollars and a tank of gas. They decided to go out of the city and hit some small towns, pick up what they could. They were approaching a small town in a farming community when Auntie spotted a cow. It had gotten through a farmer's fence and was standing by the side of the road. She yelled at her partner to stop. He didn't know why she wanted to stop, but he did it anyway. Auntie looked around, didn't see any traffic coming either way. She got out of the car, went over to the cow and pulled it by the ear. Shoving and pushing it, she eventually got the cow into the back seat of the Cadillac. They turned the car around and headed back down the road to the meat-packing plant; Auntie, Cory, and the cow in the back seat of the Caddy. When they pulled up to the meat-packing plant, her connection there almost had a heart attack. He took the cow and paid them five hundred dollars. How does Dexter know this to be true? Dexter was the guy who introduced the paraplegic to Auntie. When Cory dropped Auntie off at the end of the day, he went straight over to Dexter's house. He wanted to know what kind of nut he had introduced him to. Dexter's answer was, "Well, you wanted to work didn't you?"

Cory responded, "You didn't tell me I was going into "rustling!"

They both broke out in laughter. Cory drove off shaking his head.

When the hold-up game faded, Auntie went into the Drug Game. In her prime, she could move fifty keys a week, no sweat. She never touched cocaine personally nor did she ever sell it. She was strictly hash and grass. Auntie was good friends with Sylvie.

Sylvie had married a fellow who was in the *midnight auto supply* business. He died of cancer at a young age, and Sylvie started to work in a bar as a barmaid. Eventually, she ended up managing the bar. She was a pretty woman, petite and very well proportioned, with long black hair and big brown eyes. For such a nice looking woman, she had one glaring defect. Her two front teeth were crossed and slightly bucked. When she didn't smile, she was quite a looker. When she did smile, she would cover her mouth so as not to expose her teeth.

She was a very intelligent, quiet and shy person. She worked long hours in the bar that was the proverbial dump. It had a cement terrazzo floor, the usual wooden tables and chairs, one TV over the bar and a side room with two small pool tables. People on welfare would go there and cash their paychecks. When they had spent it all, the owner would give them a line of credit until the next welfare check. The Bug was high-class compared to the bar where Sylvie worked.

Dexter started meeting the Doc there instead of the Bug, because the Bug was under surveillance by the Man. He didn't want to bring any heat onto the Doc. The Doc was his ace up his sleeve. If Dex wanted to meet with the Doc, he would get word to him. The Doc knew the meeting place was at Sylvie's bar. When Dex walked in, Sylvie would bring him a beer; if there weren't any police in the place, she would bring him an O'Keefe. If the Man were there or if the Man walked in after Dexter arrived, she would bring him a Molson. The Doc was also familiar with the same signals. Sylvie knew all her customers by name. She cashed their welfare checks and listened to their griping, week-in and week-out. If a stranger walked in she knew it wasn't a tourist. In this manner Dexter could meet the Doc comfortably and know that neither he nor the Doc was under surveillance. Doc was only valuable as long as the Man didn't suspect him. Dexter wanted to keep his ace securely up his sleeve.

Dex set up a meet with the Doc. Sylvie gave them the all-clear signal. Dexter explained his problem to the Doc and added the sad news that he would have to wait another three months, maybe longer, for a bonus check. The Doc sat there listening attentively. After Dex finished breaking the news to him, they made small talk. The Doc wasn't really into the conversation. Dex could sense his mind was somewhere else. Dexter was about to leave when the Doc made a suggestion.

He told Dexter that he might be able to get hold of the shipping papers before customs had a chance to see them. If he could, he would hide the shipment under some other cargo and notify Dexter. If Dex were willing to pick up the shipment himself, the Doc would kick it out the door. He couldn't make any promises, but he'd give it a try. The one thing he stipulated was that Dexter had to pick it up himself. He didn't want to meet anybody. His experience with Hank and his friends was etched in his mind. He trusted Dexter and no one else.

Dex sat back in his chair mulling the proposition over. He had done his time in the trenches. He had opened, delivered and collected the money from many hash deals himself. He had too much to lose. Once he had made it over the hump, he never touched the hash or grass again. But the Doc's proposition was sound; he trusted him. Nonetheless, he would be taking a big chance. He paid people to do that work for him now. He never asked anybody to do anything he hadn't already done or could do. It was a matter of moving up the ladder. You make less by paying people to do the work for you; but at his stage in life, he didn't have to take any unnecessary chances. People who did the heavy lifting were grateful for the opportunity to work and make money, and Dexter was happy to step back. Without Dexter to organize the deals, they wouldn't be making a dime. The Doc was a case in point. However, the Doc was adamant. No one but Dexter to pick up the shipment. All of which was contingent upon the Doc being able to grab the shipping papers before customs and upon the shipment not arriving at the warehouse hot. It was a big move for Dexter at this stage and time in his life. He thought about Ajmal and the Putz. His temperature started to rise. He believed Ajmal and the Putz had their own secret agenda. If he could jam them, not give them any excuse to take their business elsewhere, he would eventually call their hand and find out exactly what they were up to.

Dex leaned forward in his chair. Looking the Doc in the eyes he said, "You know what you're asking me to do? I have people who will pick up the shipment gladly. None of my people have ever given you any problems. Why now, why change the game plan now?"

The Doc looked back at Dexter and said, "I've never done anything like this before. If you'll do it, I'll do it. If you won't, I won't."

Dexter's mind was spinning. He knew the rules of the game. The Doc was simply asking him to "back up his action." In doing so, he would be giving the Doc confidence in himself. Dex agreed.

The Doc was not a man of higher learning, but he wasn't stupid either. He laid out the price for his labour. Dex smiled and agreed. People in the Drug Game often bitch and moan about how little money they are making in comparison to someone else. The bottom line is you get paid what you ask for and not for what you're worth. This is also true in the legit world. If the Doc had asked for his usual fee, Dexter would have paid him that amount. He didn't, he asked for a helluva lot more! He was worth it! He would be paid what he asked for. Don't ask, don't complain.

They made their plans that afternoon. When the shipment arrived, the Doc would go for the papers. If he got them and if the deal wasn't hot, he would stop by and see Sylvie the same day. She would get hold of Dexter. The following day, Dexter was to be at the warehouse door at 10:45 a.m. sharp. That was the time the coffee truck pulled up. Everybody, including the customs officers, would be busy buying a snack. The Doc would have the warehouse door open. Dex was to back the truck up to the loading platform. The Doc would dump the shipment into the back of the truck and Dexter would get his ass out of there!

Dexter had two warehouses, both of which were under surveillance. He needed a place to open the shipment, to weigh up the hash and distribute it. He spoke to Sylvie. They had become good and trusted friends. Sylvie was a separatist; however, Dexter was a bloke she liked. They agreed to never discuss politics. Other than politics, they discussed everything. Sylvie was getting tired of her job as a barmaid and manager. She walked around in high heels, fish-net stockings and a bathing suit, all day long, listening to wolf whistles from guys who had a hard time paying for their beer. In short, she was fed up. She wanted to do something with her life.

Because they were such good friends, Dexter felt comfortable telling her to get her teeth fixed. He would have loaned her the money, had she asked. She was a very proud person. She never asked. Dex knew if she wanted to have another career dealing with the public she would have to do something about her teeth.

He made her a proposition. If the deal went down, he would use her house to open the shipment. She and Auntie would deliver the hash to his customers. Sylvie looked at Dexter, sizing him up. Was he just another guy trying to use her, or was he giving her a shot at the roses, a chance to get out of the bar business and move on. Sylvie was a country girl who had come to the big city. Before meeting her husband, she had run into a few losers who had used her. She was very wise in her ways. She was no longer a country bumpkin falling for a line some fast-talking guy was throwing her way. She told Dex she'd think about it.

The deal arrived. The Doc grabbed the papers like a gambler grabbing a deck of cards. He checked out the shipment. Everything looked cool. On his lunch hour he squirrelled over to Sylvie's. She contacted Dexter. Dexter went over to see Sylvie immediately. She passed the message on and agreed to work with Dexter and Auntie, opening and delivering the hash.

The next day, Dexter pulled up to the warehouse door in a big five-ton truck he had rented. The Doc was standing in the doorway giving Dexter the back-up signal. When the truck was at the loading dock, Dexter heard a thump. He gets out to see what's happening. The Doc was backing-up inside the warehouse on a fork lift truck. He waved Dexter to leave. Dexter jumped back into the truck and pulled away. His stomach muscles knotted tighter than laces on a pair of skates. His mouth had that dry Sahara Desert, sandpaper taste. He knew he had a minimum of ten years riding along with him in the back of the truck. He headed straight for Sylvie's. She and Auntie were waiting in front of the house. Dexter backed the truck up and they off-loaded the shipment into her garage. Dexter returned the rental truck, then went back to see the girls.

Ajmal had done it again! Two hundred keys of quality and one hundred keys of garbage. Dexter sold the hash, paid everyone off and headed back over to Pakistan.

Sitting in a chair in a hotel room, Ajmal started whining and crying when Dexter refused to pay him for the garbage. The Putz sat in a corner not saying a word. Dexter wanted to know why he changed the shipping product. He wanted to know why he couldn't send three hundred keys of quality hash. He wanted to know what in the hell was going on! Every time Dexter confronted Ajmal on an issue, his eyes rolled around in his head. He had no answer. He knew he was wrong, but rather than admit it, he "saves face" and says nothing. They agree to do another deal. Only this time Dexter is going to send over his man to approve the quality before it is sent. He also underlines the importance of shipping the goods as instructed. Ajmal agrees. Dexter returns to Canada.

Back in Canada, Dexter received an invitation to a wedding. An old Mafioso, whom Dexter has known for years, was throwing a big do for his daughter. Dexter wouldn't miss it for the world. He liked the old guy. Dexter often sold him some of his hash and grass. They had a respectful arrangement. You can deal with the mob if they respect you. If they don't, they'll put you on the arm quicker than Jack the bear having a crap in the woods. Dexter never had any problems with the old guy. The old Mafioso had to keep his boys employed, so the arrangement worked out well for everybody.

At the wedding, Dexter bumps into a guy known as the Duck. The Duck had made serious money as a vault man. He thought he was super-intelligent. After all, only smart people like him make big money. It wasn't that he was so smart; in fact, he was a goof. He had cultivated a bug man who could shut down almost any bank vault alarm system, including some of the most sophisticated ones. The bug man was the Duck's intro to some big bank vault jobs. It was the bug man who had the brains. Doofus went along for the ride. This being said, the Duck had a super ego, an ego as big as all outdoors. He visualized himself as some kind of big-shot bad-ass criminal genius!

Dexter didn't think too much of the Duck one way or another. The Duck had connections down on the wharf in Montreal, but he had no connections for hash on the other side. Had he approached Dexter with a business proposition (vis-à-vis teaming up with Dexter's connection in Pakistan and clearing the goods), Dexter would have considered the proposition. He never approached Dexter, and Dexter didn't approach him.

After the meal, the Duck goes up to Dexter and starts telling him that the Putz is a good friend of his. Dexter listens attentively. It is obvious to Dexter from the comments the Duck is making that the Putz has been in contact with him. When the Duck is finished bumping his gums, Dexter makes the picture very clear. Any connections the Putz has over in Pakistan are Dexter's. This can be verified by the Old Bandit, who is also attending the wedding party.

Dexter says to the Duck, "No one had better fuck around with my connections. I brought the Putz over there as a favour to the Old Bandit. The Putz was so broke he didn't have bus fare. I'd better never hear of the Putz or anyone else trying to back-door me."

The Duck answers, "Maybe some day you and I will go down to the corner store."

The Duck was making an indirect threat to Dexter. He meant that maybe some day they would get it on. The Duck had beaucoup money. He knew a lot of people — old hold-up people, mob people, and drug people — but he wasn't from the old school. He talked a heavy game but the only shooting he ever did was in a penny arcade. However, the asshole had such a big ego, he thought he could threaten Dexter, albeit indirectly. Perhaps he thought Dexter would run for the hills. Whatever he was thinking, his little brain was goaded on by his big ego.

Dexter looked at him and smiled. Then he responded, "If you come down to my corner store, you had better never let me catch you with your hand in my cookie jar."

With that the Duck smiled and walked away. Dexter could smell trouble brewing. He knew the Old Bandit and the Duck were very good friends. Strangely enough, they had hardly talked to one another at the wedding party. Dex stored all that had passed and carried on with the merriment.

He contacted Checkers. They had a meeting several weeks later. Dex asked Checkers if he would go over to Pakistan and approve some hash for him. He told Checkers he might have to stay there for two or three weeks. He wanted the Pakis to come up with the good shit. He explained the problems he was having. The Pakis agreed to let Dexter's man decide the quality of the hash and to put Dexter's label on it.

Dexter told Checkers, "Call it anything you want, any name that comes into your head. It doesn't matter what the name is, as long as the shit's real good. Just give it a name that hasn't been used before. I want something original. Call it Goldilocks, I don't care!"

All his expenses were to be paid, and in addition he would receive two thousand a week as long as he was away. A great deal for the big "C" and insurance for Dexter to receive quality hash. All Dexter wanted was quality. Checkers got off on the idea of giving the hash his own brand name. He agreed to leave in a couple of weeks. The real incentive for Checkers was that he could sell all or part of the deal when it came in. When Checkers wanted to work, the boy could move hash. He could sell three to four hundred keys of hash in a week. If Checkers said the shit was good, nobody stood around looking for a sample or thinking it over. The dealers would buy with both hands full if Checkers gave the shit his blessing. Checkers wouldn't have to put up a dime. Dexter would front it to him. Checkers would be buying the hash at wholesale price, which meant he could add anywhere from seven hundred to a thousand dollars' profit per key. It didn't take a mathematician to calculate the kind of end he was looking at. It was therefore in his best interest, as well as Dexter's, to get prime quality hash. Dexter knew Checkers was fully motivated. The Pakis were going to have their hands full, if they thought they could wear him down. He wasn't going to accept anything other than the best. After a few weeks Checkers left for Pakistan.

Arriving in Pakistan, he was taken up into the mountains to Peshawar. Peshawar is no man's land, a place where even the Pakistani army has no real control. Signs are posted warning tourists that the Pakistani government is not responsible for their security. Little twelve-year-old kids run around with Kalashnikov rifles, hand guns — you name it. This is tribal country that borders on Afghanistan. Thousands and thousands of refugees from Afghanistan are camped there. Not a place for tourists. It's a drug center for everything from heroin to illegal booze. Dexter didn't tell Checkers about the scenic drive up the mountain roads. Why deprive him of the pleasure of experiencing the panoramic vista encumbered by anothers' impressions? If he had told him about the suicide drive he was about to embark on, Dex figured he might not want to go.

Checkers was a lover, a doper, a boozer; he was not a thrill-seeker. He was not endowed with a whole lot of courage.

He met the Putz with Ajmal. Checkers wasn't impressed with either one. He told Dexter that the Putz kissed Ajmal's ass so hard the big *hodj* must have hickeys on his butt. They tried to play the delay game with Checkers. The Big "C" was in no rush. He was getting paid his two G's a week. He was motivated to get the good stuff, which would simplify his work and ensure a big payday for himself. He had booze, broads and hash. He was as close as he'll ever get to heaven. Pakistan is a stringent Muslim society, but that never stopped Checkers from finding a woman to charm.

One time in Morocco, he was riding a train accompanied by another friend from Canada. They were seated in a compartment with two Muslim women who were covered head to foot in black. Checkers starts a conversation with one of them, who spoke a little English. During the course of the conversation, he learns that they are both married and their husbands are going to pick them up at the train station. Checkers can't even see their faces. He has difficulty communicating with them. His friend keeps running interference, trying to prevent Checkers from making a pass at the ladies. Morocco too, is a very strict Muslim country. You can get your balls cut off for less. Checkers keeps on truck'n. The train arrives at the station two hours early. Checkers, being the gentleman he is, helps them off with their luggage. He also realizes that the ladies have to wait around for their husbands, who probably won't be there for another hour or so. Somehow, using pidgin English and sign language, Checkers persuades the ladies to go over to his apartment, where they can have a quickie. When the taxi driver saw two western guys get into his cab with two Muslim ladies, he freaked! He didn't want to take them. Checkers hopped in the front seat with the driver and threw him a wad of money. The cabby peeled out of the train station parking lot like a bandit wheeling away from a jug. Checkers tells the cabby to wait. The driver doesn't want to. Checkers offers to double the ante. The driver agrees. He says to Checkers, "Enjoy quickly Sir, this is very dangerous!"

The crazy Canucks take the ladies in for a quickie. A real quickie. When the one Checkers was with took off her veil, he asked her to put it back on. He didn't want to ruin the ambience. When the happy event came to a climax, the girls left with a very nervous taxi driver. No doubt about it, that man could get laid in the North Pole. One of a kind! Back in Canada, his friend would laugh about the experience, but he never went on another trip with the Big "C." Some might say he was a bad man; others would say, that's Checkers! Peshawar might have posed a challenge for Checkers but nothing insurmountable.

He sat stoned there for almost three weeks. He kept rejecting the various types of hash they presented to him. He knew quality hash as well as any Paki. Eventually they brought him some of the good stuff, not Mazar, but very good quality — hash that Checkers knew he wouldn't have trouble moving. He gave it a name, went over the shipping instructions one last time and made his way home.

Dexter kept himself busy waiting for Ajmal to ship. One day, when he stopped in to see Duney at the Zoo, Mother looked a little down. They began to make their usual small talk when Mother told Dex he had just lost two hundred pounds of hash. A guy by the name of the Mouse had paid him a visit. He was middling two hundred pounds of hash for an importer. Mother was interested, so the Mouse comes back with a sample. They agree on a price and Duney buys the two hundred seats. He gives the Mouse the cash and arrangements are made for the pick-up.

Duney uses a runner he has never used before. He was a young twenty-one-year old college student with no criminal record. The kid was just picking up some pin money. He didn't hang around with criminals or deal drugs. He was as smooth as a baby's bottom. The kid picked up the hash and took it to his apartment. He left it there and decided to go out to a local bar and have a drink. He had a few drinks, no hassles, then he returned home. The next morning the cops come crashing through his front door. The runner and the hash go down. Mother is out the money he paid for the hash, plus he has the legal expenses for the runner. The story the cops give for having a search warrant is that the kid went to a bar that was under surveillance. They shadowed him home and kicked the door in the following morning.

The search warrant is no good. The cops offer the kid a deal - possession of hashish. No amount and no drug trafficking charge. The choice is left up to the runner. He can fight it and eventually win or he takes the hit and puts it all behind him with time served in jail. Mother had him bailed out in a day or two. The runner takes the deal, cops a plea and put it all behind him.

Dexter looked at Mother. They have known one another for sometime. They both know the story didn't add up. They both know there is a rat somewhere. It can't be the runner. He went down. It could be the Mouse or the hash importer. Mother has decided to blow it off. He's seen enough violence. He prefers to accept the cops' version rather than to investigate the matter further. He's thinking of getting out of the hash game completely. He tells Dexter that hash is bringing him nothing but headaches. The candy game is quicker, more profitable and the players are more serious. Dexter knew his old friend was looking for a way to back out. If he did pinpoint the rat, he's gotta have him whacked.

Dex had his own suspicions. He didn't push it with his friend. The next day he stopped by to see the Mouse. The Mouse is jumping out of his skin. He's leaving Montreal. He wants to get out of Montreal as soon as he can. He doesn't give Dex any reason for the sudden change of heart. When Dex pushes him on it, he blows a lot of smoke up his ass. Dexter doesn't say anything about the two hundred seats of hash he knows the Mouse middled; instead, he invites him out for a couple of beers the following night.

The next evening Dexter is sitting in the Bug with the Mouse, knocking back a couple of pints and shooting the breeze. The Mouse seems more relaxed than the day before. He's still talking about moving to Toronto but not in the panicky mode of the day before. Dex notices a well-known coker walking into the Bug. He's looking around for someone. He spots the Mouse and goes charging over to him. He whispers something in his ear. The Mouse starts to change colour.

Dex over hears the Mouse say, "What's that got to do with me? I can't help him with his bail!"

The coker indicates his friend is counting on his help! The Mouse is very upset. He turns to Dexter and says, "That's why I want to leave this town. Everybody thinks their problems are your problems."

He looks at the coker and tells him he'll meet him at his house once he finishes his beer. Dex casually inquires what that was all about. The Mouse is a Class-A bullshitter, but he's a little shaken up and he's off his game. He starts to lay some bullshit on Dexter, but it's not coming out right. Dexter played the ass with him, "Mouse, you're not making any sense."

The Mouse then tells Dexter he middled two hundred seats of hash for the bozo. Then the guy wanted a key of coke to party with his friends. The Mouse arranged for him to get the coke. Now Bozo gets busted and he expects the Mouse to help him. The Mouse figures the hash man's problems are his own. He doesn't want to get involved, Dex thinks to himself. The Mouse didn't mind getting involved for the two hundred pounds of hash and the money he made off the transaction; he didn't mind getting involved for the key of coke he middled to the hash man and the money that came with that deal. It seemed he would only disturb himself as far as he could make money, no further. Maybe helping someone out who thought you were their friend was against his morals. The Mouse finished his beer and left. He never mentioned anything about the two hundred seats of hash that went down. Maybe he forgot. A moment after the Mouse left, Dexter was on his way out the door heading towards the Zoo.

He finds Duney sitting at his table alone.

"Mother," he says, "you know I don't stick my nose in the candy business, but this may be for your benefit. Did you sell the Mouse a key of coke?"

Mother nodded his head. The skin on his face became taut. His eyes glared back at Dexter.

"What's up?" he asks.

"The guy the Mouse had the coke delivered to went down with it!"

Dexter can sense that Mother's wheels are spinning. Mother hesitates, then asks, "What about the Mouse?"

"He's OK. I just left him twenty minutes ago."

"Is he gonna get charged?"

"No, I don't think so. He's talking about moving to Toronto, not about getting busted."

Mother doesn't ask any more questions. He doesn't have to! The Mouse is in the middle of two deals that go down on both ends and he doesn't get charged. You don't have to be a rocket scientist to figure that one out. Dexter did what he had to do and that was to pass the information on to his friend. It wasn't his problem to resolve. He didn't push the conversation with Duney. They started to make small talk. Dex could see his old friend wasn't enjoying the game as he used to. He wasn't doing much fencing anymore, and now he was backing away from grass and hash.

The blood that Jake the Snake had spilled had left its mark on Duney. To some degree, he blamed himself, even though Jake did what he did without Mother's consent and often without his knowledge. In spite of this, it still bothered Mother that Jake had murdered in his name.

Before getting arrested in the States for bank robbery, Duney had met a lovely gal. She was a country girl who had moved into the city. She was an honest, hard-working woman who, as fate would have it, met this *meshuggena* and fell in love with him. When he was busted in the States for hitting a jug, she told him it was all over. He wrote her from prison and asked her to wait for him. She made one stipulation. He had to promise her he would go straight. He did; during the seven years he spent in prison, he was as straight as an arrow. When released from prison he was deported back to Canada. She was waiting for him, and they got married. Asking a guy like Duney to go straight was like asking a prostitute for a refund. Mother loved his wife dearly. They started to raise a family, and he was very happy. But the lure of the street beckoned him. In no time at all, he was back in action.

He did a few hold-ups, which bankrolled him into the Drug Game. His wife had no choice but to make her life with him. She was in love with the lug. He always spoke adoringly of his wife and family. They never wanted for anything, except perhaps more of his time. He worked hard. He'd put in twelve-hour days as a matter of routine, five or six days a week. That's not unusual for successful people. If you have any illusions about making big money and not putting in the effort, buy a lottery ticket!

As Dex and Mother were talking, the desk clerk from the motel came into the bar and went over to Duney. He had a U.S. fifty-dollar bill sticking up in his white shirt pocket. He whispered something in Mother's ear. Duney gets up and goes over to a table where Apache and a few of the boys were sitting around having a couple of drinks. They leave their table and go with Duney into the motel. Five or ten minutes later they all come back into the bar. Mother joins Dexter. He explains to Dexter that a bounty hunter from the States had checked into the motel and now he's just checked out. He goes on to explain that the bounty hunter shoved a fifty-dollar bill in the desk clerk's pocket. He told the desk clerk he wanted some information on a Canadian who had jumped bail in the States. He showed the desk clerk a picture of the guy and asked if he had seen him around. The desk clerk told him he hadn't. The bounty hunter then tells the desk clerk to ask around, see if he can come up with something. He takes his key and goes to his room. The desk clerk went straight to Duney.

Duney rounded up a few of the boys and went knocking on the bounty hunter's door. When the bounty hunter opened the door, he was looking down the wrong end of the barrels of four thirty-eights, all pointed at his head. Mother tells the guy he has ten minutes to check out of the motel and one hour to be outside the city limits. If not, they would ship him back to the States in a box. The bounty hunter is a big guy who stands about six three, weighs approximately two hundred and fifty pounds. He has a build like a football player — thick neck, large arms, barrel chest and hands like shovels. He's probably a martial arts expert too. Still no match against four guys with pieces pointed at his head. His eyes widened like saucers when he saw what he was confronted with. He turned around went over to the bed where he had thrown his suit jacket. He picked it up and put it on. He went to the closet, grabbed his suit bag, his suitcase and his briefcase and walked slowly past the entourage standing in his doorway. They followed him out the door. As he passed the desk clerk, he gave him a dirty look. The desk clerk still has the fifty sticking out of his shirt pocket. The desk clerk looks back at him and says, "Well, you told me to ask around!"

The Zoo was losing its luster but it still had a little sparkle left. The bounty hunter never returned. We never did hear of another one coming up to Montreal looking for Canadians who jumped bail. Guess the word got around.

Mother chuckled. They both knew how close the bounty hunter had come to cashing in his chips. Apache was a little punk psychopath who had started hanging around the Zoo shortly before Jake the Snake's demise. He was president of a local chapter of the Hell's Angels Motorcycle Club. A little sawed-off runt who hid his lust for blood as a biker. I'll make this short, because I don't want to waste the paper on a psycho-punk like him. He was arrested for possession of an illegal weapon, a gun. He's looking at doing nine months in the can and rolls over. He spills his guts to fifty murders he has committed or has committed with others. He puts a bus load of people in the joint for murder.

Our government gave him seven years for all those murders. At his sentencing the judge says, "C'est un cadeau." His sentence was a gift.

He did two years and was released with a new identity somewhere in Canada. The police felt it was more important to clear up the paperwork on fifty murders than to keep a psychopathic killer off the streets. You can be sure he's out there murdering people to this day. Why? Because he was and is a psychopath; he likes to kill people. He enjoys it. Now, if society had wanted real justice and security for the honest hard-working citizenry, they would have put him back on the streets without any help or new identity papers. One thing for sure, he's not in Montreal!

As Dex looked around the Zoo, he could sense the change in the people and the atmosphere. There were people in the Zoo who would never have stepped foot in the place before. The word had gotten around. It was almost becoming a tourist attraction. It was filled with punters, wannabe's and rounders and, undoubtedly, stool pigeons. Not like before. Dex's friend was changing too. The game was getting to be a burden. It wasn't fun for him anymore. You could see it in Mother's walk and his attitude. Dex stopped going to the Zoo. He wasn't getting good vibes in the place.

Ajmal had sent Dexter a letter. It was more bullshit. More delays. Dexter waited, trying to get a handle on Ajmal's angle. He received a phone call at his office. It was the Newspaper Man. He wanted to stop by and see him. The Newspaper Man was a big fat guy who was a well-known rounder and punter.

Rounders are people who hang around criminals looking to get into the action, except they don't have the balls to jump into the pool. They hang around the fringes of the criminal element, picking up the crumbs of money they can from illegal deals, without getting too involved. They usually know just about everybody. As a rule they have legitimate fronts, and it is this connection that many criminals find useful. They bridge the gap between the criminal world and the legit world. They're wannabe's who think they are using the criminals; but it's the criminals who are profiting the most. Rounders pride themselves in not having gone to the can; but they know everybody in the can. They can also be stool pigeons or people who can't take the heat if they get pulled in and grilled by the Man. You had to judge each one on an individual basis. Dexter was extremely cautious with any rounder; he played it by the rules, never being overly trustful.

The Newspaper Man was one such individual. He knew Dexter well. He stopped by Dexter's office with a proposition. He'd met a guy who had just come out of the can. This guy has the movie rights to a famous book. He is in desperate need of a financial backer to help him bring the movie script to a movie studio. No one will take him seriously because of his criminal background. The Newspaper Man shows Dex the movie script as well as the guy's contract for the movie rights. Everything appears to be legit. Dex is constantly travelling in connection with his legitimate business as well as his monkey business. The Newspaper Man wants to know if he will be in town for awhile. When can he set up a meeting with the guy with the script. Dexter was busy at the time. The movie proposition wasn't a priority. He told the Newspaper Man he would call him some time the following week or the week after that. If the guy hadn't found any backer by then, Dex would meet with him. The Newspaper Man leaves, assuring Dex on the way out that this is a great deal, a deal he shouldn't miss.

The following week Dex calls the Newspaper Man early in the morning. He inquires if his friend has had any luck in finding a financial backer. The Newspaper Man says no, the guy is broke and he's desperate for any proposition. Dex tells the Newspaper Man to call the guy to see if he is available to meet him for lunch. Dexter goes on with his business, waiting for a confirmation of the luncheon meeting. The Newspaper Man calls back at around eleven o'clock and suggests they meet in a restaurant on the other side of town. Dexter tells him he doesn't have the time to leave his office and drive half way across the city. If the guy wants to meet with him, it will have to be in a restaurant near his office. If that's not convenient, he can stop by his office in the afternoon. Whichever, Dexter is not driving anywhere. He is just too busy. The Newspaper Man calls Dexter back and tells him the guy can't make it. Would Dexter make another appointment with them? Give them a little more advance notice. Dex says he'll check his schedule and call him back some time near the end of the week.

When Dex gets off the phone, he has bad vibes about the call. He can't understand why he's having bad vibes. He just has a feeling something is wrong. He returns to more pressing matters at work and tries to shake off the uneasy feeling that has come over him. It just didn't add up: the guy was desperately looking for a financial backer one minute, and then the next minute he can't get himself to an appointment because he needs more advance notice!

A couple of days later he bumps into an acquaintance who just happened to be waiting in line at a restaurant that Dexter frequents. He starts making small talk with Dexter. Throughout their conversation, the friend constantly interjects questions relating to Dexter's schedule. Is he going to be in town for a while? Does he plan on doing much travelling? Is he planning any golfing excursions or holidays? It was as though the guy wanted a copy of Dexter's itinerary. Once again Dexter starts to have bad vibes. He knows the guy more as an acquaintance than a friend. Dexter has lunch with him. All the while, Dexter's trying to figure out if he's the one who is losing it or if there is something to these bad vibes which keep overwhelming him.

After lunch he returns to his office and tries to put it all behind him. The phone rings, and it's the Newspaper Man. He wants to set up a meet for next week, in a restaurant in the suburbs. He's buying. The hair stands up on the back of Dexter's neck. The bad vibes came rushing over him like an early morning shower. Dexter's schedule is open, but he tells the Newspaper Man he can't make it. They will have to postpone it. He's going down to North Carolina for ten days to play some golf. He promises to give him a call when he gets back.

The next day in his office he receives a call from Nummers. Nummers is a close and trusted friend who is finishing up his time on a beef he got thirty-nine months for. They go back a long way. Nummers was into a lot of different scams. On one occasion Dexter rescued him from a jackpot he'd gotten himself into, and Nummers made some very serious money out of a bad situation. Dexter never asked for a dime of the money Nummers had made. He had done what he had done as a friend helping a friend. Nummers was very appreciative, and Dexter thought it bonded them even tighter as friends. Dexter saved Nummer's bacon by firing the lawyer he had, and hiring the lawyer Dexter normally used. Nummers' original lawyer had advised him the best Nummers could expect was five years. Dexter went to his lawyer and explained Nummers' circumstances. When the lawyer suggested two years was what Nummers would get, Dexter fired Nummers' lawyer and replaced him with his own. The lawyer also got Nummers out on bail and, while he was out, Dexter brought him in on some action. It netted him several hundred thousand dollars. Nummers eventually went to the can to do his time, but at that point all his affairs were in order and he had a bankroll waiting for him when he got out.

Nummers was staying in a minimum security prison that had evening visitations. He wanted Dexter to visit him the following evening to discuss something very important. The weirdest thing happened to Dexter. It was as if an electrical shock had zipped out of the telephone receiver and run all the way up his arm to his neck. He listened attentively to his old friend, and promised him he would visit the following evening, but he couldn't seem to shake the negative feelings he was experiencing.

That evening, Dexter accompanied his wife to the local supermarket to do some grocery shopping. In the shopping center he ran into a street associate. The guy exchanged small talk then, in a passing comment, he mentioned that Dougie had been asking around about him. Dexter knew Dougie as a player, but they were not friends or even associates. They had never exchanged more than ten words. Dexter asked as to what kind of questions Dougie was asking. "Nothing specific," the guy says, "Just things like, have you seen Dexter around the Zoo or Nittolo's lately? Is he travelling? Does he have a new hangout? General questions like that." Dexter didn't make an issue of it, but now he had a hunch something was up;, and whatever it was, it revolved around him.

When he got back home, he went to his stash and picked up his trusted revolver. He told his wife about his bad vibes. He still couldn't figure out what was going on, but he wanted her to be careful. He loaded his shotgun and placed it near his bed. He didn't like walking around with a gun, but when you know there is a problem or have a hunch that something is wrong, it's always better to be safe than sorry.

When he got to the office, he was greeted by another letter from Ajmal. He opened it and read it carefully — another delay, more bullshit. One line in the letter jumped off the pages at Dexter: "I'm only waiting for you." It was out of context with the rest of the bullshit in the letter. It was almost as an afterthought, or an extra measure of reassurance, that he had added that little comment. Dexter started to have a hunch that Ajmal, Putz, the Duck and the Old Bandit were his problem. Dougie was an associate of the Duck, but still no connection. He decided not to visit Nummers that evening — now, he thought to himself, he's really getting paranoid, he's even questioning his old buddy Nummers. The day passed uneventfully. There were no strange phone calls at the office and everything else proceeded normally. He left work early. He decided it was time to take the wife and kids for an impromptu holiday. Two weeks in the Caribbean would serve everybody well. He discussed the idea with his wife — who had been getting a little uptight too — and she agreed. She would take care of the travel plans as well as arrange for the kids' academic studies to be kept up to date.

The following day he received a letter from Papa Gee. He would be in Singapore in a month, and he wanted to meet Dex there. He had good news. Dexter analyzed all the thoughts whirling in his head. He decided to send a FedEx letter to Ajmal, asking him to meet in Singapore in a month. He'd also FedEx a letter to Papa Gee confirming their meeting in Singapore. He had instructed his secretary not to forward any calls, just take the messages. During the day, Nummers had called him three times. His secretary said he was very eager to speak with him. Each message was underlined "important." Dex thought to himself, whatever it was, Nummers could wait. He had a few things on his mind that rated a higher priority.

The following day he left with his wife and children for a two-week holiday in the Caribbean. While there, he called some contacts he had run into along his journey in life. They were Vietnam veterans. They had returned home disillusioned and scarred. Sometimes a bullet wound is better than a psychological wound — a bullet wound heals fast, but a psychological wound festers deep and long. In any event, they were Canadians who had gotten caught up in the fervor of war, defeating those dreaded communists and all that bullshit. When they arrived in Vietnam, they realized that their main objective was to survive and make it back home. In the meantime, they had to stay and fight and kill. For the Canadian vets, it meant three or four tours of duty, not one like the American boys who were drafted into service. Not welcomed in the States, they returned to Canada. Here they were greeted with even less enthusiasm. After a year or so in Canada, some of them decided to go back to the States. They needed a Green Card. They were told to get to the back of the bus and wait, because Cambodian refugees, Vietnamese refugees, Cubans, and Haitians had preference. Many integrated back into society; some, like the ones Dexter knew, felt used by society and got involved in drugs. Their attitude was, they had killed people for ten dollars a day, so why not do it for more money? They weren't psychopaths — well, not all of them anyway. They thought of themselves as soldiers for hire — mercenaries. If governments of the world could and would hire them, so could drug dealers. And the drug dealers paid more. Dex made his contact with them and asked them to be on standby. It was all set. Dexter had a hunch he was going to war. It's not as Hollywood portrays it. A war, whether in the underworld or in the legitimate world is not a whole lot of fun. In fact it's downright stupid. All wars are fought over money or ideology. In the drug world, it's always and only over money. It's stupid, because the cost to all involved can be financially devastating. It is a result of the bestial level man sinks to when he cannot, or will not, communicate; when he won't compromise. War is a time when man is ruled by greed or ego, or both. Not pretty, not nice, just war.

After he'd returned from Jamaica and settled the family in, Dexter went to see Nummers, unannounced. Nummers was surprised to see him.

"What's up?" Dex asked. "You left some urgent messages at my office. Sorry I couldn't get here sooner, I was on vacation."

Nummers was at a loss for words. He started explaining about how this guy has the movie rights to a book. Dexter sat there half listening to his old friend. His mind was fluid with thoughts of how he helped this guy out when he was in a jam. How he had made close to seven hundred thousand dollars because of Dex. Dexter realized his friend was babbling and it annoyed him. The bullshit kept rolling out of his mouth like sewage from a sewage pipe. He knew that Nummers had done some time with the Duck. He wondered how the Duck could buy his loyalty. He felt like asking him, but he didn't. He did not want to tip his hand. He did not want them, whoever they were, to know he was hep. So far, Dexter was still going on his hunches, his vibes, his feelings. He still did not have anything concrete. He was boiling inside. Outside, he was as calm as a southern gentleman sipping his gin gimlet under a willow tree. Nummers kept looking around as though he wanted to signal someone or make a phone call. Dex watched his every move. Nummers began to ask questions about his friend's plans — was he going to be traveling soon? Did he stop by the Zoo or Nittolo's as he usually did? — things of that nature. After about a half-hour of the head games, Dex pushed his chair away from the table, reached out, shook his friend's hand and said good-bye.

Walking out into the parking lot of the minimum security prison, Dex looked around. The place was dark and deserted. A perfect spot for a hit. The kind any dime-and-dollar hit man would jump at. Dex would have left his gun in his car. He would have been unarmed, a clay pigeon tossed into the sights of a parking-lot hit man. Easy pickins, except that somebody had been watching over Dexter, making life difficult for the conspirators who planned his demise. He knew without having been told that Nummers had tried to set him up. The urgent phone calls were because Dex had not shown up when he was supposed to. Nummers was trying to find out when Dexter would visit, trying to pin him down to a time. Dexter thought to himself, he must be getting big money for selling me out. He wondered what value to place on true friendship. If it worked out the way Dexter thought it was going to, Nummers would be on his hit list too.

When he arrived at his office the next morning, Checkers was on the phone. He's not too happy, and he lets Dexter know it right off the top. He wants to meet with him as soon as possible. Dex takes a reality check. He can sense the Big C is pissed off about something, but he's not getting any bad vibes. To be on the safe side, he asks Checkers where and when he wants to meet. Checkers says, "Anywhere, you name it." They set up a meet and Dex leaves his office.

He arrives at the meeting a half-hour ahead of Checkers. He surveys the surrounding area. Nothing is out of place. He goes into the restaurant and it's empty. He takes a table at the back of the café and sits with his back to the wall, his eyes on the front door.

Checkers shows up about five minutes early. Dex watches him through the window as he parks his car and walks toward the restaurant, alone. He enters the restaurant, recognizes Dexter, walks over and sits down. Usually Checkers has a big smile and a friendly handshake, but today he's all business. Dexter looks at him, waiting to hear what's on his mind. It doesn't take Checkers long to say what he has say.

"You know Dex, I've known you for a long time. I've always respected you, because you were straight up. I did what you asked me to do. I stayed in that fucking hole for three weeks. I got the job done. We had a deal. I was supposed to have a crack at selling all or part of the shit. Why are you fucking me?"

Dex looked at Checkers. "Checkers, what the hell are you talking about?"

"The Black Gold."

"What Black Gold?"

"Come on, Dex, that's the name I gave the shit I approved!"

"I never asked you what name you gave the shit. This is the first time I heard of it. What has that got to do with you thinking I've fucked you?"

"The Black Gold is in town and you haven't given me a call!"

"Wait a minute. Are you saying what I think you're saying?"

Checkers could see that Dex didn't have a clue. It was also true, Dex had never asked him what he had called the hash. They both sat there for a moment, lost in their own thoughts. Then Dex spoke up.

"I don't want you to tell anybody what you know or even that you talked with me. I want you to go back to Ottawa and find out who is moving the shit. Don't let on to anyone what you know. I want you to buy some of the shit and sell it. Find out what you can as to who is behind it."

"Well I already know it's coming from Montreal and apparently they don't want the Black Gold label moved in Montreal just yet. They also have another label, not as good as the Black Gold but a commercial product just the same. They brought in tons of the shit. The Paki fucked us, didn't he?"

"Yeah, but he couldn't have done it without the blessing of some smart asses in Montreal."

"Dex, I'll do what I can. I'll get as much info for you as I can, but you know I'm not into the gun thing. Are you going to let it slide?"

Dex didn't answer. Checkers answered his own question.

"No, I didn't think so. Why would that bastard screw us after all the hard work and patience you've shown him? Three weeks, three fucking weeks, just so that bastard would get it right!"

"Well, Checkers, that's what happens when you get a Putz involved in your business. That's what happens when you're stupid like I was. Oh well, too late now. Gotta do what I gotta do. Remember, you haven't seen me or talked to me. You have never mentioned Black Gold to me. Got it?"

Checkers nodded his head. They finished their coffee and left.

Dexter went to see a hash dealer he knew well and asked him if he had any hash. Yeah, there was a gang of it in town. Who was behind it? The Duck. Dex knew that the Duck would want everybody to know he was into the hash game in a big way. He had that kind of ego. The dealer told Dex that he had two kinds; however, for now they were just moving the one brand, the Sphinx. The other label he hadn't seen. Dex asked the dealer to forget about their visit and their conversation. The dealer promised to keep his beak closed. Dexter left.

First on Dexter's agenda was to call in the troops. He had a meeting with them where he explained the situation from A to Z. Their price was a hundred and fifty grand, ten grand a head for every cadaver they dropped on the street, big shot or punk, a body was a body. Dexter would decide who and when, except in the case of a shootout. If that happened, they did what they had to do. If Dex won, they would get a million-dollar bonus. They agreed.

The first thing Dexter wanted was to have one person stay with his family. He would pay all expenses. They were to bring their own equipment. They had a trunk full. Once he knew his family was secure, he would do some homework on the Duck and the Old Bandit. He didn't know much about the Duck, so he had to do some quick learning. The Old Bandit was in the candy game. Dexter had some contacts with some French-speaking ex-bandits in the East End of town. He went to see them first. He began asking questions about the Old Bandit. Right away the boys sensed trouble brewing. They didn't like the old bastard. He was a mouthy son of a bitch and a bad-ass to boot. They were more than willing to pass on whatever info they could come up with. The Duck they knew as well. They didn't like him either. In no time at all, Dexter had a book of information on the Duck and the Old Bandit. He advised his crew he was going to Singapore. He wouldn't be gone long. When he returned, the shit would hit the fan.

RULE NUMBER EIGHT
LISTEN TO YOUR VIBES

We all get vibes — sometimes we call them "hunches" or simply feelings. In the Drug Game you have to pay attention to them. It is not a question of becoming paranoid, it's a matter of life and death or going to the can. Talk to any guy who has gone down. Chances are, he will tell you he felt something was wrong before he jumped in that canoe going down shit creek without a paddle. It's difficult to tell the difference between a hunch or a feeling that is real and one that is based on paranoia, or feelings that cokers develop after a long use of cocaine. The cocaine paranoia, I can't help you with. The only thing I can say is, don't do cocaine and you won't develop fantasy paranoia. For the rest of us, it is a question of listening to our vibes.

Not every funny feeling is a vibe. Sometimes you'll meet someone you don't like. Someone, say, who reminds you of your old Uncle Bob, who was a mean old bugger. Now, you'll automatically project your dislike of Uncle Bob onto the person you are meeting. The person may not be anything near what Uncle Bob was like, but you've decided not to like him anyway. That's not a vibe. A vibe is a feeling that comes over you for no rhyme or reason. Somehow you sense that something is wrong or about to happen. It's like a premonition, except it's only a feeling; not based on a dream or anything tangible. If you are driving in a car on a slippery ice-covered road with a fool who has the pedal to the metal, you may develop a feeling that you are in a dangerous situation, but that's not a vibe, that's common sense. Vibes are not predicated on what you can see or touch, they come out of the blue. If you have a bad feeling that's so strong you become nervous or agitated for no apparent reason, stop and listen to your vibes. They are telling you that something is not kosher!

In Dexter's case, the hair will actually stand up on the back of his neck. It has happened to him more than once, when death was knocking on his door. He might not understand it or have any clue as to why it is happening. That is not important. The important thing is to take note of your surroundings and what's going on in your life. Ignore it, and you'll wish you hadn't. In the legit world, you see it happening all the time. A person walks into a casino, goes over to a particular slot machine and bingo, before you know it, bells are going off. Ask them why they picked that particular machine out of the hundreds around them, and they will tell you they had a feeling. A mother jumps up from her living room sofa and checks on her child, who is thought to be sleeping. She opens the bedroom door to find the child playing with matches. She did it because she had a vibe or a feeling something was wrong!

For example, when Dex had a bad feeling when making a delivery, he would stop and check it out! It was listening to his vibes that enabled him to survive many disastrous situations. Forget the macho shit about never passing on a deal or being chicken or paranoid. You are playing with your life. Listen to your vibes. Sometimes they may turn out not to be what you were concerned with. Big deal! No harm done. You're not in the can. Go against them out of machismo or greed, and guaranteed you will get slammed. It is something Dexter tried to remember and share with his associates, but very few listened.

CHAPTER TEN
LAW OF THE GUN

When he arrived in Singapore, Dexter checked into the Sheraton Singapore Hotel, a beautiful modern hotel located right in the center of this city nation. Singapore is a marvelous city to live in. It has year round mean temperatures of about seventy-five degrees Fahrenheit and lush manicured green grass, in a spotlessly clean setting of modern buildings and Asian architecture. Spitting on the street, chewing gum and jaywalking are just a few of the seemingly minor indiscretions that can land you in the can. It is a city that throbs with the hustle and bustle of any major metropolis in the twenty-first century but without the sham or drudgery of most of our western bastions of commerce. From its cleanliness, its organization, its civility and its culture, Singapore is a country that exudes order. The death penalty is freely given in cases of drug trafficking and murder. No sympathetic courts of appeal. The government rules authoritatively and severely against those who would sully its reputation.

Dexter checked with the front desk to see if there were any messages awaiting him. The answer was negative. Neither Ajmal nor Papa Gee had attempted to contact him. In the afternoon, Dexter went for a long walk around the vicinity of his hotel. He wanted to familiarize himself as well as he could with the locale. He walked for hours and hours, for miles and miles, eventually returning to his hotel room exhausted. It was important for Dexter to know the neighbourhood around his hotel like the back of his hand. Important because he had a plan.

He envisioned one of two scenarios. Ajmal would show up at his hotel and call him from the lobby, in which case Dexter would not invite him up but meet him there. Greeting him in the lobby, he would suggest they go for a little walk, for some fresh air, some exercise or whatever would sound appropriate. The second scenario would be that Ajmal would call and invite Dexter to visit him at his hotel. In such a case, Dexter would be right over.

Dexter had a simple plan. He had brought along his little twenty-two magnum, four-shot derringer. He believed that Ajmal would show up with the Putz and one, possibly two, bodyguards. He would have to be prudent if Ajmal showed up with the Putz and two bodyguards; however, he had an added accompaniment — a switch blade. He was confident that no matter which scenario unfurled, his raging anger would compensate for any deficiencies or lack of equipment.

He spent the second day sitting in his hotel reading about the sights and culture of Singapore. In the afternoon he took a sightseeing tour. Singapore has a magnificent forested park right in its heart. He thought to himself that this was one of the few cities he had ever visited where, after such a short period of time, he knew he could enjoy living. In the evening, he went for another long walk around the vicinity of the hotel refreshing his memory about all the little side streets and alleys one could take back to the hotel. After several hours of dogged priming of his senses, he was confident he could disappear into one of the side streets. He could make his ghostly way back to his hotel without being seen. He returned to his hotel room and waited for the phone to ring.

On the third day, he decided to call Pakistan. Ajmal's residence gave him the "Pakistani shuffle" — everyone who answers the phone doesn't speak English. The odd thing about that was that if he called when he owed Ajmal money, everybody spoke English. Getting nowhere with that line of communication, he called Papa Gee.

Immediately Dexter sensed that someone was with Papa Gee. He informed Dexter he was unable to make it to Singapore as scheduled. Dexter knew this wasn't right. From the letter he had sent Dexter, he indicated he was extremely eager to meet with him and start a program. Now he couldn't make it! Dexter let the old man talk. He didn't even offer an excuse for not being in Singapore or for not coming. He simply said he was sorry he couldn't make it. Dexter listened carefully to the old man as his conversation changed from that of a depressed sounding individual to one who was very inquisitive as to Dexter's plans. He began to interrogate Dexter. It was evident that someone was priming him with the questions.

He asked Dexter if anything was wrong. Dexter played it very nonchalant. Other than the fact that he had flown all the way to Singapore to meet Papa

Gee, he had no problems. Papa Gee hesitatingly suggested that Dexter should fly to Karachi. The old man was saying the words, but the manner in which he spoke them made it clear they weren't his. Dexter declined the offer to meet with him in Karachi. Papa Gee then asked Dexter where he was going when he left Singapore. Dexter told him he was going to Bombay. Dexter once had a girlfriend in Bombay and he knew Ajmal was aware of it. The old man asked for her phone number. Dexter told him she didn't have one, as was very common for people in that part of the world. He had long ago broken off contact with the stewardess; however, this bit of information seemed to satisfy whoever was listening on the phone with Papa Gee. The old man's way of saying good-bye was strange: he said something to the effect that Dexter should be prepared, and then he hung up.

Dexter had his answer. The big *hodj* and his bumboy weren't coming to Singapore. It was easy for Ajmal to order his men to run across the India-Pakistan border, to get shot at, to risk their lives and to die. Yes, he could give the orders; but when it came to crunch time, the big *hodj* was yellow! He knew what was going on and he suspected Dexter knew as well. Dexter figured Ajmal's next move would be to go to Bombay with an infantry of bodyguards, mostly from his Indian contacts, and wait for Dexter to show up. He would give the orders, and the rupee hit-men would go into action.

If Dexter had had a better piece, he would have gone to Bombay and held court there. Not having the proper equipment, nor the time to hire some rupee hit-men of his own, he decided to book himself on the next flight back to Montreal. There was no point wasting time in Singapore. Dexter hoped that Ajmal would communicate the information about his going to Bombay to his friends back in Montreal. This might put them to sleep and make Dexter's return work at home a little easier. The element of surprise is always a big edge. Thus far, Dexter hadn't tipped his hand to anyone. He wanted to keep it that way. Dexter thought to himself, maybe the big *hodj* would call Montreal and tell them he was going to take care of Dexter. He had that kind of ego, as long as he wasn't anywhere near the action. Ajmal was a real mamma's boy. He'd crow about all his smuggling exploits and never be anywhere close to jeopardizing his ass. Hindsight is twenty-twenty vision. Dexter realized what kind of sleazebag Ajmal was, but unfortunately, he realized it too late. The *hodj* and the Putz would have to wait for another day. Court would be held on the streets of Montreal!

When he got back to Montreal, he gathered his crew. The man in charge was called Sergeant. The three other members respected and followed the Sergeant's commands to the letter. They operated just as though they were back in the military. The Sergeant had the final say, and no one questioned his authority. The Sergeant, in turn, respected Dexter's word as final. The chain of command was clear and concise. Of the group of ex-Marines, only one fit the bill as a psycho. He was called Beatle because of his love for the music of the Beatles. He was a short dumpy guy about five-foot-eight or nine, black hair slicked straight back and eyes that reminded you of those dolls that were so popular in the eighties with those extra-large black eyes. He had a beer gut and thin spindly legs that appeared to stick out of his torso.

Cappers was about six feet tall with a thin build, Marine brush-cut hair, a square jaw and a scar that rippled across his forehead, a souvenir from Vietnam. The fourth man in the crew was called Don. He had a light brown goatee and moustache and shoulder-length light brown hair that he sometimes wore tied back in a ponytail. He was as quiet as a cat stalking a mouse. He hardly ever spoke or laughed. His steel blue eyes were like ice. When he did speak, he always talked in short abrupt sentences. He was not a man of words.

They stayed in two separate motels and moved every two weeks. Dexter went over the information he had on the Duck and the Old Bandit. The Old Bandit was now a full-fledged cokehead. Trying to nail a cokehead is like trying to catch a monkey on a football field. They're all over the place. Sometimes they can go for forty-eight hours non-stop. They decided to concentrate on the Duck.

The Duck lived in a high-rise condo downtown. The security was very tight. Not only did it have a doorman and video cameras, it also had a concierge on duty twenty-four hours a day. Getting in unnoticed was next to impossible, and then if one managed to sneak in, there would be no guarantee the Duck would be in his apartment. They scrubbed the idea of making any kind of a move on him once he was in his condo. They sat around his building for a week.

Once, two of the boys almost had a run-in with the local gendarmes. They were parked on a side street near the garage exit of the condominium, and the patrol cops asked them what they were doing. They played dumb, saying they were waiting for their girlfriends, who were at the hairdressers. The cops bought the party line; but from then on, Dexter and crew had to keep alternating every hour. Sometimes they would stand on the corner as though they were waiting for a ride or catching a bus. It was long hard work. It made Dexter respect police officers who sit around on stakeout duty for days and weeks on end. Not his cup of tea — the hours can stretch on endlessly. The Duck had a country place and an office. Dexter hadn't gotten a line on his country place, but the office and surrounding area had been well scoured. It appeared to be the prime spot to confront the Duck.

They noted that the police had two regular patrols past the Duck's office. Once in the morning between nine-thirty and eleven and the second in the afternoon between one-thirty and four. There was the usual traffic in the industrial park where the office was located, but nothing that caused any great consternation to the crew. The only other oddity was the canteen truck that stopped by in the morning and again in the afternoon. When it was there, it would attract a crowd of twelve to fifteen people. The rest of the time it was relatively quiet, except for the normal car and truck traffic.

The Duck was still walking around with his head up his ass. He went out to bars and other favourite haunts in the evening. They could have made a simpler move on him at night, but Dexter passed on that idea because he wanted to send a clear message to the underworld. A daylight move sends the message that whoever is behind it is serious. A daytime move means that the people involved will go anywhere, anytime. A daylight hit means that the people perpetrating it are professionals, people who will take on anybody who tries to stand in their way. It sets them apart from the hundreds of parking-lot hit men who strut their stuff in the shadow of darkness. Dexter wanted to establish this level of commitment from the outset. The Duck had many contacts, and Dexter wanted everyone to know that the Duck's enemies were not weak, nor would they be intimidated.

The Duck didn't go into his office every day. He had no set schedule. This meant that Dexter and his crew had to sit around his condo and wait for him to go to his office. Finally their patience paid off. The Duck left his condo and headed out on the expressway to his office. Realizing where he was going, the boys passed him and tried to get set up for his arrival at work.

The parking lot in front and around his office was full. They were forced to park the panel truck and back-up car a hundred and fifty yards away from his office and wait. Cappers and Don were in the back-up car, Dexter was with the Sergeant and the Beatle in the panel truck. Just as the Duck pulled into his office parking lot, a car pulled out and left him a spot almost in front of the door. There was no time to react. They sat there watching the Duck go into his office. The Sergeant ordered one of the boys to stand at the bus stop across the street from the Duck's office, where he could watch the front door to the office. He would signal when the Duck started to leave. The panel truck would pull up and Dexter would hop out and approach the Duck.

Dexter opted to approach the Duck himself. The Duck would not know or recognize any of the crew and that might have led to problems. The Duck had a reputation for being vicious at times. It was not known if he was carrying a gun; however, under the circumstances they assumed he would be packing. Dexter felt that when the Duck realized who he was being confronted by, he might want to settle amicably. If not, oh well!

Drug wars are always and only fought over money. It's not about honour, fairness or integrity; it's about money. Anyone who knew Dexter knew he was a man who could be reasoned with. He had sat down at many a table and resolved issues without a shot being fired. He also did what he had to do when individuals decided, for whatever reason, to go the other route. He wanted to give the Duck the option, by presenting himself personally. Settle financially or hold court. The only way to give the Duck that option was to confront him directly and personally. (It's also called "backing-up your action.")

Cappers signalled the Sarge. The Duck was on his way out. The panel truck pulled up beside the Duck's car and Dexter hopped out. He started walking toward the Duck. The moment the Duck recognized him, he froze in his tracks. He just stood there shaking like a wiggily old tit. Dexter kept walking toward him. When he was about three feet away from him, Dexter spoke out.

"Duck, we have to talk. You put your hand in my pocket! You either get in the panel truck with me or we'll settle it right here and now!"

The Duck didn't think it was a big yuk-yuk anymore. There were no smart-ass comments about going down to the corner store. He knew he was at the corner store! He knew Dexter had caught him with his hand in the cookie jar!

Dexter stood face to face with the Duck, observing his hands, watching his body language. The Duck just stood there shaking, like a big bowl of jelly. Dexter could smell the wood burning as the Duck groped for something to say.

Dexter repeated his command to the Duck, "Get in the van!"

The Duck stood there with a goofy look on his face, vibrating as though he had a live wire up his ass. Dexter was aware of footsteps coming up from behind him. He didn't turn or look around. He kept all his attention focussed on the Duck. He showed the Duck his piece. The Duck's eyes shifted in the direction of the oncoming footsteps, which were nearly on top of Dexter.

Then he said in a low, almost inaudible voice, "No."

Dexter could see that the Duck was looking in the direction of the person who was now almost beside Dexter. In tense situations like this, it's as if you can read the other person's thoughts. Dexter knew what the Duck was going to do. He was going to try to grab the person walking by and use him as a shield.

Dexter started to say to the Duck, "Don't…"

The Duck jumped toward the person who by now was passing them. Dexter opened up. The Duck went down. The innocent bystander just stood there, mouth agape, suspended in animation — no doubt a shocking way to start the day. Then the bystander continued on his way. Dexter always believed that if you keep innocent people out of your affairs, they will generally stay out of yours. He took a step toward the prostrate Duck for the insurance shot, when out of the corner of his eye he noticed the police patrol car coming down the street. It was not more than a hundred and fifty yards away. Dex wheeled around and headed back to the panel truck. He figured all hell was going to break loose. He wanted to make it back to the panel truck, because once there he could get his hands on some heavy equipment — it was loaded for bear. The two boys in the back-up car had FN semi-automatic rifles and revolvers. Dexter knew that making it back to the truck would make all the difference in the world.

He jumped in the front seat and closed the door. The Sergeant started the truck slowly rolling forward, waiting for a chance to exit the driveway. The Beatle had his FN locked and loaded. He passed Dexter a sawed-off riot shotgun, loaded with SSG magnum shot. The police cruiser with the two police officers crept in front of the panel truck blocking the driveway. The police officers kept their eyes straight ahead, they didn't even glance at the occupants of the truck. After they passed, the truck pulled slowly out and headed in the opposite direction. The Sarge kept his eyes on his side-view mirror, observing the police cruiser distance itself down the street. The Beatle watched from the back of the van.

In a matter of seconds, they were on an expressway heading downtown. Switching from one expressway to another, they made their way back to the motel. Dexter took a quick shower and a complete change of clothes and headed back to his office. He knew, that if his calculations were right, the Old Bandit would be giving him a call. Now he played the waiting game.

In the afternoon, one of the boys went back to the Duck's office. When the canteen truck appeared, he went over and bought a coffee and mingled with the customers, listening to their conversation. It was all about the shooting that had happened that morning. From what he heard, the Duck was seriously hurt but not dead. He returned to the motel to advise the Sarge. He, in turn, beeped Dexter.

Dexter went over to the motel where his crew was. They discussed the game plan. If the Duck rolled over, they were to wait for instructions from Dexter. The war wouldn't stop, even if he were in the can. Dexter felt the witness would mind his own business, so he didn't concern himself with that. He believed the Duck wouldn't talk, because rolling over would finish him completely in the Drug Game. There is no excuse for a stool pigeon! No matter what, people who play the Drug Game are supposed to keep their mouths shut and settle their problems by the law of the gun, if it comes down to that. If someone rolls over for whatever reason, they are finished if found out. Anyone who rolls over, for whatever reason, is finished if found out. If they're not taken out by the person they rolled over on, then eventually someone else will do it. Nobody cares when a stool pigeon gets dumped. Living on the police protection program is not a whole lot of fun. The cops don't like or respect stool pigeons any more than anyone else. Dexter felt the Duck would take his lumps and come roaring back like a lion.

Early the next morning, not too long after Dexter arrived at his office, the phone jangled. It was the Old Bandit: "Dexter, have you gone nuts, are you fucking crazy? You're in deep shit boy, you had better cool your jets. I'll do what I can to straighten this mess out, but for now you had better lay low! I can't believe what you did! Are you on drugs or something?"

Dexter listened to the Old Bandit. He was now trying to con Dexter into leaving town. He was going to be the white knight in shining armour. He was concerned for Dexter's welfare! Dexter couldn't say much on his telephone. He knew it was tapped. While listening to the Old Bandit, he was thinking of how to respond. Then he said, "You know that song kids always sing at Christmas time — You better watch out, you'd better not pout, Santa Claus is coming to town. He's making a list, ... and you're on Santa's fucking list! You got that?"

For a moment there was silence on the other end of the phone. The Old Bandit was trying to come up with a new approach. He realized coming to Dexter's rescue wasn't the good plan. Dexter wasn't buying.

"Dexter, what's come over you. Are you crazy?"

Dexter cut him short. He didn't want a lot of conversation on the blower. He said, "You listen to me and you listen good! You assholes want to settle this or do you want to hold court? Take your pick. I'm not gonna run off at the mouth on the phone. You know my phone is hot. Think it over and be in touch. You don't have a lot of time because Santa has a long list and you're next. He wants to get cracking. You decide what you want for Christmas and let Santa know. Good-bye."

Dexter left his office. He went to see the boys, who were anxiously awaiting the news. Dexter drafted a letter for the Duck. It was very brief and to the point. He told the Duck he knew about the double-cross and that he could still straighten it out with money, if he wanted to. The choice was his. One way or another, it was going to be settled! He gave the Duck his terms for settling out of court. The wounds he had received were interest payments on money owed. Dexter had been kept updated as to the Duck's physical progress. He was weak but he was going to survive. Capper took the letter and dropped it off with the concierge at the Duck's apartment.

The Sarge looked at Dexter and said, "The Duck must be a good Catholic to survive that one. That's not luck, that's a blessing."

Dexter thought the Sergeant was a superstitious fellow, maybe even religious. He thought he had been through enough to know the difference between luck and divine intervention. The Sarge would often say that luck was something calculable, but that divine intervention defied all odds and calculations. He put the Duck's survival in the divine intervention category.

Dexter went to his office the following day. He had a message from a business associate of the Duck's. The man was a legitimate, hard-working stiff, not involved in any of the Duck's criminal activities. He wanted to see Dexter urgently. Dexter went over to his office unannounced. The receptionist informed the associate of Dexter's presence. He invited him into his office. He closed the office door, went around his desk and gave Dexter a sealed envelope. Dexter opened the envelope in front of him. The Duck protested his innocence. He was willing to forgive Dexter for making a terrible mistake. He wanted to know how he could assure Dexter that he had nothing to do with whatever Dexter thought he had done?

The Duck's friend sat behind his desk. He obviously didn't want to get involved and he didn't want to lose his friend the Duck. He was doing what he could to ameliorate the situation. Dexter looked up and spoke to the Duck's associate.

"You tell your friend I don't buy the bullshit. If he wants to go down the road of denial, tell him it's going to be a hell of a rocky road; and when he gets to the end of the road, I'll be standing there. What he got was a sample. He might be a good Catholic, but if he thinks he's going to bullshit his way out of this one, tell him he had better be a very, very good Catholic."

The Duck's friend sat behind his desk shaking his head from side to side. He wanted to say something but he realized his friend was in a different court of law, and there really wasn't anything he could say. He wanted to help resolve the situation, but he could see that words weren't going to cut it. Dexter thanked him and left.

Dexter called his office. His secretary advised him someone had left a letter for him. They said it was very important and it was for his eyes only. He stopped by his office, picked up the letter and left. He got into his car and opened the letter. It was a very terse note. They were threatening to kill his wife and his children if he didn't stop and leave town. The Sarge could see the black rage in Dexter's face. Dexter handed him the letter.

"What's our next move, Dex?" said the Sarge, after reading it.

"I'm going to secure my family and let those bastards know two can play the same game!"

In the meantime, the Old Bandit was running around town trying to drum up support. The Duck's an angel, he is an innocent peacemaker, and Dexter is nuts. He's telling everyone who will listen that Dexter is blitzed out of his skull on drugs. He's saying that Dexter is on one of his horror-show drunks, and that he's got to be stopped. Those who knew Dexter knew that what the Old Bandit was saying was bullshit. They let him bump his gums, listening sympathetically to his tale of woe, but no one volunteered to assist him in quashing this madman Dexter. It was "mind your own business" time.

Dexter secured his family then sent a note to the Duck. It stated clearly what Dexter would do if anyone touched his family. In essence, he told the Duck that if anyone went near his family, he would kill the Duck's mother, father, aunt, uncle, brother, sister, wife, kids and his cat and dog! The response came quickly.

The Duck's friend called Dexter and asked him to stop by as soon as possible, which he did. The friend made it plain that he did not want to get involved. He was a good man, not involved in crime. Had the Duck levelled with him, he probably would have negotiated a peace. He was offering his assistance, because he was against the violence he could see brewing if the issue weren't resolved by any other means. Dexter informed the Duck's friend that his family had been threatened first.

Dexter was simply dotting the i's and crossing the t's. He wanted to let everyone know that once they started down that road, there would be no turning back!

He asked the Duck's friend if he could guarantee that no one would take a run at his wife or his children. The Duck's friend said he would speak to the Duck and get back to him. He wanted Dexter to know he didn't believe the Duck had anything to do with threatening his family. He was simply trying to resolve the family issue because the Duck had asked him to do so.

The next play the Duck made was to move his family four hundred miles away. He now felt secure about his family. There was no more talk about settlements or guarantees for Dexter's family. It took Dexter a month, but Dexter was able to find the Duck's family in New York. They were living in a high-rise condominium development. The security was very tight. They sat on the condo for two days and finally figured out the weakness in the apartment building's security. The apartment numbers were not listed on the registry board. Instead, everything was coded. If you didn't know the code, you couldn't ring the apartment. Dexter knew the apartment number, but not the code; so he slipped by the security, rode the elevator up to the eighth floor and knocked on the door. Assuming it was the janitor or the concierge, the Duck's wife answered the door. She would never have thought it was an outsider. When she saw a well-dressed man in a business suit, she asked him what he wanted. Dexter handed her his business card and said, "Please tell your husband I stopped by. Thank you."

Dexter left the apartment building and returned to Montreal. The following day, he went to his office. There was a DHL Express letter waiting for him from Ajmal. It was a brief note. It stated that he wanted Dexter to talk to the Duck. Settle the problem like businessmen. Please, please, he wrote, be reasonable. Dexter took the letter over to the Duck's friend. He showed him the letter. Before reading the letter, the Duck's friend told Dexter he didn't want to get involved in anything illegal. Dexter assured him that the contents of the letter weren't specific enough for anyone but the parties involved to understand. He simply wanted him to read the letter, verify where the letter had come from as well as the postage and date mark. The friend read the letter carefully. He checked the markings for the date and then he looked up at Dexter. Dexter asked him to inform the Duck of the letter and its contents. Then he said, "Tell the Duck, I don't want to hear any more bullshit about his innocence!"

The next day Dexter received an answer. It wasn't from the Old Bandit or the Duck's friend, it was from the Duck's silent partner. Dexter returned his call. The silent partner was known as the Dough Boy. He wanted to meet with him. They arranged to meet at Dexter's office. Dexter had two of the boys outside watching the office building from the front and back. One was in the hallway at the elevator banks on Dexter's floor. The Sarge was in another office next to Dexter. The Dough Boy showed up on time and alone. The secretary escorted him to Dexter's office. The Dough Boy started off by proclaiming his innocence. He's got nothing to do with anything. He's just trying to help his business partner resolve his problem. Other than that, he's not involved. When he finished babbling, Dexter lowered the boom.

"I have never met such an innocent bunch of sons of bitches in all my life. Now you hear this! You are the guy who plays, "Happy days are here again" on the computer. I know all about your scam down on the docks. Don't bullshit me. Your friend couldn't clear the Madonna if it weren't for you. You're involved right up to your eyeballs. Now, do you want to settle this thing amicably or do you think miracles run in your circle of associates?"

The Duck's partner sat across from Dexter, fidgeting with his hands, avoiding eye contact. He looked up at Dexter and agreed to settle. Dexter gave him the terms. He nodded his head in agreement. He was nervous about coming to Dexter's office again. Dexter suggested they meet at the airport. He could buy himself a ticket to Toronto, pass through the security check and meet him at gate four. In this manner they would be meeting on neutral territory. Dexter would have the address for the drop and the time the drop was to be made. It looked as if the war was going to wind down without another shot being fired. There was no more talk about women and children getting involved either.

The following day, Dexter received a call from the Duck's friend. The meeting place had been changed. Instructions were with the Duck's other legitimate business associate. Dexter met with the guy briefly in his office. He handed Dexter a sealed envelope. He did not know its contents nor did he want to know. He felt as if he was getting sucked into the mess. He pointedly said that he would not be passing messages back and forth any more. He did not intend to get involved in his friend's or Dexter's problem. He had offered to help all parties concerned in order to avoid violence, but he wasn't about to become a party to a criminal conspiracy. Dexter thanked him for his candidness and for what he had done. As he was leaving, he turned to the guy and asked who had delivered the letter.

Duck's friend didn't want to answer, but Dexter insisted. If he didn't want to get involved, he should at least be honest with both parties. The friend agreed with Dexter's logic; and anyway he had not been told to keep the identity of the messenger a secret.

The messenger was a guy known as the Berry. Dexter wasn't familiar with the name, but nonetheless he would check it out. The note changed the meeting place from the airport to a garage on Wellington Street, the following day. Dexter and the Sarge went for a little drive. The garage was located in a working-class district. The garage itself was on a street that fronted on a park. It wasn't on Wellington Street. There was a small park with several benches, a few large old oak trees and a path that crossed diagonally. The park was a square, about half a city block in length and was surrounded on all sides by short streets. At the foot of the park was a bank.

On the next street running toward Wellington Street was a house and the garage was adjacent to it. Wellington Street ran across the top of the park, and on the far side was another short street. On the corner of that street and Wellington was a small tobacco store, and several residential buildings that filled up the rest of the block. Facing the park on the other side of Wellington Street was a railway station.

The moment the Sarge saw the layout, he told Dexter it was a set-up.

"Looks like the boys don't want to part with their money. At least not without trying to get their licks in."

The Sarge was a man who could spot ambushes in a jungle at night. Dexter didn't question his observation. He drove the Sarge around the park slowly. The Sarge drank it all in. He asked Dexter to drive him around the neighbourhood. After several passes, Dexter pulled up behind the train station. From this vantage point they could see the garage, the park and the streets surrounding the park. They sat there quietly for about ten minutes. The Sarge made mental notes of the area, and he asked Dexter to try to remember as many of the vehicles that were parked on the streets as he could.

The next day Dexter and his crew arrived at the train station at about ten-thirty. The meeting was set for twelve. The Sarge wanted to be really early, to observe the bush-whackers setting up. Beatle and Cappers were in a back-up car. The Sarge, Dexter and Don were in the panel truck. Everyone watched and waited. The Sarge had mapped out the park in military time. The bank was at twelve o'clock, the garage was at nine o'clock, the restaurant on the corner was at three o'clock and so on. A cream-coloured panel truck pulled up and parked on the same street as the garage, about fifty yards from it. The driver got out, said something to someone in the back, and went into the garage. A small man with graying hair, wearing a baseball cap, checkered work shirt, jeans and work boots walked out of the garage with two other men and went to the park. The casual dress of the two men helped them fit in with the locals. They took up their positions on the two park benches. They watched the little guy with the graying hair and the baseball cap walk around the perimeter of the park. Sometimes he would stop in at the corner store to buy cigarettes or a drink but he kept on walking around on his patrol. Sometimes he would stop and talk to the people in the back of the van and other times he would walk into the garage for a moment. When he cut across the park, he would say a few words to the two men on the park benches, then continue down the path and walk around the perimeter all over again. They were getting dizzy watching the little guy.

Dexter and his crew were waiting for one or two of the principals to show up — either the Old Bandit or the Dough Boy, or both. The Duck was still unable to travel. When you get into a fight with a snake, you cut off the head, not the tail. There was no point in whacking a bunch of local yokel hit men. That would solve nothing. Dexter and his crew watched and waited. It was now one o'clock, and neither of the principals had showed up. Dexter lost his patience. He was going to go into the garage and give them all a taste. He reached for the door handle, but the Sarge's big hand grabbed his arm.

"Dexter, calm down. That won't solve a thing. We could blow everything for a bunch of hick hit men. Calm down."

Dexter knew the Sarge was right. Those doofusses wouldn't know what hit them, and even if he did get away with it clean, what would it solve?

The local gendarmes had passed the bank on patrol that morning while they were sitting there. They knew the police patrol car would swing by at least once in the afternoon, but they didn't know when. They had not had time to recon the area, they were winging it. Dexter sat fuming. He wanted to do something. All he had been getting from the Old Bandit and the Duck was bullshit. They needed another taste, another message, to make them capitulate. The Dough Boy had wanted to deal. Something had changed his mind. He felt it was the Old Bandit. The Duck's ego had been clipped big time. The Old Bandit was the only one left with a big cokehead ego. The Sarge broke the silence.

"You see that little guy walking around the park? He's the leader of the band. Now maybe if we take him out the Duck and his partner will come to their senses. We'll make one pass at him and then we're out of here. OK?"

Dexter nodded his head in agreement. The Sarge passed the message on to Cappers and the Beatle. The Beatle volunteered to do the hit. The Sarge started the van rolling down the street when he saw the little leader of the band coming through the park. He turned the corner and waited for Cappers and the Beatle to make their move. Once the boys made their move, they would pass the van and head straight back to the motel. The Sarge wanted the van to follow the boys as they made their getaway. If the other panel truck decided to give pursuit when they saw their little leader go down, it wouldn't get very far.

They heard the Beatle say they were about to make contact, then nothing. The car rounded the corner and pulled up beside the waiting panel truck. The Beatle's gun hadn't gone off. He had that turkey all lined up, squeezed the trigger, and nothing. He wanted to go back for a second pass. He was sure the little gray-haired hit man hadn't seen the play. He wanted another shot. The Sarge shook his head, and ordered everyone back to the motel.

The Sarge told Dex it was a bad omen. Two guys who should be picking up their shovels and reporting to work were sitting back on their duffs having a beer. Not a good sign! Or maybe it was a sign from a higher power telling them to back off!

They didn't consider the Duck's hired crew to be any real threat, because it was obvious they were all locals, doing their thing in their own familiar territory. They could disappear into the woodwork in that part of town without a problem, but they weren't the type to work outside their own backyard. Dexter wanted to get a line on the leader of the band. He put the word out and in about a week, he had his name, address and where he worked. He was called the Berry because he had a bulbous red alcoholics nose on the face of a cherub. He was also a known associate of the Duck. Dexter thought of using him as an example and a message for the Duck and company.

They couldn't tag down the Old Bandit. They had come close several times. He was quite a party boy. Every time they got a line on him, he would be gone by the time they got to wherever he was last seen. They located the house of one of his girlfriends and they knew where he lived. They just hadn't been able to be at the right place at the right time. That was the trick. For eight months the Old Bandit had had a horseshoe up his ass.

He never realized how many times he had come close to getting popped. Some fluke thing always seemed to happen at the last moment that prevented Dex and the crew from eliminating him.

Dexter was also trying to get a line on the Dough Boy. He wasn't well known, he didn't hang around clubs or bars and he didn't have a criminal record; so it was hard to get a lead on him.

They knew Dexter hadn't forgotten about them. Dexter had word the Old Bandit had told some associates in confidence he would rather be in the can than have Dexter on his ass. This was encouraging, but it still hadn't yielded the results Dexter wanted. Finally, the Old Bandit called Dexter on his cell phone. He wanted a meet and he wanted it pronto. He suggested they meet at the airport in an hour. Dexter and crew went to the airport. Dexter wanted to pop him right in the airport terminal. He knew if the Old Bandit were out of the picture, the rest of the opposition would fold. But with all the equipment they had, they didn't have a piece with a silencer. He made a few calls. One guy said he would bring one over immediately. Unfortunately, the guy didn't make it on time and Dexter had to go to the meet and just talk to the Old Bandit.

The Old Bandit was up to his eyeballs on coke, and he was very cocky. He told Dexter he wasn't putting up with his bullshit anymore. He began cursing and swearing, saliva coming out of his mouth as he barked away at Dexter. Dexter stood listening, not saying a word or reacting to the Old Bandit's threats. The Old Bandit rambled on about how he had dug a hole in the ground for Dexter. How he was fed up and how he wanted to get this thing finished with. He said, "If you touch one hair on my head, one hair on my head, you've had it!"

When the Old Bandit paused for a break, Dexter decided to end the conversation, which wasn't going anywhere. Besides, people were starting to look at them, because the Old Bandit was making quite a scene. Dexter spoke up.

"I won't touch one hair on your head, but I am going to put six bullets into that sleazebag coconut of yours. You're the one who doesn't want to settle. Your partners want to settle, but you're the cokehead who doesn't want to. You are my primary target and I am going to get you and the Duck, and the Dough Boy, and Nummers, and the Berry. I am going to get everyone of you sons-a-bitches. Now tell me where you've dug the hole for me. I'm going to put you in one. So you might as well save me the trouble of doing all that digging!"

The Old Bandit changed from night to day. Not only were there no more threats, but he became conciliatory. He calmed right down. He realized that all his bad-ass threats were like mud to a pig as far as Dexter was concerned. He offered to go and speak to his partners and come to terms. They parted with that.

When Dex told the Sarge and the boys, they all seemed relieved. This thing had dragged on for over nine months. The end was in sight. In the meantime, Dexter had placed two of the boys at the train station on Wellington Street. They took pictures of everybody and every vehicle that pulled into the garage. It paid off. The Dough Boy showed up one day. They got his license number and from there Dexter had his address. They decided to put a little pressure on the Dough Boy. Dexter drove up to his house and rang his doorbell, he didn't come to the door; he called the cops instead. The Sarge was listening on the police scanner and whistled to Dex to move out. As they drove down the road, the local police cruiser went screaming by. Dexter now had the pressure point he needed to bring this thing to a close.

The next day at his office there were no messages. Dexter decided to set the Berry up using his old friend Auntie. She invited the Berry out for lunch. She had a proposition for him. He was a very nervous hit man. He would go no more than a mile or two from the garage. He felt safe on his home turf. That is an illusion that most parking-lot hit men feel. That's one of the distinguishing marks between your parking-lot hit men and "heavies" who will go anywhere, anytime. To a "heavy" there is no such thing as home turf.

Auntie had arranged to meet the Berry at a restaurant of his choosing not more than a mile from the garage. The Sarge and Dexter were in a car parked back from the restaurant. The other boys were in two cars nearby.

The Beatle wanted first dibs on the little leader of the band. The Sarge gave him the green light. Dexter looked up and saw Dougie, a friend of the Duck and the Dough Boy, walking on the street checking the cars in the area. He spotted two of the boys and called on his cellular. The Berry's beeper went off. He left lunch quicker than a fag going to a bum party.

As soon as the Berry hit the restaurant door, the boys converged in on him. Almost at that instant, a truck double parked to make a quick delivery; the whole area was in an instant traffic jam. Had Dexter and crew stayed where they were, the little hit man would have come right to them. Instead, they moved out to nail him and they all got tangled up in the traffic. The Berry drove out right behind them. The Sarge sat there holding the steering wheel and shaking his head. He couldn't believe the luck those guys were having. They went back to the motel. The Beatle was talking to himself. The Sarge looked at Dexter and said, "I'm getting a bad feeling, Dex. Either we get this thing over with or we're all going to the can."

On his way home, Dexter stopped by his mother-in-law's house to pick up his wife, and found them both upset. The police had called in the afternoon looking for Dexter. They said he had been involved in a hit-and-run accident. They were going to call back at five-thirty. They wanted to know how to get in touch with Dexter.

When Dexter heard the story he smiled. He told his wife (who was beginning to get angry with him) to relax. He knew right away that it wasn't the cops, it was the Old Bandit trying to set him up. No one had his mother-in-law's phone number except the Old Bandit. Why would the police call his mother-in-law's house looking for Dexter? They didn't have the same last names, and besides he hadn't been in any accident. He told his wife to answer the phone when the phony cop called back. He told her to tell them that her husband was having dinner at a restaurant called Le Vieux Pêcheur at eight-thirty or nine o'clock that evening. His wife looked at him.

"Are you crazy? They'll be there looking for you. Do you want to get killed?"

"No," replied Dexter, "But I do want to get this over with. I'm going to reverse the set-up on them. Please do as I say."

The phone rang at exactly five-thirty. It was inspector so-and-so on the line. Dexter's wife told the inspector exactly what Dexter had asked her to say, except that when the inspector asked for directions to the restaurant, she answered, "Well, if you are a police officer you should be able to find it for yourself!"

Dexter gave his wife the big eyes, as if to say, "Cut it out!" Dexter knew they were stupid, but he didn't think they were that stupid.

The guy answers back, "Hey, hey, madam, don't talk to the police dat way."

The conversation was over and the game was in play. Dexter left the house and rounded up the crew. He explained the situation to the Sarge and the boys. They were all in for a showdown. They arrived at the restaurant at about seven-thirty; plenty of time to get set up. Dexter stayed in the van with the Sarge. The Sarge and Dex were at the apex of a triangle and the boys were at the other corners. Anybody walking into that set-up was deader than a turkey on Thanksgiving. They waited patiently for the bad-asses to show up.

A panel truck pulled into the parking lot up near the front. Parked in that position, it could drive by the front door at a moment's notice. They could nail Dexter the instant he walked out of the restaurant. Dougie and a fat guy walked inside and stood at the bar checking around to find Dexter. The driver of the panel truck got out. Before leaving, he stopped and said something to someone who remained in the back of the truck. The driver walked around behind the restaurant parking lot toward Dexter and the Sarge. A Camaro or Firebird pulled into the restaurant parking lot and zoomed around back. It stopped right in front of the Sarge and Dexter. Dexter looked at the Sarge and said, "Sarge, none of the principals are going to show up, you know that. Let's kick ass!"

The old Sergeant wanted some action, too. He nodded his head and started to pass the green light onto the others. Dexter opened the door and stepped out with his FN semi-automatic rifle. The guy in the Camaro caught a glimpse of Dex and floored his car, screeching it out of the parking lot. The driver of the panel truck, seeing his buddy take off, turned around and ran between the parked cars to the back door of the restaurant.

Another car was just pulling in, but it made an about-face and left. The treachery in the underworld is legion. Dexter and his crew couldn't hang around, because maybe the bad-asses that left might call the cops on them. They were obliged to leave the scene. They weren't interested in a shootout with the cops. If it came as a result of having committed an offense, that was one thing; but if it was just stupidity, that was irresponsible.

The boys returned to the motel and did a little brainstorming. They were still going around in circles. The Sarge felt that sooner or later they were going to have a run-in with the police. Driving around with all that equipment, it was just a matter of time. He looked at Dex and said, "Do you believe in guardian angels, Dex?"

Dex smiled and shook his head.

"Do you believe in God, Dex?"

Dex looked at the Sarge; he was serious. Dexter didn't want to get into a religious discussion with him; but he answered honestly, "I think that God created the earth and man. I also think he looked down on what he had created and said, "To hell with it." He left a long time ago, and he's not coming back."

The Sarge looked at Dexter and said, "Son, I've never met an atheist in a foxhole. I'm beginning to think He's trying to tell us something."

"Oh yeah, Sarge, what's that?"

"I am beginning to think He's trying to tell us that He has special plans for these boys and we're not included in those plans. And if we don't heed what He's telling us, He will take us out of the picture!"

Dex looked at the Sarge. He was serious. Dexter thought maybe he was trying to say he wanted out. It was as though the Sarge read his mind. He spoke out again.

"I'm not telling you that we are gonna pull up stakes in the middle of the battle. I just want you to think about it. There should be more bodies than in a Turkish bath lying on the street, and yet there's not a one. It's not because those assholes are so brilliant or tough, and it's not because we're not trying. It seems to me it's just not in the cards. We are with you for the duration, Dex. I just want you to know, if at anytime you want to walk away, it's OK with us. Just keep it in mind, will ya."

Dex turned to the Sarge, nodded his head in acknowledgment, and then asked the Sarge a question.

"If you believe in God, how can you be a mercenary? How do you come to terms with killing people?"

"Easy enough," he said. "I killed lots of people in war. I didn't do it because I liked it, I did it to survive. When I was, 'back in country,' my best talent was soldiering. I hired out and supported one side of a war or another — did what I had to do. I hoped I was on the right side and all of that bullshit. Now you're in a drug war. You have impressed us, because you operate with a conscience. We saw that when you moved on the Duck. You gave him a chance, and the witness a chance. You can't be all that bad. Believe me, there are worse bastards in the bureaucracy than you. Ever hear of a soldier starting a war? The thing of it is, Dex, a war is a war. Your war is illegal because the government says so. When a government goes to war, who can say it's legal or otherwise? I believe in God, Dex. Maybe someday if you have the time, you'll see how He works in your life on a daily basis, too. I haven't read anywhere, not even in the Ten Commandments, that smuggling is illegal. You're supposed to give Caesar his due, but if he don't want it, to hell with him. To me, Dex, this war is like any other, except you pay your boys a hell of a lot better."

They all chuckled over the Sarge's punchline, and the conversation ended there.

They decided on two points of action. Dexter was going to drop off a note at the Dough Boy's house. He had been sitting back comfortably, watching the action undisturbed. Now they were going to disturb him. They told him to move his wife and kids out of the house. They didn't want to hurt innocent people. They were going to burn his house down around his ears. If he stayed there, it was his problem! The idea was to put pressure on him to settle. The second approach was to concentrate on the Old Bandit full time. Forget about everybody else. He had to be taken out if this thing was going to be settled. They went over the notes they had on the old cokehead.

There wasn't any definite pattern, but there were certain things he did that lead them to believe they might be able to predict where he would go or at least the general direction he would go in when he left a given spot.

The next day they packed a lunch and supplies and went on the road looking for the Old Bandit. They were on the road for forty-eight hours straight, catching some sleep in the van or their cars. People kept calling, telling them where he was last seen. Each time they got there, he was gone. They would move on to where they expected him to go next but no luck. He just disappeared. After their marathon effort, they decided to go back to the motel and get some proper rest. Dexter went home, but he only slept for a few hours. He decided to go back out on the road alone and drive around and try to get a bead on the Old Bandit.

He drove in an area where the Old Bandit hadn't been seen for a long while. Still nothing, not even a whisper of his whereabouts. Dexter decided to go back to the motel and rouse the boys for more canvassing.

On his way to the motel, he stopped at a traffic light. A blonde woman pulled up on his right in a Nissan 300ZX sports car. Dexter looked over at her. He saw a guy sitting in the passenger seat who looked like the Old Bandit. He looked again. It was the Old Bandit. When the Old Bandit looked over at Dexter, he shrunk down in his seat. Dexter rolled down the window on the passenger side, picked up the 357 magnum that was resting on the front seat and pointed it at the blonde bombshell. She looked over at Dexter and saw the barrel of the 357 pointed at her head. Dexter cocked the hammer back and took careful aim. He figured she would do what anybody would do if they saw a gun pointed at their head. She would duck! This would give him a clear shot at the Old Bandit.

Now, you have all heard the old wives' tale about blondes being dumb. Dexter will tell you it's not an old wives' tale — it's true! Instead of ducking, she turned sideways and stared down the barrel of the 357 magnum. She opened her mouth as if she were about to sing "Oh Happy Day" and froze in that position. Dexter was saying to himself, "Come on bitch, duck!" She continued to stare at Dexter, her mouth frozen in a perfect "O." All of a sudden the 300ZX lurched forward. The Old Bandit must have pushed her foot down on the accelerator. Dexter wound the Ford out, chasing after them. The 300ZX left the Ford in its dust. Dexter kept the gas pedal to the floor. He figured they were going to get on the expressway a half-mile down the road.

The blonde bombshell was not the greatest wheelman in the world. She slowed down as she entered the on-ramp to the expressway. It was one of those on-ramps that twists down and around almost in a complete circle. Dexter hit the on-ramp full tilt, his tires screeching and sliding. He makes up for the lost distance. By the time they hit the bottom of the ramp, he's practically on their bumper. He's hoping she'll move out to the middle lane or the passing lane so that he can move to the inside and have a clear crack at the Old Bandit in the passenger seat.

She stayed on the inside lane with Dexter on her bumper. Then Dexter sees the Old Bandit climbing out of the window of the car with a snub nosed thirty-eight in his hand. He started banging away at Dexter. Bullets were bouncing and pinging off his car. He slowed down and backed off. He continued to try to follow them, but even with the Ford humping along in excess of a hundred miles an hour, the 300ZX pulled away easily. Dexter lost sight of them off in the distance. All Dex could think about was the dumb blonde broad. He has never dated a blonde woman since.

The next morning Dex met with his crew. He told them of the previous night's episode. The only comment the old Sarge made when he heard of Dexter's exploit was, "I'll bet ya that's one broad who has gone from filet mignon to hot dogs."

Dex changed his rental car and went to see his old psychiatrist. He was a very professional, kind, refined old man. He had helped Dex sort out many of his problems. Dex had always been perfectly candid with him. He knew who Dexter was and what he did. He never sat in judgement. He had always tried to help Dexter deal with issues as Dexter presented them to him. He had Dexter's complete trust and confidence. The old shrink didn't specialize in criminality. He probably found Dexter a little refreshing after his usual clients who complained about their cat or dog not loving them any more. In any event, he did what he could to help Dexter untangle the mixed or screwed-up messages we all get from our families or friends or society, without offering a whole lot of advice. He just pointed Dexter in the direction he should look for his own answers, without being pious. He had made a profound change in Dexter's life. He had cracked the wall of denial Dexter lived in and made him look at life realistically. He probably never knew the great influence he had been on Dexter or the degree to which he had brought him out of a wilderness of confusion. Dex still wasn't home, but he was making progress.

The appointment wasn't about Dex. He wanted to see the psychiatrist about the Old Bandit. Dexter wanted to know what made him tick. He wanted to see if the old shrink could give him some kind of profile on the cokehead. He started off by saying he had a friend who had a serious problem with a guy who was a cokehead. He filled the shrink in on the details of the Old Bandit as best he could without dotting the i's or crossing the t's. He knew the old shrink wouldn't get involved in anything criminal, so he made his request in a general sense. After filling him in as best he could, he simply asked the shrink what he thought the cokehead's reaction would be under a given circumstance.

There was a bit of a Santa Claus sparkle in the old shrink's eyes as he leaned back in his chair, stared up at the ceiling and pondered the question. After several moments of contemplation, he sat up and leaned forward on his desk, his hands clasped together. A little smirk crept out to the corners of his mouth, and he said, "If your friend pushes his buttons one more time, he'll jump!"

Dexter hadn't told the old shrink his friend wanted to kill the guy. He made out that his friend was trying to get him to negotiate.

"Jump? Which way will he jump?"

"That I can't tell you. All I can tell you is that he will jump to a decision. It won't be well thought out or rational. He'll just jump to a decision. It may be that he'll sit down and negotiate with your friend or he may just run off. Don't expect a rational decision from him. He may sit down and settle the differences with your friend, or he may do something else. I have no idea which way he's going to jump! He will, however, panic and jump to a decision. That's the best I can do. Tell your friend to be careful!"

He sat down with his crew and discussed what the shrink had said. They decided to go on another marathon prowl to look for the cokehead. They figured he was not going to jump to negotiations, so they were going to have to cancel his seat at the table. They started out on their rounds. Dexter received a page on his beeper. He called the guy. The Old Bandit was having dinner at a restaurant called Papagallo's. They barreled over there — they knew where it was, they had missed him there once before. The two places they figured he would go to after leaving the restaurant were to a girl friend's house not more than a mile away, or to his other girlfriend's apartment that was about four miles away.

They arrived at the restaurant. The Sergeant went in and had a bite to eat. Cappers and Don parked their car on the street behind the restaurant. Dexter and the Beatle stayed in the van parked across the street. An hour later, the Sarge walks out and joins Dexter and the Beatle. The Old Bandit is sitting at the back of the restaurant, his eyes on the front door. There's another guy sitting at the back of the restaurant. He's on the other side of the room, with his back to the wall and eyes on the front door. The restaurant is packed. If they go in, innocent people are gonna get hurt. They decided to wait him out.

The restaurant closes at two o'clock in the morning. At one o'clock, the owner starts locking the front door and letting the people out slowly. No one goes in. The back door is well secured. They can't get in, so they sit and wait. At two o'clock, some of the employees leave; but still no sign of the Old Bandit. He was apparently having a coke party with the owner and some of the employees. They didn't know for sure, but that's what they heard later. The Beatle suggested they throw a grenade through the front window and go get him. The Sarge nixed that idea. Patience was running thin with everyone. The Sarge reminds everyone that this could be their last shot at the old bastard. He didn't want to blow it. He wanted it to be perfect, no if's and's or but's. They waited some more.

At three o'clock, the Old Bandit steps out and jumps into his car as quickly as a married man grabbing a strange piece of ass at lunch time. He races his car out of the parking lot. If he went to his right, he was going to his girlfriend who lived no more than a mile away. If he went to his left he was going to the girlfriend who lived about four miles away.

He banked to his left. Sarge radioed to Cappers and Don. They were on their way. They would take up a position near the apartment building's garage door. To get into the garage the Old Bandit would have to stop and put a key in the entrance box to open the door. He would be impossible to miss. Dex drove the van on another route that took them in front of the apartment building. They didn't think he would, but in case he parked his car on the street, he'd walk right toward them. Cappers radioed he was in position. Dexter parked the van on the street. He jumped in the back and the Sarge took the wheel. He leaned the seat back making it look as though the van was empty.

Cappers wanted to be sure he didn't miss. He got out of his car and crawled on his belly to the garage entrance key box. Cappers was so close that when the Old Bandit rolled down his window to put the key in the box, he could have shoved the barrel of the FN semi-automatic down the Old Bandit's throat. They weren't going to miss this time!

The Old Bandit pulled his car up and parked it fifty yards down the street from the boys waiting in the van. A block south of the apartment building was a large police station. It had as many as forty patrol cars going in and out at all times. This probably made the Old Bandit feel secure. If anyone attempted anything on this street they would have to continue on down past the police station. The boys didn't give a shit! The Old Bandit was going down, and that's all there was to it!

He started walking up the street toward the van. The Sarge was almost lying down in the front seat. He's looking through the steering wheel, marking off the distance the Old Bandit is away from the van. The Sarge is the one who will give the order when to make the move. The Beatle wanted to make the hit. Dexter overruled him. This was personal! The Beatle put his hands on the handle of the van's sliding door. When the Sarge gave the word, he would throw it open and Dexter would jump out blasting.

The Old Bandit was about five feet away from the van. The Sarge whispered, "Now!"

The Beatle yanked on the door. His hands slipped off the door handle. The clicking sound alerted the Old Bandit, who sprinted for a field between the apartment buildings. The Beatle grabbed the door handle again and ripped it open. It only opened a quarter of the way. Dexter had to stop and push it open enough to jump out. This couple of seconds delay gave the Old Bandit a thirty or forty-foot head start into the field. Dexter finally hit the street and opened up on the Old Bandit. The old cokehead kept on truck'n, bouncing and hopping through the field. Dexter didn't stop shooting until he had emptied the forty-shot clip. The Beatle, still in the back of the van, opened up with his nine-millimeter handgun, right over Dexter's shoulder. The Old Bandit kept hopping through the field like a bunny rabbit. Not a shot skinned him. Lights started going on in the apartment buildings. The Sarge whistled and Dexter climbed back into the van. As they moved out, he radioed to Don and Cappers to move out. Cappers wanted to wait. He figured the old bastard would come in by the garage on foot. The Sarge barked into the radio, "I said pull out. Pull out now!"

No one spoke on the way back to the motel. Don and Cappers walked in and sat down in chairs at the corners of the room. They hadn't said anything, but "What happened?" was written all over their faces. The Sarge grabbed a can of beer from the little fridge, tossed one to each of the boys, then sat in his chair beside the TV facing them and popped his open. Dexter sat in a chair on the other side of the TV. The Beatle was sitting on the edge of the bed with his head bowed down.

The old Sarge broke the silence. "Well we know how he's gonna jump. He jumps like a rabbit."

From then on they referred to the Old Bandit as the "Wabbit."

The Beatle was beating himself up. He couldn't believe how he had fucked up! He had opened the sliding panel door of the van a hundred times. Most times he would open it with two fingers. This last time, he had his whole hand on the handle. He wanted to fire the door open wide with laser-like speed for Dexter to clear the deck. He just couldn't believe how he had fucked up! The Sarge sat in his chair not saying a word. Two things came to mind. First of all, the Beatle was trying too hard to do everything right. It happens all the time. Sometimes we want so badly to do something perfect that we overdo it and invariably screw it up. "Murphy's Law" came into action.

The Sarge wasn't talking, but everyone knew what he was thinking. Surprisingly it was Don who summed it all up: "The Wabbit must be living his life at the foot of the cross."

The Sarge nodded his head in agreement. The Beatle and Dexter groaned, as if to say, "Don't start that again." The Sarge looked over at Dexter. He didn't say a word. He just looked over with that "I told you so" look. There really wasn't much else to say. It had been a long night. Dexter decided to go home and crash for some long overdue sleep.

Dexter felt that his last hope at cracking the opposition lay with the Duck's silent partner. He didn't want to jeopardize his crew, so he hired some guys to go and torch the Dough Boy's garage. Then they would wait to see what his reaction would be.

When the hired torchmen set fire to the Dough Boy's garage, they got the answer they didn't want. Fifteen unmarked cars came screaming out of nowhere, racing down the road to the Dough Boy's house. They were so eager to get there, they passed the torchmen on the road. It was as though they were expecting a shootout. All the cars were unmarked. Some of the cars had those flashing red lights in the grilles. The local police patrol cars didn't answer the call. Dexter wasn't there, but he checked out the story by talking individually to the three torchmen who were. Each one told the same story. The Sarge had been listening on the police scanner and had heard nothing. Dexter drove by the house and saw that the garage had indeed been well torched. It meant only one thing. The Dough Boy had rolled over to the Man.

Two days later they read in the newspaper that the horsemen found a truck with two tons of hashish. No arrests, just two tons of hash confiscated. Dexter walked out of his house. He saw the Man all over him, big time. He knew the game was up. If he persisted, it would only mean that he and the Sarge and the boys would all wind up in the can. He went to a pay phone and called the Sarge. He explained he had company. It was time to pack it in. The Sarge responded, "Dexter, someday you'll see. We just don't fit in with the Good Lord's plan. I'm telling ya, watch for it and you'll see. If you need us, you know how to get in touch. We'll work with ya any time."

Dexter was feeling depressed. He went back home, picked up his equipment and ditched it off to a friend, who in turn dropped it off at his stash. He took his wife and kids for a holiday in Mexico. He was long overdue for a change of scenery. He kept thinking about the Sarge's words. He didn't want to believe them, but they kept haunting the recesses of his mind.

When he returned from his holidays, he heard that the Duck had gone down on a charge totally unrelated to Dexter and was doing time. The Wabbit also got slammed on a beef that was not related to Dexter and he, too, was in the can. It seemed that those criminal geniuses were trying to make money in the middle of a war. Deals started going down on the wharf like hamburger patties on a grill at McDonald's. Dexter didn't follow it that closely. He didn't know if the Man just grabbed deals and no bodies, or if people went down with them, too. He checked on the Dough Boy. He had resigned his job on the docks and drifted off into the sunset. The Duck's business associate called Dexter up. He wanted to see him. Dexter stopped by his office unannounced. The Duck's friend had a message from the Duck. He was broke and in the can. He didn't want any more trouble with Dex. There were no hard feelings on his part. He just didn't want any more trouble with him. The friend also had the same message from the Wabbit. He was in shit up to his eyeballs, and he wanted bygones to be bygones. Dexter listened to the business associate and responded by saying, "It was all over money and if they're both broke, what's the point. Tell them I have hard feelings, but I'll let it slide. You can also tell them that if I ever hear of those guys having a wet dream about me, we'll pick up where we left off! When they come out of the joint — they walk their side of the street, and I'll walk mine."

Dexter had to cool his jets, because the Man stayed with him for quite a while after that. When the heat finally backed off, he went out west to see his friends. They were doing OK. They had started growing grass and life was mellowing out for them. Needless to say, they were available for Dex if he ever needed them. When he parted from the old Sarge, he was given a big bear hug and words of remembrance: "Dex, did you do any thinking about what I told ya?"

Dexter smiled, nodded his head and walked away. He had been doing a lot of soul searching, inspired by the Sarge's words.

RULE NUMBER ONE
THE LAW OF THE GUN

This is the first rule of the Drug Game. It always has been and always will be the first rule of the dark side. If you think you can play in the Drug Game and not adhere to this rule, forget it! This rule is often forgotten, overlooked or dismissed by people who think of themselves as too good to kill someone. Many people who play the Drug Game try to bullshit their way around this rule. It doesn't work. Sooner or later some shark is going to challenge you, and take a run at you, and you are going to have to defend yourself.

The majority of people in the Drug Game are in it for the money. They are not in it because they want to hurt or kill anybody. They are in it for the money! Dexter has met many who kid themselves that because they are small time dealers, they won't ever face a situation where they'll have to use deadly force. The smaller you are, the more likely someone is going to take a run at you. The closer to the street you are, the more vulnerable you are.

The higher up the ladder you go, the more respect you have. The little sharks out there know that if you're a big enough fish, you have the power to crush them. The higher up in the drug world you climb, the fewer sharks you have coming at you, but the sharks that do come are a hell of a lot bigger. No one in the Drug Game can escape the fact that, at some point, they are going to have to defend themselves against violence.

If people owe you money, or there's a problem with quality — whatever the case may be — never, never go to a meeting where you know there is a conflict without carrying a gun. Dexter is emphatic about that. In the drug world, a lot of people won't compromise, won't be flexible. In most cases, it's a question of greed or ego, and usually both! Generally speaking, guns will get you into more trouble than they'll get you out of; but there are situations where you'll need more than your mouth if you want to get out alive.

Unfortunately, there are people out there who try to solve most of their problems with violence, rather than by using their heads. You may be the kind of person who will use your head, try to work things out. Do not project that onto the other party. That's the way you are, and it's a good and proper way to be; but don't take it for granted that the other person is going to be equally cerebral. Chances are that if they think they can solve the problem quickly by using a gun, they'll use it. It's not a toy, and taking it out and playing with it or trying to impress people that you're some kind of bad-ass can only get you killed. Using a gun must always be the option of last resort, but an option you must be willing to use.

If you have to use a gun it means the situation has deteriorated to such a low level that you and the opposition have been reduced to basic instincts, such as that of simple self-preservation. Why take a gun if it means you have to act stupid and maybe use it? It is better to have a gun on you and not have to use it, than to be in a situation where other parties are going to use one on you, and you are sitting there with nothing but your dick in your hand. Not a good feeling! The Drug Game is about surviving.

Dexter once sat at a table on behalf of a small dealer who was about to get dumped. Mother had given a guy by the name of Sonny fifteen keys of hash. Sonny only paid Mother for ten. He said that his little dealer had ripped him off for five keys. Sonny was going to hit the small dealer for the supposed rip-off. When Dexter heard about it, he went to Mother. He said he wanted to sit down with Sonny and work the matter out. He knew the little dealer was honourable. He wanted Sonny to know where he stood.

Normally in the underworld, people mind their own business. Dexter adhered to this rule also, except in this case. He knew Sonny was a rip-off artist himself. He knew of some of Sonny's dirty dealings, but up till now he had always kept his nose out of it. Dexter didn't get involved out of pure altruism, he had a vested interest in keeping the little hash dealer healthy.

Mother called the table at the Zoo. He told Dexter and Sonny to come alone and not to be carrying any pieces. He was guaranteeing everyone's safety. Dex showed up and sat at a table at the back of the bar with Mother. Moments later, Sonny walked in with three guys. The three back-up men sat at another table with their backs to the wall, watching Sonny, Dexter and Duney at the other table. Mother cut right to the chase.

"Sonny, Dexter says the little dealer is honourable. He has spoken to him and he says you only gave him ten keys. He paid you for the ten keys the following day. He even told Dexter the denomination of the bills he paid you in. He knows nothing about the other five keys. He was afraid to come here, so Dexter is here on his behalf. You owe me for five keys. I want to get this thing resolved tonight."

Dexter spoke up. "Sonny, I've worked with this dealer for over five years. He has always been right on with his count, right to the gram. I won't allow anyone to take a run at him. Somebody touches him, they touch me."

Mother piped in. "Now relax boys, I'm sure this is all a misunderstanding. Sonny, do you think it's possible that your runner made a mistake? Maybe the five keys is still at your runner's stash?"

Mother was being diplomatic, and that's what a good peacemaker has to be when they are asked to hold a table. Sonny thought about it for a minute, then he said he'd verify the stash himself. It was obvious Sonny wasn't going to go to war over five keys of hash. Especially when he knew, and Dexter knew, that he didn't really lose the five keys.

Mother wasn't finished. He then laid into Sonny about bringing the back-up he had with him and also for carrying a gun. He had a thirty-eight stuck in his belt, and he let Dexter and Mother know he had it. Mother told him straight up that what he had done was disrespectful. Mother's word was gold, and here Sonny was ignoring it. Mother went on to say he wanted a solution immediately, right then and there. If either Dexter or Sonny should violate their word, the party doing the violating would answer to him! It was clear to both parties that Mother meant what he said. Sonny agreed to pay Mother the balance of the five keys the next day. He also gave his word that he would not touch the dealer, even if he couldn't find the five keys. They all agreed the matter was settled, and Sonny and crew departed.

After they left, Mother laid into Dexter. "You've got a big mouth, do you know that? Has anyone ever told you that before? I called this table to settle a problem intelligently. You saw his back-up walk in with him! You saw he was carrying a piece! Did you have to go bumping your gums like that? If any shooting starts here, I'm sitting between you and them. Are you nuts? I'm glad about one thing. At least you respected my word and didn't bring a piece with you."

Dexter bowed his head shyly, opened up his suit jacket, and showed Mother that he did indeed have a piece on him.

"You son of a bitch! You, too!"

Dexter laughed and said, "Mother, it's not about having no respect for you. I know that guy. I knew he wouldn't come alone and I knew he would be packing. He knows me, too, and he knew I wouldn't come alone and that I'd be armed also. It's not about you, Mother. I know that guy, 'way longer than you. I had to come prepared. He respects you, Mother, that's why he came to the table; but a leopard doesn't change his spots. You be careful with that guy. Never let him run such a high line of credit that he might decide to take a run at you."

Mother was a little miffed at both Sonny and Dexter, but Dexter knew he would blow it off. Dexter had his people outside watching his car, just to be on the safe side. It is just another example of how you never go to a meet without being prepared. It all worked out with no violence, but it could have gone the other way. If it had gone bad, Dexter was prepared.

A couple Dexter once knew were small grass and hash dealers. Nothing big, maybe a kilo every two or three weeks. They had regular jobs and peddled a little on the side to supplement the family income. They had a nice scam going for several years. For the most part, their customers were office people, working people like themselves. One night there was a knock on the door. The wife opened it and four punks came charging in. They stole a little grass and some hash. On their way out, they tied the man and his children up and then they gang raped the wife in front of the family. The man was not a violent person. He couldn't go to the police, because he was a drug dealer and so was his wife. The incident ruined their marriage and scarred all of them for life. They never dreamed it would happen to them because they were just punters.

The underworld is pure capitalism. Pure capitalism is no better than pure communism. It is the survival of the fittest and the strongest. In our western society, we live in a free democratic capitalist system. It is not pure capitalism. Our society has its checks and balances, anti-monopoly laws, price controls and so on. Pure capitalism has no checks and balances other than "might makes right." What makes might in the underworld is the Law of the Gun. If you don't live by the Law of the Gun, or if you are unable to accept it, you perish. It is as simple as that!

Beaucoup bodies never show up on the statistics chart, because the corpses are never found. The numbers are a hell of a lot higher than the reported deaths. Many are just listed as missing. Many others are just not reported!

Dexter saw others try to get around this rule by hiring someone to do the dirty work for them. Eventually it backfired on them. You may try and be the nicest, sweetest, most honest, straightforward-dealing person on this earth, figuring that will get you by. It won't! A lot of people play the Drug Game without having to resort to violence. And because they are successful, they think they can get away with it forever. They don't! They will eventually have to accept huge financial losses, go to the can or die. Don't bullshit yourself or others. You will be tested; and when you are, bullshit walks and action talks.

A young man Dexter once knew was a runner for a fair-sized coke dealer in the East End of town. One day they sold two keys of coke to a party on the other side of town. The runner delivered the coke and returned to his boss. The next day the people returned the coke. They said the quality was not what was promised. The boys in the East End checked out their coke and found that it had been stepped on. They knew their coke was not cut, because they imported it directly from Colombia. Everyone had their backs up, and the guns were ready to come out of the closet. Two days later the runner was blown up in his car. The people on the other side of town admitted doing it, because they held the runner responsible for the cut coke. He was killed because he was the one responsible for all the problems. The people from the East End of town went to Dexter for some information on the people who had blown up their runner. Dexter checked it out for them and told them they were no good. They were sleazebags; however, they were dangerous sleazebags. It was obvious that the runner was totally innocent. The people in the East End didn't go to war; they had lots of coke to sell, and besides they would peddle the cut coke in o.z.'s and make their money back. They reasoned that a war with a group of deadly sleazebags wasn't worth the trouble or the financial effort. The runner was written off.

The young runner never carried a gun in his life. He was not a violent person. He had proven his honesty over the years. Things like that happen all the time in the drug world.

The only reason a shark will stop its attack is if he knows you play by the rules, all the rules. When the sharks do take a run at you, they only get one shot at the roses. If they miss, you're coming back! If they don't, well, your troubles are over anyway. If you can't live by the Law of the Gun, you can't back up your action. If you can't back up your action…

CHAPTER ELEVEN
PAY ATTENTION TO DETAILS

Dexter's Rule Number Nine is a rule that is all too often overlooked. "Details," Dexter says, "Most guys don't pay attention to the details." Chances are, you're not going to go to jail because you didn't see a major issue. Everybody recognizes big issues. For example, the police park a regular patrol car in front of your house. When you leave your house, you see that it is following you everywhere you go. You are not going to miss that, and you don't need a warrant for your arrest to tell you that you have heat. You'll obviously back off from whatever it is you are doing or going to do. Why? Because to continue is suicide. That's an exaggerated example, of course. The point is that you should be able to spot a major problem when it's in front of you.

It's very rare for a big issue to put you in the can. It's the small details you have to pick up on. It was his attention to the small details that made Dexter a difficult target for the police. Many people Dexter befriended were just too lazy or too goofy to pay much heed to the small details. They paid for it by spending years and years in jail. Some of these slowly, in drips and drabs, doing life on the installment plan; others by taking a big hit right off the top.

Paying attention to the small details will increase the percentages against getting caught. Ignore them and you'll wake up one morning with your life in a toilet bowl.

Dexter learned how to listen to people when they talked to him. Sociologists will tell you that most people don't really listen to what other people are saying to them. They half listen. This is true in the legit world as well as the criminal world. For example, a man asks a woman out on a date. The woman hears the man asking her to get laid. A man asks a woman to get laid and the woman hears the man asking her to marry him. People don't really listen to what another person is saying to them. If they did, they would hear an awful lot more and perhaps get the real sense of what the person is saying to them. It is so simple, and yet so few people actually listen attentively to what is being said to them.

Dexter saw an ad in the newspaper for a continuing education course in communication offered by a local college. It was open to the public. It was an eight-week course, two hours a night, two nights a week. Dexter took it out of curiosity. It was one of the most enlightening courses he ever took. It wasn't difficult or even demanding. The professor demonstrated how people don't listen. He selected students out of the class and gave short examples of how one or the other hadn't listened.

Dex met a person he had known for a long time, a guy he trusted completely. He'd never had any occasion not to. They were making small talk when Dexter realized that the guy was asking questions more than making statements. This can be a normal course of events in any conversation, but it was out of character for his friend. He wasn't the inquisitive type.

From out of nowhere, the friend asks Dexter if he knows a guy by the name of the Colonel. Dexter knew him. He was a player in a city over a hundred miles away. He would come to Montreal now and again to score some hash, grass or whatever. Dexter's friend didn't explain why he was asking about the Colonel, he just asked Dexter if he knew him and waited for Dexter to run off at the mouth.

Dexter's answer was a simple yes. He didn't volunteer anything else. The friend comes up with another question about the Colonel. He asked Dexter if he had seen the Colonel around. From the two abrupt questions the guy had asked, and also his sly demeanor, Dexter knew he was fishing for some information. Dexter thought that his friend was behaving strangely. If he wanted to know something about the Colonel, why didn't he just fill Dexter in? Maybe he had a problem with the Colonel, or maybe the Colonel owed him some money, or maybe he just wanted to meet with him. His friend didn't have to go into details, but as he and Dex were good and trusted friends, he could have been a little more forthright. Dexter found his friend's approach weird. He decided to throw him a little curve. Although there was only one "Colonel," Dex asked him if he was talking about the tall skinny Colonel or Colonel Bill. The guy was stumped. He didn't know if the Colonel was tall and skinny or what his name was.

Dexter started getting uneasy vibes. He now noticed how his friend's conversation turned to other friends and associates of Dexter. His friend was normally guarded, but now he was being a very inquisitive boy. Dexter decided to terminate the conversation and leave. Dex then did a little snooping around on his own. He inquired along the grapevine to find out if anything could explain his friend's strange behaviour. The word was that he was broke and he had a coke beef. People didn't seem to know too much about his coke beef. There were at least three different stories: that he'd been busted; that he'd just been pulled in; and that he'd been pulled in, charged and then released. The details of his friend's problems were at best sketchy; no one seemed to have the straight story.

Dexter's guard was piqued when his friend started asking questions about people he didn't even know. Why would he be asking questions about people he didn't know? The only answer Dexter could think of was that the Man had put him up to it. Dexter wasn't a hundred percent sure the guy was a stool. At the time, he kept his suspicions to himself. The only way you ever really know that a rat is a rat is when the bastard stands in court and points the finger at you. Then it's too late, it's all over but the crying.

It was a small detail in their conversation that alerted Dexter to the possibility that the guy might not be kosher. Prior to the conversation, he had trusted the guy implicitly. If his friend hadn't slipped up, Dexter would have done business with him. His conversation seemed odd, especially coming from a person who should have known better than to be playing twenty questions. Dex got bad vibes, so he stayed away from him. He didn't run around accusing the guy of anything. He just stayed away from him.

Later a rumor made the rounds that the inquisitive friend had set some people up on a bust, and that had bought him a shallow grave. Whatever, he's not around anymore and nobody cares. Not all rats make it to the courtroom or live long enough to collect their pensions.

By paying attention to what people were saying to him, Dexter was able to hear discrepancies in their stories. Many times it was nothing major — we all bullshit a little bit now and again. When it's a serious matter, then it's entirely different. Many times stool pigeons give themselves away by screwing up on the small details. Even the cops make small mistakes. Dexter found that, by being alert, he could pick up on the snakes crawling around after his freedom in exchange for theirs. Often it was some small detail that would tip him off about something not being right with the person. The difference between criminals and the cops is that they can make a hundred mistakes, but most times criminals can't afford one.

Most people in the Drug Game are self-centered hedonists who care about number one, and only number one. You can pick this up just by listening to them. Most criminals have no interest in the plight of people elsewhere in the world. They're quick to tell you what they want out of life; but you never hear them say how fortunate they are to have what they have. They don't appreciate what they have. Their attention is on themselves.

Dexter recalled an associate who bragged about ripping someone off, cheating some asshole out of his end or whatever. He thought he was smart. Dexter could tell from that conversation that the associate was not to be trusted. He never did business with him because he knew that he'd try to rip him off the first chance he got.

Little details make all the difference to a smuggler. If the paperwork is wrong or some minor detail is incorrect, it may alert customs to look into the shipment. One time, Dex was doing a deal from India. He had a shipper in India who was a well-known exporter to Canada and a well-established importation company in Canada to receive the shipment. They sent the deal in and it was busted. It wasn't the fault of the exporter. He was clean. The paperwork was done correctly. They couldn't figure out why they had a problem clearing the shipment. It seems the Canadian importer was on the blacklist. He was suspected of having done a shot with another crew. When customs punched the shipment into the computer, the importer's name came up on the blacklist. No one was arrested with the bust, but the shipment was lost — all because of a minor detail that Dexter was unaware of. The importer had never mentioned he'd had a brush with customs several years back. He had considered it a small detail, because he hadn't been arrested or even questioned by police. He had, however, been queried by customs and that was enough to put his company on the watch list.

Another crew lost a deal because the Canadian importer was going broke and had not paid overdue customs duties from a previous shipment. When their deal came in, it was seized. When the importer came up with the money he owed, it was too late. Customs had already started snooping through the shipment, and bingo!

On one occasion Dexter was meeting an associate to discuss business. They decided to meet out of town, go for a walk on a nature trail and talk there. The associate shows up with his runner. Dex and the friend go for a walk down the nature trail. The runner stays ten to fifteen feet behind them as they go strolling along. The friend had brought his runner with him because he had something to do later. Dexter didn't introduce himself to the runner. His friend understood that it was because Dexter was always cautious about meeting new people. He asked his friend to tell the runner to distance himself from them a little. He didn't want the runner to be a party to their conversation. As they walk slowly down the trail they are passed by other nature lovers who are moving along faster. All of a sudden the runner comes up to his boss and says in a low whisper, "Cops."

Dexter and his friend look around casually, but don't see anything. An elderly couple had passed them earlier on, but they were way out of sight by now. A younger couple had passed briskly by them and were well out of listening distance by now and continuing on their way. There was an old white-haired lady gathering leaves and acorns, but she looked to be in her sixties and harmless. Dex and his friend turned back to the runner, who was now standing with them. Dex's friend asked, "Where?"

The young man leaned in close and said, "The old lady with the leaves: look at her shoes!"

Turning around nonchalantly, Dex and his friend looked at the old lady's shoes. She was wearing high-heeled shoes in a nature park. They cut their conversation short and agreed to meet later on, when the heat blew off. Neither Dexter nor his friend had seen any steam on them that day, but they knew the young man was right. Women don't go walking down nature trails in high-heeled shoes. It would have been easy for Dexter to have dismissed the runner's observation as meaningless. Experience had taught him the danger of attempting to put things that are out of place into proper perspective. He knew that rationalizing his instincts and observations away was a ticket to trouble.

Two days later, Dexter had a meeting in a coffee shop he had never been in before. He sat down and ordered a coffee. Five minutes later the old lady he had seen on the nature trail came strolling in, accompanied by a man about the same age. They sat two tables away from Dexter. Dexter gulped down his coffee and left. The friend he was scheduled to meet entered the restaurant as he was leaving. Dexter made eye contact with him and walked right on by. The associate knew what that meant. He continued into the restaurant, ordered a coffee and read his newspaper. Dexter cancelled all his meetings and hustle until the heat backed off. Why did Dexter have so much steam? Maybe some stool pigeon dropped his name, maybe the Man had information he was up to something, maybe someone intentionally dropped his name on a phone to give him steam, who knows? The only thing of importance for Dexter was that he had heavy surveillance, and that meant it was time to fold his tent and wait for another day, week, month or year.

What saved his bacon was the observant runner noticing a small detail like the old lady's shoes. Small details can make you or break you all the time. Many people in the Drug Game are too lazy to even pay attention. Their laziness usually results in their having lots of time to sit around on their duffs in the bucket. Going to the can is no badge of honour, although some winners seem to think it is!

One way to spot a cokehead, is their gall in telling outrageous lies. It also tells you something about the drug itself. Dexter learned to listen and watch for the small details in their stories. He was able to see quickly where they were coming from. Cokeheads may keep the big picture of their story in focus but the little details will change like leaves on a tree in the autumn.

Whenever Dexter was introduced to someone for the first time, he was on his toes. Sometimes the cops use stool pigeons to introduce undercover cops. That way, they get in on the ground floor or closer to you than you would like. Sometimes they stand up in court, but mostly they work behind the scenes and that's what makes their betrayal so deadly. If a guy says he met

Harry in such-and-such a joint or in jail and he's relying on Harry's reputation as a good guy in order to do business with you, check it out, listen to the details. He may say he met Harry inside in nineteen-ninety or whatever. Find someone who was in the bucket in nineteen-ninety. Ask around. If it comes back tilt, stay away. Do you really need more friends? Dexter would ask himself if it makes sense for the guy to make the intro just out of the goodness of his heart. If the small details didn't add up, then Dexter might decide he has enough friends already. If there's an angle, you'll see it by the details of the conversation. Dexter saw many of his friends go down for some big time, all because they ignored the street rule about details.

Dex had a good friend who was in the can. He heard the guy was having a rough time in the joint because he was broke. The friend got transferred to a minimum security center. Dexter visited him, and in the process he smuggled in a pound of hash. It was an opportunity for his friend to put some money in his kick. It was a gift to his friend, not a business proposition. The friend was thrilled and thanked Dexter heartily. Dexter made it clear that he did not intend to start smuggling hash into the joint. It was a one-time deal to give his buddy a boost.

A month later the guy's wife calls Dexter and asks him to go see her husband, he said it was important. Dexter visited his friend. They sat outside in the yard and shot the breeze. All of a sudden, his friend waves a guy over to their table. The friend introduces the guy as the salt-of-the-earth, a real solid dude. They shake hands and the guy sits down at the table with them. The conversation turns to hash and how this guy has an "in." Dexter knows where the conversation is leading. When they finish talking, they turn to Dexter. Dexter tells them he can't help them. He doesn't have any hash, and he can't get any. He was really pissed off at his friend for introducing the salt-of-the-earth to him. They tried to abba dabb around the conversation. Dexter cut it short and left. The following week his friend was called up to the front office. He blew ten days' good time because the salt-of-the-earth was a stool pigeon who had informed the front office of what Dex's friend was up to.

When the friend got out of prison, he went to see Dexter. He was gregarious, a great personality and solid as the Rock of Gibraltar; but he was a goof. He would talk on telephones (in code of course) and rationalize whatever didn't suit him. In the end, Dexter realized that his good friend was a very self-centered individual who didn't give a damn about anyone but himself.

His friend thought that because he was solid, it gave him a pass on stupidity. By listening to the details of his conversation, Dexter realized what kind of person his so-called good friend really was. His exuberant personality dazzled all those who came in contact with him. It was only by listening to the meat of his conversation that one could see through the facade. He was an accident looking for a place to happen. Many people tried to give him a chance, but because he was really only looking out for number one and never giving a thought about anyone else, he fucked up more opportunities than a doorman working in a bordello. He would try to buy people, so that they would like him, so that he could control them. If he couldn't buy you, he felt threatened by you. Naturally, you can't buy real friends. He rejected those that might have been real friends in favour of the takers who were much like himself, along for the ride at someone else's expense. They are out there. You won't see them unless you learn to listen and pick up on the little details.

Dexter's friend the Grump had some small dealers who would sell two to three keys a week. The Grump would supply them with whatever they needed. One time, one of them asks the Grump for thirty keys. The Grump mentions it to Dex. He looks at him and asks him to explain. The Grump says that a long-standing client of the little dealer wants to buy ten keys, cash up front, and he'll take another ten the following week. Dexter asks the Grump how much this long-standing client usually bought. He responded that the guy would usually buy a hundred to two hundred and fifty grams — roughly half a pound — at a time.

Dexter tells the Grump the guy is a cop. The Grump passes the tip on to the dealer. The dealer, motivated by greed, doesn't listen. The Grump won't front him the hash, so he takes his business elsewhere. Eventually, the dealer goes down for trafficking in hashish. The long-standing customer was an undercover police officer. The courts are jammed up. They don't want to be bringing people in for a hundred or two hundred grams of hash or grass. It's a waste of everyone's time. Dexter was very wary when people suddenly went from one level to another. It applied to the bigger dealers as well. If a guy normally buys ten or twenty keys, watch out if he tries to move up overnight to fifty or a hundred. You can extrapolate that on up. In the coke game the numbers are smaller but the formula is the same.

The rules of the game don't change with the name of the drug.

Dexter says that small details are the cornerstone of the big picture. They can clue you in to a person's angle and that'll save your ass every time. If you are too lazy to make the effort to pay attention, and thereby overlook the small details, you'll pay the price. Unfortunately, you may be the cause of many of your friends' downfall too.

Dexter would often size up a person by how they dressed. A fifty-year-old man who wears running shoes and a gold chain around his neck is a loser. Many of the younger people today dress as though they picked up their clothes at the jailhouse laundry. How a person dresses is a reflection of what's going on inside. If you dress like a loser, you'll act like a loser; and eventually you'll become a loser. You don't have to go around with a blue suit, shirt and tie all the time, but you shouldn't go around dressed like a loser all the time either. It is not a question of being an old fuddy-duddy. It's a matter of your personal image. Yes, you can dress funky and casual at times, but not all the time. If you are too lazy to make a small effort about your personal appearance, what is going to inspire you to make the effort to play the game by the rules?

How you dress may seem like a small detail, but it's a proven fact that your clothes affect your self-confidence. When you feel good about yourself, your mind is more alert. When you dress up the outside, the inside shines, too. When Dexter sees young people walking around with their pants hanging down to the crack in their ass, he knows their head is not far away from their pant line. Dress as if you have been defeated, and defeat is not far off.

Frequently, old-timers just released from prison will show up at a bar or one of the hang-outs trying to look hip, trying to get back into the action. If you knew them before they went to the can, you knew them as smart dressers. Now, when you meet them, they are wearing running shoes, jeans, a t-shirt and maybe a baseball cap. Dexter recognizes it immediately: the system, the years, the life, has beaten them down, and now they are going on instinct; much like a boxer who keeps on swinging even though he's knocked out on his feet. They don't have the sense to quit, and they think they can fit in by dressing like a bum. After all, for the last ten or fifteen years all they wore was jeans and sneakers. They feel comfortable with the beat-up look, because they have been thoroughly beaten by the system.

You're right — it's a small detail — but those small details are what have kept Dexter and his friends from going down big time. Ignore the details and you'll be working on one before you know it! Dexter doesn't think of this attitude as snobbery, it's a simple observation that over the years has guided him away from problem people and from trouble. When Dexter walks into a restaurant or bar, he checks to see who comes in five or ten minutes after him. He watches where they sit, watches what they eat or drink. Again, it is not a question of being intelligent, it is simply a matter of being observant. It is a matter of practice.

When Dexter thinks he's being tailed, he doesn't make his suspicions obvious to those who may be following him. Sometimes guys realize they are being tailed and being smart asses, they let the cops know that they see them. Dexter has found that this only aggravates the cops and turns up the heat. Being a smart ass doesn't pay. If you're charged and it comes out in court that you demonstrated to the police that you were aware of being followed, then the judge can rule that you were acting in a counter-surveillance manner. Square-johns don't do counter-surveillance and neither should you! To many, Dexter is a mystery, to Dexter, he's just an average Joe, trying to make ends meet in a tough game.

RULE NUMBER NINE
DETAILS

Do not judge the value of the rule by the size of the chapter. Watching out for small details was essential to Dexter's survival in the Drug Game. Living his life by these rules molded his character and his personality and undoubtedly his success. Each rule is vitally important and each rule is dependent on another. When Dexter ignored one, he found the rest collapsed like dominoes. Dexter likes to say, "If you walk around looking and acting like an asshole, remember there's a place for assholes — it's called the can!"

CHAPTER TWELVE
THE LAW AND THE LAWYERS

No one would ever consider playing a game of football, baseball or hockey without knowing the rules. You would never consider placing a big bet on a game in which we didn't know the percentages. When you play the Drug Game, you're making the biggest bet of your life. You are, in fact, betting your life. Most people who gamble with their lives in the Drug Game never stop to consider the odds of their being successful; they don't know the rules so they can't begin to understand all that is against them. Dexter felt he should, at the very least, know something about the law. It is definitely an important part of the game. You don't have to have a college degree in law, but you should know some pertinent facts. Ignorance of the law is not an excuse, nor can it be used in your defense. For example, pissing in the park is not against the law. Pissing in the park on the flowers is. A small difference perhaps, but in the Drug Game a small difference can be all the difference in the world.

A prominent lawyer once told Dexter that the law is very ambiguous. It is subject to interpretation by a judge and a jury, by the prosecution and the defense. The law is not cut and dried, it is not black and white. It is, in most instances, shades of gray.

The hook that law enforcement agencies most frequently use to convict people is the law of conspiracy. It is the easiest law to be convicted on and the one least understood by players and punters in the Drug Game.

Whether they're on the fringes of crime or deeply involved, most people in the underworld are concerned about "possession." A valid concern no doubt. Naturally, if you are caught in possession of an illegal substance you are history in ninety-nine percent of the cases, except in rare circumstances such as those where the police make an illegal search. People are, therefore, constantly mindful of what they are doing when they take possession of a drug. It should not be necessary to elaborate on this particular aspect of the law. You simply have to keep in mind that possession is nine-tenths of the law.

When you buy a drug, sell a drug or transport a drug, you are up to your ass in alligators if something goes wrong! You obviously know that because at that point, you are in possession!

Conspiracy to import, buy, sell or traffic in drugs is probably the least understood law of the land and the one most voraciously applied. Under the conspiracy law, you can be in possession of a drug without actually being in possession of the drug. How does that work? Let's use this example. An individual approaches you and offers to sell you grass, hash, coke or whatever. You sit down with that person and agree to purchase the drug. Even though you don't know where the drug actually is at that present time, you are deemed to be in possession of the drug, because you now have control over the drug. You have control over the drug, because you and the other party have reached an agreement for the sale and purchase of the drug. If the Crown Prosecutor (District Attorney in the U.S.) can prove that you had an agreement to purchase the drug, you are guilty of conspiracy to traffic in drugs as well as possession of drugs. How does the law prove this? By wire taps or by using quislings to stool on you. By rolling over, the informers cut themselves a better deal in court. The rules of proof of conspiracy are very elastic. They vary according to the country, state or province you are in. When Dexter saw many of his friends and associates going down because of the conspiracy law, he vowed to be less talkative and more attentive to his surroundings. Conspiracy itself occurs when two or more individuals make an agreement for the sale or purchase of a drug or participate in the negotiation of a drug transaction. It's not conspiracy if, when someone offers to sell you a drug, you say "no" or "I'll think about it." But if you say, "How much? When?" or "Where can I get it?" You have entered into negotiations and an agreement for the sale or purchase of the drug. You are guilty of conspiracy even if you don't take possession of the drug! The simple fact that you agreed to the purchase or sale of the drug may well be enough to send you to the can for a very long time. Dexter learned that in law, the word "agreement" is not cast in cement.

Many people are convicted of conspiracy, not because of something they said but because of what other parties have said. For example, someone offers to sell you a drug. You say, "I'll think about it." They leave. Then they tell someone else or discuss with someone else, on a hot telephone or in a bugged car or house, that you are thinking about buying such-and-such. You have no knowledge of this conversation, and you are not a party to the conversation. The person comes back to you and you agree to buy the drug.

Once again, the numbnut you are dealing with talks to his partner or associates on the phone. He or she says that you are going along with the proposition, "Set everything up for tomorrow."

You are not aware of this conversation and you are not a party to it either. You weren't even present when the guy made the remark or the phone call. Let us say that during the night you changed your mind. You meet with the guy the following day and tell him you are not interested. That very same day, he and his associate go down somewhere else with the drug. You are arrested and charged with conspiracy. What proof do the police have? Let us assume the guy or gal you were dealing with is solid. They won't roll over and sign a confession implicating you and they won't take the stand against you in court. You're home free, right? Wrong!

You may be on your way to the bucket for five or ten years. Why? Because the conversations the dealer had on the phone with his associate can and will be used against you. Add this to the meetings you had with the individual, and it's good-bye. If the Crown Prosecutor (or District Attorney) can prove you had knowledge of the drug and that you had meetings concerning the purchase of the drug, chances are you're history. How can they prove what you and the dealer were talking about? The Crown doesn't have to prove what you were talking about, because the definition of "conspiracy" takes into account the circumstantial evidence and matches it to the drug dealer's telephone conversations. They use those telephone conversations against you. Do people who are not guilty ever get sent to prison because of the conspiracy law? You bet. It happens more times than you would care to imagine! How is it that such an ambiguous law can be administered in such a callous way? To a large degree it is the paranoia that comes with the drug cult permeating our society. The bottom line was that Dexter became very sensitive to this approach by the Man. For Dexter and his friends, it meant keeping their circle tight and their conversations on the telephone to a bare minimum. You have drugs stashed at a runner's house. You have been observed in the company of the runner and in constant contact with the runner via telephone. Then the runner goes down with the drugs in his house. Although you have never touched the drugs, nor been to the runner's house, you are deemed to have had covert conversations with the runner on the telephone.

A covert conversation is one in which people are talking in codes. Let's say you said, "Bring ten black cars to number two's tomorrow. Mr. Rocket says you must be going to Weight Watcher's because you lost about two hundred and fifty grams in weight. Stop by and see me, I want you to explain your loss in weight."

If you are standing before a judge, you had better be in the automobile business or a member of Weight Watcher's yourself. The judge isn't stupid. If you can't explain the conversation in a rational manner, he will accept the prosecution's argument that you were indeed engaged in covert talk. If he decides that, then he will probably find you guilty under the conspiracy law!

Not having a college degree in law, Dexter made the effort to learn the law more fully. He didn't wait until he was sitting in a prison doing twenty-five years to start researching the law. Many people without a formal education who have gone to prison for long stretches become experts in the law in order to defend themselves. They are commonly referred to as jail-house lawyers, and many of them can walk circles around lawyers who have their sheepskins hanging on the wall. Dexter learned about the law by talking to other criminals about how they were convicted. He stopped by a library and read up on the generalities of the law. He asked a lawyer questions about the law, without telling him he was doing such-and-such. If he had, then the lawyer would have been guilty of "conspiracy."

When Dex was uncertain as to where he stood in a particular situation vis-à-vis the law, he would ask a lawyer. He would give the lawyer a hypothetical situation involving a mythical "friend" who was charged with a crime, or he would say, for instance, that this "friend" had been approached with a drug deal proposition, and he wanted to warn him of the dangers, maybe talk him out of it. Dexter would then take action according to what the lawyer told him. He wanted his lawyer's opinion as to how his friend stood. Depending on the lawyer's response, Dexter would then act accordingly. Sometimes he would pay the lawyer a retainer and wait for the shit to hit the fan.

Most who get involved in the dark side have an aversion to education. They believe that if they live long enough and are lucky enough not to take a fall, they will eventually graduate with a Ph.D. from the streets, from the University of Life. They scorn education. It's a waste of time. Education is for nerds. Education is for the weak, not for the tough, smart, street people. To most, their formative years in school were a joke, a waste of time. They were itching to get out onto the streets and make money, to get into the action. When a teacher said that a college graduate made X amount more money than a person without a college degree, they'd laugh and sneer. What did he or she know about making money? A drug dealer could make more money in two years on the street than a college graduate could make in two lifetimes. Education was a waste of time. Most people who get involved in the Drug Game trash their time in school, because they see little use for it on the street. Many leave school without having the ability to read, or write or calculate. They think, and say, that you don't need it on the street. This was what Dexter thought when he was young. However, the more experience he gained on the street, the more he realized how important an education is. The more he regretted having wasted the opportunity to acquire one.

By arming himself with an education, Dexter enhanced his ability to survive in the Drug Game. It didn't make him any smarter, just more aware of life and all its variables. If you're just a small player or punter from a background that gave you no advantages or privileges, there are all kinds of grants, scholarships and government loans to help you get an education. In Dexter's opinion, playing on the dark side without an education is like jogging down the middle of a four-lane expressway hoping you won't get run over! Take it to the bank, you'll get creamed! You don't have to be a brilliant student, you don't have to be a Rhodes Scholar, but you do have to know how to read well, write well, and handle numbers, and think. Education is a form of exercise for the mind. In jails and prisons across the land, inmates exercise daily with weights. They take care of their bodies by exercising. What do they do for their minds? Exercising your mind is just as important as exercising your body. In the Drug Game, Dexter found that if your mind is not quick enough to grasp a situation, the sharks will sense it and either use you or set you up. If your mind is not performing well, you become easy pickings for the Man. Take your choice, the sharks or the Man, one of them will get you if you don't exercise your brain every day. Dexter decided it was better to exercise his mind on the outside than to exercise his body in a cage.

Dexter learned not to scoff at the opportunity to educate himself, and not to put down those who made the effort to learn. Those who did have the common sense to want to better themselves and survive, by educating themselves, were the ones he wanted to team up with. If you're going to associate with someone, do it with a winner, not a loser!

To Dexter, being a winner meant making the effort, whether in track and field, hockey, football, basketball or whatever. Winners make the effort, losers are too lazy or feel too sorry for themselves to try. It is easier to make excuses than it is to make the effort. Dexter discovered that most people in the underworld prefer to make excuses for their shortcomings, rather than make an effort to improve themselves.

The longer you play the Drug Game successfully, the more apt you are to be considered a part of "organized crime." Persons who the law deems to be "organized criminals" get heavier time than those who constantly revolve in and out of the penal system. Therefore, being successful in crime doesn't give you bragging rights; and if you do brag, you pay a hefty price. When the Man does nail you, you are gonna go down a lot harder and a lot longer because you were successful! In Dexter's case he found that the Man was a lot more willing to make the extra effort to nail him because, as a successful criminal, he was considered a part of "organized crime."

Edward L. Greenspan, a noted criminal defense attorney in Canada and author of the book, *The Case for the Defense*, has made many interesting observations about criminals and the law. Allow me to share two of his observations with you.

"When criminals conspire, they most often conspire with other criminals. After all, who else would they conspire with? They can't conspire with priests or philosophy professors. They can't conspire with law-abiding people in any walk of life. So, as a rule, they will conspire with contacts they have made during a previous stint in prison, or maybe with childhood friends. They conspire with people they think they can trust. One needs an introduction to the world of crime in much the same way as one needs an introduction to high society."

He goes on to make the point that criminals are often labeled "organized crime" people because of their ethnic backgrounds. Italians are assumed to belong to the Cosa Nostra, Jamaicans to Posse Gangs, Jews to the Jewish Syndicate and so on. When people are labeled in such a manner it is easier for the prosecution to demand stiffer sentences.

Being successful in crime has its perks and its pitfalls. You shouldn't think that because you're only a successful punter, you're not significant. The minute society labels you as a member of organized crime, the price on your head goes up!

The second observation I wish to share with you from Mr. Greenspan is:

"It is in the interest of informers to keep accusing other people of crimes. Their living, and at times their lives, depend on it. When they stop, so does the money and perhaps the protection of the authorities (or the money and attention from the media in a few high-profile cases). This does not mean that informers never tell the truth about their former associates; it only means that they lie about them often and easily. They lie about them for profit, and they lie about them to save their own skins. As a defense lawyer I have always been concerned with anyone having to face a charge based on the evidence of a former criminal associate, without corroboration or at least confirmation by some independent evidence..."

A stool pigeon or rat gives tainted or self-serving evidence. As stated before, the jacket the police build on a criminal is filled with information supplied by informants. You may well be a major "organized crime" figure in their eyes. You don't know what the hell the bureaucracies have in their computers on you. The point is, don't ever consider yourself a small insignificant player, especially if you haven't read your jacket! This was a lesson Dexter had a hard time accepting. He never considered himself a big player or a part of "organized crime." When he read his jacket, he didn't recognize himself.

Some judges pimp themselves and prostitute the law when they allow their own personal prejudices to circumvent the legal process. They are human beings and subject to the same frailties as the rest of us. A good lawyer will have more than just a superficial opinion about the judge who is going to preside over your case and your life. It is an integral part of a lawyer's repertoire of defence. For instance, your lawyer should know if there's a particular judge who is weak on the law and ignorant of the drug problem that exists in our society. That is to say, if you are brought before a judge on a drug charge, and the judge has a reputation for being particularly severe, unfair and close-minded when it comes to drug offences, then your attorney should do whatever he or she can to get a change of venue. Some judges are nothing more than political hacks. They have no respect for themselves, their profession or the law. They kiss ass to get their appointment (or in the United States, to get elected). They are ignorant of the law, and the result is a vigilante approach to justice, which they propagate as a result of their own ignorance.

A good attorney not only has to know the law, he must also know his adversaries as well. If a judge is a proper judge, that is to say, respects himself or herself, respects the law, and what goes on in the courtroom, then your attorney has but one adversary, the prosecution. If the judge is arrogant, prejudicial and biased against the defense from the outset, you've got troubles. If your attorney is any good, he or she will not be intimidated by a judge. If he or she is weak in the courtroom, your chances for victory are also weak. If you listen carefully, you'll hear the jailer's keys jingling in the background. Dexter believes that knowing his attorney is as important as it is for a boxer to know how to box.

There is a small select group of top-notch attorneys in Montreal, and that is also true in most cities around the world. A top-notch attorney is worth his salt, and a lousy one is not worth having. But an attorney is only as good as his client. If you are arrested and the evidence against you is overwhelming, don't call an attorney, call a priest! Lawyers don't make miracles. They can assist you in triumphantly defending yourself, but miracles don't come with their law degree.

If you have little hope of winning in court, but your attorneys have earned the respect of the prosecutors, they will be able to negotiate a better sentence for you. The Crown would prefer to avoid a lengthy trial, because there is always the outside chance of it backfiring on them. Dexter also discovered that he could buy time. That is to say, instead of getting a sentence of ten years, he could pay a fine and get a five-year sentence.

How did Dexter know which lawyer was a good lawyer and which one was a schlepper? Dexter talked to other people who had experiences with lawyers. He talked to a lawyer before he had a beef. If the lawyer talked down to him and did not listen to him, he knew the lawyer couldn't help him because he couldn't help the lawyer. If you can't help the lawyer, go for a plea bargain and cut your best deal. If you play the game long enough, eventually the shit will hit the fan, and Dexter was no exception.

Dexter hit the bump in the road when an acquaintance of his was arrested and charged with importing two hundred kilos of hashish for the purpose of trafficking. Dexter was arrested and charged along with his friend and other people involved in the deal.

The deal had arrived and Dexter had met with one of the accused who was eventually convicted. To make a long story short, Dexter had met Mr. Ames seven or eight times over a period of five weeks.

When the Man finally came down on the deal, Dexter was dragged before the courts and charged with conspiracy this, conspiracy that, and conspiracy for whatever they could think of. The other people charged were caught dead bang. If they had had any chance of beating the beef or defending themselves, they made short work of that by blabbing their big yaps on the telephone. All in code you understand.

Dexter was in a different position. Most of his conversations were brief: "Meet you at two, or ten, at a doughnut shop, McDonald's," or what have you. Several other conversations tended to support Dexter's defense that the meetings were pertaining to the purchase of a racehorse.

The Man wasn't buying the party line. When they smelled Dexter's involvement, they opened up the purse strings and broadened the scope of their operation, all in the hope of roping Dexter in. Eventually the operation would employ 120 undercover agents supported by helicopter and airplane surveillance, wiretaps and video camera surveillance, over a five-week period. The horsemen wanted that asshole Dexter so bad they were willing to trade in a few of their prized horses to get him.

Out on bail, Dexter went to see his lawyer of twenty years. Over those years, Dexter had been picked up, bounced around, and detained for questioning — but never charged. However, this time was different! The Man thought they had enough goods on him for a conviction. Deals are for stool pigeons or a time-saving device for a guilty plea. In this instance, it would be winner take all, and all they wanted was Dexter.

The Crown's case boiled down to the numerous meetings Dexter had with Mr. Ames, the interpretations they could slant in their favour, and some embarrassing paraphernalia found in Dexter's garage, such as an electronic scale, a money-counting machine, a knife with hashish resin on the blade, and a bulletproof vest.

Dexter's lawyer believed Dex had an excellent chance of winning; however, he believed that Dexter would have to take the stand and explain the reasons for the meetings, give his explanation of the various conversations, and dilute the impact of the paraphernalia found in his garage. He was also arrested with a substantial amount of cash and a copy of a faxed contract to buy a horse. Not pretty but not earth-shattering either.

Dexter took the stand in his own defence. The reason for the meetings with Mr. Ames was the purchase of a racehorse. This was supported by several of the intercepted telephone conversations. The questionable objects found in the garage were explained in part by the fact that Dexter was renting the house and not all the property in the garage was his.

When Dexter got off the witness stand, his lawyer was satisfied with the way things had gone. They could have been better, but all in all, no serious damage. The next day the Crown and the defense summed up their arguments to the judge.

The judge in the first trial was very humane. He got animatedly involved in the cases before him. He had a sense of humour and a no-nonsense approach to the timely dispensation of the court's time. This made the trial move along at a rapid pace. He had a reputation for being quick to decide guilt or innocence — usually he leaned on the side of guilt, but he was not harsh in his sentencing.

Among the legal profession he was considered a cowboy. The impression one got was that he looked at the accused and said, OK if you have the goods on this asshole, let's hear it. Then it was, salut, bonne chance, merci pour la visite! Because of his tendency to rush to judgement, his convictions were frequently set aside in the Court of Appeal.

In Dexter's case, the judge wanted to find him guilty because he believed he was. However, the Crown didn't really have the goods, so the judge decided to pick up the slack. Dexter's attorney provided the judge with that opportunity. Basically, the judge said, "If I believe the story about the horse, I find him not guilty; if I don't, he's history." He didn't buy the party line about the horse, because Dexter's lawyer never qualified the contract for the horse. Dexter's attorney never brought in the lawyer who drew up the contract or the legal secretary who typed up the contract. So the judge discarded it. In other words, the judge had the option to accept it or to dismiss it as hearsay evidence.

In pronouncing his guilty verdict, the judge stated that because the defence had not brought the lawyer who had prepared the contract for the horse into court, he didn't accept the contract as valid; therefore, Dexter's horse story was full of manure. Salut, bonne chance, merci pour la visite!

Outside the courtroom Dexter's lawyer wailed away at the judge's decision. He looked at Dexter and said that the judge couldn't dismiss the contract for the horse. Dexter looked back at his lawyer and said, "He just did!"

Regardless of the outcome, Dexter liked the old judge and didn't dwell on it any further. It was off to the Court of Appeal.

When it came time for Dexter's lawyer to make his spiel before the three-judge appellate court, he informed Dexter that he didn't want him present in the courtroom. He told Dexter that his presence might be intimidating to the judges. Dexter wasn't buying his party line. Dexter is a very unassuming individual. If he walked into a room and no one pointed him out, you wouldn't notice him. He suspected that his lawyer might not have the right stuff and didn't want Dexter to see through him.

The day arrived when Dexter's appeal was to be heard, he showed up in court with his old friend, Uncle Harry. He simply asked Uncle Harry to sit in the courtroom and tell him how he saw things progressing. An hour into the proceedings, the court adjourned for a brief recess. Uncle Harry walked out of the courtroom and headed directly over to Dexter, who was sitting on a bench in the corridor.

"Well, Uncle Harry, how's it going?"

"Dexter, get yourself another lawyer. You'll be lucky if that guy doesn't blow your appeal completely."

Dexter didn't expect to hear those words, although deep down inside those were his haunting fears. After the recess, Uncle Harry followed Dexter's lawyer back into the courtroom, and thirty minutes later he exited with a little grin on his face.

"You were lucky Dex, you have been given a new trial."

Dexter's lawyer also informed him of the news. He was all gung-ho to go for trial number two. It was then that Dexter informed him that he wouldn't be his attorney in the second trial. Dexter said sorry, but in this game, two strikes and you're out; three strikes and I'm out. Dexter knew his lawyer had worked hard and did the best he could, it was just that his best wasn't good enough. We all make mistakes and the lawyer's little slip-up of not qualifying the purchase contract for the racehorse gave the judge the opportunity to discount Dexter's testimony. His lawyer had made an almost perfect defence, but... They are still friends today. No hard feelings, Dex just turned the page and began searching for a new lawyer.

Dexter and his lawyer both felt that they had been robbed of an acquittal, but that's life — it doesn't always go the way it's supposed to. The judge knew who Dexter was, and he knew the heat was on big time. He looked for an opportunity to find him guilty and his defence attorney had inadvertently given it to him. Dexter knew there was no margin for error in the second half of the game. There would be no one to blame but himself if he didn't hire the best legal defence he could find.

He interviewed several lawyers reffered by people on the street. They were all good men and women, intelligent, with decent track records. In the end, he decided on a Dream Team of his own, not one lawyer but two — one very intelligent, conservative lawyer, whom he knew and trusted and one *vedette* or star. His Dream Team was Maître Nicole Bergevin and Maître Guy Poupart. On the street, Maître Poupart is known as The Terminator; his cross-examination technique is legend. He can turn a rock-solid witness into a marshmallow. When you have twenty or more cops testifying against you, a few marshmallows can help the defence immeasurably! Dexter and his Dream Team were ready to wage war with the opposition.

In the first trial, Dexter had boxed himself in with his testimony, so he had several land mines waiting for him the next time he took the stand. His lawyers prepared him well. They wrote down every question they were going to ask him when he took the stand. So that there would be no surprises, Maître Poupart played the part of the Crown lawyer and it was then that Dexter began to get a sinking feeling that he wouldn't be able to skate his way around the prosecution, as he had done in the first trial. Dexter continued to study his testimony as the trial proceeded.

Right off the top the RCMP officers' testimony began to change. A little embellishment here, a lie there, and a little more polish. The gloves were off. Both sides knew they were playing for keeps. Whatever the decision, there would be no room for an appeal. Hollywood could not have written a better courtroom drama than the one that was being played out by the lawyers locked in a battle for Dexter's future residence.

Out of the blue, a veteran police officer testified that she had followed Dexter to the warehouse where the hash had been delivered and stored. On a large map displayed in the courtroom, she calmly took pen in hand and traced out the route Dexter had taken when she had followed him on that day. Even though it was a lie, it was deadly, devastating evidence against Dexter, and it could sink him. As Maître Poupart rose to cross-examine the RCMP officer, the judge adjourned the trial for a twenty-minute recess. Dexter walked out of the courtroom and began pacing the courthouse corridor. He could hear the cell door slamming shut in his mind. Maître Bergevin approached him and said, with a slight smile, "Why Dexter, are you all right? You look so pale."

Dexter looked at her, and wondered how she could still be so confident after the testimony they had just heard. He didn't know what to say. Maître Poupart joined them and said, "Don't worry, Dexter, I'll make her eat those words before she gets off the stand."

Dexter wanted to believe in his lawyers, but he couldn't see how they were going to make a veteran police officer recant her testimony on the stand. Thinking it was all over but the crying, he was numb as he walked back into the courtroom to take his seat. Maître Poupart began in his gentle way, asking questions here, there and everywhere. Dexter wondered where in the hell he was going with his questioning. Suddenly, it all came into focus, like when a master painter brings all the strokes of his brush into harmony to reveal his masterpiece. It wasn't a pretty picture — well that depends from which side of the room you were on — it was the picture of a veteran police officer recanting her statement on the stand. Indeed, she had never followed Dexter into the warehouse grounds. That wasn't the end of it: other police officers tried to lie or embellish their testimonies in order to hang Dexter. As before, Maître Bergevin and Maître Poupart chewed them up and used their bones as darts to pick holes in the Crown's case. Dexter's Dream Team was operating on all twelve cylinders.

Dexter began to breathe a little easier each time a cop got on the stand and began to spin a web of deceit. It was like putting two bears in a honey shack, the more the witnesses embellished their stories, or out-and-out lied, the easier it was for the lawyers to demolish their credibility.

The reality is that no one goes into a courtroom and tells the truth, and nothing but the truth, unless they're suicidal. Good lawyers can make a hangman's noose out of the truth and stick a witnesses head in it. Judges understand that people tend to tell the truth as suits them best. The embellishment of testimony to enhance one's position is the norm on both sides. The trick is to be careful not to over-indulge in this embellishment. Credibility is the cornerstone of a witnesses testimony, putting too much butter on the bread leads to indigestion.

Fortunately for Dexter, his Dream Team was up to the challenge. Or, to put it less politely, the more bullshit the cops told on the stand, the more of it blew back in their faces. Maître Poupart and Maître Bergevin were absolutely demolishing the Crown's case. They knew it, the Crown knew it, and the horsemen knew it. Yet both the Crown and the horsemen continued to display an air of confidence. Dexter noticed this, and wondered how they could be so calm, in the face of decimation by the defence attorneys. He discussed this apparent contradiction with his attorneys, and it was then that they broke the sobering news to Dex.

"They're waiting for you to take the stand, Dex! You are the one who can make this case for them! They have the contradictions in your last testimony, and they intend to bury you with it. It's your call, but we recommend you sit down and keep your big box shut. Let us handle it!" Dexter wasn't sure about that strategy. His first lawyer had convinced him that it was absolutely imperative for him to take the stand and explain things. His Dream Team was saying the opposite. What to do?

He thought about the difference between the first trial and this one. The cautious, conservative reflectiveness of Maître Bergevin; Maître Poupart, the Jedi knight wielding his laser sword, slicing and dicing the witnesses like Zorro. The decision was his: to go with what his defence had been able to accomplish; or to take the stand, peddle the party line and hope and pray that the Crown didn't have the goods to contradict his British Science. As the trial continued, Dexter held off making the final decision. To testify or not to testify, that was the question.

The final witness to testify against Dexter was an old retired RCMP officer. He had retired after twenty-five years of service, most of it spent as a member of the surveillance squad. Without going into all the sordid details of the case, it is important to note that one of the principal details of the case was to paint Dexter as very nervous and paranoid. Up to this last witness, the Crown had failed to do so. On the contrary, Maître Poupart had been able to elicit from the previous testimony that Dexter had been observed acting in an appropriate, normal and rational manner.

The now-retired police officer had testified in Dexter's first trial. The defence expected no surprises from this witness and felt his testimony was redundant at best. The witness walked into the courtroom wearing a checked black and gray sports coat, black shirt, black pants, black cowboy boots, and as a final touch, a black and white tie with a picture of Elvis Presley on it. His hair slicked straight back, his barrel chest fully extended, he looked the judge straight in the eye, raised his right hand, and was duly sworn in. He started off his testimony by stating that he had observed Mr. Ames and Dexter in the parking lot of a restaurant. Dexter had been nervously looking around at the other parked cars in the parking lot and constantly glancing over his shoulders as he walked and talked with Mr. Ames.

Dexter glanced over at his attorneys. They were relaxed and composed. Maître Bergevin's fingers danced on the keys of her laptop computer, taking notes as the witness colourfully described the scene and the apparently nervous, paranoid behavior of Dexter. The old cop looked boldly at the judge, a slyly confident smile at the corners of his mouth. It was apparent to one and all that he was the one who was going to put the nail in this smart-ass Dexter's coffin. The Crown turned the witness over to the defence. Dex thought to himself, "Old man, you just volunteered to put yourself through a wood shredder!"

Maître Poupart rose from his seat at the defence table. He slowly approached the witness on the stand. In a low bass voice, he greeted the old cop. Then he began his cross-examination. After some initial, inconsequential questions, he moved to the heart of the retired horseman's testimony. The old cop must have heard the lawyer's laser sword warming up as the questions began to pierce through his arrogant facade.

Maître Poupart never hacked away at his witnesses; his laser sword-like questioning just sliced away at his opposition, piece by piece. In no time at all, the old cop was jigging all over the stand. His sly smirk had changed into a partial grimace, as each swipe by the lawyer cut the British Science from the truth. When his testimony was stripped down to the bare bones of truth, the witness was forced to recant his previous testimony.

"Thank you. No more questions your Honour," said Maître Poupart.

The witness stumbled off the stand, totally humiliated. He was a liar, he knew it, and he knew that everyone in the courtroom knew it, too. The old cop had wanted to end his career with fireworks; instead, he ended it with a fart!

There was one very pertinent element in Dexter's defence left to be established. It was the cornerstone of his defence, the qualification of the contract to purchase a horse, in order for it to be accepted as uncontradicted evidence. The purchase agreement or contract had been found in Dexter's possession when he was arrested. It had been produced at his first trial along with other articles found in his possession. In the first trial, the judge had considered the contract for the horse as hearsay evidence, and he threw the contract out, and Dexter in!

The lawyer who drew up the purchase agreement for the horse had been Dexter's civil attorney for approximately fifteen years. Shortly after Dexter's arrest, he had been appointed to the bench. The lawyer who handled Dexter's first trial didn't think it was necessary to call in Judge Anthony DeMichele to verify or qualify the contract, by testifying that he was the lawyer who had prepared it for Dexter. After all, it was the Crown that had produced it into evidence; and besides, at the top of the contract was the fax number of the law firm from which it had been faxed. Added to those facts was Dexter's testimony supporting the contract and its origin. Therefore, he did not see the necessity of qualifying its authenticity any further. This was a major oversight on the part of Dexter's first lawyer; and as a result of it, the judge had the opening he was looking for, and Dexter got slam-dunked.

Dexter's Dream Team was not going to let that ball drop in the second trial. Maître Bergevin contacted the law firm that Judge DeMichele was formerly with. She spoke with his former partner and asked him if he could get in touch with Judge DeMichele and have him sign an affidavit attesting that he had indeed prepared the purchase contract for the horse. She was assured that there would be no problem. Judge DeMichele was presiding over a case, and the moment it was over he would have time to prepare and sign the affidavit. Dex's lawyers then concentrated on other aspects of his defence.

Dexter's second trial had started and still no signed affidavit from Judge DeMichele. Maître Bergevin called his former partner again to see what the delay was. It seemed that Judge DeMichele was having a lapse in memory. Dexter and his lawyers decided that, given the gravity of the situation, they would subpoena Judge DeMichele and declare him a hostile witness. This was not good for the judge, but he was leaving them no choice. Maître Bergevin made another call to Judge DeMichele's former partner, this time stating her intention to subpoena the judge, and everyone knew the subsequent fallout that could ensue. Anthony's memory began to improve, but the affidavit was still not forthcoming.

On the morning of the twelfth day of the trial, the Crown was wrapping up its case, and the defence would have to commence with theirs. The decision for Dexter not to testify had all but been made; however, if the contract for the horse was not qualified, Dexter might be obliged to take the stand. At the beginning of the session, the judge announced that they would have to recess at eleven-thirty because he had been called to a special, unscheduled meeting. They would resume court in the afternoon at three o'clock. The Crown wrapped up its case at eleven-twenty, and court was adjourned.

Dexter and his Dream Team went for lunch. Maître Poupart was trying to be upbeat. With or without the affidavit, he didn't think Dex should testify. His lawyers tried to put a positive spin on the situation. Dexter was getting that old sinking feeling. After lunch they walked somberly back to the courthouse. Before entering the building, Maître Poupart excused himself. He saw an old friend and stopped to chat with him. During the course of their conversation, he explained his dilemma. His friend stated that he knew Judge DeMichele. He offered to give him a call in order to avoid a potentially embarrassing situation for all parties. If what he heard was true, he could see no reason why Judge DeMichele would want to put himself through such an ordeal. He would call him immediately and try to simplify matters. Maître Poupart really didn't want to call a judge into court and have him declared a hostile witness, but he was so pissed off, he would have done it!

Suffice it to say, the phone call worked. Maître Poupart went up to Judge DeMichele's chambers and Maître Bergevin played the stall game when court resumed. The judge ruled against her motion, but that was OK, because at ten after three, Maître Poupart walked back into the courtroom and joined his consoeur at the defence table. Dexter didn't see any papers in his hand, but he caught the wink Maître Poupart gave Maître Bergevin. The defence was now ready to proceed. They submitted the signed affidavit and advised the judge that it was the only evidence the defence was prepared to make. The Crown and the horsemen were rocked by the news. That meant no Dexter on the stand, no bombs to throw at him and no land mines for him to step on.

Dexter had received an eleventh-hour reprieve. The unexpected and unplanned delay in the trial, the chance meeting by Maître Poupart with an old friend, and Judge Antony DeMichele's last-minute capitulation were all too much to be attributed to chance. Dexter heard the words of the old Sarge echoing in his mind: "Someday Dexter, someday you will see for yourself, there are no atheists in a foxhole!"

This incident raised Dexter's faith to a much higher plane. There was no doubt in his mind that the Good Lord had been watching over him. Why? Well he still doesn't have the answer to that one.

The Dream Team took the ball and shoved it down the Crown's throat. The defence attorneys wove a web of doubt based on inconsistencies and lies in the testimony of the Crown witnesses. They built the resulting doubt into a formidable defence. After a full day of pleading, the defence rested. The Crown basically threw in the towel. The Crown's presentation lasted forty-five minutes and they were out of there. The judge would reveal his decision in ten days. This time Dexter walked out of the courtroom feeling a lot more comfortable than he did after his first trial. His lawyers felt confident they would get a not guilty verdict; however, they cautioned Dexter that it's not over till the fat lady sings. They told him that if the judge really wanted to find him guilty he could and would; however, they believed the judge would have to work a lot harder than the Crown Prosecutor had. The norm was that judges make their decision based on the presentation of the facts placed before them and not based on their ability to assume a biased view.

Dexter counted his blessings, a great law team, a fair-minded judge, an unscheduled delay, a chance meeting that brought a politically-appointed flunkee (whose head had become as big as his ass) back to reality.

Three weeks later Dexter was back in court to hear the judge's verdict. Dexter figured that a little bird must have whispered in the judge's ear. In spite of all that had passed in the courtroom, the judge still didn't give Dexter the benefit of the doubt. He found him guilty and dropped the hammer on him. So much for a fair-minded judge.

I asked Dexter if he was angry with the cops or the judge for not giving him the benefit of the doubt. He said, "No, that's the way it goes in the major leagues." The lesson Dexter learned was that if he were ever to go to court again it would be before a judge and a jury, not just a judge. The bottom line for Dexter was that there was no one to blame but himself. He always maintained a positive attitude, even in the face of a guilty verdict. He didn't look for excuses or try to blame anyone. He just wanted to do his time, turn the page and get on with his life; and that's exactly what he did. It was also easier for Dexter to take that attitude because he was doing short time. If he had been whacked with a ten or fifteen-year pop, his attitude would have undoubtedly been different. Getting popped was one thing, getting slammed would have been something else.

What Dexter looked for in a lawyer was one who was respected by the police, the prosecutors and other lawyers and judges. If you're nailed dead bang, a good lawyer isn't going to bullshit you into believing that a long, drawn-out trial is the answer. What you need is a lawyer who has a good reputation for negotiating with the powers that be for a reduced sentence and one who has a sincere interest in your welfare, which is not always the case!

Some lawyers are so greedy and hungry for money that they make you feel like a dollar sign when you walk in the door. Dexter prefers a lawyer who tells his clients up front, "This is what I think I can do. You don't like it, shop around." You can see when you talk to them that their work is a labour of love. They enjoy what they do, and they do it well. Top-notch lawyers are expensive. Expensive lawyers are not necessarily top-notch.

Dexter's experience is that a good attorney will have a least two or three attorneys working with him. The reason is simple. An attorney, no matter how brilliant, cannot do all the research alone. He needs assistance in this area. Also, if he has associates, they can brainstorm to develop the best defense. Attorneys who work alone will lack the support they need in defending you.

Normally, the prosecution is swamped with cases. Frequently, they handle a dozen at a time. They lack the attention to detail and the preparedness that a small to medium-sized law firm has. They rely heavily on police testimony and truthfulness; this can be as helpful as throwing a drowning man an anchor.

To Dexter's mind there are basically two types of lawyers. The technician — a lawyer who excels in knowing the law and all its technicalities. He is up to date on the latest jurisprudence and changes in the law. Technicians are the professors of law. If you can imagine your lawyer as a professor of law, lecturing students on the law, then you have what Dexter calls a technician.

The other type of lawyer is a *vedette* or star. He or she will be marked by an air of confidence, of *savoir faire*. A lawyer who is a star is like a salesperson. If you can visualize your lawyer as a good salesperson, then you understand what Dexter means by a vedette or star. They have the gift of gab and shoot from the hip.

Rarely is a lawyer both a technician and a *vedette* at the same time.

A good lawyer knows how to walk and talk in and out of court. Most cases are settled out of court. If your attorney doesn't know how to wheel and deal, you're the one who pays the price, not him. Deals are cut out of court, as a matter of expediency. If every case went to trial there would be a five-year backlog of cases. The prosecution has to settle cases out of court. If you don't think you are getting a good enough deal out of court, you might have to push it to trial. Usually there is a meeting of the minds that is convenient to all concerned.

If you're not represented by good attorneys, you place your head in the hands of the prosecutor, and that's generally not a good idea. Justice is for sale, and if you can't afford to pay the band, get off the dance floor. You've got to hire the best attorney you can afford. Like it or not, that's the way the game is played. Lawyers don't hire out on the installment plan. The gist of that is, you have to have a cash stash for those times when money talks and bullshit walks. Dexter learned this early on in his career and saved himself a lot of time pushing weights.

The reason attorneys don't like to put their clients on the stand, is that their well prepared case can be destroyed if you screw up while testifying. At some point, your lawyer will have to turn you over to the Crown Prosecutor who will come at you from all angles. Your attorney can only hope and pray you don't fuck up.

If it has been decided that you will take the stand in your own defence, demand that your attorney write down all the questions he or she is going to ask you on the stand. Every single last one of them. They do not like to do this, because it is a lot of work! That's the only reason. You're the one paying the piper. Absolutely, positively demand that every question you're going to be asked when you're on the stand be written down! Make it clear that once you are on the stand, they cannot ask you any questions other than the ones submitted to you. These are painful lessons some of Dexter's friends have experienced as a result of not being properly prepared by their attorneys before testifying. Once you get in the box to testify, there's no turning back, there are no time-outs.

A seemingly innocent question by your attorney, one you hadn't discussed or thought about, can set you off. When it's all over he may ask you why you fumbled around so much when he asked you for your mother's maiden name, and why, after that, you blew all the rehearsed answers out the window. You explain that you don't know who your mother was, and that it's a secret you have never discussed with anyone. If the attorney had rehearsed the question beforehand, you would have been prepared for it. He didn't prepare you for it, and instead, he touched a nerve deep within you that set you off your game plan. By that time it's too late. If you have taken the stand and screwed up, you'll be the one walking down that yellow brick road. Attorneys often overlook the fact that their clients are under intense pressure when they are on the stand. They also don't want the work of sitting down and making up a detailed questionnaire. If your attorney won't do it, get another lawyer. Lawyers are in court every day, they're used to it; it's a foreign environment for you.

If you think attorneys give good testimony as witnesses, you are in for a shock. Many times, when the shoe is on the other foot and they get on the stand, they babble on or freeze up. Don't let your attorney bullshit you. He says you have to take the stand to win, fine! Do your homework and make the effort to be prepared. You don't want any surprises from your attorney when you're in the box.

Do not assume for a moment that your lawyer knows the law. When he or she is planning your defense, ask for the specific point of law on which they are basing your defense. They should be able to furnish you with a brief description of the law and how it applies to your particular case. In other words, ask questions. If you don't agree where your lawyer is coming from, say so.

The one law you should all know is the "KYMS" law — Keep Your Mouth Shut. When you are arrested, interrogated or just questioned by the police, remember KYMS. If you don't know that law, ask your attorney about it. If he doesn't know it, get another lawyer!

Whenever Dexter was dealing in foreign countries he always inquired about the laws and customs of the land; failure to do so can bring you heat and a lot of unnecessary problems. If it was a Banana Republic, he got to know who the top bananas were and how to reach them. Moroccans, like Pakistanis, are infamous for their custom of betraying the people who work with them. Don't fight it or argue about it, accept it. If you walk on the wild side in those countries, know how treacherous the people are. For example, in most third-world countries the police do not follow you in another car. Usually they will ask your taxi driver for a lift. If you see this happening don't panic, let him come along for the ride. Just don't sit there bumping your gums with your associate in the back seat, because most times the police officers speak English and other languages. Ignorance of the way the police operate in third-world countries can only end in hardship and some hellhole prison.

Rule Number Ten
The Law and the Lawyers

It is self-evident that you need to have some idea of the laws of the land in which you operate. It is equally important that you cultivate the names of several good attorneys in whom you have confidence to defend you when you are "unjustly" accused. Justice is for sale. Hire a cheap attorney and get free accommodation and a photograph for the family album thrown in as a bonus. Hire a good attorney, and you may not have to stay as long as the penny-wise and pound-foolish player who assumed justice was for all!

CHAPTER THIRTEEN
SPIRITUALITY

People who commit crimes are human beings who have feelings, emotions and family values like everybody else. We sometimes stereotype them into faceless, nameless people who live somewhere else. The reality is they are with us everyday; we meet them in the shopping centres, malls, grocery stores and coffee shops. They are our neighbours, our co-workers and members of our local community. They support the same hockey or football teams and share many of the same common interests as the average citizenry. Often, what is lost in the headlines and sensational journalism is the humanity of those lost in the sea of crime. Dexter believes "spirituality" is in each of us from the moment of birth, regardless of our social or religious background, race, colour or creed. He believes it is an undeniable, unrelenting need within each of us that demands fulfillment. It is the voice within all of us that asks the questions: What is life all about? What is my purpose in living? Is there a God? Why am I not rich? Why am I rich and still not happy, when I have so much? Why, why, why?

For the best part of his life, Dexter was an atheist. He tried not to think about the void, the hollow, empty space inside of himself. It seemed impossible to sedate, to replenish, to satisfy! Like most people he met, he just didn't talk about it. It was a personal matter, not something to be discussed or shared with others. Finally, he began to sense that the voice that reverberated in the hollow space deep inside of him was being quieted, being stilled by his growing spiritual faith.

To him, spirituality is the belief in a God who interacts with us in our daily lives. He says it's the only thing he has found that can fill that void, that vacuum, that emptiness that rested within him. Dexter likens it to the swirling mass of outer space. It has no beginning and no end, it is just there! He could not live contentedly without addressing its taunting calls to be filled, to be satisfied.

Dexter has met people who cower behind their intellect to muffle its call to their consciousness. Others, like Dexter himself, try to bury it in materialistic possessions and pursuits. He found that it cannot be bought, sold, or stifled by intellectual pride. He could not run from it by hiding behind his work or profession. He could not numb it out of his consciousness with alcohol or other drugs. He could not deny its presence or its ceaseless demand for attention.

I suppose it calls to each of us in different ways, but the call is always the same. Where is happiness? Why can't I find the peace and happiness I see in some? We all hear its call — even in a crowded room with friends and family — we hear its aching, haunting call.

Sometimes Dexter could blanket it away from his conscious thoughts for a time; but it always came back! There was no peace for him from the voice within. He couldn't ignore it. He couldn't deny it. He tried, but he couldn't buy permanent peace from it. He could not extinguish it from his consciousness with drugs, materialistic adornments or self-centered interests. Spirituality, the belief in an omnipresent God in his life, was the answer. It was an answer he didn't accept easily. It was a path he was directed in by the old Sarg.

One can know the joys of this world and accept the hardships that the school of life teaches us if one embraces a spiritual belief. At least that is the way Dexter has come to see it. He discovered that if he truly wanted to live a contented life, he had to incorporate some spirituality into his life. That didn't mean that he had to become a fanatic, a Holy Joe, a saint or a martyr. He found that the more he focussed the centre of his life in spirituality, the more he came to know happiness, the more calm his innards felt. He had to learn what was important and what was only his egotism, goading him down the road toward dreams that were doomed to be broken. A life spiritually centred, is a life of fulfillment and acceptance. He came to believe that he could make a difference, and that it was up to him to do so.

Dexter concentrated on his legitimate work when he got out of the can, and eventually the Man backed off. Some time thereafter Papa Gee arrived in Montreal. He called Dexter at his office and they set up a meet. The old man looked old once again. His lifeless, thinning hair, once dyed dark brown, was a mousy gray. He no longer had a spring to his step. He looked old and scowling. He was all business. He wanted to know if Dexter was interested in heroin. He had several airline stewardesses doing body trips. He was getting set up to do four or five keys of pure smack a week. He had one contact in the States for distribution, but the contact could only do one key every two weeks. He needed a contact who could distribute bigger quantities.

Dexter looked at Papa Gee sitting across the table from him. From day one, Dexter had made it very clear to Papa Gee that he would have nothing to do with heroin. His anger was about to explode, when Papa Gee spoke up abruptly. He knew Dexter was not interested, but he had hoped that he would introduce him to some contact. Dexter answered with a simple no. He wasn't interested and he would not introduce him to anyone.

The old man seemed to sense Dexter's anger, even though Dexter hadn't expressed it verbally. There was a momentary silence between the two men as they sat there looking at one another, each with his thoughts. Neither said anything, but they both knew this was the end of their friendship. Dexter broke the silence by inquiring about Shama. Immediately the old man began knocking her, putting her down. She wasn't really his daughter, he confessed. She was a low-class street person whom he had befriended and tried to help. She was not a good woman. No man would marry her.

Dexter listened to the old man trash a beautiful human being. He listened to the old man describing what a big heart he had, how he had tried to help a poor waif. When Papa Gee stopped talking, Dexter asked him what Shama had done. What had turned him against her so?

His answer was a bullshit story about how Shama had been running around and had gotten pregnant. He, Papa Gee, had paid for her airline ticket and expenses to send her to Singapore for an abortion. The back-room abortion had been successful, but when she returned to Karachi she had a mild infection. As she lay weak and left alone in her one-room hovel, the infection spread. Papa Gee said he was unable to get a doctor in Pakistan to attend to her. Maybe he did try to get her a doctor. Maybe he was too afraid to even try — a pregnant unmarried woman in Pakistan can mean a death sentence for the woman and for the man who got her pregnant! A week later Papa Gee stopped by to see her and found her rotting corpse. According to him, God had punished her!

The old man had used her for his pleasure and wasn't careful. He was the one who was responsible for her pregnancy. He had lost the best friend he ever had and was too selfish, too self-centered to know it! Dexter felt like a heel himself. He should have brought her to Canada, regardless of any deals. Dex had his excuses, but inside he felt that he too had let Shama down.

He told Papa Gee that he didn't want to see him any more. He asked him to remove his phone number from his notebook. This the old man did in front of him. They parted company. Dexter didn't offer to shake his hand. He simply said good-bye and walked out of the restaurant. A year later Dexter heard from another contact he had in Pakistan that Papa Gee had been busted in the States with heroin. He would never see daylight again.

Dexter stopped by to see Auntie in her old age home. She informed him that Sylvie was dead. She had died of cancer at the age of forty-three. Sylvie was a very dear friend to Dexter. She hadn't wanted anyone to see her dying. She had blossomed into a beautiful woman, but in the end, cancer had made her ugly. Sylvie had helped Dexter a lot during his one-year war on the street. She had fed him a ton of information. She had always been available to sit with him and listen to his problems. Many times, she had given him very wise counsel. Dexter remembered their last luncheon and her parting words, "Dexter, get out of da game before da game gets you. It's changed, it's not like before, mon ami. Quit, maudit anglais!"

She gave Dex a big hug and a kiss. They walked quietly to her car, not speaking another word. She was a dear, sweet and true friend.

Mickey, a runner for Dexter, had been frequenting the Zoo. One day he charged over to Dexter's office all excited. He told Dex that he had seen an old friend of his at the Zoo — René. Mickey was popping buttons because Mother introduced Mickey to René as a friend of Dexter's. Mickey figured he was moving up in the world. René was now employed by Duney as his new enforcer. René had bought Mickey a drink and asked him to tell Dex to stop by.

Dexter had always liked René. He was an easygoing guy with a great sense of humor. He was one of the boys from the old hold-up school. He had gone down on a bank job in the States with Duney. René did more time than Duney because of his attitude. Once in the can, he changed. He refused to work. He refused to partake in any of the self-help programs offered to him. In short, he refused to play the game. The Americans didn't care and rightly so. René just sat there doing his time, and as a result he was turned down for parole several times. In the end, he was deported to Canada. Whatever it was, René had snapped. He wasn't the same old René. Mickey was going on about René and all that he had said, when he stopped and asked Dexter a question. "Why does René wear two black velvet gloves all the time? Is there something wrong with his hands?"

Dexter looked at Mickey, a young twenty-two-year-old setting out on his life-long journey of crime. He was very naive for a person his age, especially in the Drug Game. Mickey sat across from Dexter waiting for an answer.

"Mickey, I want you to stay away from René. He's very dangerous. He wears the black velvet gloves as a sign that his hands are the hands of death, and he wants everyone to know it!"

Mickey's jaw dropped open. He nodded his head. He understood and agreed to stay away from him. What had happened was that Mother had started having problems with the punkers, the sleazebags, and the stools who had begun to hang around the Zoo after Jake the Snake's demise. Duney didn't want to hire another coconut. He just wanted an enforcer for show. He thought that this time it would be different. He thought he could control the situation better because of his experience with Jackie. It didn't work out that way. Six months after René started working for Duney, he started flexing his muscles. He half-ass threatened Mother on one occasion.

The final straw came when René collected a hundred thousand dollar payment for Mother and kept it! Mother sent him to Toronto to collect another debt. René had become a skitzy psycho with his nose in a bag of coke all the time. A very dangerous animal! When he arrived in Toronto, he went to see a contact to buy some personal coke. After he bought the coke, he returned to his hotel room and sprinkled out two big lines on the cocktail table. He sniffed one line down each nostril. Then he picked up his shovel and reported to work! The coke was pure, and cut with fifty percent pure heroin.

When that mixture went into his blood stream and hit his heart, it was all over. Mother never hired another full-time enforcer after that.

Later on, Dexter bumped into Mother at the Lachine Hotel. He wasn't the same person anymore. He was almost out of the hash and grass business altogether, and he was talking about stepping back, way back, in the coke game.

It was vacation time for Dexter and his family. They packed their bags and left for the Grand Cayman Islands. Dexter used travel to educate himself. It was also a way for him to enjoy his family, to get out of the pressure cooker in which his life was usually encapsulated. Looking back, Dex regretted not having taken more time off to spend with his family.

One night, Duney was sitting in the bar of Nittolo's Motel having a drink with friends. The Punch; a big coke player, walked in and approached Mother. He, too, was one of the boys from the old hold-up school who had made the transition into the Drug Game. He was, like so many who get involved in the coke game, a big user himself. Some coke players don't take coke themselves; but most do, and the Punch was no exception to paying the price caused by cocaine's web of destruction.

In the beginning, cocaine gives the user a false sense of happiness, of power, of invincibility. In the end it takes everything back with a vengeance. The paranoia sets in and the bouts of depression overwhelm the user coming down from the night before. You become completely unscrupulous in your efforts to feed the addiction and the cocaine ego with more of the "sucker's elixir of life." Cocaine was touted as the jet-setter's drug of choice, but it's not. It's the "loser's recipe" for self-destruction. Crack cocaine is even worse. Dexter witnessed many a young ball player with the Montreal Expos throw his career and life away with cocaine. He once talked to a young ball player who had a good career in the making as a pitcher for the Expos. He loved living in Montreal and playing for the club. He battled with cocaine and lost. He went from a three-hundred-thousand-dollar-a-year wage earner to picking up garbage for the sanitation department in Tampa, Florida.

It's hard to understand why anybody would play with Satan's "opiate of the People." Our society is strewn with destroyed lives left in the wake of cocaine. It happens to athletes, movie stars, doctors, lawyers, businessmen and women. Dexter often asked himself why people who appeared to be winners opted for the cocaine trash bin? Was it because they were losers to begin with? Maybe they couldn't handle success. Success scares many people. For those who have had the "misfortune" of becoming successful when they weren't capable of handling it, or prepared to handle it, cocaine is the easy way out! Losers always look for the easy way out!

The Punch was never a prince to begin with, but for those of us who knew him, he was a James Cagney character. If you met him, you knew he was a hood. There was no mistaking him for a brain surgeon. Still, in all of that, he had his attributes. Cocaine had erased any positive factors he had in his character. It reduced him to the lowest status to which the "sucker's elixir" can reduce a human being. Mother considered him a friend — not necessarily a buddy — but a friend from the old school; a pal who was now doing his thing in the Drug Game.

The Punch had a proposition for Mother. He told him he had twenty keys of pure uncut coke. The price was right! He told him he had the coke in a room at the motel. He offered to show it to him immediately. Duney left his friends at the bar and walked out with the Punch to the motel room.

Punch opened the door and Duney walked in. The Punch closed the door behind them. Big Fat Larry stepped out of the closet with a shotgun in his hand. Mother didn't need a map or a written contract to know what was going on. The Punch had the doorway blocked. The only other way out was the large plate glass window. He grabbed a chair and threw it through the window. He raced toward it and attempted to jump out of the motel room. Fat Larry blasted away with the shotgun, killing Mother on the spot. There was a third man hiding in the bathroom. His name escapes Dexter at the present, and he's not about to go around asking who it was. Anyway, the guy's dead!

The Punch, Fat Larry and the other guy fled the motel. Their game plan had been to kidnap Mother and hold him for ransom. Mother knew that even if the ransom had been paid, he was a dead man. He did the smartest thing, under the circumstances. He made a play and hoped for the best. The point of initial contact is always the weakest moment for any criminal who tries to abduct, rob or hold someone up. If you're gonna try to defend yourself, that's the time to do it.

The police teach women not to comply with an abductor, if they ever find themselves being accosted in a parking lot or on a street. Don't get in his car. Don't let him get in your car. Your best chance for survival is to do whatever you can on the spot. Once you comply with the abductor, you are giving him more and more control. The best thing to do is to make whatever move you can make right off the top. Mother did what he could, but it wasn't in the cards.

Dexter was on the first day of his vacation. They had spent the day on the beach, playing in the ocean and having a great time. They all went to bed exhausted. In the middle of the night, Dexter was jarred out of his sleep. He sat up in bed with such a jolt that he woke up his wife. She asked him what was wrong. He told her he didn't know. All he knew was that something was wrong. He had a hard time getting back to sleep. In the morning he called the Newspaper Man at his office and found out about Mother's death. The Newspaper Man didn't have a lot of details, but he was going to make the rounds that night and find out. He'd let Dexter know what was going on.

The reason Mother was killed was twofold. The most obvious reason was money. They thought they could milk millions out of Mother's kidnapping. The second and even more powerful reason was envy! Envy is one of the "seven deadly sins." It is never more prevalent than in the underworld. People are jealous of you if you are successful. They envy a successful person's stature in the underworld. Egos are crushed or offended. This is especially true of old timers or people who started off on the street. The realization that you have become successful and they haven't eats them up. They think you should give or loan them money — you were just luckier than them. They believe they are better than you.

Their egos tell them they deserve to be on top of the pack, or at the very least, as successful as you.

Cocaine is rocket fuel propellant for the ego. People on cocaine all have big egos, it comes with the drug. So, it's no surprise that people in the Drug Game were green-eyed with envy of Duney. He was the biggest. He was the number-one man in Montreal and in Canada. Years later an associate of Mother's was convicted in the United States for trafficking in cocaine. He was said to have been the biggest catch since Manuel Noriega. The associate had many of Mother's actions dumped on his back. The point is, Mother was big, and a hell of a lot of cokeheads had their egos out of joint. The hit never would have happened if tacit approval hadn't been given by those cokehead sleazebags. Envy is a deadly weapon in the Drug Game, a weapon you have no protection against!

Mother's death rocked Dexter. It weakened his gradually developing spiritual faith. He asked himself why, if there was a God, why would he have let a bunch of cokehead sleazebags murder a man who in his own way had helped a lot of people? It just didn't seem right to Dexter. It gnawed away at his fledgling faith. Six months after Mother's death a newspaper article about him noted that if he hadn't been murdered, he would have been arrested and deported to the United States for trafficking in cocaine. Apparently, a secret Grand Jury in the U.S. had indicted him on cocaine charges. The papers were in the process of being drawn up for his arrest and deportation. He would have been found as guilty as his associate was. He would have spent the rest of his life in a seven-by-eight-foot cell, caged like an animal until his eventual death.

Reading this, Dexter felt comforted knowing that God had spared his good friend such an inhumane existence and death. Duney wasn't a pillar of the community by any stretch of the imagination, but he wasn't an evil person either. At least with Duney you knew who he was and what he was, unlike the thousands of politicians, bureaucrats and civil servants who pursue their careers to glory without regard to the untold suffering and destruction they leave in their wake. Dexter was and is proud to say, "Mother was a friend of mine."

The Punch went into hiding. He was holed up in a high-rise apartment complex waiting to see which way the wind was going to blow. He needed a TV, so his trusted friend Apache Trudeau arranged for one to be brought to his apartment. Inside the TV was a bomb. After it was delivered, someone flipped a switch, and the Punch and some of his associates found out the wind was blowing them all to hell.

Apache Trudeau pleaded guilty to his part in the bombing along with the fifty other murders he had participated in. He received a seven-year sentence. The bomb almost killed a couple living in the apartment next door, along with their infant son. That was of little concern to the police because they made their statistics look good for solved murders. Trudeau got a slap on the wrist!

Fat Larry rolled over and joined the police protection program. He got a better deal than Trudeau. As a result of his co-operation, he never went to prison. The third man in on the murder of Duney was held to a more serious court of justice; friends of Mother's turned his lights out permanently!

Canadians have an expression that says, "Two mountains never meet, but two men do." Ajmal and The Putz are still out there and maybe someday, *inshallah* (God willing), Dexter will meet up with them!

With Duney's death came big changes in the Montreal underworld. The Drug Game never missed a beat. It was business as usual, except no one could fill Duney's shoes. Many tried, with varying degrees of success. They plodded along, but there was no more focal point. There was no more cohesion. Everybody went off into smaller groups and did their own thing. There was no more "conscience" in the Drug Game. It became a pure money play. Small potatoes were making big money, sleazebags were making big money, stool pigeons were, and are, making big money. The Drug Game is a violent, self-serving, ego-centered pursuit of self happiness, without any conscience, regard for others, or concern for society. There is no camaraderie in the Drug Game. Mother was the last remnant of the old school of those who felt a concern for others on their side of the fence. The Drug Game here, like everywhere else in the world, has been overcome by the "wilding" phenomenon of America.

"WILDING IN AMERICA" COMES TO CANADA

Officially, "Wilding in America" came to Canada on the 13th of May 1991. Word on the street has it that orders came down from on high in the RCMP to execute criminal defense attorney Sydney Leithman. Subsequently, criminal defense attorney P. Beaudry was murdered by RCMP officers. Ironically, Mr. Beaudry had worked for the RCMP prior to becoming a criminal defense attorney. Also within the same time frame, two Cali Drug Cartel members were executed in Montreal by RCMP officers. It was all part of a cover-up by the RCMP officers to close the potential leak of their involvement in the Drug Game. The cover-up has persisted to this day.

"Wilding" is a phenomenon first identified and named in America. It is the biggest threat to our stability, our security, our financial well-being and our freedom. It was first brought to light by Professor Charles Derber of Boston College. His most recent work on the subject is called "The Wilding of America"' (St. Martin's Press, New York). Professor Derber writes;

"Although much of wilding is criminal, there is a vast spectrum of perfectly legal wilding, exemplified by the careerist who indifferently betrays or steps on colleagues to advance up the ladder. There are forms of wilding, such as lying and cheating, that are officially discouraged, but others, like the frantic and single-minded pursuit of wealth, are cultivated by some of the country's leading corporations and financial institutions. Wilding is… careerism, and greed that advance the self at the cost of others,… antisocial self-centeredness made possible by a stunning collapse of moral restraints and a chilling lack of empathy. Wilding includes only individualistic behavior that advances or indulges the self by hurting others. The line between corporate self-interest and economic wilding is blurring in today's global economy."

Another description of a society in wilding is:

"You that trample on the needy, and bring ruin to the poor of the land… and practice deceit with false balances, buying the poor for silver and the needy for a pair of sandals…" (Amos 8:1-7)

Wilding has permeated every niche of our society from the financial sector, the political sector, to government and religious institutions. It is a virus that has germinated in America and is spreading around the world. Perhaps wilding started with the massive use of cocaine in our society. Dexter noticed the social change in the underworld with the onslaught of cocaine. Maybe it was the catalyst in our legitimate society. Recently in Montreal, there was a court case known as the Matticks Case. The Matticks and other associates were charged with smuggling twenty-five tons of hashish into Canada. That's what they were charged with. They were suspected of smuggling a big bunch more!

When their day in court finally arrived, their lawyer pointed out to the judge that the police had manufactured evidence against his clients. The frame-up was clear to the judge. Judge Micheline Corbeil-Laramée threw the case out of court! In essence she stated that she was not going to preside over a trial and have to distinguish between factual and manufactured evidence presented by the police. Justice Corbeil-Laramée demonstrated to all parties that she had respect for herself, her profession, her court, and most importantly, "the law of the land." Many police officers were upset with her decision. What those police officers failed to understand is that she may have saved the lives of other police officers, and of many private citizens, by deciding what she did.

If the criminal element of our society gets the impression that they will not get justice in a courtroom, they will hold court on the street. Why not? Better to take your chances on the street, if you believe that you have no chance in a court of law! Many of you who read the earlier chapter, *Law of The Gun,* must have thought it is vigilantism. It is! So, too, is it vigilantism when a jurist denies an accused due process of the law. When a jurist pimps himself or herself and prostitutes the law because of their own personal bias or prejudice, that is vigilantism, that is wilding! The problem today, as Dexter sees it, is that individuals are being rewarded for their wilding attributes, rather than being scorned.

Criminals have always been part of every society from the beginning of recorded history. The underworld is a mirror reflection of the society in which it exists. The United States has the most violent society of any modern nation. The drug world is in a state of anarchy — what does that tell you about the society in which it exists?

Recently, a sociologist on one of the talk shows stated that Black Americans and Hispanic Americans live in a much more violent society than White Americans. Is it the colour of their skin? No, I think not! Is it because they have come to believe that there is no real justice for Blacks or Hispanics in American courts of law? Real or not, if that is their perception then the Americans will have to do something to eradicate that perception or the violence on the street will continue and even escalate.

Of course a society engaged in "wilding" will not have compassion for those lives who are locked in our prisons forever and a day. It will spare no conscious thought for the human lives that are wasted, that are destroyed, in order to perpetuate our growing bureaucracies, to extract our last ounce of vengeance and revenge. A society totally consumed in its own pursuit of wealth and self-aggrandizement will have no compassion for the waste of humanity. That is not to say that psychopathic killers, rapists, pedophiles and serial killers shouldn't be locked up forever. They, however, make up a minuscule proportion of the people warehoused in our penitentiaries. We should not have our judges throwing out life sentences like Santa Claus handing out candy to kids at Christmas. There is always hope an individual will change.

To place a human being in a cage without hope is the most cruel and inhumane thing a person or a society can do to another human being. Dexter has seen the results of individuals treated in such a manner. When they get out of prison, they are time bombs ticking away to countdown. Usually when they explode, their victims are the most defenseless of our society. The thought of all these coconuts making it out onto the streets is terrifying. A man who has nothing to lose is the most dangerous animal of all.

Dexter has lost his zest for the game or the chase. The society that once provided Dexter with thrills, laughter, excitement and profit no longer appeals to him. The Old Sarge's words had taunted Dexter so much that he began his own search for the spiritual truth. As he looked back on his life, it was easy for him to see that there was a power working in his life that had kept him out of the hands of disaster, out of the hands of death. Dexter reviewed his life with honest candor and, in the end, he concluded that for whatever reason, he had been spared from a life of ruin. It wasn't a matter of being careful, smart or lucky — there were those unexplainable situations where Dexter wasn't the master of his life and circumstance.

Dexter investigated the claims, traditions, history and theological teachings of all the great religions. He concluded that there was some good in all of them, some truth in all of them. Dexter believes that each person must go on his own spiritual journey and find his own spiritual path.

Embracing a spiritual faith has made many profound changes in Dexter's life. He is no longer on a materialistic merry-go-round, always chasing what he doesn't have, thinking it will bring him happiness — until the next want comes along. Today, he appreciates the simpler things in life. He is grateful for all that he has, and doesn't envy those who have more. Life has taught him that with every gift we receive there comes a responsibility that, in many cases, is greater than the gift.

His mind no longer throbs with the rapid pulse of a racing car piston grinding out to the max. He has a wide variety of interests, which he actively pursues. When he was younger, he never allowed himself the time to take stock of what was really of interest to him. In those days, he had but one interest — making money. He has faith that his God will guide him on other paths before his journey is over; paths that will bring him joy in helping others and not in gilding his cage.

Dexter dotes over his grandchildren, savouring every moment of their growth and development. He knows they will grow up to be productive members of society, rather than rebels without a cause. He hopes they will have the fire in their souls not to accept mediocrity but to face a challenge with spirit and conviction, knowing that they can and will succeed. If Dexter's grandchildren turn out to be simple punters in life, he will love them just the same and just as much, because he knows that for some, the pain of failure is beyond their capacity to survive. It is better to be a punter and enjoy your station in life, than to be a player who never succeeds and pays the price.

When Dexter looks back on his life with the wisdom of age, he can hardly recognize himself. The fiery heart is tempered now, but the flame still flickers deep within. He must always be vigilant so as not to fall back into "looking for a crisis." He knows there are crises out there waiting to be discovered — age can slow down a reckless spirit, but there is no cure.

Even today, the Man hasn't given up on trying to nail Dexter. Hell they've come closer to nailing Dexter more times than an old whore's ass has been pounded into a mattress. Today, Dexter is considered to be an old campaigner, not easily deceived or tempted. He knows that the shark who can deliver his head to the Man will get a platinum-plated license to work the streets, or a get-out-of-jail card. And so it is that Dexter continues his journey in life, savouring his freedom and pursuing interests that have no monetary value but are rich in meaning and purpose.

The boys from the old school always used to say, "If you want meat, go to a butcher; if you want money, go to a bank."

Uncle Harry, a friend of Dexter's, once said, "Show me a man who has never made a mistake in life, and I'll show you a man who has never done anything with his life."

Plato once said, "An unexamined life is not worth living."

Dexter likes the saying, "The joy of life is in the journey, not the destination."

Robert Menton once said, "Crime is a product of a disparity between goals and means."

Always remember The Eleventh Commandment — "Thou shalt not get caught."